Praise for *My Cleaner*

'This beautifully observed, intelligent and moving novel is one of those rare things – a small, carefully wrapped surprise that gets better and better with the unravelling. Gee does not pull her punches. She has a strong message to put across about familial love and about awareness, or lack of it, of other cultures.'

The Scotsman

'Much of the joy of reading Maggie Gee derives from her ability to take control of a complex and multilayered narrative and render it as accessible and satisfying as a television soap. Her prose is rich and gossipy; it mixes the highbrow with the vernacular, and is, at times, shockingly cynical … *My Cleaner* is a moving, funny, engrossing book.'

The Observer

'*My Cleaner* is both simple and subtle. It is structured around an elegant juxtaposition of the inner lives of two opposites: its texture comes from the blunt repetition of their ungenerous thoughts, punctuated by occasional gusts of provisional warmth.'

TLS

'Gee satirises the liberal conscience of the chattering classes with uncomfortable perception in this hugely enjoyable novel … her portrayal of Britain's new underclass of immigrant workers is presented with her trademark stinging clarity.'

Metro

'Maggie Gee is a superb and pitiless analyser of middle-class angst. Elegant, humorous and surprising, this is a classy performance.'

The Times

'It's amazing how many details, characters, stories within stories, Maggie Gee's unquenchable exuberance crams into this comparatively short book.'

The Spectator

'An intelligent and satisfying read.'

The Sunday Times

'A masterful study in Africa/UK relations which manages to be supremely uncomfortable without being cynical, and clever without being calculating.'   *Big Issue*

'Maggie Gee's new novel is a smart satire on a subject central to most women's lives … we either keep our houses clean, or pay someone else to do it. It's a queasy thought … and [one] you will never brush casually aside again after reading *My Cleaner*.'
Daily Telegraph

'*The Flood* was chillingly predictive. *My Cleaner* is a calmer, happier novel. Yet a gnawing tragedy lies in the shadows, all the more poignant for the deftness with which it's brushed aside.'
The Independent

'*My Cleaner* is another successful attempt on Gee's part to inhabit the mind of someone who is quite unlike her: in this case, a black Ugandan … Gee gives all her characters, white and black, male and female, the dignity of knowing that they live according to the choices they have made.'   *New Statesman*

'*My Cleaner* is a delicate dissection of middle-class anxiety and the fear of otherness.'   *Literary Review*

'Must Read: we get the trademark Gee humour and also a thoughtful, moving read.'   *New Nation*

MAGGIE GEE

MY CLEANER

TELEGRAM

British Library Cataloguing-in-Publication Data
A catalogue record for this book is available from the British Library

ISBN 1-84659-008-6
EAN 9-781846-590085

First published in hardback in 2005 by Saqi Books, London
This edition published in 2006 by Telegram Books

TELEGRAM
26 Westbourne Grove
London W2 5RH
www.telegrambooks.com

For Hilary and Irene Soper, with love

I am grateful to Sarah Smyth, Adam Pushkin and Cheltenham Literary Festival, whose 'Across Continents' commission sent me to Uganda in 2003, and to the Society of Authors for an Authors' Foundation grant which allowed further travel to Africa.

To read vivid contemporary Ugandan writing, contact Femrite publications (femrite@infocom.co.ug) or their distributor, African Books Collective in Oxford (01865-726686).

Thanks are due to many people who helped me in Uganda. To brave Margaret Achan Loum, Nakalanda Sanyu Francese, Beatrice Kabasambu Manyinde and Sarah Young. To all the 'Femrite' writers in Kampala who made me welcome, particularly Jackee Batanda, Winnie Rukidi, Lillian Tindyebwa, Hilda Twongyeirwe and Ayeta Anne Wangusa. The critical intelligence of Jackee Batanda and Hilda Twongyeirwe saved me from making many more errors. Thanks to my friend Charles Sempiira; to Pamela Acaye; to Syed Jafar Ali; to everyone at Blue Mango, particularly Annette Kibuuka; to Sandra Hook at the British Council, Kampala; to Nick Minogue, Kirsty Hutchinson and Becky Walker; and to Carol Lindsay Smith (CLS.dev@lineone.net) who helps Ugandan NACWOLA to distribute 'Memory Books' for families affected by AIDS.

Thanks always to Christine Casley. To Sue Jay, Graham Mort, Jacqueline Nkusi, Nick Rankin, John Ryle, Hanna Sakyi and Dan Shepherd for information and encouragement, to Hannah Henderson at the British Council, London, for sending me to Libya, and above all to Anna Wilson, Rebecca O'Connor and everyone at Telegram.

Part 1

1

The sun is shining on Uganda. Today is Mary Tendo's birthday.

The sun is shining on fields of white sheets in the hotel linen-store Mary keeps. Soon she will walk to the Post Office and find a letter that will change her life.

2

'I sent a letter to my cleaner – '

In London, it is warm and grey, already warm at nine am, though tomorrow it will be cold again. Most of the summer has been rather chilly, which gives the British a lot to talk about. They creep closer to each other under veils of cloud.

It is three hours earlier than in Kampala. Vanessa Henman has been up for half an hour and is feeling brisk and pleased with herself. She is on the phone to her best friend, Fifi.

'– Oh, you're just eating your breakfast, I see. As usual, I've been up for absolutely hours. So anyway, today I'm feeling more hopeful. Last week I sent a letter to my cleaner – you won't remember her – my former cleaner – Yes, black. Yes, young. Well Justin adored her. She went back to Africa years ago. I've asked her to come back and help with him. No I didn't see her when I went to Kampala, of course I didn't, I was terribly busy, to be frank it was all rather high-powered, embassy parties and what-have-you. No, writing the letter was Justin's idea. He says I never listen to him, so I thought if I wrote – Yes, exactly. But who knows if we'll hear from her?'

A slight noise behind her makes Vanessa look up. She shrieks, loudly, and almost drops the phone. A tall young man is standing in the doorway, long and white and soft and naked, with a string of amber beads round his neck. As she screams, he covers his cock with his hand. 'What's the matter, Mother?' he asks, irritably.

In her ear, a tiny voice is worrying: 'What on earth's the matter? Are you all right, Ness?'

'It's Justin. I didn't expect to see him up. Justin, why are you up at this time? I'd better go. Kissy kissy, Fifi.'

She puts the phone down and glares at him accusingly. How long has her son been listening?

'You ought to be pleased that I am up.' His flesh has a greyish, unlit look. The lines of the muscles have lost definition, she thinks, anxiously assessing.

'I am pleased darling but you gave me a shock. I was just telling Fifi that I'd written to Mary.'

'It's the fourth of July. It's Mary's birthday.' He suddenly smiles a radiant smile, and colour returns to his big, loose mouth, and his cheeks lift, and he is very handsome; but his pointless happiness enrages Vanessa.

'How can you *possibly* remember?' Suddenly he irritates her beyond bearing, his great pale nakedness, his soft sulky voice, his haywire corona of uncut yellow curls, the fact he is here in her study in the morning when normally he sleeps until four pm, his ridiculous pretence of remembering Mary's birthday –

When only a few weeks ago, he forgot his mother's.

She sits and stares at him, vibrating faintly, wondering if he is really her son.

He turns and leaves with a sudden turn of speed, his eyes on the floor, his arms clasping his torso, his cock swinging round and semi-unfurling like a big soft lily in a nest of golden filaments, then stubs his toe on a pile of books, and hops on, swearing as offensively as possible, the orange beads bouncing below his collar-bones, hard on the softness of his flesh.

His mother watches him go, despairing. He will not get up for the rest of the day.

Vanessa stares at her crowded desk. The in-tray is layered like puff-pastry, collapsing, sliding at both sides. An old-fashioned birthday card sits by the desklight, with sugary roses and a scattering of glitter. It gives her a strange feeling, this birthday card. It was sent from the village where she was born, which she's hardly revisited since she left home. Vanessa is proud to be a Londoner, a sophisticate, a creature of the city. And yet her village is still out there, somewhere. Somewhere down motorways and dim summer lanes. The card makes her feel guilty, but also happy, because the link is not quite broken. But the card is hideously ugly. Vanessa sighs, and shoves it out of sight.

(But two days later, she will write a letter to the cousin she has not seen since girlhood.)

Outside her study window the sky is low and lidded. Vanessa Henman frowns at the clouds.

She thinks, I need light. I am a creature of light. The sun must be shining on Africa.

One year ago, I was in Kampala.

3   Mary Tendo

Today is my birthday. It is a great day. The sun is shining on Kampala.

Thank God for my birthday. 'It's Mary's birthday.' Little Benedicta, the third room-maid, who wants to please me, told the porter, who helped me to the lift with my bag, which was heavy because it held the Memory Books I am printing out for my friend in NACWOLA. They will go up country, for the women with AIDS. The porter doesn't realise that I'm used to carrying, because in England I worked like a dog. I have strong muscles underneath my pink blouse. But I smile sweetly and let him help me.

Here I am important, the Linen Store Keeper. It is a good job, only just below the House Keeper. Perhaps as a graduate I might have done better, but everything doesn't go to plan. The years of wandering, years I lost, times that I don't need to think about, for I have done well, I have found my place. I wear a smart suit, and the thin gold chain that Omar gave me when I was his wife.

It must have been a good day for my parents, thirty-eight

years ago, back in our village. I wish they were here to be glad with me. Though we did not count the days, in the village. There were no dates, there was no diary. I was the child who came with the harvest. Later we had to fill in a form, and that was when they invented my birthday. In Britain, my birthday became real. My Omar gave me a birthday card. And every year Justin drew me a picture – Miss Henman's boy, like my second son. That little, white-haired, white-skinned boy. And my real son, Jamie, covered me with kisses. My English birthdays made me happy.

In this country we have learned to be happy when we are not frightened of a revolution. Maybe people in the government are lining their pockets, but politicians always line their pockets. At least now the army is under control. Later this year there is another election and maybe we'll have to be frightened again, and rush like crazies to hoard tins and packets, and wait for rumours, like we did the last time –

But everything is better than it was when I was little. The butchery and terror of Amin, Obote. So we live for today. Live in the day. There are things we have lost, things we have suffered, but now, today, there is a ring of sunlight. We're a long time dead, so let us be happy!

In the village it seemed we were always happy, despite the gunfire we heard at night, despite the killings not far away. The laughter still flies like birds in my ribcage. My days, my days. They are all still with me. The riches that my birthday brings me.

Jamie, Jamil. My beloved son.

Today I received a letter from England. A letter from UK, and my heart started drumming. Maybe Jamie had managed to get to London.

I walked to the *posta* in my lunch break. Occasionally

Omar still sends me letters, and other friends from other countries, and I tell them to write to my PO Box (although it is a nuisance when I forget my key) because in the hotel trade nothing is certain. I like to think I could resign tomorrow, then no one has any power over me. Sometimes I threaten to leave, and they raise my wages, though actually I like my job, and for the moment I mean to stay.

The Post Office stands opposite the big foreign banks on the red main road of our capital city. The road is pot-holed by heavy rain and then baked dry in the sun again. I am used to this road, with its rivers of traffic, shaking and honking in all directions, though when I first arrived it made me sick and dizzy. I came from the village a lifetime ago, but now the city has entered my veins, dusty and bright and bursting with faces, shining black, almost blind in the sun, rushing me with them into the future.

The future grips us in its jaws. Once this was the City of Antelopes. Now there are no more golden *kobs* jumping away down the green slopes. So many shops selling mobile phones, dozens of them, hundreds, though many people buy them, then can't afford to keep paying for air-time. So the city is littered with dead metal beetles. But the shops keep on springing up cheerful and hopeful, decorated in bright yellow plastic, with tidy staff in the South African style, smiling at us all in sky-blue uniforms. And there are South African burger bars, too, copies of American burger bars, where confident young people sit and smoke and talk and wave their mobiles at each other. Though surely they cannot like the food. It is ten times the price of smoked beef and *matooke*. They make the burgers from the animals' entrails, teeth and hooves, stuck together with fat. My friend who works there told me about it. The ice-cream is nice. Sweet and creamy.

I sit in the linen store. Here I rule. *Nze Kabaka wa wanno*.

The linen store of the Nile Imperial, one of the biggest hotels in the city. Queen of these orderly white fields. It is very quiet. I am in control. I make sure the paperwork is done. Some of the newer maids are slovenly, but I soon teach them how to fill in the forms. And little Benedicta is always helpful. She sharpens my pencils, and brings me tea.

There are straight-edged bales of cloth like new snow. I never saw snow until I was in England. But I had seen it in the nursery rhyme book they taught us to read with at primary school, and there were pictures of pretty, chilly white children, and strange dark pointed Christmas trees. Later I bought my own tree, in London. My friend Abdu Mawanga helped me carry it home.

I'm a woman of the world. I have travelled, seen things. The months and years in other places. I count them up like beads on a string. Most Ugandans have never left home. I must remember I am lucky, happy. *Katonda anjagalanyo.*

The sun setting over Leptis Magna. Omar, my husband, took me there. It is a great ruined city in Libya. He took me there, as a wife, a lady. He had a camera. He took pictures of me, by the severed stone heads of the snakey-haired women. There were fifty of them. They were all different. Each of them looked sad in a different way. And those sadnesses survived two thousand years of history.

But we were still young, and very happy. Happiness never turns into stone. Happiness gleams like sand in your hands. We tried out the echo in the open air theatre. Beyond the stage, more sand, then sea. The sky was bright blue and had no edges. There were no clouds. It was full of hope. There was sand in my pockets for years and years. Hard bright grains to press with my fingers.

It is not only Omar's fault that we parted. When you're far from home, marriage isn't easy. *Munamawanga.* You are different, and people are distant and suspicious. Neither of the families can support you. Nobody understands your problems.

But Omar was good. He taught me to drive. Some of his Arab friends didn't want their wives to drive, but Omar taught me, and was proud of me. Yes, at first he loved me, and encouraged me. Our car was a second-hand Nissan Bluebird. In England, bluebirds mean happiness. A blue tin box of happiness. We closed the windows, and were warm inside. For years it was enough for us. I forgot my degree, I forgot my ambitions.

But I do not forgive him for taking my Jamie. Jamie, Jamil. Beloved boy.

Still I am glad that my husband loved me.

The sun rose over the bridges of London as my bus ran along the burning Thames. Going home from my work as the sun came up and office workers were beginning their day. The same sun we have in Africa, but there it is wrapped in white spider-thread. I got up every morning in the dark and cold while my husband Omar was still fast asleep, because he had studied until two in the morning. I did my work like the other foreigners, cleaning the offices of the sleeping English. They arrived, yawning, as we went for our breakfast, we hundreds and thousands of people from the empire. (They say that Uganda was not part of the empire, they say it was just a 'protectorate', which makes me laugh! Protecting us from what? From the other competing *bazungu* empires.)

The British Empire was already just a memory. And yet, these office workers were still our masters. They never knew us or talked to us, but we knew about them, from their wastepaper baskets. I wanted to arrive in a suit, as they did, and drink the coffee from the coffee-machine, and use their phones to call my family, and drop old chewing-gum like them, as if the ground would swallow it up. I wanted those people to know my name. (We had names for them, too, they knew nothing about: 'Hair Shedder', 'Sticky Pants', 'Snot Finger'.)

Later in the day I went to their houses and did the same job for less money. It was the only way to enter their houses, to feel what English lives were like. Some of them pretended I was not there. I walked through their rooms, dusting their dust, *shush, shush, shush, shush*. I was their guest, I was their ghost.

But now I have a good job, in Kampala. I wear shiny high heels imported from Dubai, which are cheap to me, at 10,000 shillings, so I have three pairs in different colours, and pink-and-blue Masai beads from Kenya, and my flat has a T.V.-clock-radio and white plastic furniture you just sponge clean, all done in seconds, as good as new. And a small refrigerator with an ice-box. And a special bin for the sliced white bread I buy whenever I feel like it, and a tin for the cakes I enjoy at weekends.

I have a shelf of books left behind by hotel guests and another shelf I have bought myself, although books in Uganda are very expensive. (I own three books by Ernest Hemingway. He was a foolish man in some ways, but I like his short sentences – short sentences help you to be truthful. He told the truth about being young and having no money to buy books, like me. And about how first love slips into the past, which is also something that happened to me.) Soon I shall buy a second-hand computer, and my friend the accountant will help me to use it. I can type already, so it will be easy. Maybe I will write my own story.

I go to church regularly, of course, although my *kabito* does not come with me. I arrive early, and sit near the front, and sing out the hymns from my family hymn book. The pastor knows me and I am respected, though I do not rush up to the altar and bear witness in the new, American evangelists' style.

A lifetime ago I left my village. I shall go back some day, when I have more money. I wanted to take my son to see them. The old ones deserved to see my son –

But I haven't returned. It is my goal for the future. I will go back rich, with sugar and paraffin. Take them a netball, and a football.

I will go back with Charles, my friend the accountant. He will drive his car, and wear his suit.

(Will anyone remember me? My parents have gone, but there are still aunts and uncles. The cousins. I had so many cousins. My friends who sat on the ground with me. We sat in the shade of the mango tree. It was big, and old, with a crown of pink fingers. Sometimes we held hands, and watched the giant ants, wobbling through the dust with their long black bellies. We told each other stories about the village, and made up tales about the city, where Queen Elizabeth might be visiting our king, Kabaka Freddie. Though later the Kabaka died, in England, and people whispered that he had been poisoned.)

We children always knew we had to leave the village. In order to come back. More, better, different. It was our parents who told us to go. They saw us as teachers, lawyers, dentists, doctors, even presidents. Did they not see we might be porters and cleaners, taxi drivers, parking attendants? Despite our degrees and certificates.

My father was a farmer, for most of his life, though he worked in Kasese, when I was little, and later, when he was old, he got sick. But most of the time he was what people call a peasant. Although in the village our family was important. Our land grew bananas, maize, sorghum, black and white beans, tomatoes, sweet potatoes. My mother kept him at it, for he liked *waragi*, and as he grew older, he liked it more, but he never beat my mother, like the other fathers. One day, though, he fell off our bicycle under the wheels of a bus from the city, and his leg was broken, and the bananas were ruined, and after that he couldn't ride the bicycle. In our district women don't ride bicycles, except as passengers, side-saddle. The village men don't like women who ride. They think sitting astride does something to a woman. So we had to pay one of the uncles to sell our bananas, and he always complained that the bicycle was crooked.

My mother sold maize and potatoes by the roadside, and beautiful pyramids of tomatoes, as neat as the triangles I drew at school. I loved the hot sweet smell of our tomatoes. The *bazungu* in jeeps paid good prices for our vegetables, white people travelling through Africa, and thanked us too much, and took photographs, although we had doubled the price for them. I practised my English: 'Hallo, how are you?' Some of the other children had bad manners: 'Hallo, how are you, give me money.' Then the *bazungu* looked pink and unhappy, and got back into their jeeps and drove away.

We had five books. My family was lucky. My father was a barman when he was young in the big hotel for white people near Kasese, near Kilembe mines where they mined copper and cobalt. All the young men wanted to go to Kilembe, to make their fortunes and have adventures, and my mother said it was all the fashion to be courted by a Kilembe boy. My father sent home money, and he brought things back with him, some sheets and pillows, and knives and forks. He said he was happier after they sacked him, when he came back home and looked after the farm, but if so, why did he drink so much? He brought us three novels in English, which careless *bazungu* had left in the hotel. I read them until they broke into islands.

Her Destiny, *The Shores of Love*, and another title I cannot remember where everyone was stabbed in an English castle. You had to guess the murderer. I did not really care about it. And we had a Bible. And a hymn book.

The Bible is the single most beautiful book. I read it nearly every day, at home. And we had a copy of *Hymns Ancient and Modern*, pages 49 to 306. Though many of our neighbours had the everyday prayer book with the hymns we usually sang in the church, no one else had *Ancient and Modern*. The covers were lost, with hymns 1 to 73. When I came to Kampala, to university, Maama sent it with me, and in the nearby church, it was the book they used, but they had half a dozen copies for five hundred people. So I sang from our book, and was the envy of others. The rest just stood there humming and moving their lips, trying to say the words after me. Maama said the book was mine, when I left Uganda. By that time, though, I had read hundreds of books, all the shelves of my friend the professor who taught me at Makerere University. I loved Charles Dickens, and Chinua Achebe. I loved Mrs Jellyby, and Becky Sharp. For a week I wanted to be pale like Becky. I wanted to make a life, like her. I loved the poets, and the playwrights. But I was still grateful for our family hymn book.

We children played outside as dusk fell. We were the only house with a jacaranda. Most people had purple potato trees, which had no special evening sweetness. The sun drew the perfume from the creamy yellow flowers. There were little gold weaver-birds which danced and settled. We chattered like birds and ate sugar cane. Being a child was light, and easy.

(Yet every so often we were woken by gunfire. Sometimes there were rumours that soldiers were hiding from other soldiers in the bush near by. One thin man, haggard-faced, very important, came and stayed the night with us, and I was told to tell nobody, and not to speak to him, or look at him. But I risked a glance, and he was handsome, and he smiled at me as if he had seen me. I thought he was a hero. My secret hero. Now he is in the government, and people say things about corruption. I think it is harder to be a hero, once you become the power in the land.)

Our parents told us to go to the city. At night, they talked about the city lights. They said they shone like stars in the distance, though all we could see was low dark hills. The first time I saw the lights for myself was when my father took me to boarding school. There they were, a line of stars on the horizon, and a kind of humming, like a thousand bees. A thousand bees going after money. And they did shine like stars, growing brighter and brighter, until I was dazzled, and forgot about the village.

I managed to move from the country to the city. I made the great journey between worlds. It kills some people, and drives some of us mad. I did not want this to happen to my children. You see them, walking on the streets of London, the ghosts of Africans attacked by spirits, with matted hair, laughing and shouting. I thought, 'My children will be born in the city. My children will never suffer like that.' I meant to have three, or four, or five, not the nine or ten they have in the village. I was proud I knew about family planning. And yet my life has not gone to plan.

In the end, I had only one child, a son. And no one can predict what their children will suffer. Sometimes I find I am arguing with God. Is it true that he sees every sparrow that falls? Can he see Jamil? Does he care for him?

I had names for my daughters, but they never came. Life in London was all rushing and running. I loved Omar at first, and we knew such happiness. He made me laugh, as my father had. He liked my cooking. We liked our car. But later there was never enough money to pay the instalments or the petrol or insurance, and my student grant from the government lapsed, and I stopped my MA and became a cleaner. After all my dreams, and my parents' dreams, this was the future I had seen on the horizon. The shining lights were just empty offices that had to be cleaned before the sun came up. And a hundred dusty bulbs, in dusty houses.

I thank Jesus that those days are over. Now when the maids come for sheets, they knock politely. It calms my soul, the clean, blank whiteness, the way the maids bow their heads to me. 'Happy birthday, Miss Mary.' 'Happy birthday, Miss.' The older ones don't know their own birthdays, but the young ones think they know it all. I do not let them take liberties, though I praise Benedicta, who is polite.

I am proud to be the Linen Store Keeper. Now I am important, and my life is in order. The white sheets muffle the noise of the city, and the noise of the past, all those foreign cities, the dirt and the mess of the years I lost.

The sounds in the village were always the same. The city is a muddle of shouts and machines, but the sounds in the village spoke to me. The thump of the wooden pestle on its mortar as the women crushed ground-nuts for ground-nut sauce. *Thud-ah, thud-ah* like the beats of my heart. And little quick voices of weaver-birds. They dart through the branches like bright yellow thread.

But now my blood has grown red and loud. When I close my eyes, I am still in the city. There are horns blaring and beggars begging, their feet tipped like flippers from polio. They sit in a line outside the phone-shops. When I lie in the darkness, I no longer see my family home's white jacaranda, with its buds that opened into yellow-white stars. I am in the city, and it is in me.

I picked up my letter from the Post Office. It is a strange building, flat and red. They say government spies live on top of the *posta*. The spies, if they're there, are welcome to watch me. I do not care about the government. The queues were long because I went at lunchtime. There are fifty queues, and the rules are always changing. I went to my box, clutching my key. The metal felt slippery and hot in my hand. I held it so tight that it marked my palm.

I was so excited when I saw there was a letter. God had sent me a letter on my birthday. I am not a child, wanting cards and presents, but a letter from my son is my heart's desire. Jamil had remembered my birthday, a miracle! I felt the whole post office was smiling at me. Trying to hurry, I dropped my letter, and had to clutch it up from the dusty floor.

I saw my own name, in blue ink, swimming closer. At first I was sure it was Jamie's writing. My eyes caressed it; my heart leapt and thudded.

Then it snapped into focus, and everything was wrong. Neat angular writing. Not my Jamie's. I recognised it, somehow, but it was not his.

And then my skin stood up in small pimples like the legs of a chicken dead on a table.

The writer-woman's writing. Yes, it was her.

I am still not ready to open it.

4

Justin is dreaming about his childhood. It is six pm, and he is still in bed. He has thrown off the thick cloud of duck-down duvet his mother got out for him yesterday and lies sprawled on his back in a sheen of chilled sweat, streaks of blonde hair slicked across his pillow.

In the dream, all his school-friends have come for tea. He is still at his local primary school, so the friends are every shape and colour. It is his birthday, they are smiling at him. Mary Tendo is making the tea, plates and plates of white bread and red sweet jam, the food he always liked best as a boy, though his mother never allowed white bread. Mary used to buy it when his mother was out. And chocolate biscuits, and crisps, and baked beans.

But now they are eating a small white giraffe that Mary has bought for him as a treat. The giraffe is quite tough, and starts wriggling, but he wants to eat it to please Mary, though the other children push it away. Now it cocks up its head and looks at him, big reproachful eyes, a long tremulous lip. Suddenly it gets up from the table. It is his mother, who has just come home. Her teeth are big and sharp and yellow and she smells very strongly of giraffe.

Justin cries out, afraid, and wakes, and sits up, and sees he is alone in a darkening room. Outside the window, it is raining again. He scratches furiously, and goes back to sleep.

Two rooms away in the big suburban villa, bought for a song twenty years ago, Vanessa Henman is exercising hard, driving herself through her hundredth stomach crunch, her neck tendons cording, her vertebrae clicking. She tries to support her head with her hands but it's almost impossible to relax it: the head seems to go on working on its own, such a heavy head, such a narrow neck, too long, far too long, for the rest of her body. 100, 101, 102 – and then she remembers she need only do 100, but a voice in her head insists she go on, and for neatness she aims for 110, but the demon drives her to 120. Until ten years ago she ran every day, but the bones in her hips began to ache.

'You have to accept you are getting older,' the doctor had said to her, quite gently, when she went to ask him to deal with the pain, a decade ago when it still seemed new. 'None of us is getting any younger, Mrs Henman. It's probably best to give up the running.'

'*Dr* Henman, actually,' she'd snapped at him. (She flushes pink now, remembering.) 'I can't give up running, it's part of me. In any case, I'm only in my forties.'

Had she known the future, she would have kissed him. For after that meeting with Dr Truman, she had taken up Pilates instead of running, made friends with Fifi, her Pilates teacher, and co-written a book which had made her name and earned them both a lot of money, *The Long Lean Line: Pilates for Everyone*. It hit the beginning of the craze for Pilates: Vanessa was on every radio show, though Fifi, who was younger, got the television dates, and starred alone in the video, which had almost caused an argument between them, and Vanessa had to be forgiving. They had followed it up with another three, *The Long Lean Line 2, 3* and *4*.

Though it seems the vein might soon be exhausted. She's had a phone call from her editor. 'I'm talking to Marketing, Vanessa darling. Maybe we're coming to the end of the line. No, sorry, of course I'm not trying to be funny.'

In any case, novels are her *métier*. She published two novels in the 1980s, which were 'very well reviewed', as she always points out. On the strength of them, she got the job she still holds, as Lecturer in Creative Writing at one of the new universities. She started that department, and designed the course, which over the years has grown increasingly popular.

But the students always ask her what she's written recently. They only half-smile, and look slightly disappointed, when she tells them about her Pilates books.

'They have made me a *lot* of money,' she assures them. 'Remember there is money to be made from non-fiction.'

'Most of us want to write fiction, and novels,' a brave, and ignorant, student protested. She gave him B- for his next two assignments.

Creative Writing, she has come to understand, is a magnet for the unteachable. Two in ten students are actually mad. In recent years she has too often caught herself listening to a student describing the plot of his novel, the two-hour tutorial extending like a desert, as a voice in her ear hisses, quite loudly, 'This person is insane. Both of us must be. The story he is telling me is not worth telling. Nothing at all in this exchange is real. Why aren't I writing my own novels?' She is starting a new module this term, called 'Autobiography and Life Writing'. Perhaps this will encourage the students to make sense: or perhaps the madness will just come out.

At least she is still all right for money, though there is the enormity of Justin, the problem of Justin, a limp dead weight, sucking up her energy, her time, her money, weighing on her like a mountain of debt. Every time he breathes, he becomes more costly. How can she write novels with him in the house?

Vanessa frowns as she trots downstairs. And the stair-carpet's filmed with a faint spume of hair, her own yellow-blonde hair, which tends to fall out. She is temporarily without a cleaner, since the last one met Justin naked on the landing. 'I just don't feel right with men around,' the woman had whined, as she handed back their keys. Vanessa told herself she could manage without; these days one had to pay cleaners a fortune, and they didn't do it half as well as oneself. But she's finding herself too busy to clean, though she sometimes attacks a pan or a surface with furious vigour for ten minutes or so.

Justin is a liability. How can she keep cleaners with a nudist about?

It is time for another conference with Tigger – her nickname for Trevor, Justin's father. She gave him up two decades ago, once she realised he had no ambition, and refused to take things seriously; including her writing, including her. He wouldn't read the parenthood manuals she bought him. They separated when the boy was just a baby, one and a half, just beginning to talk (it hurt that he said 'Dadda' before 'Mumma'). But Tigger still hung around the house all the time. Though in the last year, since things went wrong for Justin, Tigger has too often been otherwise engaged, falling for a stupid young would-be artist not so much older than his son, some kind of Indian who doesn't speak English.

Typical, she thinks, typical of men. All right, he still phoned and he still sent money, he even came round to do trivial jobs, but he seemed to think his loyalty was to this young girl, just because she happened to be living with him.

Vanessa chops carrots into crisp orange rings, so forcefully she almost cuts off a finger. Usually she is too busy for vegetables, except for the pre-cooked, supermarket kind, but Fifi has suggested that Justin ought to have some, that he is simply short of vitamin C, and that is why he lies in the dark and sleeps. So Vanessa has bought a book called *Salads for Life*, and is making a mixed salad to share with Justin, though the last one simply sat by the side of his bed, growing limp and brown as the shadows lengthened.

It doesn't matter, she won't give up, she will do the right things, even if no one else does, though Justin's father has let her down, though Mary Tendo has not answered her letter, though Fifi is often unsympathetic, and her hips still ache, and her students are thick. She will keep up standards: she is a stoic.

These thoughts are comforting. She chops less fiercely, approving the marriage of reds and oranges, tomatoes and carrots, garnet-bright grapes, of apple-white celeriac and slivers of spring onion, the light and dark greens of the moonlets of cucumber, the silver-pale edges of the iceberg's frills, the curves of the onion like the bole of a lute, and all of it sitting like grace on the plate, indisputably good for them, and she has made it.

It matters to Vanessa to do things right.

5   Mary Tendo

It is early morning. The sky is red as kisses, the passionate kisses of my friend the accountant who said goodbye to me ten minutes ago. (That is what I call him when the bolder young maids try to find out about my private life. In fact, I am happy that Charles is an accountant, and I like to think of him that way, though in my heart I also call him my *kabito*, my sweetheart.)

There are too many people on this taxi. It is a joke, the law that says maximum fourteen. The driver is greedy, and instructs the boy to hang out of the door and take on more people from the crowds of early morning workers at each stop. There are seventeen of us now, and three live chickens which squawk as we rock into the ruts of red earth where the heavy rains have dug into the road that roars up and down the hills of Kampala. A man in front of me has AIDS, or TB. He is very thin, and coughs horribly, and cannot hide it with his bony hand, and everyone tries to move away, but we are packed together like the dried bananas I took with me when I went to

London. I think the chicken is pecking my calves, but my legs are pressed hard against a sticky plastic suitcase that belongs to the fat woman next to me, and I cannot turn round to shoo it away.

I am holding my birthday present on my lap. It is the computer I have always wanted. Not the big heavy thing I had imagined, but a silver laptop, a thing of beauty. It is nearly new, and it is easy to use. I love it more than anyone can imagine. I have longed for one for years, so I can write down the stories unravelling in my head like pieces of ribbon. I will write about my youth, like Hemingway. Already I have written a sentence on it. 'dear charles thank you for my present. it is my new baby! yours sincerely mary.' I have not got the hang of the capitals yet. I am clutching it tightly, in case it gets dirty.

At least the boy keeps the sliding door open so air without germs comes into the taxi. It smells of warm rain and earth and flowers, the red-tulip-flowered trees called *kabakanjagala* which means 'the King loves me'. (King Ronald still loves us, though he does not really rule us. Now we are ruled by Museveni, and he loves us so much he doesn't want to leave us. So people whisper he might rig the elections. I think it would be better if he loved us less.)

I spent last night with my friend the accountant who lives in a new flat in the suburb of Bukoto. Charles took me to a smart café, western-style, which opened recently on the Jinja Road, where we had a big table with a white cloth just for the two of us, and small portions, and the waiter was a boy who called me 'Madam', though I thought he was laughing at me behind his eyes, and most of the other guests were *bazungu,* nearly as white as the tablecloths. I think I would rather have gone to Jimmy's, where you eat smoking hot pork under the stars, delicious *muchomo*, with your fingers. But in the end

I had a very nice birthday, a very nice night with my friend the accountant, and was too busy to read my letter. Now it is morning, although in London it will still be the middle of the night.

Henman is in London. Henman is sleeping. Does she still live in that big empty house, so much too big for only two people?

I worked for her, nearly a decade ago. Miss Henman. Vanessa Henman. Nessie. I spent eight years with her, at first twice a week, then every afternoon, because she found me useful. With her son Justin, who was like my own, but what? But easier to love. (Not that I loved him more than Jamie. I have never loved anyone more than Jamie.)

Easier to love, because not mine. I did not have to fight with his father. Indeed, I liked the little boy's father, though the writer-woman seemed to despise him, and talked about him jeeringly, both in his presence and his absence. She called him 'Tiger', an animal's name.

In fact this Trevor was very clever. He mended the washing-machine and the boiler. He made the radiators work one winter when there was snow on the ground outside and the heating broke and we nearly froze to death. I became worried about Justin. English children are pale as ice. His little fingers were blue like the sea, the blue-grey sea that is a wall around England. But he said, 'My dad is coming soon. I know my dad will be able to fix it.' And his mother was screaming, 'Why isn't he here?' But then Trevor arrived, and like magic, fixed it.

Little blond Justin. Pointy nose, grey eyes. I think he looked very like his father. An English face with sharp small features, except his mouth, which was round, like a rose. He liked to be kissed. He liked to kiss. He liked to be with me when I worked in the kitchen. I liked it too. Children make me smile. All my adult life I have felt short of children.

He wasn't allowed in his mother's room. He couldn't be around her when she was working. He was always with me. I liked him there. The more I liked him, the less I liked her.

I met the writer-woman through a postcard in the newsagent. 'Nice friendly family requires trained cleaner.' Trained? What did she mean? Not to do *doo-doo* on her floor? I was trained to be a teacher or a writer like her. I have been to Makerere University, 'the best university in Africa'. (Everyone says that who hasn't been there, and I always smile and agree with them, although bits of Makerere are falling down.)

I went round to see her, smiling, smiling. She shook my hand as if we were equals (I was never equal to the people I cleaned for. I knew all about them, all their dirtiness, the secret habits that no one else knew, the places they left snot, or sanitary towels, the fruit they left to moulder in the bins meant for paper. And so, I was superior.)

And yet, not all of them were bad. Even the Henman is not all bad.

That day she was alone with her small son, who was pulling at her skirt and snatching at her sleeve. I saw she could not make him behave. I saw he needed her to look at him. At the same moment, I started to love him.

I asked her, where was the family? She looked puzzled, and then she laughed. 'You are from Africa, of course. This is a single-parent family. That means, it is just me and my boy. Women like me rather like it that way.' She said it with a strange, show-off face that made me think she did not really like it.

'Women like me'. She meant modern women, not African women with too many children and aunts and sisters and grandparents. I thought, well somewhere there must be a father, unless this woman is the Virgin Mary, but I said nothing, only smiled politely, and looked at her as if I admired her.

(But how can you be happy not to have a family?)

I asked her what the job would be.

'Oh not very much, I'm not a fussy person.' Her smile was thin and nervous. She wanted me to like her, but I knew what they were like, these thin smiling women. 'Just wash the floors, vacuum, dust and polish. I *do* like a really clean kitchen and bathroom, and sometimes I'm afraid that means hands and knees.'

It took me a moment to see what she meant. She thought I would kneel down to clean her floor. 'Yes, yes, Madam,' I said, smiling, smiling. She was stupid, so perhaps she would pay me well. 'How much is the hourly rate, Madam?' (I would never call her 'Madam' again, but at interviews it makes a good impression.)

Suddenly she looked both mean and ashamed. 'Two pounds an hour, take it or leave it.' Her mouth shut tight like an envelope of money. In those days, no one paid less than two pounds. It was the least you could pay, to the least of people.

I stopped smiling, but I accepted. I took from her, and later I left her.

One day she caught me in her garden, chasing a frog down her path with a broom. I was shouting at it, driving it forwards. 'It's only a frog,' the yellow-haired one said, her thin lips angry, but trying to smile. 'Leave it alone, Mary. They're sweet little things.' It lolloped away, jerky, slimy. She watched it as if it was her own baby.

These people are dirtier than in our village, something my mother would not believe. Ugandans know about animals. Frogs are worse than cockroaches.

This woman had books that were covered in dust. She never read them, or lent them to me. Her rooms were lined with them, like tiles or plaster. Big piles of them stood in the hall and bedroom. Without being read, they were slowly dying. I saw the pages were going yellow.

I am an honest woman, but I used to take them, in batches of three or four at a time, whatever had risen to the top of the pile. I hid them in her cupboard, and waited for a while. If she missed one, and asked me, I 'found' it for her. If she didn't notice, they were justly mine. I have always been a reader, but she never offered. She never asked me if I wanted them. Perhaps she didn't think I could read, though I read her letters when I got the chance.

The only book she missed was one she had written, which only goes to prove how big her head is.

I was glad she told me. I put it straight back. I didn't want her stupid writing on my bookshelves. She probably wrote poems, 'Little frog, I love you. I save you, Froggie, from the big fat African.'

(The truth is, I did read some pages, later. She wasn't a poet. It was prose like a desert, going on to the horizon, and nothing ever happened.)

Her bottom was flat and white as a *chapatti*. I saw her once, coming out of the bath. 'Sor-ree, Mary,' she said, and giggled. If she saw what she looked like, the thing would have cried.

I left her one day. I left the country. I travelled the world, then I came back to Kampala. Without my husband, without my son. Home, but not home. Still far from my village. Each night I tell myself, I'll go there soon. But for now I have a respectable job, a decent position with okay wages, and save my money whenever I can.

Why am I afraid to open her letter?

6

Justin wakes up at three am ravenous, hollow and sad in the heavy moonlight, and gets out of bed to raid the fridge as he often does once his mother is sleeping, and steps on the plate, and crushes the salad, and leaves it there spilled on the fitted carpet.

On his way back to bed, Justin pauses on the landing, outside the door of his mother's room, and drops, briefly, to his hands and knees. He listens, sniffs, alert like a fox, his shoulders white in a panel of moonlight, his pale hair stiff as a ruff of ice, and then crawls closer and closer in until he thinks he can hear her breathing, and noses the door, and kisses it, then stops, stone still, as her light clicks on, and lopes dog-like to his own room.

Her light goes out again. The house is silent.

7   Mary Tendo

The envelope is too thin to contain money. It was the first thing I looked for, of course. She must owe me money for the work I did. Here what she paid me would be a fortune, but not in London, where even breathing cost money.

I have opened the letter. It does not begin well. *'I hope that you and yours are healthy and happy. I myself am well, but there is bad news'* – bad news on my birthday, that is unlucky. *'Justin, who you were so sweet with, is ill. In fact, very ill. He never gets up. He has been back home with me for six months now, and I am looking after him hand and foot '*– well, she never did that when he was little – *'but the future does not seem very hopeful …'*

Does she mean he is dying? That stabs my heart. How old must he be? Twenty-one, twenty-two. Surely only Africans die so young. *'I thought of you, because you always loved Justin.'* Then it goes on for several paragraphs. *'If you happened to be free, or looking for a job, I would be so grateful if you came back to help me. Promise me at least to consider it. Please do ring soon. I will ring straight back.*

Affectionately yours,

Dr Henman'

She'd left space for a signature, but forgot to sign it. I know her real name. Vanessa H Henman. Her friends called her 'Nessie', but I called her 'Miss Henman.' Nessie is the name of a monster in Scotland. I know she wanted me to call her 'Doctor'. Now Dr Monster comes begging to me.

I sit staring at the linen. Blank, blinding. Scotland is a pale place, all ice and snow. I never had enough money to go there. She was a cold woman. A mean woman. I cannot go back, not even for Justin.

Then I think about him. He was rarely ill. He was never allowed to stay away from school, because his mother had to do her writing. Is it really possible that Justin is ill? It makes a small pain, under my rib-cage.

And then, on the reverse, I see an ink postscript.

'PS. *Obviously we should pay return airfare. And reward you VERY HANDSOMELY.'*

Suddenly, the future lights up like a necklace. If I had enough money, I could go to my village. I could come back rich, and go to my village. Without asking my *kabito* for money.

It comes out of the blue. It is chance, or fate, but perhaps God wants me to leave my country. Now I'm back in Kampala, I don't want to leave, but …

My life is a story of arriving and leaving.

8   Mary Tendo

The first time I left it was chance, not choice.

My father's brother had a very large wife. They had both been close to the guerrilla soldiers who based themselves near the lands of my family as they fought the liberation war. After the victory, my aunt moved away from my uncle, and lived in the city, and became famous. She had many friends in the new government, and beautiful *gomesi*s in many colours with sleeves puffed up like a butterfly's wings, and shiny new cars with small frightened drivers. She became the new Minister for Women's Affairs and the Protection of Public Morals.

My aunt had five sons but no daughters. She sent for me just before I graduated, and asked me why I had not come to see her. I did not say that in my family we believed she was a proud and cruel woman who was unfaithful to my uncle. I said that I had felt unworthy.

'But the state needs modern young women like you. Our new president wants to encourage women. My job is to encourage young women. If you are a good girl, your aunt can help you.'

Her house was on Kololo Hill, near all the embassies, where everyone is rich. She had a pretty garden full of bougainvillaea, in three colours, white, peach and pink. Dry, papery bougainvillaea. The pink was a killing, brilliant pink, the colour of a *muzungu*'s lipstick. She wanted me to cut it back so the timid white and peach could flourish. She told me that her *shamba* boy was ill, but I knew she just wanted to see me humbled. I worked all day in the blazing heat, and in the evening she called me in and told me to wash, then the house-girl brought supper.

She said there was a new presidential scholarship that paid for women graduates to study abroad. Probably it would mean a future in the government. Certainly it meant at least a year in UK, and the chance to gain an MA from London. She wanted me to apply for it.

'But Aunty, I am not the best student in my year.' The goat was tough, but I made myself eat it. Her big white teeth cut through it like scissors. She shouted at the girl who served it, but at me she smiled, a wide blank smile.

'You are my niece. You will win the scholarship. I wish I had daughters, but God did not wish it.'

Four months later I was on a plane to London, flying through the sky for the first time, thinking about what my father had said. He had come to Kampala to see me off. I think he had never been there before. At any rate, he got lost for a day and was found by some people from our village who were selling clothes in Owino market. My mother couldn't come: she was supervising the harvest. She sent me, wrapped in a banana leaf, a package of fried ants, delicious *enswa*, although the leaf was bruised and torn. Perhaps she thought I would take it to England. It would not have made the right impression!

My father was very proud of me. 'At last, someone from our family is flying.'

I didn't say, 'But we often flew, we children playing round the mango tree. We used to raise our wings and fly like hummingbirds.' I didn't want to think about the mango tree or the cousins I was leaving behind. I sat on the plastic seat beside him and told him I would buy them presents.

'They say London is very expensive,' he told me gravely. 'Daughter, you will have to be wise.'

Suddenly he looked smaller and older. I didn't say what was in my mind, that he had never been to London, that he would no longer be able to advise me. 'You know your daughter can live on nothing.'

He tried to think of a last piece of advice. I think he was recalling my childhood. I used to run faster than the boys, and came into the house with my knees bloodied where I had fallen on stones or acacia thorns. The scars were still there under the nylon tights I was wearing to look European.

'Don't run around on the plane, daughter. They say they fasten you down with a belt. If you wriggle too much you will rock the plane.'

I left him sitting there, not moving. Alone, as if he was learning something. How hard he had tried to be a good father. He had made himself say nothing about children, or marriage, although I had already left it too late according to the customs of our village.

I was young, and proud. I was going to England. The plane took off, and I looked down on Uganda. The buildings shrank as the view increased. Where was my father in so much space?

I remembered his words as the roaring plane broke through into the sunlight above the clouds. The journey levelled and became easy and the stewardess said we could unfasten our seatbelts. She had a smart uniform and shiny lipstick and her hair was flat-straight like a European. She obviously knew about flying, and London. I smiled at her and undid my seatbelt so I could lean over and look at the sun, and there was heaven. I was rushing towards it. Africa was lost beneath brilliant whiteness.

I imagined my family, small as insects.

When we landed in London they sprayed the plane against mosquitoes. My throat grew tight. As I came out on to the high steel steps, the light was like ice. I stared out at London, and nearly fell forward.

But this time I'm a woman, and everything is different.

I look at myself, tiny, all those years ago. One day I mean to write that girl's story. I hear her voice in my head at nights. All her mistakes have become my wisdom.

Now I do not need to beg money from the government, or work like a dog in my fat aunt's garden. Now I am too sensible to fall down the steps. Now I have flown on countless planes. Now I am too old to become a cleaner.

The letter starts to tingle in my left hand. How much would Henman pay me to go to England?

9   Vanessa Henman

When she rang today I nearly said, 'Not now!' She sounded like all the other opportunists who ring up and bother you when you can least bear it: foreign, and flat, without affect. She said, 'Is it you?' as if she didn't like me, but of course, it is just that she isn't English, shyness rather than anything else. Her voice had got deeper, as well, with the years. I was slamming the phone down – because let's be frank, these firms do mostly use foreigners, so a foreign voice does make me suspicious – when I suddenly realised it was Mary.

'Mary! Is it really you?'

'Yes, Miss Henman, I got your letter.'

(Of course Mary always pronounced 'Mrs' as 'Miss'. It was one of the irritants I'd almost forgotten. I'm sure I had told her that I was a 'Dr', but she'd looked at me blankly, in that African way. Perhaps it was because I was a single mother. I resolved that this time she should call me 'Vanessa'. Mary and I had to make a clean start.)

Yes, she was well. She had a very nice job.

I started to tell her about Justin, his terrible depression, his refusal to eat, the way he was getting less and less mobile, the succession of doctors who could do nothing. 'Justin hates everybody, Mary. Except you. Of course you know how much I love him.'

There was a silence on the line. I thought for a moment we were cut off.

'Miss Henman, I need money for Jamil. He has a place at Al-Fateh University. His father says he will be a vet, but he has to pay to get into al-Fateh.'

Jamil was the son; I had forgotten about him. Of course, the father was Libyan. Naturally there would be deals to be done. In any case, this was the African way. When they dealt with white people, they bargained upwards, just as they beat people down in the markets. I understood things better now I'd been to Africa. 'Mary, I know we can work something out.'

'Miss Henman, now I shall give you my number. It is the number of my mobile. When you decide about the money, you telephone again.'

This was a new Mary. More confident … bossier. More avid for money, which took me aback. Unwilling to trust an old friend. But I'd been to Africa, I understood, for in Africa, everyone is poor, poor things, even the richer ones aren't quite like us, so I made allowances, and rang off, gratefully, and did some calculations on an envelope.

She doubled what I offered, and I agreed.

Of course money is problematic, with Africans. They don't understand that we borrow everything, that we are poor in a different way. That my house cost me more than she could earn in a lifetime. They never understand we have money troubles too. That life in London is hideously expensive. I suppose it is a failure of imagination.

Although, to be fair, they themselves have nothing. The

monthly wage of a house-girl in Kampala is not much more than five English pounds.

In any case, now I feel happier. Mary is coming. All will be well.

Of course she will have changed. All of us have changed. Justin was a boy, when she was here, and such a darling, so clever and happy. I was still struggling to make my name. Mary seemed like a girl to me.

Though she can't have been a girl, she had just had a baby. She started with me as an hourly paid cleaner. I remember how deferential she was, calling me 'Madam' at the interview. (She must have thought she embarrassed me, because she never did that again. Not that I was sorry, but it sounded quite sweet. Her voice was lilting, like a little dark bird's. The 'Madam' fell on my soul like balm.)

I think that Justin was only three. Such a beautiful boy. Red lips, blond curls, smile of an angel, though he did have a temper … Gifted. Oh yes, he was very gifted. Walking at ten months, talking at eleven, trying to read the cornflake packet at two, admitted to school nearly a year early – at my insistence, but they were pleased to have him. Already a fluent reader, of course; they slowed him up, if anything. And oh, so charming, and amusing. Though tiring, of course, when one was working hard. Motherhood's never an easy option.

Justin made all the other parents jealous. They must have got tired of hearing all his achievements. Their own children seemed to have all kinds of problems: eczema, asthma, dyslexia, dyspraxia, while Justin was wonderfully lexic and praxic. Yes, and his skin was like silk under glass.

I don't understand what has happened to him, why he lies there dully staring at nothing, not reading books, actually *not reading* when his room is full of wonderful books, not writing anything, though once he wanted to be a writer, not combing his hair or washing or smiling. I suppose that part of me is angry with him, but the other parts of me are racked with sorrow. It isn't in the family, this kind of depression. Not on my side of the family, at least. Just my mother's brother who killed himself, and that was because he had the wrong medicine. Admittedly my mother was sometimes unwell, but she never actually stayed in bed. Once or twice she went away to hospital. But the rest of us are perfectly cheerful. My cousin Lucy was such a happy girl.

It must come from Justin's father's side. Of course, Tigger would never admit it. He doesn't believe in introspection.

That is my only reservation about Mary. She got on too well with Justin's father. It's the African way: defer to the men. They tell me that is changing now. Perhaps she will come back a feminist! In which case we shall get on better. I myself have always been a feminist, though not, of course, a man-hater. And after all, Mary is now divorced. She mentioned this in a letter she sent that may or may not have been asking for money – there were hints, I suppose – three years ago. Both her parents were ill in the government hospital. The hospital was free, according to Mary, but the drugs had to be bought from a private clinic. It seemed a peculiar system to me, but I sent a little money by Western Union. It's true that Justin more or less insisted. One was happy, of course, to have been of use. She wrote again later. The parents died. It would be heartless to think it was a waste of money.

When she first came to us, Mary was probably in her early twenties, though she looked like a teenager. She and Justin hit it off at once. He certainly wasn't as old as four. She began by cleaning two days a week, and ended up coming every day to look after Justin when he came home from primary school. I was a slightly older mother, thirty-eight when I had Justin. I didn't feel old: I was slim and fit. Older mothers can be better mothers. We have more resources – to be frank, more money – and more knowledge, and of course we value our children more than some teenage alley-cat casually dropping a litter of kittens.

Justin was a very *wanted* child. I keep telling him that, but it seems he can't hear me.

By the time Mary arrived I was in my forties, though she probably assumed I was in my thirties. Having a baby takes years off you. As long as you have help, as I did (a maternity nurse, and then a nanny until Justin started nursery school).

Mary, of course, must have had help too, because she was busy till late at our house. She came to me at one every day and stayed until Justin went to bed. She probably had some cousin or other looking after Jamil while she was with us. She did once ask me if she could bring her son along to work with her here when he was poorly, but I had to say, 'No', lest he infect Justin. Sometimes she baby-sat for me, though she started to ask for extra money, and sulked if we got back after midnight, claiming she had to get up very early. Perhaps she did have to get up early – in fact, I believe she did several jobs, because the husband wasn't earning. He was some kind of perpetual student, at that time. Later she claimed he was a diplomat.

Now I think perhaps I got some things wrong. Justin was always very sweet with little children. Perhaps I should sometimes have let Mary take him back to her place, to play with Jamil, as she asked. There would have been advantages for her son, playing with a clever, articulate boy. But then, Justin had so many activities: judo, maths for gifted children, drama, *Français pour les jeunes*, chess club, gym, kiddy Pilates, Fun with Yoga. Mary was always driving him somewhere, and he loved his activities, I'm sure he did.

(Curious that now he is completely inactive. The doctor says that his muscles are wasting.)

I would come in to the kitchen unexpectedly and find them cuddled up at the table, singing. He used to make up nicknames for her. She taught him all sorts of African songs which must have increased his cultural awareness, though it gave me a strange feeling when he sang them on his own and I couldn't understand a single word. It was like living with an African boy! So I bought a tape of nursery rhymes and asked her to teach him some English songs.

Of course there is no competition between us. We shall be united in caring for Justin. Perhaps I was a tiny bit jealous of her when she started to let him call her 'Aunty'. It was an African habit, not appropriate for England. The child had real, blood aunties, and it only confused him to call Mary 'Aunty'.

It was as if he loved Mary more.

More than his real aunties, not more than me. He can never have loved her more than me.

I do believe in being honest with children. I sat him on my lap and explained to him, one evening, that I paid Mary to look after him, and that if I didn't pay her, she wouldn't do it, whereas Aunty Becky and Aunt Isobel loved him for nothing.

It suddenly comes back, what he said to me. He must have thought I was attacking Mary, when I was only trying to give him the facts.

'Who is Aunt Isobel?' he asked. I couldn't believe he had forgotten his godmother. Of course she lived a long way away. 'And I only see Aunt Becky at Christmas. Why don't you pay them too? Then they'll love me more. They hardly ever come to see me. Mary comes to see me every day.'

He left me winded, with nothing to say. He was staring at me with eyes like stones, and his fists were clenched as if he wanted to hit me. His father had a temper, and so does he.

Then he said something worse, shouting, crying.

'Why hasn't anyone paid you to love me?'

10   Mary Tendo

Leaving again. I am leaving my country. The plane climbs unsteadily up through the clouds. It can't seem to get clear. Perhaps we shall die. I keep my seatbelt on, remembering my father. So proud, so afraid when I first left Uganda.

Once I hardly knew that I lived there.

When I was a child, I lived in the village. My village was the whole world to me. But I saw it was not, when I came to Kampala.

Then I left the city, and saw my country, and all the golden land around it.

Now there are no more clouds below us. I peer down, and see tremendous spaces. Trees that stretch away like a sea. And in the distance, yellow desert. And all these lands are African.

That was what I saw, when I first left home. Although England is famous, it is very small. I saw, from thousands of miles away, that I had come from Africa. That I belonged to Africa. I was Ugandan, and also something more.

So I am who? *Baampita ani?* I am an African woman, thanks be to God. It extends behind me, the mountains and forests that air travel allows me to see. The green and the gold going on for ever.

The valley of time, stretching back to Adam, as I read in a newspaper headline in London: 'ADAM AND EVE WERE AFRICAN. Rift Valley Origins of First Man.' So *Adamu* and *Eva* belonged to us! I carried the cutting in my handbag till the paper was yellow and dropped into dust.

It helped me to see their littleness. The little lives of the rich *bazungu*. They are rich and clever, but they are like *nsenene*, swarming insects that cover the sun. They will fall away, as the insects do.

Thank God I am an African woman.

Part 2

11

When Mary Tendo flies into Heathrow it is a cold clear evening in mid-September and she is nervous about Immigration. She checks her passport once again, and her pink notebook with Miss Henman's number. Her fingers leave damp prints on the cover and she wipes them on the hard webbing of her seatbelt, telling herself, 'In a few hours it will be over.' Yet looking around her, on the plane, at the anxious faces of younger Ugandans, licking their lips, staring out of the window, she guesses she's one of the very few with a job to go to and a place to stay. For her, getting a visa was not impossible. Her bank statements could pass the test, with a cash injection from her friend the accountant, and of course Vanessa Henman, at the other end, was a doctor, a householder, a college lecturer, which made Mary's paperwork look good. In time, the agency issued the visa. Yet the process has left Mary feeling like a criminal. They even took prints of her index fingers! When she first went to London, all those years ago, everything had been so much simpler.

Why have the British grown afraid of her?

And having the visa is no guarantee. Mary knows that even

with a visa Ugandans are turned back at Heathrow airport. If that happens, she will be paid nothing. She half-wishes she had stayed at home.

It happened to a *boda boda* man Mary knew, one of the hundreds of men in Kampala who rent out the pillions of their scooters to passengers, lining up on street corners near the big hotels. After a mile on the bumpy roads, most passengers are glad to get off. This man was kind; he was nicknamed 'Smiler', and sometimes he gave Mary a lift home for nothing, because she was pretty, and looked tired. Smiler always wanted to better himself. His father had died when he was seven, and Smiler had had to try and work the farm. First he grew maize and cassava, and sold his harvest until he could afford to buy coffee. Then he planted coffee and sold it each year until he had enough money to buy a bicycle. Then he used the bicycle to take loads of green bananas to Kampala, where he sold them for a big profit. He did that for four years in a row (though he was so thin he could hardly keep the bike steady, weighed down by a great curving anchor of bananas) until he had enough money to buy himself a second-hand *boda boda*. Then he got it in his head that he must move to England, to pay for his five younger siblings in the village. So he sold the scooter he'd spent years saving up for, to pay for his visa and airfare to London, where several cousins had promised him work.

He was back in Kampala the day after he left, rejected by Immigration at Heathrow, without an explanation, without his scooter, without the money he had spent on the airfare, without any hope of getting entrance to England, fifteen years of his life blown in a day, too shocked to take in what had happened to him. Mary saw Smiler alone on the pavement, his pupils grown small and stunned with loss. She bought him lunch at the Curry Pot. Soon he had managed to rent another scooter and was back on the street, but his eyes were still different, and she always paid him, and tipped him well.

Now Mary, too, has taken a risk. She has sub-let the flat she loves so much to a second cousin whom she thinks she can trust. But she hasn't given up her good job at the hotel. She has told the manager a small lie to the effect that she has a female condition, something delicate (so her male boss won't pry) and serious, so she needs some time off. If things don't work out, she will be magically cured! In the meantime, her job remains open.

But the loss of her flat preys on her mind. She was happy there. Her life made sense. Things were going well with Charles, her *kabito*, and they were talking about marriage. Has she risked all this for the chance of making money?

Besides, her last memories of the UK are not rosy. They run through her mind as the plane circles lower, roaring awkwardly through banks of white cloud that stream fitfully across the blue English sky.

When Omar left her, Mary's life fell apart. She'd gone back to Uganda with almost nothing, for she had put everything into the marriage, both the money she earned so hard by cleaning and the hours she cared for her family unpaid. She knows that in Kampala people thought she was a failure, a returnee who came back with nothing, a *nkuba kyeyo* who did not manage to earn enough money to change her life. This time Mary will have to do better. No wonder she is sweating as she steps out of the aircraft, though the London air feels cold on her skin.

Miss Henman has said she will be there at the airport. Mary wonders if Justin will be well enough to come. In any case, would she recognise him?

All at once her heart lifts with happiness. She feels certain she will recognise Justin. Of course she will be able to help him. She is not in UK just for the money. *Jesus, I thank you for bringing me back*. God will make Justin well again. Mary rejoices to be back in London.

Now she looks at the long slow queue of non-EU nationals, snaking heavily along beneath the harsh airport lights, in the vast concourse, a great vault of plastic ten times as big as Namirembe Cathedral, the dark red Anglican cathedral in Kampala. Mary joins the slow queue. Disdainfully, because she is almost a Londoner, she has married and given birth in London, and lived with its citizens for nearly a decade. She does not want to be lumped together with these village virgins, these foreigners, who are gawping around at the airport, awed, because they have never been beyond Entebbe.

In the end she gets a limp, pale pink immigration officer who has the regulation unsmiling face. He stares at her photo, and then at her, then, frowning, back at the photo again. Mary is ready for what comes next. 'Is it really you?' he says, with raised eyebrows. 'This photo doesn't look like you.' She knows she must not get upset, or show anger, so she makes herself smile and says, 'Yes, it is me. Perhaps I was younger.' He does not smile back. 'You are married?' Mary says, 'Yes', without thinking, and dare not correct herself in case he thinks she's lying. Just for a moment, her heart beats hard. But she only hesitates for one split second when he asks if her husband is in London. The answer 'He is in Libya' would probably detain her for several hours. Instead, she says, 'He is in Africa.' She finds herself staring at the man's lower teeth, which are grey and uneven, patched with off-white. British teeth which have seen better days. Fortunately, before his next question, one of the hard-eyed solitary men who stare at all incoming passengers comes hurrying over with an urgent message and the pale, bespectacled man loses interest, yields up her passport, waves her on.

Now she swings her great suitcase off the carousel,

rejoicing in the strength of her arms, and pushes her trolley gaily through Customs. 'Nothing to declare', naturally, though she has brought all sorts of presents for Justin, knives and barbed arrows, since he always loved weapons, which the two of them will hide from his non-violent mother; to give to his girlfriends, bead necklaces (which are Kenyan, she knows, but he will not, and she bought them from a seller near the National Theatre, so in a way they are Ugandan), a smooth goat-skin quiver trimmed with soft fur, two African shirts with sunburst patterns. At the last moment she'd remembered Miss Henman, and snatched up a woven raffia basket in vivid shades of yellow and green. It is tied to the side of her trunk with string. She regrets it, briefly. It makes her look too like the humbler people in that long pleading queue.

But nothing matters now except seeing Justin. She is hurrying towards the crowded barrier where hands and heads twitch and wave, three deep. She smiles at them all, indiscriminately hopeful. The flickering screen of faces is scanning her, but only one, suddenly, reacts. It is the small bony face of an elderly lady, and two stick-thin arms have shot up in the air, waving a sign that says, 'WELCOME MARY'.

My God, she realises, it is the Henman. In eleven years, she has become this mask, topped with flat yellow hair that makes the skin look whiter. But the face is smiling, and Mary smiles back.

Only seconds later, the two women have met. Close up, she can see it is really Miss Henman, just eleven years older, thinner and tighter, her mouth showing large new youthful teeth which smile and smile in her direction. Miss Henman puts down her bag and her coat and Mary realises that she means to kiss her, but Mary decides to hang on to her case, which she drags behind her like an alibi, and her other hand clutches flightbags and passports and the free *Daily Mail* she

57

picked up on the plane, which is full of stories about a new wave of illegal immigrants, this time arriving from China and Russia.

And then something happens against her will. Mary finds she is letting everything go. She has laid her great suitcase down on its back, and dropped the small bags in a pile on the floor, and the passport and paper go fluttering after. Despite her best plans, she and Henman are hugging, the thin arms turn out to be surprisingly strong, the narrow lips peck at her cheeks like a bird, and her own lips kiss back, and she even feels tears – a warm soft stinging in her dry tired eyes – to be welcomed like this by the woman she has hated.

'Miss Henman,' she sighs, and the woman says, 'Vanessa. We must be Mary and Vanessa, please.'

12

Vanessa leads Mary away to a taxi. She has taken Mary's lightest bag, leaving Mary pulling her life on wheels, the shoes, the coffee, the arrows, the Bible, the photograph book of Omar and Jamie, her *Songs of Praise*, her two new *gomesi*s which she means to wear when she goes to church.

As they fly along the motorway, the trees amaze Mary, so thin, so golden, so perfectly matched, so lacking in birds and fruit and flowers, so often solitary, without brothers. A few are scarlet as tulip trees, and Mary remembers that this is autumn. She had almost forgotten the crisp English seasons: at home all the seasons run together. But the trees are beautiful, and she is content, marvelling anew at this effortless journey, the way the taxi has all its parts working, no corrugated cardboard, no broken windows, the fact that they did not go at once to buy fuel, the rows of identical red brick houses, the organised Englishness of it all, this smooth chill world she had almost forgotten.

The house is the same, but surely bigger, greyer. Mary's heart beats hard as she walks up the path and sees the same clouds of dried lavender heads, the same red rambling roses, grown enormous, bending over the porch and encircling the window, and the hedge now almost as tall as she is.

When she was here before, her Jamie was little. She was still breastfeeding him at night. The rosebushes were small. She had loved their scent. Her own little boy. Her precious darling. How can he have gone so far away?

Mary makes herself think about Justin instead.

As they walk up the path, she says to Vanessa, 'I am excited. I am longing to see him. I think he is tall. Tall like his father.'

Vanessa's face clouds, and Mary remembers she never thought Justin at all like his father, although the two had the same nose, the same smile. How much about this family has Mary forgotten? Yet now she has thrown in her fate with them.

'I'm afraid his father is still rather hopeless.'

'Mr Trevor? I hope he is well.'

'Tigger, I'm afraid, is a typical man. He has just got himself a teenage girlfriend. A foreigner. She speaks no English. One really can't see the point of it.'

Mary swallows hard and thinks of the money. She will make sure she gets it as soon as she can. She will keep a record of everything she earns, and add to the sum every day, every week, until she has enough to go home again, to meet her *kabito*, to go to her village.

In the meanwhile, though, she is here on her own. Where the late sun has left it, the house looks dark, and she cannot see inside the windows.

Suddenly Mary is a little afraid. These English houses are like lost worlds, detached from each other, buried in trees, overgrown with plants and strangled with secrets. Whereas life in Kampala is lived outside. The houses there have thin walls and big windows, and quarrels and weddings are all in the open, though sometimes people are beaten in secret. But here in London, *everything* is secret.

Vanessa is ringing hard on the door. 'Justin promised to get up for us,' she says under her breath, half to herself. 'I left a chicken in the oven for you, Mary.'

Mary is pleased: she smiles at Vanessa.

'Yes, as I mentioned, I have been to Uganda, so I know you cook chicken for honoured guests.'

Mary's heart lifts. Henman has killed a chicken! And then she reflects, she would not have to kill it, she simply had to buy it from the supermarket. But all the same, they are cooking a chicken.

After three more rings, Vanessa hunts for her key and lets them in. The house smells warm, of chicken. It is silent, except for a faint sound of sizzling. Vanessa cocks her ear towards the stairs. She shakes her head, with a small frown of disappointment. 'I'm afraid he's asleep. I will show you where you're sleeping. You could wash your hands, and then we will eat.'

Mary thinks, I have never slept here before. What will my dreams be like in England?

The house feels enormous. There are five bedrooms. She only knows the bedrooms because she had to clean them. She does not remember which is which. The house seems older than before. At any rate, it is safe and dry.

Mary tells herself she is not too impressed. She tells herself she will find it old-fashioned now that she has her own flat in Kampala, so bright and modern, with wipe-clean surfaces and everything within reach of her hand.

Vanessa opens a door, and looks anxious.

But the bedroom Mary will sleep in is pretty. It is larger than Mary's front room in Kampala. There is a fine bed, a small pink armchair, a dark dressing-table with a table-lamp, a framed picture of sheep in a flat green field. The room is light, because it doesn't have the insect screens which cut out the sunshine in Kampala. It has a nice view across the front garden to the road and beyond it the motorway to Heathrow. In the blue-and-flamingo-pink-streaked sky, Mary sees a plane sweeping up into the clouds. Perhaps it is leaving for Uganda. A red sun is sinking. She will see the sunsets.

My life is a story of arriving and leaving.

'I like it. Thank you for my room, Miss Henman.' She says it before she thinks about whether it is better not to thank her until she has been paid, and Vanessa is relieved, since she has spent an hour agonizing over whether to give Mary a better room, with its own basin, and a view of the back garden, the long lawn and the willow trees, which is normally the guest bedroom. But Mary is Ugandan: this must seem like a palace. 'You will see you have got your own television, Mary. And *do* remember to call me Vanessa.'

Mary hadn't seen it. It looks small and smart and she doesn't yet know it is just black and white. On impulse, she kisses Vanessa again, and Vanessa flushes with shame and pleasure.

'I shall go down and finish the supper.'

By the time Mary joins her, Vanessa is carving, her long blade shearing the white like silk. The dining room has been painted yellow, and there is a light Mary thinks very beautiful, made out of thousands of pieces of glass, hanging like a waterfall, full of rainbows. This light must have cost a lot of money. Perhaps Miss Henman has become a rich woman. Mary begins to smile with pleasure.

She sees that the table is set for three. It bears a vase of yellow roses, two shiny candlesticks, three patterned glasses, a decanter of wine, with fine writing on the side: yellow squiggles of butter like caterpillars, and creamy-pinky shells of white bread. Mary loves white bread, though she prefers slices. The curtains are soft velvet, with twisted gold cords. The walls are lined with crowded bookshelves.

For a second Mary doesn't know what to look at. Everywhere you turn there is something to see. It has been years, and she has forgotten. Life is so much barer and simpler in Kampala.

And yet it is cold. Mary starts to feel chilly. She is shy at the prospect of a meal with Vanessa.

'I may go and wake Justin?' Mary inquires.

'To be honest, I don't know what to say.'

'I'll go, Miss Henman.'

'Don't be long,' says Vanessa. She is carving the chicken, and she is hungry. She goes on slicing for three or four minutes, and pours some wine, and puts the vegetables in dishes, although that will make more washing-up for Mary –

No, she thinks, I must wash up myself. This first evening, I'll wash up myself.

Vanessa finds she wants to eat quite badly. She takes a long swig of the red wine. The chicken smells glorious, so does the gravy. *Please may we eat before it all cools down.*

She can hear a low murmur of voices from upstairs. Mary has succeeded in waking him, then. A very small, secret part of Vanessa is hoping it won't be too simple for Mary, that Justin won't just put on his clothes and come down meekly as if nothing's been the matter, that his love for Mary will not be the single perfect key to unlock all the misery.

Because if it is, what does that say about Vanessa?

Why have I been such a useless mother?

The fat on the gravy is a solid sheen. With a sigh of impatience she sets off upstairs. The murmur of voices is getting louder.

She pauses for a second outside Justin's door.

What Vanessa hears astonishes her. She feels the blood

63

come and go in her cheeks. He is actually laughing. Laughing quite loudly. She hasn't heard him laughing in ages. Curious, envious, she opens the door. Justin is entwined with Mary on the bed. Both of them are giggling. They could be lovers. Justin's face freezes as he sees his mother.

'Are you coming down to eat?' Vanessa says abruptly. She tries to smile, but her face is stiff. 'I have carved the chicken. It is getting cold.'

But Justin is retreating under the covers.

'Coming, Miss Henman,' Mary says.

Neither of them looks her in the eye. Justin is just a blind mountain of bedclothes. Mary follows the older woman downstairs. She sees Miss Henman's hair has grown thin.

Vanessa scoops out potatoes clumsily so that one rolls on to the tablecloth, tears off a chicken wing and gives it to Mary, though there are neat pale slices ready on the platter. 'Look for goodness sake don't call me Miss Henman.' Vanessa sits down and gnaws like a fox, suddenly desperate for nourishment.

But the food soon starts to work its magic, restoring the blood sugar the wine had sapped. Within minutes, Vanessa feels better again. Mary is chewing guardedly, thinking about the advance on her wages. Vanessa takes a deep breath and smiles, wondering if Mary has noticed her teeth. 'What happy times we all had together. And you are looking well. Not a day older.' She lifts her face to the chandelier, waiting for Mary to compliment her.

'It is because of our skin,' Mary says, pleased. 'Ugandan skin is very strong. It does not go in wrinkles like English skin.'

Vanessa remembers that Mary is tactless. Never mind, she is here at last. She gazes on Mary and is satisfied. She looks so solid, healthy, happy. She looks like someone who can – save the day. *Mary, Mary. Stay here and save me.*

'How did you find Justin on the whole?'

'He is tall and handsome,' says Mary, carefully.

'Thank you,' says Vanessa. 'He has always been wonderful. Everyone has always said so. Handsome, brilliant, so polite. But now he is terribly ill, you know. He hardly eats. And I never see him. If he goes on like this, I'm afraid he will die.'

'Here I am, Mother,' Justin says.

He stands in the doorway, in ill-matched clothes, heavy track-suit bottoms and a pink Hawaiian shirt, his beard gingery and formless. But he is here, and he is awake. He takes a plate, and begins to load it with dark leg meat, potatoes, bacon. '*Obviously* I'm not going to die.'

For a moment Vanessa thinks she has been dreaming, that the last six months have been a bad dream. But she knows her son has been very ill. And almost at once she starts to worry.

'Have some breast, Justin, it's better for you. There's plenty, darling. Lovely white breast.'

His hand, which is vigorously spooning out gravy as he bends right over to the centre of the table, stops in its tracks, and he freezes for a second, the light from the chandelier brilliant on his hair, which looks so blond it is almost colourless, the ash-white ringlets of a giant baby. He puts his plate down on the table with a crash. A little spill of juice darkens the cloth, a little emission of mess and chaos. He stays bent over, as if waiting for blows.

'I will get a sponge,' says Mary automatically, and gets to her feet, and pats at Justin. Then Justin straightens, and his head hits the light. There is a tinkling sound, and hundreds of pieces of rainbow light spin around the table. He puts up his hand, perhaps to calm the crystal pendants, but Vanessa cries out, sharply reproachful, 'It's a new light, for heaven's sake be careful! Honestly, poppet, you don't know your own strength!' and he changes his mind and lurches upwards again, butts at the chandelier like a goat, laughing peals of riotous, masculine laughter, and strikes it again and again with his forehead until the white skin is pitted with red. 'Goal, Mother! Three goals to me!'

And then he charges back upstairs, thunderous, a weight that will surely break the stair-treads, leaving his meat to go cold on the table.

Vanessa sits stunned. Mary wipes the stain, then thinks, I will not do this again. I have not come here to wipe the table. She wishes she could say *Mpa ku ssente*. Give me some money, you miserable woman.

Perhaps Mary looks discontented, for Vanessa reaches out one thin white hand. It shines like a hen's claw in the sharp glassy light. 'Oh Mary, so sorry, are you all right? What a *dreadful* way to welcome you. Now, I daresay you are tired from your journey. I don't suppose there's anything I can get you …?' As she says it, she gets up and walks away.

Mary is surprised to find herself saying, 'Miss Henman, I will need some money,' and after a brief pause, the other woman says, 'Yes.'

13 Mary Tendo

A hundred and twenty-one pounds and thirty-seven pence. £121.37.

I have been in London for seven days, and earned the advance that she gave on my wages. Of course I have spent a little money. I bought some postcards and some postage stamps so I could write to my friend the accountant. Soon I will buy a mobile phone, but fifty pounds is a lot of money when you think about it in Ugandan shillings. One hundred and fifty thousand shillings. Next week, when I have earned more, I will do it, and send some money to my sister in Luweero.

I also put three pounds in the church collection. The English church seems to have grown more friendly, though it has changed, American style, and we are supposed to call the vicar 'Andy'. It is strange for me not to respect the pastor. And most of the black people there are old. I must find a church where Ugandans go. It was always a problem when I was with Omar, because he did not like me going to church, but now I am free, and go where I like.

What else did I spend my money on?

Ah yes, I bought some sanitary towels. Although the travelling has upset my body, which has often happened to me before. It used to happen when I travelled with Omar – my period would come when I least expected it. I suppose Miss Henman no longer has periods.

It is too late for Justin to have a brother, though he used to pray for one every day. When I told this to Miss Henman, many years ago, because I thought she would like to know, she was angry, which was a surprise to me. 'And who will the father of this child be?' I did not see what was wrong with Trevor, although she laughed at him and called him Tigger, which is a childish way of saying Tiger.

(In many ways, English people are like children. The Henman still has a toy bear on her bed. Though I once heard an elderly, shrivelled *muzungu* sitting in the bar at the Nile Hotel say exactly the same thing about Ugandans: 'The African, you see, is like a child.' I wanted to tell him he was like a tortoise, with his wrinkly neck sticking out under his shell.)

My own Jamie also wanted a brother. Instead he had a hamster, then a kitten, then a puppy, though at first Omar said all dogs were dirty, and tried to stop Jamil having one. It is one of the things I like about UK, the way the people love animals. The English buy their dogs from a pet shop, where they are kept in bright clean boxes. In Uganda, dog-owners like their dogs, but we don't cuddle them like babies. I always enjoyed taking Jamie to pet shops. In the end Omar came to look at the puppy, and after he had seen him, he could not refuse. Jamie loved the small white and black dog like a brother, and he called it 'Liquorice', like his favourite sweet. It was very funny: it jumped up and down, and licked Jamie's face, and liked television, barking at other dogs in the dog-food advertisements. I wanted to take Justin to see Liquorice, but Miss Henman always said 'Another time, Mary', and somehow the other time never came.

I shall not think about Jamie today.

On the whole, everything is excellent. I am doing well in Miss Henman's house, though I must remember to call her Vanessa. I am finding my feet and beginning to save money.

The truth is, I am here as a detective. I thought they wanted me as a nurse, but I cannot nurse an unknown illness. In fact, I do not believe Justin is ill. He is certainly not ill as people are in Uganda, with TB or AIDS or malaria. He is not unwell like he was as a boy, the only time I remember him ill, his cheeks as fat as a football with mumps. His skin is clear and his eyes are white, and so his illness is a mystery.

Frankly I think he is ill in the head. But this is harder for me to judge, for in some ways, all the English seem ill in the head, as I found out when I lived here before. They stand in queues, frowning and worrying, touching all their bags to be sure they are still there, and when they talk, it is almost a whisper. They keep saying 'Sorry' or 'Excuse me', and if you look at them, their eyes dart away. And they usually look sad, or in a hurry. They stream into the underground, eyes down, like ants.

But Justin is what? He is a moper, a sleeper. He is not in a hurry about anything. Once I understand, I know I can help him.

On the second day that I was in England, I went to see Justin and was stern with him.

'Mr Justin – '

He opened his blue eyes, amazed. 'Mary, you can't call me Mr Justin. Won't you call me Junty, like you did before?'

'I do not know.' I had to think about this. 'Because you are no longer a baby, I will call you Justin instead of Junty. But if you prefer, I will not call you Mr.'

He sulked a little, with his lips like a Ugandan's, which make him beautiful as a woman.

'Justin, I have run you a very nice bath.'

'I don't need a bath.'

'You smell like a donkey.'

This made him laugh, and cover his face.

'If you go on this way, you will grow a tail.'

When he was in the bath, I inspected his room.

I found out why he never eats his dinner. Underneath his bed, it is schoolboy heaven. A jewellery box of sweets is spilled everywhere. (Miss Henman would see them as hellish, though. Miss Henman thinks that sweets are poison. Perhaps it was sweets that ate her teeth. My teeth are perfect, without fillings.)

I myself like chocolate and peppermints, though I never had them till I came to the city. But obviously Justin has too many sweets, and they are too easy for him to pick up, so he does not have to get up for his meals. And his sheets are full of sweet papers. When he went to his bath, they stuck to his skin. A white boy covered in butterflies.

I swept up all the sweets into a carrier bag, and changed his sheets, and opened the windows. The wind from the garden came into the room. The clean green wind, so beautiful. This house is greatly in need of fresh air.

When Justin came back he smelled warm and sweet. I did not tell him what I had done, I did not want to fight with him. I was going to put the sweets in the dustbin, although they were not really *ebanisiko*, but when I looked, it was full of food, packets of half-eaten, expensive food, and the carcass of the chicken, which still had meat on, but Miss Henman had not bothered to make soup or stew, and I did not want to add to the waste, so I hid the sweets at the back of my wardrobe. In Uganda, the ants would have eaten them by bedtime.

Justin came back clean, with slicked-down hair, but he still had the orange necklace on. He sat beside me on the bed.

'Don't go away, Mary. Please, I need you.' He held my hand and smiled sweetly. His forehead was still a mass of bruises. I cannot believe this gentle boy is the one that attacked his mother's new lamp as if he was a bull in a butcher's shop.

'Justin, why do you wear this necklace?'

He looked at his knees as if he didn't want to tell me, in the same way he did when he was only ten.

'Come on, Justin. Do not be shy.' I took his chin and turned it towards me; I am not afraid of him, as Henman is. I cannot be afraid of the child I looked after. (Of course, she did not look after him.)

'It belonged to someone.'

'I think it is a woman.'

His red lips smiled, and he looked away.

'Justin, what is the name of this woman?' And then his face began to collapse, like a balloon after the end of a birthday party. (His mother always came to his birthday parties. But I did the work. I blew up the balloons. I blew them up till my cheeks ached with blowing. Usually Tigger, his father, helped me. Miss Henman took a photo of Justin blowing out his candles, but I baked the cake and stuck in the candles. You have to be patient, since they keep falling over, and poor Miss Henman could not be patient.)

'It doesn't matter. It's not important.'

So then I knew it was important. But I let it rest, I will get there in the end. *Akwat'empola atuuka wala*. I can be cunning, when I need to.

'Justin, will you tell me why you stay in bed?'

And then he started to look disagreeable. I know that face very well. Already over a decade ago I remember how his lip would curl at the corner, and both nostrils would go a pointed shape, like a cow breathing out after it has been running. It was the only time Justin looked like his mother.

'I think you know. I bet my mother has told you. I'm supposed to be ill. Everyone says so. The doctors are doing a load of tests.'

'So are you ill, Justin? What do you think?'

'What do *you* think?' He turned the question to me.

His eyes were blue, and still very young. It was hard to tell him what I think.

I do not believe he has ever travelled. London is another world from Uganda. In my mind, the worlds clash sharply together like the brass cymbals in the church band. Maybe it is hard to know two worlds –

But all of a sudden I was very angry. I did not show it, but I wanted to strike him. I thought of the sickness in the villages. This mummy's boy should be sent to Uganda. People younger than him are still dying of AIDS, losing their lives because of ignorance, although in Uganda we educate people, with leaflets and posters and plays in schools where AIDS is shown as a gorilla or a devil and the schoolchildren attack it with spears. Maybe clever Justin would laugh at that, but sometimes it is good for a message to be simple.

Let him see how everyone works, in Uganda. Even the very ill work harder than him. The sick people are panting in the heat in the fields, till they become too tired to feed their children. Let him see how some mothers, knowing they are dying, fill in Memory Books for their children, writing down everything the little ones need, names of the grandparents and cousins, stories about the children as babies. These are the Memory Books I used to print out on the photocopier of the Nile Imperial. Justin has a soft heart, he would sob if he read them. And there's not enough medicine; some only have aspirin, while the bathroom cupboard here is stuffed with medicine. Expensive medicine, only half-used. Every kind of painkiller for Vanessa, because she is frightened of getting small headaches, vitamins for this overfed boy.

This boy who lies here all day, sucking sweets. Only the dying lie in bed in Uganda. I looked at his body. Fattish and white. I wanted to strike him, or shout with rage.

But instead, I surprised myself by starting to sing, and as I sang, I became less angry. What came from my lips was a nursery rhyme that we learned together when Justin was little, when Vanessa gave me a nursery-rhyme tape, 'Traditional English Nursery Rhymes', and told me to listen to it with Justin, because he knew only African songs. 'Georgie Porgy, pudding and pie, kissed the girls and made them cry ...' I sang very loudly, because I was angry, only two inches from his large pink ear, which made Justin jump like a startled *kob*, but then he smiled, and began to join in. 'When the boys came out to play, Georgie Porgy ran away.'

Of course, I have loved him since he was small. I know that he is sick in his soul. Now he is an adult, I pity him. And all the English. They've grown soft and weak.

'Mary, do you think I am ill?' he asked.

'Now I am here, you will get better.'

'Thank you, Mary. You're wonderful.' The smile he gave me was warm and sweet. I thought, it is not his fault he is English. I remembered they can be kind, and polite. The educated ones have very nice manners; we Baganda people appreciate that.

He took hold of my hand again, and kissed it.

'I knew that you would save me, Mary.'

I did not say any more to him. Maybe the Henman had driven him crazy, always instructing him and asking him questions. Maybe that is why Justin sleeps all the time.

I shall find the girl who owned the necklace.

14

Vanessa tells herself to be calm, and yet she lies awake worrying.

It feels as if Mary is doing, well, nothing. Vanessa instructs herself: think positive.

Of course Mary will concentrate on Justin at first. And then she will have to recover from her journey. What matters is that we all get on.

She remembers, uncomfortably, more details of how things went wrong with Mary last time. Mary was asking for more money. Perhaps Vanessa *had* got just a tad out of date, but one couldn't forever be raising wages … Happily this time she has been generous. Five hundred pounds a month, she reminds herself. She does the comforting sums yet again.

When Vanessa went to Kampala, the preceding year, she had discussed the staff question with several Europeans. They all admitted that wages were low, but most of them claimed to pay over the odds. The figures they quoted were amazingly low: 80,000 shillings a month for inside servants, 50,000 for a *shamba* boy to do the garden. ('I mean, the natives pay

their people peanuts – 15,000 a month, would you believe?')
80,000 shillings was twenty-six pounds. That worked out at
… Vanessa's excitement increases. They are paying them six
pounds a week out there, less than a pound a day! And that
was thought generous.

Looked at in that light, Mary is rich. She is earning more
than one hundred pounds per week. Thirteen times the wage
of a servant in Uganda. Not that Mary is a servant here, of
course. But Vanessa hopes that Mary will be grateful. In fact,
perhaps Vanessa is paying her too much.

She doesn't want Mary to think her foolish.

Vanessa tosses and turns, thoughtful. It would be awkward
now to lower the wages, but perhaps she can approach it from
another direction.

Does she really have to employ a new cleaner, now Mary
is living here with them? Surely she will expect to clean, since
that is what she did before? 'I will leave it to her own common
sense,' Vanessa tells herself, and begins to doze off. 'I will get
out the cleaning things, and leave them in the kitchen, next to
the vacuum and the mop. And perhaps a shopping list, and
some money, and the car keys, and perhaps the secateurs, as
well, because Mary used to help Tigger in the garden, when
he came round at weekends, and the roses do need pruning …
Africans, after all, are basically farmers.'

'While you settle in, I will do the cooking,' she had said
to Mary on her third day, after Mary had overslept again. 'I
expect you have jet lag. Never mind.'

And Vanessa does do the cooking, at first, and the shopping,
as usual, from the supermarket, where she reckons she can 'fly
round' in quarter of an hour and get enough food for the next
few days. It isn't her style to make a list, shop in bulk, fill up the
freezer: she's a working woman; she has no time. But on days

when she isn't at the university, she sometimes drives to the supermarket early, enjoying the feeling of virtue that brings, darts haphazardly down half-empty aisles, scooping up items that take her fancy, and then, when she tires of it, relapses to the checkout and scoots her trolley to the coffee shop, where she buys a giant *latte* and skims the paper while the frozen food gently defrosts at her feet.

After all, she's never wanted to be a housewife. Her mother was a housewife. Life has moved on.

She comes home on the eighth day after Mary arrives with three heavy bags, hauls them into the kitchen, and feels suddenly low at the thought of unpacking them. Upstairs the house sounds far too peaceful. She's inured to Justin sleeping all the time, but the thought of them *both* in bed is maddening. So she dumps the bags in the middle of the floor – if the bacteria want to multiply, let them – makes a pot of amber-pale Lapsang Souchong, pours a tiny, delicate lagoon into her favourite, petal-thin, cherry-blossom cup, slips into her study and telephones Fifi.

'Fifi talk to me darling. I need a friend. No absolutely right, I'm not very happy. Mary isn't doing a hand's turn. They both just lie there. I am waiting on them.'

'It's their energy levels,' Fifi says. 'You have to release their energy blocks. I did tell you about the "Lettuce Plus" diet?' She hears Vanessa sigh down the line. 'When did Mary get here? She's probably exhausted. Don't forget you are *bathed* in radiation in planes. But you always said she was a good little worker.'

Vanessa clutches at this straw of encouragement. 'I don't want to sound as if I am complaining. At least Justin's shaved. Meaning, he's walked to the bathroom. Don't you think he looks terribly handsome when he shaves?'

'Ness, you have to stay calm. You have to stay focussed. You have to accept he can be a pain. Sometimes I'm relieved not to have any children.'

Vanessa pounces on her favourite theme. 'Most people don't realise how a mother suffers – '

But Fifi moves swiftly to head her off. 'Perhaps you should try him on Pilates again? We both know exercise does wonders for depression.'

Is she trying to say that Vanessa is depressed? Is she hinting that Justin is malingering? Vanessa remembers that Fifi gets jealous when Justin takes up too much of her attention. Once Fifi had actually complained that her Siamese, Mimi, doesn't get a look in. 'My son is ill,' Vanessa says, loftily. 'Obviously we all know exercise would help him, but frankly, walking down the landing is a start. At least he doesn't wet the bed any more.'

Mimi was house-trained as a tiny kitten. After such frankness, Fifi rings off hastily and goes for a long aromatherapy session.

Invigorated by their little exchange, Vanessa returns to her unpacking.

She has grown disillusioned with the "Lettuce Plus" diet that Fifi always bangs on about, though according to her handbook, *Salads for Life*, it is 'guaranteed to energise the stress-weary'. (But could Justin be stressed, after working six months and lying supine for another six?)

So Vanessa has returned to her favourite kind of food, which has always been smooth, and white, and mild, although she has a horror of sliced white bread, which Justin likes, and she forbids. The bags she unloads are packed with neat small blankets of starch and sugar and hardened fat, cook-chill lasagnes, prefilled pancakes, palped chicken breasts in white wine and cream, warm mouthfuls oozing with mother's milk that just need sucking out of soft plastic packets, bland swimmy curries that coat the throat paired with sticky sweet pastes of precooked rice, innocuous veal schnitzels in shrouds of pale crumb, butter-soft purées of neutered root.

Good, Vanessa thinks, inspecting this hoard. At least I don't have a life like my mother. At least I don't have my father to please. That grim little kitchen. The scratched steel sink. At least I don't bake bread or kill chickens.

Home is uncomfortable to think about. A thousand miles away from her well-stocked fridge-freezer, her golden infusion of Lapsang Souchong. She gulps down her tea, and does the 'Tree' position from yoga.

All she has to do is stay calm and focussed. Dear Mary will soon get the bit between her teeth.

15

At first Mary finds Vanessa's food delicious. And life in London is wonderfully easy. She does not have to get up at four to be at work at five, as she does in Kampala: she need not buy vegetables from the market and scrub and peel and chop and boil. She does not need to heft hacked shanks of meat, bloody and bony and awkward to carry, back from the butcher's to her little flat. She is happy that Vanessa is doing all the cooking. Mary's job is just to serve two plates, one for herself and one for Justin, and take it upstairs to Justin's room, where she wakes him up, and drags him upright, and tries to make him eat with her. If he doesn't eat, Mary takes no notice, but eats her own meal and lets him talk.

But after ten days, Mary doesn't feel well. She wakes up thinking, *Omutwe gunnuma. Lwaki?* She never gets headaches in Kampala. Her belly too. *Olubuto lunnuma.* She looks at her belly. She is definitely fatter. It is probably packed full of cream and soft meat. Her back aches too. She is constipated. She sits there, suffocated, stogged with pale England.

She has never lived this way before. She quite likes the idea of convenience food, because she is a modern woman, but when she lived with Omar, they rarely ate it, because she wanted to be a good wife. She told him she would learn to cook like his mother, and soon she was good enough to entertain his sisters, when they came to London, suspicious, critical. Omar had asked them, in their own harsh language, if they could find fault with Mary's *sharba libya*, lamb slowly cooked in vegetable ghee with tomatoes and *hararat* and cinnamon. Both of them admitted it was delicious. 'It is because Mary always adds parsley at the end, it freshens the flavour. It is better!' he told them, this time in English so Mary could enjoy it. After that, naturally they rounded on her when she served them delicate Libyan rice-puddings: 'You cannot make *mhalbiya* without any *atr*!' But Omar ate with gusto and laughed at them. 'Where would she find extract of geranium, in London?' He loved her Ugandan dishes too, rich groundnut stew bubbling with chillies and ginger, fibrous cassava or yam with beef. Mary would keep quiet when Ugandans in London complained that they never had time to cook properly.

Vanessa, it seems, has never cooked properly.

The next time Mary has a meal with Justin, she has to ask him an awkward question. But Mary has known him since he was a boy. She uses the words that she used then.

'Mr Justin – Justin. How often do you poo?'

She is looking at him so seriously that Justin straight away bursts out laughing. 'Mary you are funny. You can't ask me that.' He takes a big mouthful of mashed potato, which his mother bought ready-mixed with cream and nutmeg, and carries on laughing, in little hiccups.

Then Mary smiles too, and looks like a conspirator. When she speaks next, she is whispering. 'Because since I came to live in this house, Justin, I do not poo. My body must have a plug like a bathtub. Justin, you must tell me your secrets. Is it that in the UK, no one poos?'

After a lot of giggling, she wheedles it out of him. Justin, too, hardly ever poos. 'Perhaps twice a week,' he finally tells her. 'But I mean, Mary – we really don't count.'

'In Uganda, I poo at least twice a day.' This claim, made with pride and a demure downward look, makes Justin burst out laughing again.

'Mary, it's just so cool that you are here.'

'Justin, I am going to have to make changes. Soon we will be pooing every day.'

Vanessa, who happens to be walking down the landing, hears gales of laughter from Justin's bedroom, and is once more racked with curiosity. But she goes downstairs telling herself to be happy. If he's laughing, Mary is a good investment. And very soon, surely, she'll take over the housework.

It is true she has ignored the cleaning things, left hopefully out by the tall cupboard. But Justin is definitely livelier. One morning he smiles at his mother on the landing, and it is only half-past ten, and he has pyjama trousers on, which is certainly an advance on nothing. The plates Mary brings down after meals are empty. So Vanessa grits her teeth and goes on cooking. She has deferred the question of hiring a new cleaner.

Yet the house is getting dirtier: balls of hair and dandruff on the fitted carpets, a mottled skin of grey on the basins, tidemarks of brownish scale in the bath, a faint smell of urine around the lavatory. The kitchen floor bears ghosts of spilled sauces: when the oven goes on, it smells of old burnt food. Vanessa decides not to notice it. That is what Tigger always recommends. Trevor has a gift for not noticing things. It is maddening, but it keeps him contented. Vanessa feels she is learning wisdom. Perhaps she will never lose her temper again.

She does a deal with an unnamed god in her brain: make Justin better, and I'll be a new person.

Life goes on like that until the night Mary notices her innards are chock-full of white rice and precooked chicken.

The next day, Mary gets up at seven. Vanessa hears the front door closing and runs along the landing, heart in her mouth, to check that Justin is still in his room. He is still in his room, but Mary is gone. She reappears at ten with three bulging shopping bags. She leaves a sheaf of scrawled receipts on the table, torn scraps of paper from some crude market. Within half an hour, the kitchen is changing.

The earth has spilled roots out on to its lap, great brown and red tubers, white in cross-section where Mary has sawed some off for the pot. Great bullet-hard cabbages like dark green oilskins, with bulging white veins as strong as bone. Fat misshapen carrots like giant's fingers, ringed with knuckles of dirt, trailing six inches of hair; tomatoes puffed and quilted like marrows; pinky-gold mangoes smelling faintly of rot; cocoa-brown cassava as thick as a wrist; two enormous hands of black oversized bananas. And other things packed in rough paper or sacking: shiny beans like pebbles: coarse brown rice. Mary unpacks, and straight away starts cooking, dragging out an old black iron cauldron that has not been used since Tigger was here.

Vanessa hovers on the threshold, watching, uneasy at this vegetable flood, this weird invasion of living things into her kitchen, and there is Mary, in vigorous action, her strong back bending and straightening, her taut arms whirling like a Hindu goddess.

At two o'clock there is a giant lunch, after which Vanessa goes in to college feeling as if she has swallowed a farm. Her stomach makes noises throughout her workshop, and one of the MA students gets the giggles. When she comes home at six, Mary is cooking again. The kitchen has been cleaned and tidied, though the rest of the house is still in disorder, and the lunchtime washing-up is stacked dirty on the draining-board.

When Mary goes upstairs with plates for her and Justin, they are piled so high they hardly fit on the tray.

'Are you sure that Justin is going to eat that?'

'Do not worry, Miss Vanessa. It is good for him. By the way, Miss Henman, excuse me,' she says, sweetly. 'I am leaving the dishes for you to wash.'

'*I beg your pardon*?' gobbles Vanessa, her mouth choked with fibre, but Mary is gone.

Vanessa, of course, has no intention of doing it. She goes to bed, and lies there for hours, listening to the sound of her borborygmus. Then she sleeps heavily, only to wake at three am to the sound of voices. People laughing, or quarrelling. It must be in the street. She sleeps again.

In the morning, someone is in the bathroom. Vanessa has an urgent need. She doesn't want to trek to the downstairs loo while she is still in her short 'Pachamama' t-shirt. She stands outside fretfully for several minutes, listening to someone, who must be Mary, talking to herself and farting like a tuba. Then there is the sound of the loo roll rattling furiously upon its holder. Vanessa goes tactfully back to her bedroom so Mary does not find her there. After a few more minutes, tact is impossible. She emerges, crab-wise, but the door's shut again. Justin is inside, grunting like a baby. Vanessa limps furiously back to her room. By the time she gets in, the bathroom smells like a midden. This will become her morning routine.

And in the kitchen, the washing-up is still there. The work-tops are clean, but the washing-up, two lots of it, covers the draining-board, and overflows on to the dark oak table. Vanessa is incapable of leaving it. She puts on the radio, and stacks the machine.

After all, at least she has a dish-washer. Whereas Mary had probably never even seen one.

More and more exotic foodstuffs arrive. The kitchen starts to feel like a harvest festival. Many of the newcomers are unfamiliar. The bananas are not over-ripe, Mary says, indeed they aren't bananas, they are *matooke*. Whatever that may be, thinks Vanessa. And there are big dry nuts with pink papery skin. Once Vanessa finds an insect she has never seen before, a weevilish thing with a fat hairy body, and she squashes it savagely, with a phone-book, because she is afraid of it. The compost bin is always full.

'And where do you buy all this?' asks Vanessa. 'Surely most of this food is African?' And so is my kitchen now, she thinks, a little sourly; it always seems hot, and swirling with steam.

'But London is full of African things,' Mary answers. 'London is full of Africans'.

The house is much louder than it was before. Mary Tendo is not a light woman. She does not run upstairs, as Vanessa does, fleet as a bird on small stiff legs, or pad like Justin, who never puts his shoes on, and likes to be silent, so his mother does not notice him. Mary has a stately, womanly walk that Vanessa starts to find irritating. How does she have time to walk so slowly? Why is she always walking about, or clashing spoons in the kitchen, or closing doors loudly? Why does Mary have to sing hymns as she cooks?

'Where is the serving dish?' Mary asks. 'I am cooking pork ribs with cassava and cabbage and I can only find one serving dish.'

'Is it in the cupboard?' Vanessa asks, guiltily. She knows she has not emptied the dish-washer.

'I do not think so, Miss Vanessa. Can you please find me the serving dish?'

Grumpy, Vanessa opens the dish-washer, to find she has

forgotten to switch it on. She extracts the dish and does it by hand. Gives it to Mary without a word, and Mary accepts it with a curt nod.

'Dinner will be ready in half an hour.' Mary's words seem innocent enough, but Vanessa knows she has been dismissed.

Fifi rings, at nine, some time after they have eaten. Vanessa is lying on the floor of her study, trying to do her usual curls and crunches, but her stomach is still busy digesting the food, and complains as she doggedly lifts and straightens. She is glad to be interrupted by the phone, but a little disappointed that it is Fifi. Part of her expects her cousin to ring, her cousin in the village, her long-lost family.

Fifi wants to know how things are going with Mary. 'You said she had barely showed her face.'

'Well that's changed completely. She's always in the kitchen.'

'That's brilliant. You see, I told you not to worry.'

'Almost too much, as a matter of fact. In some ways, the house doesn't feel my own. In fact – '

'Well you can't have it both ways, can you? With live-in servants, you can't be private.'

Vanessa doesn't like being told by Fifi. She resolves not to show weakness again. 'Mary is a marvellous cook,' she says. 'Terribly healthy. Lots of vegetables.'

'Oh by the way, that reminds me,' says Fifi. 'Mimi has been nibbling my spider-plant. They're supposed to be terribly good for cats. But isn't that sweet? Do you think she *knows?*'

'I was trying to do my stomach crunches,' Vanessa interrupts her, irritably.

'Oh fine, fine, I was just concerned. Last time you sounded all over the place. So basically now you're happy?'

'Couldn't be happier,' Vanessa lies.

16

Next morning the phone rings at seven am. A man with a foreign voice is shouting.

'Wrong number,' Vanessa says, half-asleep.

He seems to be shouting, 'Merry Christmas'.

'This is *a wrong number*!' she shouts back, and crashes the phone back on to its cradle. She is teaching today: she needs her sleep.

Two minutes later, the phone rings again. She snatches it up, and bellows 'Yes?'

This time the voice is speaking very slowly, as if to a dangerous idiot. 'Mary Tendo please. I am phonin' from Uganda. This is her house? I must speak to Mary Tendo.'

Vanessa goes to the door, her eyes still half-closed, and bellows 'MARY!' at full volume. 'Telephone! From Africa!' Mary seems to appear from the wrong direction, from Justin's bedroom rather than her own, and brushes past her without a word, sits down on her bed, and takes possession of the phone, leaning back on Vanessa's pillows, smiling and swinging her feet up cheerily.

After three or four minutes, which feels like an hour to Vanessa, standing there frowning and rubbing her eyes, Mary Tendo rings off, and says, 'Thank you, Miss Vanessa.'

'It was *very early*,' says Vanessa, meaningfully.

'It is all right, Miss Vanessa, do not worry. I was already awake, relaxing.'

'I hope the phone-call was important. Is somebody ill? Has someone died?' Vanessa is not at her best in the morning, but the edge of irony is lost on Mary.

'Thank God, my friend is very well. This was my friend the accountant, Charles. One day you will meet him when he comes to London!'

'Oh really.' Vanessa's voice contains a wealth of meaning, but Mary has already gone back to bed, smiling a broad and kindly smile. Vanessa cannot get to sleep again.

17   Mary Tendo

Three hundred and sixty-six pounds and fourteen pence. £366.14.

I have been here three weeks and things are still going well. The money I have earned is growing like a mango pip dropped on the ground in the forest at home: by morning, there is a mango tree. Soon my life will be full of mangoes.

It is true I have had a small financial setback. I bought myself a mobile phone, for £49.99. It was one of the cheapest, pay as you go, but still it looked fine, small and neat and shiny, and the salesgirl described it as a 'clamshell model'. Of course it seemed like a good investment, so I could contact old friends in London, and also call up Charles, in Uganda. I bought it in Harlesden and on the bus home I sat listening to the ringing tones. Several seemed nice, I couldn't quite decide between 'Amazing Grace' and 'Ave Maria', so I played them over and over again until a man with a miserable face and glasses leaned over from the seat behind, tapped me on the shoulder and asked me to stop. 'I've got a sodding headache already,' he said. 'One thing I don't need is "Amazing Grace".' His face was very red, his breath smelled of wine and there was something sticky on the lens of his glasses. So I stopped playing my ring-tones, but scrolled on down and was pleased to find they had 'When the Saints'. I forgot about the drunkard and started to play it, but suddenly he snatched the phone from my hand. 'This is a British bus and you can't do that.' 'Give it back!' I shouted. 'Not till you get off.' 'I am getting off now.' 'I don't believe you.' I threatened him a little with Vanessa's umbrella, because we know how to deal with thieves in Uganda, and he said 'Mother of Jesus' and gave the phone back. I was playing 'When the Saints' as I walked back home, only as soon as I got in, Vanessa came and asked, 'Did you happen to borrow my umbrella, Mary?' While I was busy pretending to look for it (I eventually 'found' it by the bookshelves in her bedroom), I somehow managed to lose my phone. Every so often, I search for it. In the meantime, I use Vanessa's phone, which was awkward on the morning my *kabito* rang. She stood rudely by the bed, and would not go away. What if we had wanted to sweet-talk each other?

I am carrying on my detective work, all the while helping Justin get better. And I myself am quite well again, though a little heavier from eating so much. Now we all defecate every morning in order, including Miss Vanessa, although she would not like me to say so. I make these Londoners shit like Ugandans!

I am earning my money by shopping and cooking. It seems like easy work to me, but I know Miss Vanessa thinks cooking is hard. On my first week here she was doing the cooking and sighing and swearing as she did it. She left the kitchen looking red and exhausted, like a *muzungu* who has been in the sun, though all she had done was take food out of packets. I hope she is glad I have taken over.

But sometimes she comes and interrupts me and tries to talk about Uganda. She is very proud she has been to Uganda. She went last year, and she stayed for three weeks. She claims she was teaching Ugandan students to write. The British Government sent her there, together with some other British teachers, though I cannot imagine why they chose Vanessa. They stayed in an American hotel, with air conditioning and no mosquitoes. She wants to talk to me about Kampala, but the things she has seen seem ordinary to me. She is very excited by the smelly old storks which drop white birdshit all over the city. We do not like those ugly *karoli*. Ugandans think they are common, and dirty.

She also pretends to like the taxis. She calls them *matatus*, a Kenyan word. I tell her that we just call them 'taxis', even if they carry twenty people, but she thinks I do not understand. 'Oh no, I didn't go everywhere by taxi. I wanted to live like the natives, you know. I wanted to do everything like you.'

I pretend to sneeze, and go on with my cooking.

But soon she will be back again. This time she wants to talk about western Uganda.

The guests of the Nile Imperial all went there, and talked non-stop about western Uganda. They told the staff, very proud, at breakfast, 'Tomorrow, you know, I'm going to the west. I've heard it's very beautiful, western Uganda.'

'Oh yes, Madam. Very beautiful'.

'I am excited. First time on safari.'

'Oh yes, Madam. Enjoy your safari.'

Then some of them would ask us, 'Have you been there recently?'

And we always said, 'No, Madam. Enjoy your safari.'

Kampalan people do not go on safari. Only the *bazungu* go on safari. I talked about this to my friend the accountant.

'Charles, why do we not know our own country? I too would like to go to western Uganda.'

My *kabito* had never thought about it. 'Mary, why do you want to go there? There were enough animals in my village. The *bazungu* like animals more than people. They even like lions and crocodiles.'

But I am stubborn and do not agree. For a start, I myself like animals. (Jamie and I, we both liked animals. When I was a child, I grew very fond of goats, because I liked the boy who was the goatherd, and I liked Jamie's pets, even the mangy hamster, and I took him to London Zoo on Saturdays.) I told Charles, I want to see my country. It is our country; it does not belong to them, these old *bazungu* in their four-wheel drives, wearing pale brown clothes all covered in pockets, which makes them look like ancient soldiers hung about with battle-kit, with cine-cameras and walking-sticks and water bottles and binoculars. They go on safari with polite black drivers. Without the drivers they would be too frightened (yet they think they own them: they always say 'my driver', 'Could you go and see if my driver is waiting?').

One day I will have money, and time for a holiday. Most Ugandans do not have holidays. And then I too will go on safari.

But until I have been, I will not talk about it. The lion who roars too much catches no game. I will not discuss it with Miss Vanessa. She thinks she will show me she loves my country; she believes she will please me with all this 'knowledge'. But why should she lecture me on western Uganda when most Ugandans have never been there?

She gabbles on, but I say nothing. I make a loud noise with the spoon in the saucepans. After a bit, Miss Vanessa gives up. It is not her fault. She is ignorant.

18   Vanessa Henman

Oh shit oh shit it has all gone wrong. Just when everything seemed so hopeful. That is the thing, they're unpredictable. Even though I have known Mary for years. You never really know what they're thinking. Shit, shit, shit, shit.

It all began with the problem with the mornings. Except for the days when Mary goes shopping, she really is quite hopeless in the mornings. She rolls down, yawning, around eleven, when I have already been working for hours. My study is next door to the kitchen, and I have tended to stay out of her way, because it is annoying to find her there, still in her slip-slops and a thin cotton nightgown through which you can see too much of her body. She really has the most enormous breasts. What if Justin should walk in and see her? She is hardly setting him a good example.

And then today I smelled something. I am sure I smelled cigarette smoke in the kitchen. I am allergic to it, which makes me notice. I am mildly allergic to a number of things, though Tigger always laughed at me when I said so. But even a hint of smoke, and I know. It is not that I blamed Mary Tendo at all. I am sensitive, I have been to Kampala. I suppose nearly all Ugandans smoke. Bad things come from the west, and they jump at them, because they do not realise the dangers. It's a cultural thing. One understands it. One tries to be culturally aware.

When I said this to Mary, she became sulky. She did not deny that she had been smoking, but she pretended it was rare in Uganda. I felt sorry for her, and did not argue. But Mary had better not smoke in my house.

Moreover, the bitch should get up in the morning.

No, I'm not angry. I did briefly lose my temper when Mary said something inflammatory, but now I am completely calm. This whole disaster is not of my making.

I suppose I felt she was taking advantage. Taking advantage of our distress.

It wasn't as if I rushed into anything. I hadn't been able to sleep last night: too many comings and goings on the landing.

What were they doing all night long? Why did nobody but me get up in the morning? I was unable to concentrate on my marking, so I sat in the kitchen and waited for her, and that was when I caught it, that faint smell of burning.

By the time she came down, I was a little cross. I think I had been looking at the house with fresh eyes. Without my noticing, it had got filthy. The kitchen was cluttered with monstrous vegetables. That dirty black cooking pot of Tigger's was always sitting on the Aga. The rest of the house was even worse. No one had bothered to dust or vacuum. (We do have a Dyson. It's not exactly hard.) The lavatory bowl, which is always in use, has developed brown stains, and the shower is blocked. The dust on the window-sills is thick as fur.

She shambled in around a quarter past eleven, yawning and smiling, and I had to say something.

'Mary Tendo, we must have a talk.'

'Yes, Vanessa.' (I distinctly remember I had not asked her to call me Vanessa, she just suddenly did it, as bold as brass.) 'But it is not Saturday today.'

Saturday is the day she gets paid. I felt all she cared about was the money. She was only thinking about herself. I did not invite her here to be selfish.

'Mary, do you know what time it is?'

She shrugged. 'There is a clock in the kitchen, Vanessa.' She was smiling a lot, but I think she was nervous.

'Somebody has been smoking here.'

She sniffed, disdainfully, then laughed a little. 'Perhaps Mr Justin has been smoking.'

'I know my son. He never smokes.'

She looked at the ground, as if I didn't know him.

I couldn't put up with it any more. 'Mary why do you never get up in the morning?'

'Because I am tired,' she said, rather sulky. Her eyes had gone dead, in a way I remembered from a few little quarrels when she worked here before. It made it impossible to know what she was thinking.

So *sh*e was tired. But *I* was tired, I was tired from working and not really sleeping because of the noises I heard on the landing!

'Mary, *why* are you tired? You are not really working. I hoped you would do your bit with the cleaning. This is a big house. There is a lot to do. I am obviously very busy at the college. I cannot do everything here as well.'

'You did not ask me here to do the cleaning.'

I saw she was going to be aggressive. 'Mary, I am paying you very well. I brought you here to look after Justin, and obviously help in the house as well. And now you do nothing and pretend to be tired.'

And then she looked at me, full in my face, and said

something terrible I cannot remember, and I lost my temper – I regret I lost my temper, I hardly ever lose my temper, except with Justin, of course, and Tigger – and I am afraid I shouted at her, 'How dare you say such disgusting things! You are my cleaner! You are just my cleaner!'

And now Mary Tendo is upstairs, packing. It is all over.

But what shall I tell Justin?

19   Mary Tendo

I am upstairs, pretending to pack. I have done this twice at the Nile Imperial, letting them see that I was emptying my locker, and each time, they have raised my wages.

I have always known Miss Henman is crazy. But still this morning she has surprised me; I did not expect her to be quite so angry.

I told her I was sleeping with Justin, and suddenly she was screaming at me. 'You are my cleaner! You are just my cleaner!' Which shows you she thinks cleaning is something easy, and cleaners are stupid people, not worth listening to.

And yet, she asked me here to look after Justin.

(It is something strange about the *bazungu*: many of them fear us, or do not like us, and yet they give us their children to care for. They say very often how they love their children, even Henman, who used to call, 'Kissy kissy kissy' to Justin, every day, after she finished her writing, and stretched out her hands. Though often he ignored her, and clung to me.)

She should have been pleased I am sleeping with him. (It is what we always say about the *bazungu*. They speak very nicely, but you do not really know them; you never know what they are thinking.)

Justin begged me to, and I thought about it. I thought about it, and then I agreed. I knew if I slept with him it would help him.

Besides, I enjoy it, although it is tiring. The Henman does not know how tiring it is.

When I tried to tell her, she screamed even louder.

And so I have come and started my packing. I am banging my case about on the floor. Soon she will come and apologise. I hope she will come and apologise. I cannot leave now. I have to earn more money.

(£2,000. That is what I need. £2,000 is six million shillings. I do not much want to buy land or build houses, because I have seen it go wrong for others without quite enough money to bribe the officials. My friend Charles thinks he knows all about the system, the *bibanja* and *poloti* and the KCC, though sometimes his fingers have been burned, as well. My *kabito* puts his fingers in too many pies. He is an accountant, but he deals in cement, and sometimes lends money to other businessmen, and sometimes gets it back, and sometimes not. Still, let him get rich for both of us, and rent rooms to thieving tenants, if he wants to. I have my own plans for the six million shillings. I will not say why I need it for Jamey, but I need it for Jamey, most of all.

It costs a lot of money to find people. And some people can never be found –

I must think of the other things I shall do. Buy smart new dresses at Garden City, instead of going to Owino Market. Fill up Charles's car with sugar and paraffin, with tea and coffee, with rice and aspirin, with shoes and hats and shirts for the children, and English books for the primary school, and my friend the accountant will drive us to the village.

So I cannot go back to Uganda till Christmas. It will take four months to earn the money I need.)

It is possible there has been a slight misunderstanding. I thought of this after she really started screaming. Surely even Miss Henman would not believe that I was doing bad things with her son? I Mary Tendo! A Ugandan Christian!

And then I started to laugh a little. And then I started to laugh a lot.

Of course, nothing bad is happening. Nothing, at least, that could make me pregnant. Of course it is different with my friend the accountant because he has promised to marry me. God is my witness, I'm an honest woman.

Many things Miss Henman does not understand, but this is the one that made me so angry that I had to pretend I was going home.

Because I was her cleaner, she thinks I always will be. When she looks at me, she sees 'my cleaner'. When we had the argument, she called me 'my cleaner'. *She thinks that Mary Tendo is a name for a cleaner, like Vanessa Henman is a name for a professor.*

(And when I was here before, eleven years ago, the Henman made me laugh when she talked about me. She thought I was too stupid to understand. But I noticed that, after I started looking after Justin and tidying up a little in the afternoons, she changed what she called me from day to day, when different people came to the house. Sometimes she said, 'This is my cleaner' and sometimes she said, 'This is our nanny'. So she got two servants. But she only paid one.)

In fact, Mary Tendo is educated, as educated as Dr Henman. I am BA Hons, Makerere.

And when she screamed at me, I answered her politely. 'I *was* your cleaner. I'm not your cleaner now. I *was* your cleaner, Miss Henman, Vanessa.'

The Henman thinks that cleaning is something easy. But Henman never really cleans her house. Every now and then when she cannot do her writing she chooses something small, like a light or a bath tap, and polishes it like a crazy woman. She rubs it like a wasp that is trying to sting. She shines it as if it will light her path to heaven. Then she comes to me and shows me her work. 'You see how nice it looks when one makes an effort.'

I do not say, 'But it took you two hours. When I was your cleaner I had only three hours to clean the whole house, which is big, and old, with five dusty bedrooms and three sitting rooms.' I repeat what she says, and look at the floor. I say, 'Very nice, when one makes an effort,' but it comes out wrong, and I almost laugh, and she notices, and looks at me strangely.

In fact, I am starting to rebel against her, because I am tired of pretending to be humble. I remember a story about Idi Amin, who was our leader when I was a child. He was a terrible man, but also very funny. When the British economy was in trouble, he started a 'Save Britain Charity Fund' in Uganda, and telegrammed the UK prime minister to tell him he was sending 10,000 Ugandan shillings 'from his own pocket', and a lorry-load of vegetables from the people of Kigezi.

The British government ignored his offer. Probably the British think Ugandans are simple, and do not recognise our sense of humour. And yet Amin renamed himself 'The Conqueror of the British Empire in Africa in general and Uganda in particular'!

Part 3

2 0

Justin lies awake in the moonlit dark, looking at the back of Mary's head, its crisp curls just visible, springy and resilient, tough enough to survive, and save him. Mary could not sleep with the curtains closed, and so now he sleeps with the curtains open. Everything is different now Mary is here.

Perhaps he does not need to wake her up. Perhaps the panic will not come tonight, the feeling of falling and falling for ever, the demon voices that come and accuse him of all that he has left undone. Sometimes it's enough just to see her there. To know that someone is there just for him. Someone who will let him reach out and touch her. Who came round half the world to find him.

His mother had tried to send her away. Although she denies it, he knows it is true. Two days ago he woke to the sound of voices, and his mother was screaming at Mary in the hall. Mary stood there with her coat on, a poor cotton thing with big shoulder-pads and shiny buttons, and her cases beside her, ready to go. She was calm, but she was talking loudly. Neither of them was listening. Mary was wagging her finger at his mother. Justin stood on the stairs, his heart in his mouth. Both of them were ignoring him. In this house, Justin is still a child. But he made himself go down and join them.

'Are you driving her away?' he remembers shouting. And other things he should perhaps not have said. 'I hate you, Mother. You're driving her away.'

'You don't understand.' She had turned on him. Her mouth was thin and furious, her pupils were tiny, her nose big and bony, like a witch. He had been shocked by how old she looked, which made him wonder, for a second, whether his mother was going to die, and then he could go and live with his father, if his father would let him live with him.

Will he always have to live with his parents?

But he loves his mother, painfully, deeply. He is like a sucker, still joined at the root. How would he live without his mother? How would he live without Mary?

All his life he has felt abandoned. He has been left at so many places: Baby Reading, Junior Einstein, gym for toddlers, swimming for tiddlers.

How could he stop what was happening? 'You've driven her away, you've driven her away,' he had sobbed, stupidly insistent. 'Mary is the only person who can help me.' But it only made his mother scream louder.

And then his father rang on the door. They had all stopped dead, in total silence.

Before he rang again, Justin managed to say, 'If Mary goes, I will never forgive you.' His mother stared at him, eyes wild.

Then his father came in and it all calmed down, though Mary refused to go from the hall or move her cases till his mother said 'Sorry'. She did say 'Sorry', which astonished Justin. His mother has never said 'Sorry' to him.

And his father made them all a cup of tea, and then his

parents had begun to quarrel, as they usually did, and life went back to normal.

In the end it turned out it was his father's fault, according to his mother, for not being there.

How could his father cause the quarrel by not being there?

It is true that his father's been away more than usual. He has a new girlfriend, whom they've never met. His mother had told him she was practically a schoolgirl, but later he found out that this wasn't true. Soraya is twenty-nine, and an art teacher. His mother calls Dad 'the cradle-snatcher', which makes Justin feel ashamed for his father.

Of course his father is really old, so Soraya must be blind, or desperate. All the same, Justin would like to meet her. Perhaps she is easier to live with than his mother.

Sometimes he thinks that his mother is a demon. Sometimes she makes him feel hopeless, useless. His heart starts beating too fast again. Can he ever be good enough to please his mother?

Mary stirs in her sleep and snores gently. The sound is soothing, like a pigeon cooing. Justin stretches out his hand and feels the heat of her shoulder, very gently, not quite touching her, just sensing the living, easy warmth, and his body relaxes, and he breathes deeply.

He thinks about some of the things Mary says. He knows his mother believes she is stupid, although she has never actually said so: but when he was a child, and Mary looked after him, he used to pass her sayings on to his mother, and she would get a strange, superior expression, and say, 'Remember she is African. They have a different way of doing things. Remember that you are an English boy.' And he would feel embarrassed, and wish he had not told her.

But now he thinks Mary might often be right. For example,

she believes that his father is clever. Justin has been brought up to despise his father, but Mary claims he is interesting.

'But as Mother says, he is not educated,' he said to Mary, a few days ago.

'Sometimes education makes you stupid. Your father is not a stupid man. Your father is clever, but also kind. You, Mr Justin, are very like your father.'

'My mother says I am the image of her.' But even as he'd said it, he knew it wasn't true. He is big, not bony: he is slow and lazy, not jerky and speedy, like his mother. (*Now* he is lazy. Once he was not. Once he worked so hard that his brain burned out.)

'I think you should get to know your father.'

As he lies in the dark, he remembers Mary's words, and thinks, 'I shall try,' and falls asleep gently.

But half an hour later Justin wakes up sweating, his heart thumping, from a terrible dream. His mother has discovered him down on the lawn, which is dry as straw, in midsummer. He's drinking beer with his father and his father's girlfriend, who is nine years old. She is pretty, and happy, and Justin is as young as her, and he suddenly knows that this is his sibling, the sister he has always wanted, and his mother has kept him away from her. They are pouring the beer on to the yellow grass, and it pushes up instantly, dark green and shaggy, a wonderful game they can go on playing, but suddenly they hear his mother screaming, and she bursts from the house, yelling, 'Justin, get up! Get up and get on! You are all useless!' and he sees that the glass door she came through is shattered, and daggers of glass stick out from his mother, and she is bleeding, and it is his fault, and everything that happens is always his fault.

He reaches for the sweets underneath the bed, and then he remembers that they are not there, and turns over, and reaches out for Mary.

21   Mary Tendo

Every night, Justin is frightened of demons. He cannot sleep deeply, he dare not wake.

When I was a child, I never slept alone. Of course, all the children slept together. And later when I was at Makerere, whenever I went home I slept with my sister. The English make their children sleep alone. It is not surprising that demons attack them. Of course, I am educated, and do not believe in demons, which are a projection of the unconscious mind. Belief in spirits drags us back into the darkness that hangs like a shroud over the north of my country, where Kony listens to spirit voices and then makes children eat other children. His army cuts off lips and noses. The war in the north goes on for ever, too terrible to think about, for no one who travels that way is safe –

The people of Uganda must escape from spirits! And yet, they can attack you when you sleep alone.

Every night when the Henman is asleep I fetch my duvet and my pillow and take them along to Justin's room. He puts a low couch beside his bed. The first night he told me to move it myself. I told him no, I would go back to my room. So after that, each night Justin did the moving, and put it back each morning, in case the Henman saw it.

I lie beside him and comfort him. For the first few weeks, each night he sucked my breasts, which gave me a sharp feeling like pain in my belly. It was like pain, but also like wanting. I said nothing, I accepted it. I have always wanted another baby. Now I have no milk, but I can still give comfort. Soon Justin will no longer need to do it.

When I was here, Justin was like my baby. He was three years old, but I suckled him. Because he butted at me like a goat, like the skinny goats back home in the village who push their muzzles at their mother's teats.

I did not do this when the Henman was watching. I knew from my friends who were also nannies that the mothers did not like us to do this. But many of us did it. I had plenty of milk, I was still feeding Jamil, though because of my work, I could only feed him in the evening and the morning. Maybe Justin drank more of my milk than Jamil.

I know he drank more of my time than Jamil. When I remember this, it makes me angry, and so I shall not think about it. Yet this is what happens to very many women. We look after other women's children, not our own.

I dream that in heaven it will be made right. Our children will be young again, and we will care for them. God will put Jamie in my arms.

The Henman is very proud of feeding Justin. Some English women do not feed their children. She told me this, when she finished in her office, she took Justin from me and tried to hold him, though he wriggled and kicked and reached out to me. 'We are very close, as you can see. I breastfed Justin for two whole years. It was very tiring, but I'm glad I did it.' I smiled and said, 'Very nice, Miss Henman.'

I did not tell her that in Uganda, we breastfeed our children till they are four or five.

There are many things that I have not told her. One day I am going to speak my mind, once Justin is better, and I have earned my money. In the meanwhile, I will write everything down on my precious computer, which is sitting in my bedroom.

I have decided I do not hate her. She is old and alone, and will not live long, because she told me she will soon be sixty. Though some of the *bazungu* live for ever. I hope she will learn something before she dies.

I have told Miss Henman that she needs to hire a cleaner. It was easier to say because Trevor was here, and when Trevor is here, there is one sensible person. We were drinking tea after the argument. Trevor always smiles at me as if he likes me.

When I said, 'Miss Henman, you must hire a cleaner, because I think your house is dirty,' her face went very red, although I smiled politely. But after a bit, she said, 'Very well.' Then I told her that I would help her to find one, and she said, 'This beats all.' Which must mean, 'Good idea', so I told her, 'Please write an advertisement, and then we shall stick it in the newsagent.' And then Trevor laughed and said to Vanessa, 'I bet you would like to tell her where to stick it'.

But in fact she stuck it where I suggested, which is where I found the postcard, all that time ago. And she wrote the same thing, about the 'nice family', though she didn't say the nice son stays in bed, and walks around all day without any clothes on. Since then many people have been calling the house, and I have a shortlist of seventeen. I have told Miss Henman I will interview them. I thought she would be pleased, but she did not look happy.

22

Trevor Patchett approaches the house rather gingerly.

Last time he was walking up the path he heard screaming inside, at the same moment as the rose scratched his arm and made an awkward triangular tear in his new work shirt. He is still wearing it: a battle scar. Last time he arrived they were all crying except Mary Tendo. It hurt to see his tall son crying, big teardrops running down and soaking his beard. And Vanessa screeching and crying with temper. And Mary Tendo wagging her finger and talking in her sing-song African way. All of them turned and stared at him. 'I'll make us a cuppa,' he had said, as usual, and made a pot of her Earl Grey rubbish. By the time he left, everything was calm.

They were mad, of course. All of them barmy. But most women are. He is philosophical.

The boy, though, he cannot abandon the boy.

And so he is here again, as usual, on call, with his tools, his teabags (since he can't stand Earl Grey, and Vanessa will have nothing else in her kitchen) his sugar-cubes, his phlegmatic patter. It was her own word for him: 'phlegmatic'. At first he thought it was another insult. Then he looked it up, and saw she had a point. You couldn't say she was a stupid woman (though he often does, and will again).

This time, at least, he does not have to duck, because Mary Tendo has cut back the roses, and he sees that the upstairs curtains are open, the curtains of the bedroom that imprisons Justin. Is that a good sign? Probably. He listens, carefully. So far, all quiet.

The rose has produced some last small red flowers. He remembers, wryly, that he put the thing in, maybe twenty years ago, maybe nearer thirty, when he still believed he would be living here. He sees his own reflection in the window. He still looks like a man who can get things done. He comforts himself that he is not old. When you're self-employed, you cannot grow old. He still looks strong, sturdy, doesn't he? Soraya even says he is handsome, but then, she's an art-teacher, and short-sighted.

He takes a deep breath, and rings on the door. Vanessa insisted that he keep his door key, but each time they get burgled, she changes the locks, and by now he is several sets of keys behind.

A strange blonde girl answers the door. For a moment, his heart soars like a song bird. My boy has a girlfriend, he thinks in that flash. He's got himself a girl, he must be back to normal.

'Hello,' she says, very doubtfully, with a foreign accent and a big white smile.

'And you are?' he says, grinning back at her, plonking his bag of tools on the doormat.

But straight away he realises he is wrong. She looks too shy, and she says, 'Please. I am nobody, I am just here for job. Can I help you, sir?'

Then Mary Tendo appears behind her. Last time he was here she was standing in the hall surrounded by her bags and

Justin and Vanessa, and the enormous row was going on, so Trevor didn't really notice what she looked like. Now he sees Mary is plumper, older than before, but still attractive, still very much a woman. Her hair is even shorter now, which might look boyish, but her neck is long and soft, and she is curvy, bosomy. Once Vanessa had accused him of fancying her. He blushes, suddenly, and looks away. He has known Mary for years. Of course he doesn't.

'Hallo, Trevor. I hope you are well.'

'Hallo, there Mary. How's it going?'

And then she is off, talking loudly. Trevor smiles at her benignly, but doesn't listen. Of course he doesn't listen when women go on. Vanessa has gone on at him for over two decades, so Trevor had to find his own way of coping.

But Trevor has a lot of time for Mary. Little Justin would have been buggered without her. She must have put up with a lot, from Vanessa. What must it be like, working for her? (But then, of course, Trevor knows what it's like. He's been working for his ex for over twenty years. Coming round to fix whatever needs fixing. Unpaid and rarely appreciated.) So despite what Vanessa has said about Mary, he views her with understanding and pity. To come back here, she must be desperate for cash.

She is still full of vim, talking for Britain, or Africa as the case may be. 'I am very busy. I am interviewing people. We need a new cleaner, and Miss Henman is at work, so I am taking care of everything. This girl is from Australia – '

'Austria – ' the blonde girl corrects her.

'And her name is Anna – '

'Anya, Miss.'

Mary looks as though she enjoys that 'Miss', and smiles at her encouragingly, and at Trevor. 'I just gave her a test, to open the door. Trevor, did you think she was good at it?'

'A1,' says Trevor, obligingly. 'Very good door-opening, Anya my dear.'

'I think that Anna will be good at cleaning,' says Mary Tendo, with a queenly smile.

'Well, you get on with your interviewing,' says Trevor, tickled by this turn of events. 'I'll just go and make myself a cuppa in the kitchen and then I'll get going on that toilet.'

'Trevor, you cannot go to the toilet. The toilet is blocked,' says Mary, firmly.

'Just a turn of phrase,' Trevor grins. 'Come to unblock it. Madam called me.'

In the kitchen there is another surprise. Justin is there, sitting shelling peas, shucking one after another into a big white bowl, *ping, ping* on the shiny china, and he is freshly shaved, and looks young again, because last time his scruffy ginger minge of a beard made him look like an ageing down-and-out.

'Oi up cock,' says Trevor, and punches him fondly. 'Making yourself useful, Justin lad?'

'Um …' says Justin, but he smiles at his father, that enchanting smile that once made teachers melt, and girls swoon, and his employer take him on (for the mere six months when he has been in employment) and his mother more doting than was good for him, Trevor reflects, sitting down beside him.

'Maybe one day you'll come and help your father.' Justin says nothing, but his eyes move slightly in a way that does not dismiss the idea. Trevor hurries on, encouraged, not pushing it. 'Have a cup of tea, boy. I've brought my own as usual, it won't be some of your mother's rubbish.'

Trevor waves his Typhoo teabags in front of his son.

'We've got some, actually,' says Justin.

'Never,' says his father.

'Yes. Mary Tendo likes strong tea.'

Trevor feels vaguely affronted. Ness has always refused to have it in the house. The system is changing behind his back, the insane system he has always known. And the kitchen looks different, full of fruit and veg, great bottles of oil and jars of grain, huge hairy brown things and bulgy green things. It isn't quite what Trevor is used to, and he has been coming here for over two decades. It even smells different. And Justin is here, out in the daylight. The prodigal son, the golden boy who one day slipped back into babyhood, wetting his bed and crying and sleeping. The brilliant spark who got lost in the dark. Oddly, the grief had brought them together, the sudden crushing blow of his breakdown. Vanessa, who thought she knew everything, suddenly knew nothing, and turned to Trevor.

And I didn't have a bloody clue, thinks Trevor. But maybe Mary Tendo does.

Mary Tendo appears, looking bright and masterful, trailing Anya, who looks pale and skinny beside her, just as the kettle boils for tea. 'Anna is going to do a tea-making test,' says Mary, handing her the teapot. Anya makes tea, nervously, and spills a little on the work surface. Mary *tuts* kindly as she hands her a cloth, and Anya wipes it up, too carefully.

'Aren't you going to give the girl a cup?' asks Trevor.

'She would be embarrassed,' says Mary, drinking. 'Cleaners do not drink with their employers.'

'Have I got the job then?' asks Anya, rather sharply. She has noticed Justin, and is staring at him hard. Trevor checks that his son is wearing both parts of his pyjamas, but for once he is, and the girl is still staring.

'First a washing-up test,' says Mary Tendo. Trevor notices a certain glint in her eyes. He wonders why she's chosen such a very blonde woman.

Vanessa comes home at half-past seven and Justin at once goes back to bed.

'Miss Henman, I have found you a cleaner,' says Mary.

'Vanessa,' she reminds Mary, irritably. 'But is she experienced? Is she good? Will she clean my house till it sparkles?'

('I don't want to get landed with another African,' she has whispered to Trevor, in the hallway. Several of the candidates have been black, and Vanessa is afraid they will gang up on her.)

'Anna is Australian,' Mary says. 'I think it is a very clean country. Also, I have given her several tests. Trevor heard me interviewing. I was excellent.'

'You were red-hot,' says Trevor, laughing. 'She really gave her the third degree.'

'There's not a lot to it, is there?' says Vanessa, irritated by all this praise. 'I mean, they only have to be sane, and honest. Cleaning, you know, it isn't brain surgery.'

'Cleaning is hard work,' says Mary Tendo. 'To do it well is not so easy.' She looks to Trevor for support, but he only smiles and looks away.

'I'm not an expert. Blokes never do it.'

'Men are so lazy,' says Vanessa, but half-heartedly, as if she has her eye on other prey.

'I'll be off then,' says Trevor. 'I've fixed the toilet and got that shit out of the gutter.'

'There's a tear in your shirt,' Vanessa says, critically. 'This Indian person doesn't look after you – '

'Soraya's from Iran,' Trevor corrects her. 'And I've never asked a woman to mend my shirts. Look, I've really got to go, Vanessa. Got to read a book.'

'What's the rush?'

(But he's always talked about reading like this, as if it is an urgent need, something he has on a timetable and might lose forever if he misses a moment. When he lived with her, briefly, he kept his books in a wooden chest he had crafted himself, ingeniously fitted with internal folding shelves and adjustable compartments, a cross between a tool-box and a nineteenth-century writing desk, but big enough to contain twelve dozen books, as he had told her proudly, no more, no less. 'One hundred and forty-four books,' he said. 'That's all the books I have in the world.' At which her lip had curled, slightly. Poor man, he thought he was a great reader. 'I have four thousand or so,' she replied. 'But you haven't read 'em all, have you?' he asked. 'Nobody does,' she said, amused. 'I do,' he told her. 'Then I pass them on. To a friend who might like it, or a charity shop, so the good books keep on doing the rounds. And then I buy another one, and read that. Reading's the breath of life to me.')

So she doesn't wait for him to give an answer. It's just the way he is, and always was. 'Did you paint that chip in the bath enamel? I've been asking you to do it for ages.'

'No, too lazy,' he says. 'Ta ta. Nice to see you, Mary. Keep trying with Justin. He looks a lot brighter since you arrived.'

'Cleaning is hard work,' Mary doggedly repeats, but neither of them is interested. They have wandered, gently squabbling, into the hall, and Vanessa is seeing him off into the twilight. The toilet is working, the gutters are clear, Justin's peas are eaten, Anya is hired. Things seem to work better when Trevor is around.

Vanessa pats him on the shoulder with her thin pale hand, which he has been familiar with for half a lifetime. Unconsciously, he always checks for the ring. 'Bye bye Tigger. See you soon.'

'Not if I see you first,' he says, and manages to kiss her on the cheek before she backs away from him, laughing and protesting, into the dark house where Mary waits.

23   Mary Tendo

I have nearly finished showing Anna how to clean. She tells me she is experienced, but I see as I watch her that she is not. She brushes *towards* her with the long brush, when you should push the dust *away* from you. She begins her work by emptying the waste paper tins, though as she is cleaning she will fill them up again. She vacuums the floor before she tidies, though when she tidies she will find more dust. She does not look under the cushions on the dining room chairs, but of course crumbs always creep under cushions. Still she is very quick and she smiles all the time and when she does not know, she does not worry me with questions, and her hair and her skin are very white and clean. I am surprised that I chose a white-skinned cleaner, but it is good for them to learn a new skill.

Now that I have settled the cleaning question, I can concentrate on two things which are more important. I shall do my detective work, for Justin, and make a beginning on my new project. I have set up my laptop on the dressing-table. It makes me smile to watch myself, sitting there writing in my rose-pink room. I did not have a mirror until I was fifteen.

I shall write my Autobiography and Life. In Kampala, of course, I would be too busy. I took the name from some papers that Miss Henman left on the table in the kitchen. It is the new course she is teaching at her college: 'Autobiography and Life Writing'. The description used show-off words, of course, which is not her fault, as I know myself from the years I spent at Makerere University. You cannot pass exams if you do not show off (though some people enjoy it more than others).

'There is a pervasive discontent with the traditional convention-driven narratology of novels, and people are turning to life writing to reappropriate their own narratives. This is especially evident in a post-colonial and post-imperial context.'

I am 'post-colonial' and 'post-imperial', and so I have exactly the right context. Though if anyone else said it, I would be annoyed. I do not want the empire and the colonies attached to me like a long tail of tin cans. I am going to write about my life in England, Uganda and all over the world. *My Autobiography and Life*. Or perhaps, *The Life of Mary Tendo*. Everything will be finished by Christmas. I find myself wondering who will read it. Sometimes I think, thousands of people, sometimes I think only my *kabito*.

I hope it will end with an adventure, once my work as a detective comes to a climax.

24   From *The Life of Mary Tendo*

Everything begins with the mango tree. We sat under the mango tree and told stories. Sometimes I could not wait for my turn. I hope our tree has not fallen down.

In London mangoes were very expensive when I first came here, all that time ago. My employers used to buy them, and leave them to rot. They hardly ever ate the fruit in their fruit bowl. It was me who had to throw it away. In the end I started taking the fresh fruit for my baby.

I dreamed that England would make me rich. Instead, it made me a fruit thief and a cleaner.

I cleaned up other people's mess.

Hair-balls, chewing-gum, pellets of snot.

Sperm-stiffened towels, cigarette butts, blood.

Baby sick, nappies, sanitary towels.

My professor said to me, 'Remember, Mary, you always have choices,' but once you are a cleaner, there are no more choices. Every kind of dirt becomes your business. Some people would say I was less than my parents, but I know how much I paid to get to London. I am proud, not ashamed. I am a Ugandan.

In the village, my family was considered rich. We had a square house of plaster, with a flat roof of tin. You could see the bricks of the inside walls. But most people still had mud huts, roofed with straw, little round huts like baked chocolate, with lizards dropping from their thatch like rain. My mother told me not to laugh at them. We had boys who fetched water and helped with the crops, aunties who sewed and made clothes for us, cousins who helped to cook and clean. What was there to clean? Only the cooking pans, the cook-house. No rows of books, no polished floors, no expensive carpets to brush with soft brushes. Just dust and insects when it was dry, mud and frogs when the big rains came, splashes from the cooking, ash from the fire. The bedding to be washed and dried in the sunlight, and spread flat as paper, to kill the jigger flies. Life in a village does not have to be dirty.

And in London, Paris, Tripoli, also, all the rich cities where I have cleaned, I found what? I found dust, and mud, and insects. More dust than at home, because the things were everywhere. All of the houses were stuffed with things, mirrors, pictures, toys, money, left lying around, mostly white people's money. And the dust was grey, mostly white people's dust. It came from their skins, their hands, their heads. It wasn't sand. It wasn't earth. It wasn't alive. It was dust from their faces. The city is dirtier than the country.

I cleaned in the city for ten years or more. And so I learned many things about cleaning.

Miss Henman believes that cleaning is easy. Men like Trevor and Justin cannot do it at all, and some African men never enter the kitchen, though my friend the accountant goes where I ask him.

But all my life I have tried to be clean. African people are clean people. I knew that even as a small girl. I watched the aunty who helped my mother, crouched on the ground outside the house. She washed the dishes in a big metal bowl. She used cold water and hard blue soap. Scrubbing and rinsing till they shone in the sunlight. It was quiet in the village. She sang as she worked. You could hear small sounds of water lapping and little grunts of pleasure as she finished something, and shook it in the air, gold drops flying. She did it every day after food.

I must have learned my lesson well from the aunty, because I cleaned this house for years and years. I cleaned offices too, with heavy machines, with an army of foreigners, in the early morning. Some of them clean well, some are lazy. The Australians were not lazy. I made one friend who was Australian, a tall young woman called Leanne, from Brisbane. She had big muscles, and she helped me move furniture, and she was always singing, and very clean. This is why I did well to choose Anna to work here. The Portuguese were good, but complained too much. The Spanish were proud. They did not do the work. I liked my friend Juanita. She was very funny, but she was always waiting to be rich and famous. The Africans were grateful to be working, at first. But later some became like the Spanish. The Nigerians were very loud, always shouting. The Ugandans tried to call home on the phones. The Rumanians were racist, with many prejudices.

I myself am not prejudiced. I learned this at Makerere, where everyone teaches that racism is bad. And the Bible says we are all God's children. But English people are too lazy to be cleaners. I never met English people cleaning. Only one man I remember who was mad, and had to take medicine every morning. When he did not take his medicine, he was always laughing, so of course we knew he was really crazy, because the English do not laugh very much, and never do their own cleaning. I think they must be bad at it.

All over the world people live by cleaning. I did not understand this until I was in England. In Kampala, most families do their own cleaning, except for the *bazungu* and the very rich. Most of the *bazungu* are working as 'donors', for organisations and countries that give money to our government, but to make up for it, they are mean in private. In my church I became friendly with two women, Grace and Martha, who were house servants in the same row of houses. All the people who lived there were embassy families. The houses were large and beautiful, but my two friends lived in dark quarters in the garden. My friends' children were not allowed to visit them. It broke their hearts not to see their children, but if the employers caught sight of them, they docked the wages. These people were supposed to be ambassadors, but they were frightened of Ugandan children! Do they think our children are bad, or dirty? Have they never seen them dressed for church on Sunday? One family took Grace to London for the summer. She was very excited before she went. But in fact, she spent all her time here cleaning, then babysitting nearly every evening, so she did not get a chance to see London. And afterwards the woman docked her wages, because 'it cost more to feed you in UK'! And whenever the employer's spoiled children got ill, it was another reason for docking Grace's wages, and when Grace complained, the woman gave three reasons: first because Grace had looked after them badly, and that was why they got the infection: second, she probably infected them: and third because, now the children were ill, it would be easier for Grace to look after them. And this is the way these *bazungu* stay rich. Compared to them, Miss Henman is an angel.

Yet when I start to think about Kampala, Ugandans are not angels either. For in many families there are cousins and aunties who do the cooking and the cleaning, relatives who live like beetles in the kitchen and do not have any other jobs. Of course this happened in my own village, but there most of the aunties had somewhere to live, because to build a hut is not so hard, and it is easy to grow things, or keep a chicken. It is different in the city, where families squash together. While I lived in Kampala I did not really notice. Everyone at home just says, 'Oh, she is family', and these people are family, but they are slaves as well, and some of them are desperate for the chance to escape these hard families where they work like ants, to get a real job that is paid with money.

I was good at cleaning, and in a way I liked it, because I knew the money helped Omar to study, and afterwards it helped me buy nice clothes for Jamie, and toys and books, so I was pleased with myself. Though there was never enough time to play with Jamie. And so his father taught him to read, which made me jealous, though he was a good father, and when Jamie read to me for the first time, I was proud and glad, and we were all happy, and hugged each other, and were a family.

I worked long hours, so I earned good money, although in the end I got tired of it. I cleaned houses and offices. Then later, hotel rooms, in Morocco and Paris, when I followed Omar on his first postings. When we were first together, he believed women were equal, and quarrelled with the imams who said we were not, and quoted the Koran, with passion. But as people age they become more fearful. Omar did not really want me to work any more, and yet he never earned enough money for us, and so he could not stop me working. And I think he was ashamed that I was only a cleaner.

(It was not my fault; when we went to Paris I applied for many jobs in schools and offices, but once they saw I was African, they would not look me in the eye, and usually they said the job was gone. Yet the French did not mind my cleaning their rooms, so long as they did not have to be in my presence, just the dirt and mess that came from their bodies.)

Also Omar was jealous, especially in Morocco, because I had to clean the rooms of men. He thought that, if I was alone with a man, I would not be able to stop him making love, although when we were students in London, and young, he knew I was often with other men, and I did not even notice them. Because I loved Omar, as I always would. Even when my marriage was ending, I loved him. Even when I hated him, I loved him. And even now, because he gave me Jamie, even if later he took him away.

But I never told Omar about the men who came when I was working and brushed against me, as I was bending over to dust or polish. They pressed themselves against me through my overalls, and I had to be polite, and beg them not to, when I wanted to punch them hard in the stomach. And I could have done, but I knew they would sack me. In my dreams, I push them away, even now. I have strong muscles. One day I shall use them.

I know everything there is to know about cleaning. Because African people are forced to be clean. In Uganda, there are many diseases that kill you if you are not clean.

But nobody likes to clean other people's toilets. No one wants to put their head near the stains of shit and urine from other people's bodies. The carpets smell of urine round the toilet bowl. And many people do not flush their toilets. Until you are a cleaner, you do not know this. Until you find things floating like slimy brown crocodiles. Nobody likes to clean the hairs from the bath, dark hairs from their privates, curled like worms.

Nobody likes to brush the dandruff from the dressing-tables where rich women sit and do their make-up. It lies on the wood like dirty yellow snow, not melting, and they are off dancing, or flirting with men, with stiff shiny hair, in tight-fitting dresses, smelling of vanilla or lemons or roses. Then cleaners like me, dressed in overalls or track-suits, come silently to take away their leavings. We dance with the brooms and the vacuums.

Sometimes it is cheerful, when the bosses are out, and we can play music, and shimmy as we work, and make faces at ourselves as we clean the mirrors, which are sprayed with a lacy veil of toothpaste that makes us beautiful and vague as brides, beautiful as our queen, Nagginda Sylvia Luswata, before Kabaka Ronald lifted her veil. But people like the Henman will not let you play music, because it disturbs them in their important work, which is sitting reading in a bubble of silence. Yet I can read anywhere: on buses, on trains. Today I read Hemingway on the underground. I was in another world, in *The Torrents of Spring*. I did not shush my neighbours, or frown, or complain.

You would think they were not real, these pale fragile people. You would think they did not have mouths, or arses. Perhaps they would not know the word for it. And then you find out how real they are. No one would believe how real, how dirty.

No one wants to touch used sanitary towels. These women take them out and forget about them. They are black with old blood from the women's bottoms. Or sometimes bright red. Like snow with roses. They smell like meat, like salt and iron. Perhaps the bloody ones do not think about this. They throw the things away into a bin in the bathroom, and later the bin is emptied by magic. I do not suppose they do it on purpose. But when I pray to Jesus, I pray against these women. I pray He will make them do their own dirty business.

Also, when you are a cleaner, everyone blames you. If

anything is lost, the cleaner has moved it. If anything is broken, the cleaner has broken it. Usually of course the employer is right, but you cannot clean without breaking things. You must always say it was already broken. Or else they will take it from your wages.

It is their fault because they have too many things. In Ugandan houses, there are no things. There is nearly nothing, except cooking pots and blankets, rush mats for sitting on, perhaps a table. Ugandan houses are clean and airy. British people's houses are full of little objects. They get dusty and dirty, they break and they fall, they fade and get old, there are more and more of them.

They interest me, though. These British houses tell a story. They are full of letters, and photographs, also. (If Miss Henman and Justin both went away, I could find out their story from the things they have collected. But because she is a writer, she never goes away, though she is very proud she went to Kampala. I wish she would go to Kampala again.)

In Kampala, only the rich have cameras. Most people have only wedding photos, which we keep in a shiny plastic book, and show to all visitors when they arrive. But Miss Henman's house is full of photographs, perhaps a thousand, perhaps two thousand. Shiny piles of photos of her and Justin. And other faces of white strangers, too many of them to look at, or dust, or remember. And other pretty things that are not useful. And broken things she does not put in the rubbish.

It is hardest to clean when the employer is at home. Eleven years ago when I was her cleaner, Miss Henman was often working in her study, which meant she sat reading a novel all morning, or talking to her friends on the telephone. (To be fair, I did sometimes see her typing.) Whenever she was home, I could not be happy. She was always coming through to make herself some coffee, or cook herself lunch while I cleaned the kitchen.

It did not matter that I had already cleaned the cooker. It did not matter that I had wiped the surfaces. The Henman left them covered with crumbs and grease, and always tipped the last of her coffee in the sink. It sat on my clean sink like a filthy black feather from one of the greasy old *karoli* in Kampala. Then she left the dirty cup on the draining-board, just after I had whitened it with bleach.

And I had to hear all her advice about cleaning. The Henman is a teacher, and cannot stop teaching. 'I think you might be using too much bleach. It is very bad for the environment.' 'Mary, please put all vegetable waste in the compost' (although she dropped her apple-cores all over the house, going sticky and brown in the wastepaper tins). 'Mary, do please get the washing straight out, if it stays in the machine it gets horribly creased, and I know you don't always get time to do the ironing.' (There was never enough time to do the ironing, though she left it in a tall pile on the landing, and after I started it, she would bring me more, and because I am not lazy, I did not like to leave it. So I went on ironing as I played with Justin. Once he nearly pulled the hot iron down on his head. But when I told the Henman, she only blamed me.)

She was always there, with her pale eyes staring. So I could not read her letters, or examine her drawers, which were very untidy, when I did look quickly, or try on her clothes and necklaces, or call my Omar on the telephone, or call Uganda, as other cleaners did, or watch the television with Justin, since his mother said television rotted the brain. I could not drink a cup of tea in the garden. I could not take a shower, or try on her perfume, or sip at her bottle of 'London Gin', which had a nice picture of berries on the label, or dry my hair with her hairdryer. You see how Miss Henman interrupted my cleaning!

I am glad my *kyeyo* days are over, the days of doing dirty work for nothing.

And now I am going to meet some friends from the days when I was young, and a cleaner.

25

Mary has begun to have a social life. Now she has recovered from the shock of arrival – the big dark house with its frozen inhabitants, her shrivelled, nervous, yellow-haired employer, the sleepy, sulky, ruined boy – now she has got started on her task as a detective, and feels she has deserved a little time off, she has used the phone numbers carefully written in the new pink notebook she bought in Garden City.

And as soon as she's hooked up with Ugandans in London, Vanessa seems physically smaller, to Mary. The house is less oppressive, less like a prison. Justin's state of depression, like the body of a grub very slowly burrowing away in the dark, no longer lies like a stain on her heart. She is still a Ugandan. She can be happy.

It is worth the journey to the other side of town to sing her heart out on Sunday morning with other Ugandan Anglicans who know you open your mouth when you sing. Who laugh and chatter after the service, and do not whisper, or pretend to be humble. Mary eats *muchomo* on Saturday nights with friends of her elder sister's ex-boyfriend, and the smell of roast meat is the best in the world, both salty and sweet, with burnt-sugary juices that coat the pink core in dark caramel – though they tell each other that they miss Kampala, the sprays of white stars on the blue night sky, the punters eating their pork out of doors, licking the salt off bare warm fingers. They complain, they talk loudly, they roar with laughter. They tell stories about *kyeyo* in London: one's a lawyer in Kampala, but a bouncer here: the teacher washes dishes: the senior civil servant is selling kitchens on the telephone. Most of them hold down at least two jobs, and some of them are studying as well. All of them have fallen asleep on buses, as Mary once used to, years ago. All of them find London ferociously expensive, and yet they send money home, and save, and manage to go out as well. 'We are Ugandans. We know how to party.' Now Mary remembers how to party.

She goes dancing in the early hours at Club Afrique in Canning Town, and although ten pounds is a lot of money, although there are too many Congolese, it is wonderful to hear Ugandan music, Ragga D, Trishlaa and Jingo Shoe, and Mary loves dancing, though when she was with Omar she only danced at home, with him. Now all the men want to dance with her, although she is a decade older than some of them. The beat is in her blood, her hips, her heels. She could dance for ever: she's the Dancing Queen. Oh, and here is her favourite, Chameleon.

When she comes into the street, hot and happy, at three am to catch the night bus home, she sees, sharply lit up, in the sudden chill, a familiar face, smoking a cigarette under the street light. 'Abdu?' she says, amazed. And it is him. Abdu Mawanga. Her friend from her early days as a cleaner. Now waiting to pick up two of his daughters, who are still strutting their stuff inside. They reminisce in the cold night air, sending plumes of white breath up to join the pollution, and Abdu asks Mary to lunch in Dalston, where he has a good business he wants to show her.

Next day Mary decides to invite Juanita, a Spanish cleaner they had both been fond of, in those days as fragile and twittery and bright as the pet shop budgies that Mary loves. And to her surprise, Juanita is still at the phone number she had all those years ago, still living in the same council flat, though it must be over a decade since they cleaned together.

They manage to meet, at Dalston Kingsland Station, three days later, all three of them exuberant.

'The money was good,' says Abdu Muwanga, escorting Mary along, with one affectionate arm, through a crowd of chattering, many-coloured peoples. 'Didn't we think the money was good, at the time?'

'It was riches,' Mary says. 'Not the houses, but the offices. And it wasn't lonely. We did have some laughs.'

They are picking their way between the blowing striped awnings of the market stalls at Dalston Kingsland. Ridley Road is smarter than it was ten years ago, with more brick-built shops and less rubbish on the floor. It is a weekday: business is quiet. Yet the young men are out there with lavish displays of bright red meat, surely too red to be true, shining rich as velvet in the fresh cold air. The fish-stalls have jewel-like sweeps of crushed ice from which the heads of fish poke up like beaks, pink and turquoise, with round veiled eyes. Even the thinnest stalls have something to sell: dull stumps of brown manioc or cassava. An old woman sits by a tiny pile of pastries. '*Oly otya Nnyabo,*' Abdu says.

'*Jendi Ssebo,*' the woman replies.

'*Story ki?* Business *egenda etya?*'

'*Bwetyo. Tuuli waano tugenda mpora.*'

131

'Is everyone here from Uganda?' asks Juanita. In some ways the little Spanish woman is unchanged. She has the same squeaky voice, the same short, breathless body that taps along on too-high heels, never quite catching up with Abdu and Mary. But her face is less happy, and more lined, and the vivid rose of her cheeks is painted.

'The lady with the pastries was Ugandan,' says Abdu. 'Most people, not. Lots of Nigerians, Ghanaians.'

'You Africans,' says Juanita, at least half-disapproving. 'You everywhere. Not bein' funny.'

They are going to have a look at Abdu's business. He is very proud of his success. Once the three of them had soldiered together on the early shifts for a contract cleaner: now Abdu and Mary have escaped, but Juanita is still spending her mornings cleaning and her afternoons as a school meals assistant. She has dressed up more than they have, to make up for this. Later they are going to a café on Mare Street that serves Ugandan and western food. Mary knows that Juanita will shriek in horror when she sees the steaming mounds of carbohydrate.

Abdu's shop is on the side, solidly built, solidly roofed. He has several people working for him, who smile respectfully as he arrives. He sits Mary and Juanita down at the back, and begins to show them what he imports. 'This Chicken Curry Masala you can only buy here. People come from all over London to get it. Authentic Ugandan spices, of course. I am building up my chain of supply. If you have a good product, people will buy it …' Mary listens to him talk, with shining eyes. She is happy that Abdu has become successful. When they were both young, he was kind to her, hauling machines for her that she could have carried, always asking after Jamie and Omar, showing her the respect she needed. And he has stayed the same, though he is plumper, more substantial. His hair is thinner, and he wears good shoes.

Juanita is impatient, and darts around, picking things off shelves and putting them back, sniffing suspiciously at unfamiliar vegetables, glad when she finds something she can name.

'Peppers,' she says. 'Red peppers. Nice?'

'Those are special,' says Abdu. 'I'm proud of those. They come from the same seed as Caribbean peppers. But there's something about the Ugandan soil. Don't you agree, Mary? *Ettaka lya Uganda lilina akakondyo!* And the Ugandan weather too. These peppers are delicious, they have more flavour but they're not too hot. No one thought I would be able to sell them here. I began with one box a week, a few years ago. Now I can shift two hundred boxes a week! *Nekolela maali wano*, not bad money!'

'Big man,' says Juanita, a little mockingly, lifting her tiny nose towards him. Her hair is full of small combs and decorations, too girlish for her, and her eyebrows look surprised, a thin black arch that she now raises even further. 'You have become a very big man, Abdu. But I am starvin'. Some of us still workers! My afternoon off, I always get a nice lunch.'

'Time to go', Abdu agrees, and aside to Mary, *'Naye kati enjjala enzitta.'*

'It's the weather,' Mary says. 'I am always hungry here.'

They set off towards the café through the cooling wind. Can this really be London? Mary wonders. Only ten percent of people are *bazungu,* and some of those are probably Spanish, like Juanita, or maybe Eastern European.

A tall handsome man with a huge purple turban and one long earring like an elephant's tusk emerges, half-dancing, from a side-alley from which reggae music ebbs and flows. He embraces Abdu like a brother.

'This is the Doctor,' Abdu says. 'And this is my sister, Mary.' They shake hands. 'And my other sister, Juanita,' he adds, almost too late, pushing her forward.

'Are you from Uganda?' Juanita asks, suspicious.

Abdu bursts out laughing, and pats the tall man on the back. '*Nawe ori munauganda?* Which part of Uganda are you from, my brother?'

'Don't use your barr-barous language with me, Abdu. I'm from the Ca-rib-bee-an, miss,' he spells out, laughing. 'The Doctor is my name. Everyone knows me.'

Juanita nods without understanding. 'So what part of Africa did that tall man come from?' she asks, once they are settled in the warm café, with its view of the street and all its peoples.

'Montserrat, not Africa,' Abdu tells her. 'A tiny island. But he knew Bob Marley.'

'I know Bob Marley,' says Juanita, jealously, eager to recover from any mistake. 'Everyone knows Bob Marley.' And she gets up, laughs, and begins to dance, as if she were young again and happy, to the words she is singing, in a high cracked voice, 'Don't rock the boat … Don't rock the boat,' and Abdu and Mary sing along with her.

Abdu recommends the goat curry, and he and Mary order lots of 'food', Ugandan-style, big starchy roots of sweet potato and cassava. He tells them about other businesses he has, renting rooms to Ugandans in Forest Gate. 'I don't mind them sharing, three to a room, if that is the only way they can afford it.'

'Oh yes, very kind, very nice,' says Juanita. 'And that way you make more money, no?' She orders, with much frowning at the menu, a steak, then tells the waitress the meat is tough.

Throughout most of the meal, she complains, like a poem. Her sadness is real; her husband is ill, has not worked for years, because of diabetes, her daughter, who was clever, left school at fifteen and got involved with a drug-dealer. The fact that he was black has not endeared her to Africans: 'I'm not sayin' nothing, but he was coloured.' Now the daughter has a baby that Juanita 'never' sees (though it turns out that this means every other weekend). 'Why? Why has God done this to me?' Then Juanita has a beer and becomes even franker.

'You all do well because you stick together,' she says, tomato sauce congealing on her upper lip. 'And now the English give you all the jobs, and all the money, because you coloured. I'm not bein' funny, you two my friends. But how come you both rich and I'm still poor? I been in England a lot longer than you. Nobody does any favours for Juanita.'

'I am not rich,' says Mary. 'And no one did any favours for me. Only my friends, like Abdu and Leanne.' But she sees Juanita is very unhappy. 'You too, Juanita. I do remember. When I had to stay home with Jamey, one day, you covered for me, so I got my money.'

'Of course,' says Juanita, brightening. 'Is the story of my life. I help everybody, always.' She tells a few stories to illustrate this, which are very long and incoherent, and then they start remembering their youth, so they are all laughing again, over coffee: about how Mary put salt in the supervisor's tea: how Abdu locked a sneak in the stock cupboard.

The conversation becomes sober again when Juanita asks how Jamey is. 'Clever little boy, innit?' she says. 'Lovely dark eyes, just like his dad. Though I never understand how you could marry one of them.'

'Don't forget that Abdu is a Muslim too,' says Mary quickly, but Abdu shrugs and smiles. Mary has dreaded being asked about Jamey, but once she starts to talk, it is almost a relief. 'Ugandan Muslims aren't strict like Omar. Well he wasn't at first, but as he grew older … Remember Omar was Libyan. And he worked for the embassy, of course. Maybe he thought I was holding him back. He changed. People change. He began to believe he could find someone better. Younger, less stubborn. A good Muslim.' Now the words come less easily. 'And he thought – it would be better for Jamie too. When we were posted back to London, things really went wrong. Omar grew afraid of all the godlessness here. He thought that Jamil would be sucked in. Maybe find a non-Muslim girlfriend, because what? Because Omar himself had done the same. And so – ' Mary stops, and takes a gulp of water. It still seems shameful to tell what happened. 'Omar told me that he was going to divorce me. And before I knew it, he had gone back to Tripoli. Taking Jamil. Then he married again. I met her twice. She is not so bad. Sometimes she tells me things on the phone. In any case, things did not work out. Jamil and his father began to quarrel. Maybe Jamie blamed him for the divorce. And Omar was worrying about him again. You see, out in Tripoli, their rich young men … they are educated, they all have degrees, but later there is no work for them. They are too proud to do – jobs like ours, so they lie around all day, watching bad films and drinking.'

'So Jamil got into bad company?' Juanita's mouth is sorry, but her eyes are excited.

It is suddenly too hard for Mary to go on. Because what can Juanita understand about her life? The little Spanish woman has still got two children, whatever may be wrong with them, and one grandchild. It seems like such riches. Mary is too proud to show her cupboard is bare.

She makes herself smile. 'No, his father imagined it. He worried too much. Jamie has always been a good boy. He has got a place to do Veterinary Studies, at Al Fateh University, in Tripoli.'

'Ha! Very clever!' says Juanita, but she pouts, and is restless, inspecting her gold bracelet. 'My kids, they don't need to be brainy, do they? *No importa*, they both earning money.' Reluctantly, she returns to Jamil. 'So now he is going to be a student, you are happy, even if you don't see him for a bit.'

And Mary nods and changes the subject, because she cannot bear to finish the story, though its empty sadness runs through her body. She tries, every day, not to think about it, except at night, when she says her prayers. For although she has told Abdu and Juanita no lies – Jamie *has* won a place to do Veterinary Studies, Mary *does* believe he is a good boy – she has not told them the whole story. Indeed, she does not know the whole story. Her heart yearns towards him: *Jamie, Jamie.*

'Ladies, I am going to pay for lunch,' says Abdu. 'Juanita, I admit I am rich! As rich as Donald Trump, at least. England has been quite kind to me. I have my family. I like my weekends. And my kids, you know, they are Londoners. Though they like to check out Club Afrique, and Kabira.'

'Don't you ever miss Kampala?' Mary asks. 'It is OK where I am. The room is nice. The work is very easy for me. But I miss Uganda. I miss my language. *Tugenda kwelabiila baani betuli.*'

'Honestly?' says Abdu. 'I only miss the weather. How could I go home again, and sometimes not have electricity, for hours on end? Nowhere to shop, no opportunity? You see, Mary, Uganda is here. In Forest Gate and New Ham, it is Uganda. So many Baganda here, it is like home. We have even got our own football team! Simba FC is a brilliant team. And our own radio station, every Sunday!'

'It's just like I said,' Juanita nods but without venom, she is even smiling, this proves her point. 'You Africans are taking over, in London.'

Abdu sees that Mary is looking sad. 'Things have been different for you, Mary. Because you married a husband from another country.'

'I married a husband from another country,' she repeats. 'It is true, Abdu. So far away. I married for love – '

'So did I,' says Juanita. 'I got nothing but trouble from that man. If my girl goes wrong, is because of 'im.'

'It's my son,' says Mary, but then can't continue. 'I am only sad about our son.' And because Mary will not cry in public, she smiles a brilliant smile, and gets up from the table.

Abdu pays the bill, and then looks at them, his two friends, these two different women. 'God,' he says, 'will take care of them, *inshallah*. God will look after all lost children.'

2 6

Vanessa does not notice when her house is clean; she only notices when it is dirty. But in fact, the house is better now Anya is cleaning it. The bathroom smells of lemons again. The wastepaper baskets shed their ragged crowns of newsprint. The flowers in the dining room are fresh, and the vases are no longer surrounded by brown petals, lying on the table like a ruff of spilled tobacco. The dado- and picture-rails are white, where once they were traced with long smears of soft charcoal.

Anya likes cleaning. She is glad to have a job, and she thinks that Justin is mysterious and handsome. She wipes the mouthpiece of the phones, which she thinks must be bubbling over with germs. As she puts it down, it rings, insistently. This morning it has rung a lot.

Vanessa is irritated by the phone, because she is getting too much marking from the new Creative Writing intake. It is her day off from college, but she hasn't left her desk. The dark-eyed boy, Derrick, is quite good, and very keen, one of those who are constantly submitting writing. He has two

obsessions: pigeons and knives. They have not yet started to
drive her to distraction. She scrawls, 'Well done again, Derrick.
Juxtaposition of central motifs once more consistent and
compelling.' If the telephone shrills when she is at her desk,
encouraging, describing, validating, Vanessa tends to be ruder
than usual, and slams the receiver back into its cradle.

It is the foreigners, the foreigners again. They ask for the
wrong people, in uncertain intonations, either very tentative
or very bossy. They ring with news of prizes for 'Mr Henman',
or offers of new kitchens, or phones, or loans, or cheaper gas
or electricity, and Vanessa gets mad, and begins to cut them
off as soon as she hears a voice that isn't English, although she
would be shocked if this was pointed out.

Sometimes they ask for unfamiliar people. A man has
rung several times for 'Mistendo'. He has a faintly rasping,
Arab-sounding voice, but the person he is asking for must be
Japanese. Vanessa does not connect it with Mary. She never
thinks of her as having a surname. Because she is a cleaner,
she is only 'Mary'. Vanessa cuts him off, with a terse 'Wrong
number'.

Someone has been calling for Justin this morning, a soft
woman's voice, pretending to be shy. Vanessa snaps, 'Justin's
asleep.' 'Please will you wake him?' the woman asks. 'Certainly
not,' says Vanessa, and puts the phone down. As soon as it's
down, she has a twinge of misgiving, but the girl did not even
give her name, she is certainly someone from these horrible
companies, ringing up to exploit Justin's illness, and Vanessa
thinks, 'I was right to be firm.' But in case he gets cross with
her, she might not mention it.

In any case, Justin is still hardly speaking to her. He is not
impolite, he does not lose his temper, he just leaves any room
Vanessa enters. On the surface, things have worsened since her

small tiff with Mary. Vanessa rehearses words she'll never say, of inquiry, apology, entreaty, but he slips away while her mouth is still opening.

In other ways, Justin is certainly improving. He is somewhere in the house, vertical, not naked! For some weeks now, he has been opening his curtains, and appearing, dressed, around the house before noon. Vanessa has managed to bite her tongue and not ask him if he has any plans, though in some respects it is more difficult now than it was when he was tucked away upstairs. He does seem to like watching Anya clean. When she comes to the house, Justin gets up earlier, and even offers her cups of coffee. This is rather a relief to his mother, who was never sure that he knew how to make one. 'Could you make some for me too, while you're at it,' she had called through to Justin this morning from the study, but the grunt that came back was discouraging. She had to get up and make her own.

The phone rings again. '*Yes!*' Vanessa snarls, and feels silly when she finds it is Fifi. Vanessa pulls herself up in her ergonomic chair, and fills her voice with animation. 'Lots and lots better, thank you darling. Oh yes, having Mary here was a great decision. Not mine, by the way, it was Justin's idea. As you know I have always been a *listening* parent. My whole aim has been to empower my son. Well no, he's not actually back at work. It all takes time. You can't rush things. When you are a mother, you learn to be patient.' – This is a subtle thrust at Fifi, who at forty-eight will never be a parent.

Yet Vanessa has come to depend on Fifi, now she doesn't have a man, and her son has grown distant. There is a little story she wants to tell Fifi, wants to tell someone, at any rate. So she changes tack, and flatters her. 'Darling it's so kind of you to ring. Sometimes you're the only person I can talk to. I do think Justin and I are making progress.' And she tells her about the mobile phone.

Vanessa recently found what must be Justin's mobile phone, on top of the bookshelves in her bedroom. It is small and sharp, shiny and modern, and opens and shuts like a silver shell. Although Vanessa's not a big fan of mobiles, it seemed like a symbol of the old Justin, the one she once felt proud of, and had such high hopes for, who went off to work each day in a suit. Also, he had left it on her special bookshelves, which could only mean he had been borrowing a book, though Vanessa can't pin down which one has gone. Most important, her son had come into her room, he had *actually come into his mother's room*, after so much rejection, so much shouting, after actually saying that his mother was 'toxic'!

'Justin never asked for the phone,' she tells Fifi. 'He never came looking for it, either. I just slipped the thing back into his room, next day, at the foot of the bed, without saying anything.'

Fifi, after six years of therapy, falls eagerly upon this incident. 'I love it,' she gasps. 'You see, it was a message. He was trying to slip back into your body. The mother's bedroom means her body – '

'I don't know about that – ' says Vanessa, uneasy.

'– well not in a pervy way, of course. Think *womb*, darling, not vagina. Womb and room, that's rather good! And borrowing your book, well that was a tribute. It's terribly touching. I'm so happy. And your reaction was perfectly judged. By giving it back, you acknowledged his autonomy. My therapist would be proud of you both. By the way, what shape was it?'

'Well, mobile-phone-shaped,' says Vanessa.

'You see?' Fifi is triumphant. 'I told you so. I won't say it's phallic. But it's yin and yang. You are getting into harmony. In any case, I must rush off for my Reiki.'

'I'm never quite sure what Reiki is.'

'Oh universal life-force energy, darling. You know, the universe is made up of thought. We just have to manifest joy and abundance.'

Vanessa tries to find this reassuring.

Once Fifi is prone upon the massage table, she finds herself talking about Justin and Vanessa. It is easier to talk, somehow, hanging in a void, staring at the floor through the padded face-rest. The masseuse says, 'You always talk about them. Sounds like they're almost family.' A long pause, and then Fifi replies, 'Well I virtually have no family. My mother is dead. My brother's in Canada.' Suddenly the face-rest feels uncomfortable, hot on her face, pressing on her. She squirms and rears up like an irritated serpent. 'How are you finding the new face-rest?' the masseuse inquires, anxious, pausing for an instant. 'Actually I preferred the old one.' 'This one's more modern. It's top of the range. In fact it's the Cloud Comfort Memory Foam model.' 'Oh right, it must be me then, don't worry.' But Fifi feels less joyful, and less abundant. All afternoon, she reflects on her life.

Before supper, she phones Vanessa again. 'It's true, Vanessa, I've neglected my family. Mimi, as you know, is like my child, Mimi is warmer than the average Siamese, but there's still a strain of selfishness. The truth is, anyone could fill her bowl. I do have a family, aunts and uncles and things, but I never see them, since my parents died. Of course they're mostly in France, my lot. As a matter of fact, I have a living grandma. But I should go and see them – I'm going to go and see them. And I wanted to ask – will you come with me?

Vanessa feels flattered to be needed – her own house

seems to do quite well without her – and says, rather grandly, 'Delighted to help. Why not a little holiday in France?'

But Fifi presses on, disconcertingly, 'I started thinking about you and Justin. You're really in just the same boat as me.'

Vanessa is speechless for a second. She prefers to feel compassion for Fifi. 'Justin is not a Siamese.'

'You don't see your family either, do you? And of course, Justin is all on his own.'

'Nonsense, Fifi, he has always been sociable.'

(Yet now he lies in a room alone. She doesn't admit it, but Vanessa feels vulnerable. She has no siblings, and she never sees her cousins. Who is there to hold her to the ground? Sometimes, when she lies there in the middle of the night, she feels she and Justin could be lost in the darkness, two atoms of dust, empty, meaningless. Perhaps she and Fifi could help each other. She decides she will confide in her.)

'As a matter of fact, just a month or so ago, I had a birthday card from my cousin in Sussex, who I haven't seen since I was a schoolgirl. It started me thinking, and I wrote to Lucy. And I really have been hoping she'll get back to me. Not that I myself feel lonely, of course. I don't know, I thought it might somehow help Justin. To have more of a family than just me. In any case, Lucy hasn't written back.' The truth is, Vanessa is still hoping.

'Let's go to Paris!' Fifi says again, laughing. 'My grandma still has a house in Paris.'

'Why not?' says Vanessa, only half meaning it.

But as the evening draws on, she thinks about Paris: a little rosy gleam on the horizon. She's in need of a gleam. She's done eight hours of marking. She is still wading through the new intake class. It annoys her that Beardy, the silly old man (who, to make matters worse, is younger than she is) is arguably

better than her favourite, Derrick. But Beardy has a tendency
to cheap satire. After all the effort Vanessa puts in! It's that
little grin she keeps seeing on his face, twitching away under
the white fungus …

But perhaps she is becoming paranoid. She turns with relief
to her own writing.

And sits on for hours, in her autumn study, where unread
books use up the air. She stares at the unforgiving slopes of
her laptop, wondering if the book of her dreams, which would
sketch out the truth of her life like a theorem, a silver vapour-
trail behind her plane, might rise into being, clear and entire,
but the screen shows only burnt droppings of phrases.

She finds herself wondering what Mary is up to. She heard
her come in, around five pm, and then the usual hammerings
and slashings and thumpings that meant she was putting
the dinner on. The smell of cooking floats through from the
kitchen, but Mary herself has disappeared.

Abandoning her struggle with the dreck on her screen,
Vanessa creeps upstairs, and stands listening on the landing.
Not a sound emerges from Justin's room. She feels relieved,
somehow, that Mary isn't there. Nobody in the loo or the
bathroom. She pauses by Mary's bedroom door.

There is a curious, repetitive noise. A kind of quiet thumping
that reminds her of something. But her brain won't process it.
And then she remembers. It sounds like the noise Mary made
in the kitchen one night, grinding nuts in a mortar and pestle.
Perhaps she is preparing food in her room.

It must be some Ugandan habit.

27   Mary Tendo

All I can do is write about Jamie. On and on, about the thing that happened. Because I talked about him, to Juanita. My heart is stirred up. I am not myself.

But I am not ready. I cannot do it. I wipe it away: *delete, delete*. I have to get up and look out of the window until my mind is blank as the sky.

And now I am back at my dressing-table, in this nice room, and everything is fine. On the whole, when I see my friends, I feel better. I compare our lives, and am not unhappy. I am not living in a small shared room for which I have to pay eighty pounds per week, doing night-work in a factory, without the right visa. I have not fallen into the clutches of Nigerians who sell other Africans for a percentage. I am back in London, but I am not a cleaner. I have certainly done better than Juanita.

And yet my heart pains me, because of Jamey.

I will not cry. I smile in the mirror. It makes me feel better to see myself, sitting very straight in the new yellow sweater I bought quite cheaply at Dalston Market. No, I am not going to think about Jamey. Instead I must sort out my thoughts about Justin. This is my job. I have not been lazy.

I have found out several things about Justin.

Firstly, a woman has broken his heart. This is why Justin has given up hope. This is why Justin needs me so.

It was morning. He sat beside me on the bed.

'I wanted her to marry me,' he said, like a child.

'But Justin, you are not ready to marry.'

(But then I remembered what I felt for Omar. I was not much older than Justin is. I was alone, and lonely, in London. The money for my grant had not arrived. Every day I phoned my aunt in Kampala. But her husband was no longer the President's friend. Each time I phoned she became less friendly. In the end I knew the money was finished. But once I met Omar, nothing mattered. I knew we would be in love for ever. I still see his eyes, dark like pools in the forest. And his skin, which was like golden sand, so to me at first he looked like a *muzungu*. I will never forget his eyes, and his hands. Both of us were lonely, and far from home. In Uganda, Christians marry Muslims. We live together in the same village, so we marry each other because we are neighbours, and the families do not mind. It is ordinary. I did not understand things were different in Libya.

But Omar wasn't racist. His heart was good. *Yali mussajja mulungi nyo*. He found me beautiful. He made me laugh. My life became sunlight, until the storms came. I have never lost my love for Omar. Perhaps things will work out like that for Justin.)

'Is she a nice girl?' I asked him, very quietly, so that I would not sound like the Henman, always asking things, and interfering. I stroke his soft blonde hair with my hand, so he knows I am not his enemy.

'She was perfect,' he said, 'until she broke my heart.' And then he told me all about her. He met her at university. She is doing the famous MBA, which everyone knows is the way to get rich. 'She will soon be an international businesswoman. She won't want anything to do with me. Because I just lie here uselessly.'

I said to him, 'You are not useless. You have been ill. I love you, Justin.'

'It wasn't true,' he mumbled, at his chest.

'What was not true?' I asked him, very soft.

'She said I had another girlfriend.'

'She thinks you have another girlfriend?'

'It wasn't true. It was my mother.'

'It is Miss Henman? I don't understand.' But I began to understand.

'I always had to meet my mother.'

And so I understood the problem. This is what happens to the *bazungu*. When their children are little, they hardly see them. Later, when they grow, and are no longer any trouble, and the parents start to get old and weak, the parents want the children to love them. By then, the children do not know them. But the parents want to get to know them.

Then I thought about the evidence I had so far. I said to him, 'Did this woman give you the necklace?'

He looked down at the ground, and shook his head, so my fingers, which were caught inside his curls, pained him, and he winced and frowned as if I had hit him. He looked as he did when he was a child and the Henman asked him too many questions.

This is when I showed my detective skills, for I have not read Agatha Christie for nothing. Sometimes Miss Marple could be very gentle. 'Perhaps you borrowed it from her?'

He was quiet for a moment, but then he nodded.

And so I know this girl is important.

And I said to him, 'You must visit her,' but he said, 'She does not want to see me again.'

It does not matter, I am going to find her.

And here is the second thing I know about Justin. I know he was given the sack from his work. He did not steal things, or come late to the office, or tell lies about the other workers. He did not get drunk, as many young men do. He got the sack because he was not a woman.

He worked for an advertising agency, which paid him good money to invent advertisements. (Later I will ask him how much they paid. Probably he was paid more than me, although I am older and more experienced.) He told me the advertisements were all for women. They advertised perfume, and clothes, and cars, and cigarettes, and alcohol. And young women were their 'target market', because young women had all the money, so they wanted a young woman to write the advertisements. The reason why young women have all the money must be because they have all the jobs.

'I tell you, Mary, that's the way things are. This city is made for young women. They don't need men. We are obsolete. Just look in the papers. It's the same there. All the columnists are young women. And they spend most of their time slagging off men. We're all useless, and feeble, and wankers, apparently.'

I smiled and said to him, 'Do not worry. Young women still need men for babies.'

But he looked sad and obstinate, like a goat, and he said, 'You are wrong. They do not want babies. My ex said all men were wimps and liars.'

And this is the third thing, and the most important. I know the phone number and address of his girlfriend. I know this because I interviewed the cleaners, and had to listen to the phone messages. But one young woman did not want the job. One young woman had called for Justin.

She had a soft voice. She was called Zakira. She said she had called for him twice already. She did not leave her telephone number, but fortunately it was the last message, and I know how to find the last number.

I told Justin that the woman had called. At first he looked happy, but a minute later he turned over in bed, and groaned into the pillow. 'It is all useless. Zakira hates me.'

'If she telephones you, perhaps she doesn't hate you.'

'I know she hates me, because I am hateful. Because I am hopeless. Because I am disgusting.'

I said to him again, 'You are not so bad. I think I should telephone Zakira. She has a nice voice. It is educated.'

But he groaned again and made me promise not to. Still I did not promise not to find her.

The next night, when he was fast asleep, I got up and put the bedside light on, then dug my way through the heaps of clothes that cover Justin's bedside table. Then I started looking in his drawers. In my own bedside drawers I have pictures of Jamil, and the letters he sent me, and his school reports. They always say how hard he works. I must not start comparing Jamil and Justin.

Justin's bedside drawers were like a litter bin. Old receipts, old tickets, old bills from restaurants. So once he went out like other young men. Once he bought music and expensive clothes. At last I found some letters in careful black writing, folded neatly together, unlike the rest. They were signed with a beautiful, flowing 'Z'. Of course it was her, not *Zadam*, or *Zargaret!* But the first two letters had no address. I was very tired, and I might have given up, but God gave me patience to look at one more, and there was her address, at the top of the paper! 20 Canaan Gardens. Or maybe 30. Or even 26. It was not written clearly. But all the same, I felt so happy.

Yes, most things are going splendidly.

28

Mary and Trevor are smoking in the garden. Vanessa is at college all day on Friday, and Trevor has popped round to see how things are going. He finds Mary weeding, in her blue cotton nightgown, looking for all the world like a farmer. She smiles at him joyously. 'I like this work. It reminds me of home, when I was a child, and watched my father. But the soil is so dry. In Uganda, we have real rain. Rain that can wash your house away.' She thinks, maybe this house should be washed away, and then all the people could escape, and Justin could swim up, with his curls in the sun.

'You're not short of water, then,' says Trevor. He thinks of the Africa he sees on TV: flat yellow desert, with flyblown skeletons. But then he remembers one of the books he most enjoyed from his folding book chest. In fact, Trevor had enjoyed it so much that he did what he very occasionally does, which is to cheat on his usual system of passing books on as soon as he has read them, and deflected it to some bookshelves he's put up in the garage, where he sometimes sits and reads and potters on Sundays: *My African Journey, by the Rt Hon.*

Winston Spencer Churchill M.P. The cover has a picture of a young Churchill in a solar topee, by a cross, dead rhinoceros. 'Source of the Nile, Uganda, isn't it? I know that from old Winston Churchill.'

'The villages are short of clean water,' says Mary. 'People give them wells. But they forget to care for them. Maybe the problem is, they do not know how to. We do not look after things enough at home.'

'Well, Winston was impressed with the Uganda railway.'

'It is broken now,' says Mary. 'Do you like his book?'

She makes Trevor strong tea, with milk and three sugars, and he offers her a fag, and they sit by the rose-bushes, which have grown too tall, for Mary has only snipped off the dead bits, by the little blocked fountain with its skin of black leaves, which English people have forgotten to look after. At the end, a stand of silver-green willows, just starting to ripple with gold, for autumn. Leggy pale yellow chrysanthemums. Honeysuckle that could do with pruning, but still bears twined crescents of pink and gold, as well as semi-transparent red berries. Not long ago, this was a beautiful garden, before Vanessa grew too busy to garden, before Justin was ill, when their world was lighter.

'I did like it,' says Trevor. 'I really did. Dunno why, I just liked the cut of his jib.' Seeing her uncomprehending face, he says, 'You know, I kind of took to him. He was an enthusiast, was Churchill. I'd like to go to Uganda,' he adds. 'Didn't Winston say it was the Pearl of Africa? I'm going to look that book out again.'

'Maybe I will borrow it,' says Mary. 'I would like to see what he says about us. It is a famous book, but I have never seen it.'

'Done,' says Trevor. 'I'll bring it round ... You know that Nessie went to Uganda.'

'She tried to tell me about it,' says Mary.

'I bet she did.' They both sit and laugh and blow out white smoke on the bright autumn air. Trevor notices the roses have got black spot. 'You know you can never prune too hard, with roses. You want to have a real go at them. You have to be ruthless with a garden, Mary.'

Mary absorbs this advice, and smiles. She will enjoy being ruthless with Vanessa's garden. 'Trevor, I like the cut of your jib,' she says, and pats him on the shoulder.

But Trevor sits lost in his own thoughts. Trevor has never been ruthless with anyone. Trevor has given Vanessa her head. Perhaps he should have done more for Justin. Perhaps it is not too late to try. 'You know the boy, Mary. You're close to Justin. Do you think he's well enough to give me a hand?'

'I think it is good for him to see his father. I think it is good for him to get up and work.'

'Only problem is, the old girl won't like it.'

They puff reflectively. She says, 'Never mind. Mr Justin is young, he should be working.'

'See, she's always been terrified he'd be like his father. He was always the wonderkid, you know, super brainy. She always insisted he took after her. Whereas I was a bit of a dunce at school.'

'Once you are a man, school is not important.'

Trevor thinks, Mary is very wise. 'Well, Nessie has never got to grips with that thought. See, for her, being brainy was the only escape route.'

'I don't understand,' says Mary. The truth is, she doesn't want to hear about Vanessa. It is enough that she puts up with her.

But Trevor keeps talking about Vanessa's family. How they were ordinary country people. Her father was a farm labourer, who lived all his life in a tied cottage. 'The mother was ill, as I remember. Ness told me all about it when we were first together. By now I don't remember the details. Vanessa never wanted to go and see them. Not after we were married, and not before. So we went and got hitched in a register office. I asked my brother and my parents, but we didn't tell her lot till afterwards. She said she couldn't get married if they had to be there. Pity, really. I did love her. I know her Dad never had any money but I wouldn't have minded footing the bill, you know, if she'd wanted to push the boat out, have a church wedding with all the trimmings … When I first met the mother, I thought she was bonkers. Poor woman, she kept asking if I was cold, and making cups of tea, but she hadn't boiled the kettle. The father seemed to have given up. In any case, Nessy was a swot, and brainy, so she managed to get away from all that. So far as I know, she's hardly looked back.'

Mary stubs out her cigarette in the grass. She has tried not to listen to what Trevor says. She does not intend to feel sorry for Vanessa. She remembers his advice and weeds with vigour, pulling up the cosmoses, the seeded delphiniums, the dull-leaved peonies, the Nerine lilies, but leaves the splendid pink spires of willow-herb, which she has never seen before.

'Miss Henman always wanted Justin to be clever,' she says, after a while, thoughtfully. 'Perhaps this is why he was always studying, at this class, or that class, or doing his homework. Sometimes I thought his head would burst.'

'Well, maybe it did,' Trevor replies. 'Maybe that's just what happened to the lad. But you, Mary, are a sensible woman. You just carry on the way you're going. And let me know if I can help you out.'

Mary knows at once how she wants him to help her. 'First, you must help me to print my writing.'

'Blimey, you're not another writer.' Trevor is joking, but Mary doesn't laugh.

'Yes, so you must find me a printer. Next, tell me everything about London wages.'

'Do you mean, for a cleaner?'

'I am not her cleaner.'

She goes into the house and returns with a notebook, and listens attentively, and writes it all down.

29

Mary rings on the door as loudly as she can, to hide the nervousness she feels. Canaan Gardens is smart, in an expensive part of London, though the door itself is scruffy, with several bells beside it. It is number 20, which she thinks is right. Today November feels like winter; she knows she must go and buy more warm clothes – in Uganda, of course, she did not need them – but Mary is waiting for her next week's money. In fact, her money seems to go quite quickly, once she has topped up the credit on her mobile, which she finally found in Justin's room, and bought relaxer for her hair, and cocoa butter, all of which cost five times what they would in Uganda, and sent money to her sister through Western Union, though the notes in her bedroom are still mounting up, the delicious little stack is getting thicker.

Perhaps it is the cold that makes her feel sick. Since she came to London, she has often felt sick. Perhaps it is the grey cloud that hangs over London. It must be heaving with dirt and pollution. And perhaps Mary ate too much English porridge before she went to church this morning. She has started cooking it for her and Justin, since Vanessa told her it was 'energising'. Because it is true, the Henman has energy, always running everywhere, upstairs and downstairs, and being bossy, and doing her sit-ups, quite unpredictably, anywhere, so that Mary opens doors and steps on her hair, and then Vanessa screams, and says, 'Sorry, sorry', though really Mary sees she is annoyed. All this takes a lot of energy. But porridge just seems to make Justin sleepy, and today even Mary is feeling lethargic.

Still, she knows she must make a good impression, and tries to stand straight on the tall white steps. She is wearing her best dress, which is yellow, and her best cardigan, which is blue, and her best shoes, which are summer espadrilles, no good for walking or Ugandan rains, so her feet hurt, but she ignores them. She is carrying her notebook, like a good detective, in case there are things she must write down. There is silence inside. The big windows stare at her.

She stands even straighter, and rings again, all three bells in succession, since she does not know which one, and makes herself smile, like someone important, a private detective, a Linen Store Keeper, an Autobiographer and Life Writer. She reminds herself she bears a message from Justin, even though Justin does not know she is here. Like Cupid, she thinks, in the romantic stories, and then she thinks how unalike they are, because Cupid is white, and sweet, and fat, and this makes her laugh, as she stands on the pavement, so when the door opens, rather fast and hard, Mary really is smiling a joyous smile.

But the woman who stands there is not Zakira. She is young, and beautiful, but she is black. Less black than Mary is, but still black. She has an orange scarf knotted round her forehead. She is clutching a large plant in front of her body, with mauve daisy-heads, and earthy black roots. She has been gardening, then. She looks annoyed.

She takes in Mary and her face is stony.

'Good morning,' says Mary. 'How are you?'

'Sorry, I'm not interested,' the young woman says. 'I keep telling you lot I am a Muslim.'

Mary looks puzzled, and then understands. The woman thinks she's a Jehovah's Witness. They come to Vanessa's house, too, always smiling, carrying their Bible, and they're often black. Last time Mary actually asked them in, thinking perhaps they would pray for Justin, but they stayed for hours, talking nonsense, and she soon realised they did not believe in Jesus.

'I am not a Jehovah person,' Mary says. 'I am looking for Zakira. She is young, she is English.'

'She isn't,' says the young woman, very decidedly. They stare at each other, deadlocked, for an instant. Earth falls on the floor from the roots of the plant, and the woman kicks it away, crossly.

Then Mary continues, polite, professional. 'I am looking for Zakira. I have a message.'

'Carry on,' the woman seems to say, but this doesn't make sense, so Mary tries again. 'Where is Zakira?' she asks, very slowly. This time she pronounces the 'Zakira' differently, in case her accent has caused confusion. 'She is young. She is an English woman.'

The woman looks affronted. 'I thought for a moment you were for me. Are you for upstairs?'

'Maybe,' says Mary, cunningly. 'Is anyone there?' But she senses there isn't. The house has a hollow, silent feel.

'You're a Witness, aren't you. I knew you were.'

And with that, the woman closes the door. Mary stands outside, in her orange coat, her smile fading, her heart sinking.

She tries the other numbers, with no success. She will have to go back and re-read the address.

By the time she reaches home, she is composed again. Retreat three paces to advance one more. As she comes up the path, she cuts four red roses with the nail scissors she has in her bag, and when she is inside, she puts them in a vase.

She sits in the sitting room, her shoes beside her, wriggling her toes, which hurt from walking, and Vanessa comes through and gives her a look, down her long thin nose like an ant-bear's proboscis, so Mary lifts her foot and waves her toes at her, and Vanessa disappears into the kitchen, vanquished.

But Mary has things to say to her. 'Are you making tea, Vanessa?' she calls to her employer.

There is a pause, and then, 'I suppose so.'

Vanessa brings it through with a pale cross face. She is not used to seeing Mary in the sitting room, with her garish yellow dress and clashing blue cardigan, so very un-English, so African: and yet she is plumped down in the middle of her sofa. 'Will you be cooking soon?' she asks Mary, curtly.

Mary smiles at her. 'Do you like the roses?'

'Yes,' says Vanessa, catching sight of them, scarlet, four bright grace-notes on the dark piano. She smiles back at Mary, mollified.

'Do you see I have been digging the back garden? And I have been weeding. I am good at weeding.' And Mary smiles again, her sweet, child-like smile.

Vanessa thinks, one can't stay angry with them. Things *have* been better since Mary arrived. The garden had really been going to seed, but now there are long stretches of freshly weeded earth, though she hasn't had a chance to look at it closely. Still, she can't let Mary behave like a house guest. Vanessa tries again. 'What are you cooking today?'

'Thank you for my tea.' Mary waits for a moment, and then begins, sounding almost shy. 'Vanessa, it is Sunday.'

'It's Sunday. And?'

'Vanessa – I think I will not cook on Sunday.'

'I'm sorry? You have cooked every other Sunday.' Vanessa begins to boil up with frustration. There is no reasoning with Mary Tendo.

'Vanessa, this is why I must ask for more money.'

'Ah. You are going to ask for more money.'

Vanessa has been afraid of this. It has happened to several of her friends. People come over here to work, the wages are agreed, everything is dandy, both sides are happy, but then people claim that life is more expensive than they thought.

Mary starts again, talking faster and louder. 'I have been working all day for Mr Justin. And recently I talked to Trevor. He assures me most people do not work on Sunday. And besides, I have also been talking to Justin. I learned how much money he was earning at his work. And so evidently, I must ask for more money.'

Vanessa sits down beside Mary with a sigh. 'Mary, Justin is hardly an expert on work, he has only done it for a week or two. And trust Tigger to make trouble,' she adds, crossly. 'He knows nothing about it, he has never had a cleaner.'

But Mary sits up straight, and looks her in the face. 'I *was* your cleaner. I am *not* your cleaner.'

'Oh sorry. Sorry. I forgot for a moment.' Those wide black feet on her pale carpet.

It is all so difficult. Vanessa wants to get it right. She knows, in her heart, that the money is too little. After all, when she does a freelance lecture or workshop, she never charges less than two hundred pounds a shot. Not that there is really any comparison. How can you compare a writer with a cleaner?

They sit side by side on the edge of a gulf.

But Mary smiles at her, and tries again. 'I think Mr Justin is getting better. I think he will soon want to go back to work.'

'Yes, yes, Mary. You are doing well.'

They sit in silence, staring at the carpet. They are a breath apart, with the world between them.

Mary is wondering how she can ask for six hundred pounds per month instead of five hundred. The Ugandans she knows here earn more than that, but they are not living in, with everything paid for. Besides, this job is not very hard. Perhaps it is too much. She will ask for five hundred and fifty. That is only about ten pounds more per week. But the Henman is unpredictable. She has stopped looking cross, her face is kind. Mary turns towards her, and says very softly, 'If I have more money, I will cook on Sunday. And next week, I think we shall all go to church. It is good for Mr Justin to go to church.'

'Oh never mind that,' says Vanessa, alarmed. 'I don't think so, really, Mary.' She looks at Mary's shoes. They are wide as boats. They are made of rope and canvas, hopeless for winter. The weather is changing. Mary must be cold. Perhaps she doesn't have any winter clothes. And since Mary arrived, she does spend less on food, since Mary buys everything from the market. 'How would it be,' Vanessa says slowly, 'if I were to pay you two hundred pounds?'

Mary's face becomes blank with disappointment. So Henman thinks she can put the money down. 'Two hundred pounds. No, Miss Henman. Two hundred pounds is not enough.' She shakes her head so hard that her neck starts hurting.

'Not enough? Two hundred pounds a week not enough? But Mary, it is double what you have been earning. Two hundred and twenty a week, then. That's my last word. And I really don't know how I will manage to pay it.' (But in fact, Vanessa knows she can pay it. Her mortgage will be paid off next year. She has money in the bank from Fifi's videos. And after all, it will not be for long. Justin will get better, and Mary will leave.)

But suddenly Mary is laughing beside her. It is a beautiful, infectious sound, a laugh full of happiness. And life. And humour. Vanessa wonders, do I ever laugh like that? I used to once. Tigger made me laugh.

And then she is squashed in Mary's arms, and Mary is kissing her on both cheeks. 'God bless you, Vanessa. I love you, Vanessa.'

And for an hour or so, she really feels it. The money is real. Such a lot of money. In a month, she will earn more than in a year at home.

Soon the stewpot is boiling loudly in the kitchen.

That night, they both go to bed feeling happy, but Mary wakes up weeping at three am.

30   Mary Tendo

Through my own hard work, I am becoming rich. My wages have gone up, through my own efforts. I have saved just under a thousand pounds. That is three million Ugandan shillings! I have put it in the top right-hand drawer of the dressing-table. A beautiful fat envelope. I blow on the notes so they don't stick together. When I count them, I always hope to find one more. They rustle like the wind in the tall golden trees that wave at me from across the road.

Now I look at the planes taking off through my window and am happier, because I do not miss Kampala, or my sparkling white flat, or Charles, my *kabito,* since I know I shall go back to them soon. (*And Jamie will come back. He must come back.*) The planes jump like fish into the red-pink sky as they take off from Heathrow every evening. They swim like tilapia towards Uganda. And I shall go back, with a case full of money. This is because I have been so determined. I think I have excelled at all I am doing.

For example, I chose the right cleaner! Today I was very happy with Anna. A good cleaner can change your life.

Because today, when Justin was making her coffee, Anna asked him if she could clean his room. And to my surprise, Justin said, 'Yes'. Because usually he does not want anyone to enter. Of course, I sleep there, so I have cleaned the dust, and made it healthy for me to sleep, but I do not tidy Justin's things, just take away my duvet and pillow each day. The room is very messy and confusing, and Justin is too lazy to tidy it.

And while Anna was cleaning, Justin sat in the garden. It is the first time he has been out of the house. He screwed up his eyes at the light like a baby, and nearly came straight back inside. But I brought out a chair, and told him to sit down, and then I fetched him the morning paper – I had never seen him reading a paper.

(In Kampala, there are fewer papers. *New Vision* is expensive, and does not tell the truth, and the government keeps closing down the *Monitor*, or forcing them to run 'corrections', or print long speeches by the President. In England they are lucky to have so many papers. They sit on the underground reading them, not looking at each other, rustling the pages, and sometimes you sit opposite a curtain of papers. Vanessa's house seems stuffed with papers, so the box for recycling is always spilling over, and Anna has to jam the rest in the dustbin.

In Kampala it is very different. The vendors sit there, on the hot pavement, selling single copies of old magazines. Maybe two months old, maybe six months old, each one weighted with a big piece of glass, dusty broken glass that gleams in the sunlight, in case the precious things blow away. And Ugandans buy them, although they are old. We know that most things change very little. We value the stories, we value the pictures. Some people stick the pictures on their walls. But here in England they must always have new ones. Although mostly they write about plastic surgery, or film-stars divorcing, or diets, or depression, or how happy women can be without men, which I think must depress young men like Justin.)

Justin sat and read a story about Tony Blair, the prime minister who likes war so much, because he does not live in a country like Uganda, which has four wars going on at once. It is strange how Mr Blair is always smiling (he seems happier than anyone else in Britain!). And he likes our President Museveni, and so does Mr Bush, who came to visit. They all like war, and so they all get on, and no one tries to stop the bloody war in the north, which is killing so many Acholi children, and others, also, who try to pass through, and it is like a curse we cannot escape from; like a swamp that sucks us down.

I was glad to see Justin sitting out in the sunlight, reading a paper like a normal Englishman. He spread out his paper in the breeze like a prince and ate the lunch I had made for him. Later he can do all these things for himself, but at the moment he is still like a baby. I was glad to see him outside at last. His curls were like an angel's, fine and golden. The sun shone on his milk-white skin.

These people do not know how lucky they are. War never seems to happen here. And yet I love Justin. It is not his fault. I want him to be well. I cannot hate him.

Anna found several things in Justin's room. First of all, she found he had a television. It was hidden underneath a dressing-gown, which he had draped cunningly over the screen. It was on, but he had turned the sound down. She asked me whether to turn it off. I went upstairs and had a look. I had never seen this television. He was watching a programme called 'Parent Swap', where real children choose to swap their parents. So now I know Justin is not sleeping all day.

If this is how he spends his life, perhaps he is doing it to annoy his mother. When he was little, she always complained if she found Justin watching television. 'Surely you are not watching TV *again*?' – as if most people only watched it once.

I wonder whether Miss Henman knows her son is interested in swapping his parents.

But the other thing Anna found is more important. It shows me I have made a major error, but all detectives sometimes make errors. A good detective will learn from them.

Under the bed Anna found a photograph, and left it on Justin's table, where I found it. A picture of a beautiful black woman. On the back of the photograph is written 'Zakira'. And as I look at it, the face changes, and I see it is the woman with the orange headscarf who stood on the doorstep in Canaan Gardens. The woman who was holding the purple flower.

31

Trevor has found *My African Journey*. He sits in the garage, under a bare bulb, browsing through the book which he had liked so much. It was written in 1908, which isn't really so long ago.

Winston has a brisk, manly style. When he's got something to say, he doesn't hang about. The first chapter is called 'The Uganda Railway'. Winston seemed very impressed with this, which ran from Nairobi to Lake Victoria: 'Here is a railway, like the British Fleet,' – he'd be shocked by how small the old Fleet is now, thinks Trevor – 'not a paper plan or an airy dream, but an iron fact grinding along through the jungle and the plain, waking with its whistles the silences of the Nyanda ...'

Trevor likes that phrase, 'an iron fact'. And the way Winston made himself a butterfly net out of telegraph wire and mosquito net. Once the British were good at making things. These are the kinds of facts Trevor likes. His clients have airy fairy ideas, but he has to work them out in practice. Nessy is airy fairy too. That's why he does all her donkey work.

Winston had fallen in love with Uganda. Its polite, clever people, its animals. Not just the animals he could shoot. He really took to the butterflies. 'Swallow-tails, fritillaries, admirals, tortoise-shells, peacocks, orange-tips … flitted in sunshine from flower to flower, glinted in the shadow of great trees, or clustered on the path to suck the moisture.' And yet he also saw the horror of it. Mosquitoes, tsetse flies, death and destruction.

Trevor wonders what Mary will make of Winston. The book seems to change when he thinks of her reading it. 'What an obligation, what a sacred duty is imposed upon great Britain – to shelter this trustful, docile, intelligent Baganda race from dangers which, whatever their causes, have synchronised with our arrival in their midst!'

Didn't Mary say her language was Luganda? That probably means she is one of these Baganda. Mary is not what you might call 'docile'. Winston might get right up her nose.

'Let us be sure that order and science will conquer, and that in the end John Bull will be really master in his curious garden of sunshine and deadly nightshade.'

Trevor has mixed feelings, reading this. Of course, it must have been great to know there was an empire, so any old schoolboy could dream of a future, instead of being on benefits.

Though maybe it was only public schoolboys. And Uganda wasn't really our garden …

Winston's confidence shone out from every page, yet the world he imagined never came into being. And he was a bloody clever chap, so what hope is there for the rest of us? The man believed the railway would make everyone rich, yet according to Mary, the line has been abandoned. No more trains from Nairobi to Uganda. They've got AIDS, apparently, and old

John Bull didn't even sort them out with clean water.

Trevor switches off the light and goes back in to the house, leaving his shelves of books in darkness. What must life be like in today's Uganda?

32   From *The Life of Mary Tendo*

Mary likes what she re-reads about herself. Her *Life* now exists outside her head, outside her body, which has lived it. She likes the low hum of her laptop's engine, which reminds her of her beautiful fridge, at home. Here in London, she's inventing Uganda, for as she writes, her life becomes different.

I was a clever girl, rarely given the cane. My parents sent me to boarding school because the local school could no longer teach me. I passed senior school with thirty-five points, the highest score the school had ever had. Being clever did not help me to make friends with the others, but I did not care, I lived for the holidays when I came back to my friends in the village. And then I finished boarding school.

My father decided I had to marry, but my mother was strong, she stood up for me. 'If she's educated, the world will be hers.' 'She should marry,' my father said, sternly.

'You want her to stay here all her life? You want her to stay poor, like us?'

'You want her to be a shrivelled woman who nobody wants,

with a womb like a groundnut?' My father rarely shouted. My mother murmured something soft. I lay awake listening, willing her on.

Night after night the same row broke out. I knew my father was torn in two. He had been approached, by an old friend, on behalf of a boy from the next village, good people, with many cows, and the bride price offered was a good price.

Cows now, or cows in the future? My mother saw a blue distant sky raining cows.

I am the child of good parents. In our village, there was no better father. He called me to him after a week of storms. 'Daughter, will you marry Mwanje?' 'He is quite nice,' I said, looking down. 'Thank you for asking me, father. But I don't want to marry him.' At first he shouted, but not for long. He made me promise to work my hardest, and let him arrange my marriage later, but he did not look at me when he asked, and I did not look at him when I promised. Both of us knew I was going away.

I went to the kitchen and helped my aunty, but I watched him sitting out in front of the house, a long time, alone, before he came inside.

I went to the city, to Makerere, and in the village they were all impressed. '*Asoma e Makerere*. It is the best university in Africa.' (Yet once you have been there, you know it could be better.) Instead of gaining cows, my father sold chickens to give me money for food and paper. Books I queued to read in the library; even Makerere had not enough books, and now I hear many shelves are bare. I came home on the taxi, most weekends, racketing along on the broken road, walking the last five miles on foot.

My second year in the city, life seemed strange and oppressive. I was far from home, and we were maddened by rumour. Obote was driven out by Museveni. We hoped for better things, but change makes you afraid. The city filled up with jeeps of happy soldiers, hooting loudly, returned from the bush. Ugandans had all grown used to fear, under Amin and Obote, and we didn't know then that the new lot would be better.

But the city grows into you, little by little, like creeper, silently up from the ground. I became careless, like the other girls, and no longer wanted to go home to my family. It grew into me; I grew used to it, the pavements with only small breaks and holes, the shops with electric light inside, the *askaris* in uniform, carrying rifles I thought at first would be used to shoot me, the vendors selling fake gold chains, the big dirty taxi-vans everywhere, out of which men shouted and waved their hands, the hotels being built up to the sky, the hurrying people in their new smart clothes, busy women with square mannish shoulders and shoes with heels like blades of knives, the new cinema telling wonderful stories with colours and sounds as sharp as daylight (though quite soon I no longer bothered with films – the American directors did not know my story), the sweet perfumes in glass bottles, the powerful, hissing sprays against insects, the whispering voices of the professors, the way they smiled behind their glasses and pressed against me in corridors, the dirty old *karoli* swooping over the city, with their rusty black feathers and hanging goitres.

I worked very hard and did well at my studies, but my father's money was never enough, and I was ashamed to ask for more. I got a job, working in the Plate Café, washing dishes and wiping tables. I never told my parents this. It was hard and tiring and I missed assignments.

My professor asked me what was the matter. I will not write which professor he was, because I know some people would blame him. In fact, he had always been kind to me. I had a feeling that he liked me. I told him the truth, and he made a soft sound, a tongue-and-teeth sound that meant he was sorry. 'I'll buy you a meal tonight if you are hungry, and we can talk about your problems.' I was overwhelmed. He was kind, like my father!

He took me to a restaurant some way out of town. I didn't know the people there. I had a large glass of beer with my food, because I was nervous of talking to him. I wasn't used to beer. I told him, 'You're kind. Thank you for being kind to me.'

'Will you be kind to me?' he replied. He looked in my eyes. His were soft and hot. 'I'm an old man, but I think I can help you. We could be good friends, and help each other.'

I wanted to cry, but I felt excited. Besides, at least he had bothered to ask me. There were others who forced themselves on their pupils. That night was painful, but I did what I had to. I knew it would help me if I made him happy. When he found I was a virgin, I think he was sorry. He said, 'God forgive me', when he had stopped pushing. But he wasn't sorry until he had stopped pushing.

We remained friends for nearly a year, and I didn't go back to the Plate Café. He lent me books, which was wonderful. I read everything, both serious and funny. Dickens, Thackeray, Rider Haggard, PG Wodehouse, Chinua Achebe, and the endless wailing of Virginia Woolf, thin terrible books where nothing happened. But still I was happy to have read her. I loved the professor for his books. He had studied in UK, and knew everything. But he wasn't young, and his breath was like a goat's. I didn't look at his chest like a woman's, his round soft belly, the grey hair on his back. There was kindness, though, from both of us. And whatever he looked like, he was a good lover. He taught me things that young men don't know, as I found out later when I slept with one. The boy looked cute, but he finished in seconds. (*Later I will delete all this.*)

I quarrelled with the professor when I became too clever. With his help, reading over my essays, I started to get the best marks in the class. My subjects were English, Politics, ——. (*I will not specify, in case the man sues me.*) My friend said he didn't know about ——, so he didn't help with those particular essays, yet my marks in that field began to improve. They improved so fast that my friend became suspicious.

'The Professor of —— has many girlfriends,' he said one evening, as he did up my dress. 'One of them is sick. What do you know about this?'

'I heard the same thing,' I told him, shrugging. His fingers were rather hard on my neck. 'I think she is ill because she stopped eating. She had an abortion. Now she is too thin. '

I myself had round breasts and a behind like melons. Many men wanted to be friends with me. Of course this other professor liked me, in the same way as my first professor. The second professor called me into his office and said, 'You are clever as well as pretty.' I wouldn't let him touch me under my skirt, but maybe I had plans for him in the future. He was younger and bolder than the first professor, and had a blue car with shiny paint-work that he steered boldly through the dirty old taxis. (He smoked Marlboro Lights. Now I know their smell. They smelled of America, and those were the days when I thought I would go there, somehow, anyhow, and be a rich American woman; the days when I thought I could do anything. And perhaps I will still become rich, and fly over, but I no longer want to be American. Uganda already has enough Coca-Cola. Every village is covered with its big red signs.)

The first professor was becoming jealous. 'Maybe this girl

is dying,' he said, and he pulled me round to face him. 'The Professor of —— cannot be trusted. Why do you need more than one professor? Don't I give you enough money? Don't I give you enough loving?'

No one in Uganda has enough money, except for Asians and politicians, who spirit their money away overseas. I kissed him, and said life was very expensive, so maybe I would have to make more money. And then I was lying on the floor, and there was warm blood coming out of my mouth where I had fallen against the table. I saw he was ashamed, but it wasn't enough, and I slapped him, hard, with my strong peasant hand.

He said, 'God forgive me,' as he had once before, and pulled on his clothes very quickly, trembling, over his pock-marked shoulders and hairy pot belly.

So then I had to write my essays alone. But perhaps what he told me saved my life. I found other teachers to help with my essays, and help pay my fees, and buy me dresses. Though many were honest, some were not. But I never said 'Yes' to the Professor of ——, and six months later, the thin girl died.

Mary is happy when this section is finished. Mary, in fact, has told a lie. It is perfectly true that her professor hit her. It's true, as well, that he was sorry. But she was too young and afraid to hit back.

So her autobiography has made her stronger.

She looks at herself in the dressing-table mirror.

I, Mary Tendo, *am becoming a writer.*

33

Now Mary Tendo goes back to the smart street, with the scruffy house, with the tall white steps. She is going to get it right this time. Everything is better the second time. If she could have her life again, Omar would not leave her, she would not lose Jamie.

Climbing the stairs is like a mountain, but she hopes she is looking less like a missionary. She thought about wearing a hat, or sunglasses, so that Zakira would not recognise her, but this seems too much like a detective novel. Instead she wears plain black trousers and sweater, clothes she has bought very cheap in the market, but which make her feel like a Londoner, since everyone in London seems to wear black, with the orange coat swinging open on top. In these clothes, people treat her differently, as if she is no longer simple-minded. And she has dug up a rose-bush from the garden, which she intends to give to Zakira. The roots were a problem, but they're neatly coiled in a plastic bag inside a smarter paper one.

Mary rings loudly but nothing stirs. Still, she is so sure she will be successful that she waits for a minute, then rings again.

This time she hears heavy feet approaching, and the door opens the length of a hand.

It's not easy to see if it's the same woman. 'Zakira?' says Mary.

'What do you want?' The woman's voice is very English, like the newsreaders on BBC World Service, which Mary listens to at home with Charles. As educated as Miss Henman is, or even more so, Mary thinks.

And yet, she's thinner-faced than Mary remembers, in the half-dark of the half-open doorway. 'Good morning,' Mary says, and smiles, but the woman looks at her fixedly, coolly. Mary begins to doubt herself. 'You are not Zakira?' she asks, slowly.

'I hope I am,' the woman says, softly. 'Could you kindly tell me who you are, now, because I can't stand here chatting all day. I'm very pregnant, in case you haven't noticed.'

Mary's heart sinks with a sickening lurch. Zakira is pregnant. Has forgotten Justin. Has found another man. Mary's mission is doomed to failure. How terrible, that Zakira is pregnant. Last time, of course, she had been clutching a plant, which must have hidden her big tummy.

'I come from Justin,' Mary continues, doubtful. 'Justin has sent this flower for you,' which is not quite true, but she holds out the rose, heavy with earth in its sheath of thick paper. The woman's eyes open wide with shock. There is a pause and then she says, mutedly, 'From Justin. You had better come in,' and so Mary follows her down the stairs and in through Zakira's white-painted front door.

Mary sees with approval that the flat is very tidy. Big expensive vases, containing no flowers. Some beautiful lamps, ornate metal and glass, which have a look of North Africa. There are many books, but they are all on bookshelves. A table with a laptop, covered in paper. Of course, Zakira is doing an MBA, the famous degrees that makes everyone rich. Mary wishes her *kabito* could have such luck … Justin loved this woman, and she gave him up. She looks a little older than Justin, Mary thinks. Zakira is probably too proud, too lucky. She will have her baby, and grow powerful and wealthy – but Mary cautions herself against envy.

She sits on the sofa while Zakira makes tea. She will not allow Mary to help her, but returns with two cups, and this time she smiles. But as she sees Mary without her coat, a glaze of anxiety chills her expression and her eyes become sharper, assessing her.

'How do you know Justin?' she asks, abruptly.

'I care for him,' says Mary, smiling, and Zakira's mouth contracts with dislike.

'So did I,' she says, and half audibly, 'What a waste of time that turned out to be.'

Mary is puzzled and starts again. 'I am in England working for Justin's mother.'

'His mother!' says Zakira. 'His mother is a bitch.'

Mary cannot help laughing, and puts down her tea, in order not to spill it on Zakira's sofa. Then she covers her mouth, and becomes very grave. Obviously Zakira is not interested in Justin. No wonder, since she is pregnant by another man.

'I am sorry,' Mary says, and stands up again. 'I think I have come here by mistake. When do you expect your baby?'

'Christmas,' says Zakira. Mary's struck with sadness: how lucky to have a Christmas baby. How different it would be if the baby were Justin's. There is a long pause. Zakira, watching her, sees something sympathetic in Mary's expression, because she suddenly says, 'Have you got children?'

'Two,' says Mary, without thinking. And then realises she

is thinking of Justin. 'One,' she corrects herself. 'His name is Jamil. He had to go and live with his father. I do not know what has happened to him.'

'Jamil? That is an Arabic name.' Zakira looks at her with more interest. 'I was born here. But my parents are Moroccan.'

'His father is from Libya. A Muslim. I miss my son nearly every day. But a boy, you know. He must see his father.' Mary says the words she has said so often, but she does not believe them any more. Sometimes she wishes that Omar were dead.

'Did Justin's mother send you to tell me to stay away?' asks Zakira. 'She puts the phone down on me, you know.'

'I do not really come here from Miss Henman,' Mary hurries to say. 'I come from Justin.'

Zakira stares for a long moment, deciding. And then she says, 'Well, it's Justin's baby.'

And Mary claps her hands, and jumps in the air. 'It is Justin's baby! I am so happy! I am Mary Tendo. I was Justin's nanny.'

A small tear starts from Zakira's eye. No one has been happy about this baby. 'My God, you're Mary. I've heard so much about you. Is it really you? When did you come back?'

An hour later, they are walking together, even more slowly than Mary usually walks, towards the house where Justin must be sleeping.

Zakira has tied back her jet-black hair, and put lipstick on, and wrapped herself in an expensive purple coat which Mary envies. Zakira feels beautiful again, although she is enormous, leaning, sometimes, on Mary's arm, a painted boat on the cold river, listing as she sails towards the ice of winter. 'I love this country. If I'd been born in Morocco I couldn't have done a thing that I wanted. But I hate the weather. I love the heat.'

Mary, in her thin orange coat, agrees strongly.

The two woman have struck up a makeshift alliance, based partly on Zakira's acute need. She has spoken to no one for several days, and now she tells Mary everything. Her perfect life has imploded, this year: she has had to drop out of the top-flight MBA she was doing at Imperial College, because she was too sick to get in to classes three times a week, and fell behind with her assignments. 'Although I have finally got permission to take it up again next year.' She tries to study now, but being pregnant makes her sleepy. 'I've just been afraid that I will never manage, once the baby is born. On my own. In disgrace! You know, I'm not religious, but we are still Muslims.' Her parents are Zakira's greatest worry. They are separated in all but name: her mother has gone back to Morocco to look after her own bedridden mother, and her father, a professor at SOAS, is currently a Visiting Professor at Harvard. 'In one way it is a fantastic relief. If they were here, and knew, they would be going mad. In theory my father is a liberal, but in practice he would be so ashamed. And my mother – my mother is medieval. And at the same time, I do miss them. They have a house in Kensington. In a way they've always been too proud of me, and so I was bound to disappoint them, wasn't I? A bit like Justin with his mother ... I was a junior partner in the firm where Justin worked, the youngest ever, male or female, then I got on this high-powered MBA. My brother is the tearaway. But my mother loves him more than me!'

Zakira knows a lot about Mary already. 'You were like a mother to him, he said. I can't believe that you've come back.' She's arrived like the bringer of hope, of life. Zakira's face has lost its hard, bored expression. Her beautiful eyes are alight again. She understands Justin has really been ill, that it wasn't as she feared, that he didn't want to see her, after the bad quarrel when she gave him up. She understands now that he lost his job, that the two things together have made him ill. 'And there were some real bitches in that office, believe me. I was glad to get out and do my MBA.' Now she knows that Justin has been ill, she can feel tender: now she knows what is wrong, she will care for him.

And yet there is the obstacle of Justin's mother.

Zakira has never met Justin's mother, although she has heard too much about her, for Justin loves his mother excessively, even for Zakira, who honours her family. This woman has snubbed her several times on the phone, slamming it down when Zakira was speaking. No wonder Justin hates her as well as loves her.

But Mary tells her it is time for them to meet. Mary seems enviably confident. Zakira is impressed with her. She does not quite believe all that Mary says, about writing *The Life of Mary Tendo*; Justin has not mentioned that Mary is a writer, and nannies do not usually write their lives, and besides, Mary seems – very African, somehow – in most ways, very different from Zakira …

On the other hand, there is something about Mary, an energy and hopefulness Zakira has lost over the lonely spring and summer months of being pregnant, saying nothing to people at her old workplace in case they rejoiced that she had messed things up, and nothing to her family, and nothing to Justin, while thinking, at first, 'I shall have an abortion', and later, when she found she had left it too late as a way of never making that fatal decision, 'A child is coming, what will happen to me?' None of her contemporaries has children. But Mary has a son. She understands.

Zakira's nervous about meeting Justin's rude, cold mother. Still, at least the fear makes her feel alive, where an hour ago she was indifferent, moribund, because it seemed that no change was possible, that she would be imprisoned in the cold for ever, imprisoned in her body with its lumbering cargo. No one would visit her and no one would help her, and the big heavy baby would never be born, because out in the world no one waited for him, no-one wanted him except his mother.

Now the knot of fate is going to loosen. Zakira sways along at Mary's side.

Mary gives Zakira one last warm smile before she slips her key into the door. She leads Zakira into the sitting-room, then goes upstairs to waken Justin.

But he is not there.

The bedroom is empty.

Even more surprising, the bed is made. Mary checks the bathroom, the loo. No one. She comes downstairs and scans the back garden. It doesn't seem possible, but Justin has gone. (Though she doesn't remember this until later, she sees Justin's arrows all over the garden, sticking out of tree-trunks and flowerbeds and fences, the arrows Mary smuggled in from Uganda, pale bamboo arrows with barbed steel heads. Justin has been playing with someone in the garden. His goat-skin quiver lies on the ground.)

She is just relaying the bad news to Zakira when the front door opens, they rise to their feet, their faces alight with nervous excitement – and Vanessa tramps in, looking tired and grim as she does at the end of a day of teaching. She goes straight to the kitchen without noticing them. The tap runs, then she reappears, and is taken aback to see the two of them.

'Good afternoon Miss Henman, Vanessa,' says Mary.

'Ah Mary,' says Vanessa, with a small sigh, and encompasses Zakira with a vague smile. Soon her house will be full of Ugandans. Still, Mary has worked harder since her wages rose:

she is washing-up again, and using the vacuum.

'Miss Henman, this is my friend,' starts Mary. 'She – '

'From church?' Vanessa says, shaking Zakira's hand rather cursorily. 'Very nice to meet you. Now, Mary, do make your friend tea or coffee. I'm actually exhausted. I shall go and lie down.'

And before either woman can explain herself, she has swept upstairs, clutching a milky glass of aspirin, her lips tight and pale without their coat of crimson, her forehead creased with tiredness, a folder of marking in her other thin hand, together with the letter she has found in the hallway.

The gaps in the house become wider and deeper. They sit there stranded in the shadowy sitting room, surrounded by photographs of strangers, and suddenly they feel what they did not before, two African women in a foreign land.

Mary stares at Vanessa's African masks, which her employer is particularly proud of, staring out at them from an expanse of pale plaster, dark cicatriced faces with empty eyes. They do not feel like ancestors.

'I do not like them,' she says to Zakira.

'They are ignorant,' says Zakira, regally. She is not talking about the masks. For a moment she feels much closer to Mary. What can it be like, living under this roof? 'People like her know nothing about us. And they do not want to get to know us.' And then she pauses, and reflects. 'I think they are afraid of us.'

34

Vanessa lies upstairs on her bed. The aspirin is beginning to work. Down below, she can just hear the quiet murmur of the two women's voices like a distant river. It isn't unpleasant. It is comforting. Perhaps she and Justin have grown too self-enclosed. Perhaps it is good to meet new people, though today she had come home completely exhausted.

Vanessa's class today was a near-riot. She had asked the new intake to bring in an object which inspired their writing, and might inspire others. Usually people bring photographs, maybe ferns or shells, a stone or a feather. But Derrick had turned up with a whole dead pigeon, and two of the girls became hysterical, one because she said all pigeons had fleas (though it was a soft, pink, plump-looking thing) and the other because she suspected he had killed it. This girl, Daisy, who came from Devon, wore long hippyish clothes that were tight over her breasts, and had big, fixed eyes, rather slow and moon-like. She very often seemed to quarrel with Derrick. Perhaps she was attracted to him. Daisy had brought along a photo of her cat, which was white and fat and soft and sleepy. 'You like to kill things,' Daisy shouted at him. 'We don't want to see your victims.'

'It died of old age,' Derrick insisted. But there were two small marks on the back of its neck which looked suspiciously like airgun pellets.

Derrick became defiant and articulate. As the girls shrank away, he pushed the pigeon towards him, so it sat in the middle of the long table, almost living as its flesh-coloured feathers slowly settled, beautifully soft, from pink to pearl, a thing of wonder in its intricate detail. Vanessa started to imagine an odour, a sort of sweet-savoury, menstrual smell, but it could equally well have come from the girls. Her classes were usually a moil of hormones. Derrick had a loud, rather toneless voice, which allowed him to dominate the room, though this time he had a lot of competition. 'Salvador Dalí threw a cow from a plane. You probably don't even know who Dalí is. If that was art, tell me why my pigeon isn't?'

Soon everybody was shouting at once and Vanessa had to bang the green marker on the whiteboard, but before they fell silent, she heard Derrick demand, 'You tell me what is interesting about your fat pussy?' Whereupon half the class collapsed in laughter, while Daisy stood up and burst into tears.

By the time Vanessa had mediated, only forty-five minutes remained for writing, which Daisy insisted was unfair, since 'Some people write very fast without thinking,' looking hard at Derrick, who by now was established at his own small table in the corner of the room, where the pigeon would cause least physical violence. So Vanessa had agreed there would be no reading out, and instead she had taken all the writing in, which meant she had doubled her load of marking.

Daisy, of course, was very annoying. But Vanessa had become a little anxious about Derrick, whose scripts, though skilful, were increasingly violent. Perhaps she shouldn't be encouraging him?

It was very odd, this writing business. Looking quickly, she sees that the best piece comes once again from the infuriating man with the Father Christmas beard, who has written a skit upon this morning's class, where the teacher is whimsical and ineffectual, and the pigeon is actually crawling with maggots –

But she forgives him, since he has made her beautiful.

Vanessa falls asleep for an hour, and dreams she is writing the book of a lifetime. It spools from her fingers, witty, brilliant. She has written two thirds of the book before breakfast, though Daisy stands there, wailing and pointing, 'You went too fast! You killed the pigeon!' She is about to deny it when she looks under the desk and finds she is making love to the boy, whose penis is a fat, pearly-pink pigeon, and she thinks, 'This is brilliant, it doesn't stop me writing! I could have been doing this all these years!' She has almost finished, she is coming, she is there – but when she stands up to take her bow, she finds she is naked below her waist, and sees Justin waiting behind her, staring, hang-dog, heavy, unloved by anyone, jealous of the boy with the thin dark body, and he says, 'You see, you forgot about me. It's all your fault, you forgot about me.'

Waking, she remembers that rush of pleasure that came with the sense that she had written brilliantly. Her headache is gone, the voices have vanished. Full of resolve, she goes down to her study.

But there are so many books in there. The piles seem to loom like cliffs all round her, the base eroding, the summits frowning. She picks up a novel she has never read which is touted on the front as 'The book of the century ... Brilliant writing, subtle, heart-piercing.' She reads a few pages. It is banal. Sighing, she returns to her own writing, but she finds her mind wandering over to Mary. At five o'clock, she telephones Tigger.

'Mary seems to have made some friends,' she tells him. 'She brought this Ugandan person to the house. They were nattering away when I came home.'

'Good for her,' says Trevor. 'She'd get bored, otherwise. You're busy with your teaching, Nessie.'

'Don't call me Nessie,' she snaps, at once. 'It's a stupid nickname, honestly, Tigger. And please don't talk about me like that. I'm not a *teacher*, you know, always *teaching* people. I'm a writer. It would be frightful to be a teacher.'

'It was the summit of my ambitions,' he says. 'I always wanted to teach history. But as it turned out, I was better with my hands.'

Some dim memory is stirring in Vanessa. 'Do you know I've just remembered something. I think Mary once wanted to be a teacher. May even have trained as a teacher, over here. I think she didn't finish, the money ran out.' Which makes her feel better – Vanessa has the job that Mary Tendo always wanted.

'It's not over yet,' says Trevor, gnomically. 'There's more to Mary than meets the eye. Toodle-oo, Ness. Got things to do.'

'What are you up to?' Vanessa asks. She has always unconsciously kept tags on Tigger.

There is a pause, which in another man might have sounded guilty, and something which might almost be whispering, and then he says, 'Got to read a book.' That ridiculous urgency, as she should have predicted, as if otherwise the book might escape him.

He was like that about reading, he did it on purpose, he had to stick out and be difficult. They might have made a go of it if he had been more normal. But as it was, poor Justin did not really have a father, not a normal, useful father, that is. Justin did not have a normal family.

And then she remembers this morning's letter. She gets up and runs back up to the bedroom. It is still on top of the duvet, unopened. She sees, as she sticks her nail into the envelope, it comes from the village where she was born. The letter is from Lucy, her country cousin. Her heart lifts with real excitement. She settles against the pillow to read.

To her surprise, Lucy writes well, although she is not educated, just a housewife. Vanessa thinks, writing well must be in our family. She feels a little twinge of pride. It is stuffed with news: very little is bad. Uncle Frank, the husband of Aunt Isobel, has been an invalid for years with Parkinson's. 'I pop in and see Dad every day, but we think he can't go on forever. He's had a good innings – 83!' The rest of it is a kind of social diary: who has married, who has children, the village scandals, the new village hall, which they have been building on the site of one three hundred years old, which Vanessa remembers: dank lath and plaster. And Lucy is inviting her to the opening. 'Why don't you bring Justin down to see us? We're having a knees-up at the end of October. My place isn't a palace, but you're very welcome.'

Vanessa is shocked by how pleased she is. They still remember her. They might even love her. There is still a world to which she belongs, although she has neglected it for half a lifetime. The silent world of her mother and father. Though once she had longed above all to escape it, time has rinsed it in reminiscent sunlight. She imagines: overlapping leaves of oak trees, the soft green body of a hilly landscape. Her mother's garden, with its vegetable beds. A place where she need not be busy.

Then she checks herself. She is being sentimental. The party

will be a fluorescent-lit bore, where people will get drunk and
do karaoke. And no one will know what to say to her. Of course
she won't go. She will get on with her novel. And what will she
say, if they ask about Justin? Her contemporaries' children will
all be working, dropping babies like rabbits, chubby grandchildren; bragging about sales targets, cars, trampolines, plans
for camper-van trips to New Zealand … She pushes the letter
away, firmly.

But the past whispers on from the blue letter.

Part 4

35 Mary Tendo

The Henman is spoiling my plans again. Last night she lost her temper with Justin and Trevor. The woman should have been praising them. And me, as well, for encouraging Justin. A son must see his father, whatever the cost. (*I did not take Jamey away from his father. If he ran away, he chose like a man.*)

Sometimes I think she is possessed by spirits. Of course, I do not believe in demons, and yet she has invited them into her home, with the many hideous masks and figures that she brought back from her trip to Uganda, although most of them were not made in Uganda, they were made in other African countries which are at a lower level of development, on the Gold Coast, in Mali, in Guinea. I have said to her several times already that these masks are not good to have in the house, but she only laughed at me, and said, 'Mary, you are funny. I can't believe anyone still thinks like that. But of course it is a cultural thing.' And with that she laughed more loudly than ever, so her grey eyes turned into tiny metal buttons.

But last night she did not laugh, she screamed.

Of course I am not a person who smokes, because I know

smoking is unhealthy, but occasionally I have a cigarette – in fact, every evening before bed, in the garden.

I buy Ugandan cigarettes, from Harlesden, *Rex* and *Sportsman* cigarettes, from the Mugalu Brothers. Once I know Vanessa is in bed, or in the bathroom, I pop out through the kitchen door, and light up. Recently Justin has come and smoked with me. Although I consider this to be a good thing, because it gets him out of his bedroom, the Henman is unreasonable about smoking, and so I have not mentioned this achievement.

But last night after I had finished my writing and came downstairs to sit in the garden, the Henman was still in the sitting room, and so I hid my cigarettes in my pocket.

'Mary, I am out of my mind with worry. Is Justin up there with you, in your room?'

'No, Miss Henman.'

'I thought I heard noises.'

'No, Miss Henman. He must be in his bedroom.' And then I remember, he was not in the house when I brought Zakira back to see him.

'Of course I'm not stupid, I've looked there, he isn't.'

And then I saw how frightened she was. And I realised that she does love him. And I too was frightened, but I did not show it. It is always best to be brave and cheerful.

'He never goes out. You know he doesn't.'

She is looking very old, and thin, and white. I said, 'But Miss Henman, he should go out.'

And she shouted, 'Do not tell me things I know already!' and then she said 'Sorry, I am just upset.' Justin has been missing for several hours. But this was only the beginning of her shouting, because at that moment the doorbell rang, and she ran to the door, on her thin little legs, and threw it open, and there was

Justin, in the bright porch light, and behind him was Trevor. And to me Justin looked lovely as an angel, with the light shining down from heaven on his curls, and his cheeks were rosy, and I tried to embrace him, but the Henman was screaming and hitting her chest: 'My God, Trevor, what have you been playing at?'

'Er – hallo there, Ness. The lad's been helping me.'

'I've been painting,' smiled Justin. He was proud of himself. 'I have worked for six hours. And Dad has paid me! At any rate, he is going to pay me.' But his face started to fall as he saw his mother.

'You bastard, bastard!' she shouted at Trevor. 'I've been so worried! Why didn't you tell me what you were doing? I actually phoned you this afternoon, and he must have been there, but you didn't say a thing – ' She was yelling this right in Trevor's face, but he said nothing, just looked at Justin.

'Er – '

Then Justin started to look unhappy and worried, and said, 'I asked him not to tell you. I didn't want anyone to know. Just in case I freaked out, and was a failure.'

Then the Henman turned round and screamed at Justin instead. 'Well you can hardly be a success as a painter! Did I bring you up to be a labourer? Do you want to be a failure like your father? Oh Justin, you were always such a high flyer!'

And then Mr Trevor looked very sad.

And so I thought, time for Mary Tendo to join in, because there was no reason for all this sorrow: at last Justin was working again. And also, I wanted my cigarette.

'Perhaps we should all count to five,' I said. 'If Trevor and Justin go into the garden, Vanessa could make us a cup of coffee, and then we can talk about everything calmly.'

But then the Henman started screaming at me. She was

turning around like a white tornado, striking at each of us in turn. 'Oh and what will you be doing while I make your coffee?' she said very loudly, staring at me.

'I shall go in the garden with Trevor and Justin.'

And so I went there, but they did not follow, perhaps because they were afraid of her. Two big strong men, afraid of a woman. Trevor said, 'Better not wind her up. She's already practically snapped her watch-spring.' But I could not stay inside like a child. I sat outside on the lawn under the moon, which shone on the neat bare earth I had weeded. It was a very big moon, low and orange. Inside the house I could hear her screaming, and Trevor talking quietly, but Justin said nothing, and in the end his mother stopped screaming, and I heard the sound of the front door closing, and then I suppose that she went to bed. And so I smoked cigarettes, three in a row, because my heart was beating loudly, and I was thinking, all this fuss, and I do not make any fuss about Jamie. These people do not really know about sorrow. They do not know about missing someone.

And then at last Justin came out to join me. He had taken his clothes off, like he did before, and his nose was running, and his cheeks were slippery. He clung to me again, like a baby, but I made him sit up, and have a cigarette, and he felt very cold, and was shivering, and I went and got a rug, and wrapped it round him. Perhaps this boy would have died of cold. It is so different in England, the things you die from.

But he still dropped the ash on his naked skin, and yelped like a rabbit before I could shush him. Then the window of the Henman's room banged open, and she shouted down, 'What is going on? You all think I am stupid, but I am not! I know perfectly well what you two are up to!'

I whispered to Justin, 'We shall say nothing.' But instead, he called up, 'It's all right, Mums. I couldn't sleep, so I came in the garden.' And after a bit, she was quiet again.

And I told Justin I was proud of him. Because it is good that he worked for his father. And quite soon Justin stopped shaking and sniffing.

'I just don't know what to do about her,' he said to me later, as we slept together.

But I said to him, 'Justin, I want to help you, but I cannot make your mother too angry, or else I think she will send me away. Perhaps she will send me away tomorrow.'

'She won't. She can't. I won't let you go.'

'Do not forget that your mother loves you.'

But I have an idea, which I am sure will help her. Next time the Henman loses her temper, I shall take all her African masks off the wall, and also all the little dark figures. Some of them are victims of sorcerers who stand there miserably holding their stomachs. But the Henman just thinks they are 'sweet' and 'artistic'.

One day the Henman will lose her demons.

36   Vanessa Henman

She will have to go. It is insupportable. My house, my son are no longer my own. Even my ex-husband is behaving strangely. And now she has started this weird *juju*. I almost feel afraid of her, although that, of course, is ridiculous. She is just a simple African woman.

But sometimes she does not seem so simple.

Item one: the blue nightdress in Justin's bedroom. Anya left a pile of his things on the landing. Why was Mary's hideous nightdress among them? I asked her about it, but she only smiled, and said, 'Vanessa, it is an error', which could have meant anything, and told me nothing. But I thought of the noises in the middle of the night, and the strange thumping I hear in her bedroom.

I must not think like this. It is disgusting. Perhaps it is me who has the problem. I am open-minded, I try to be fair. I know about Oedipus, and Jocasta.

All the same, the thought makes me want to slap her.

Item two: she makes Justin set his sights low. This wretched idea of him helping his father. Of course it will do for a week or two, as a way of getting him back to normal, but in the long run, it is just a nightmare, the thought of my brilliant, gifted son, dragging around as an odd-job man. (Though Trevor got terribly cross with me and forbade me to say any more to Justin. 'Leave well alone, I'm telling you, Ness, or I won't be responsible. He's very fragile, still, our son. Don't you dare make him think you despise him. You might hide your feelings about me, as well. Or you can start cleaning out your own gutters.' Those eyes of his were simply flashing fire! For a moment he looked almost handsome.)

So I have decided to say nothing for a bit. But I'm biding my time. And I do blame Mary.

Item three: the African herbs in the kitchen. The food was one thing, but now she is bringing in strange little packets of dried root and powder, glass vials of seed-heads like shrunken pupils, wizened black plant-stuff from another world. I asked her, quite nicely, 'Are these herbs for cooking?' But she said, 'No, it is medicine for Justin. I have told him to stop taking his Prozac,' and I said, 'But Mary, that could be dangerous!' And she said, 'Vanessa, Prozac is dangerous. Especially now Justin is working with Trevor. What if he is painting up a ladder? I am sure that Prozac will make him sleepy.'

I really couldn't argue with that. I have always thought that drugs were dangerous. But obviously I have forbidden her to give him any of her coal-black rubbish. The Health Food shop is one thing: we all use that, herbs and homeopathy in proper labelled bottles. I am open-minded on alternative health. But African witch-doctors are something else.

I wonder if Mary will take any notice. It seems to me she does whatever she wants to.

Item four: she encourages Tigger to smoke. It isn't good for him. He has a weak chest. He looks terribly robust, but he does get the sniffles, and of course he often works in the open air. No one can say I don't care about him. He's the kind of man who needs the odd reminder. I mean, he hardly ever used to change his socks. But Mary has always been soft on men. Why else does Omar have custody of their son? And Mary has always admired Tigger. Now she is around, he is much more – uppity. It isn't a change that I enjoy.

Then yesterday I smelled smoke in the kitchen, as clear as day, by the door to the garden, when Tigger had popped in after a day with Justin. They were all round the table, talking very loudly. I was in my study, as usual, working, and when I came through, the room went quiet, and I could smell cigarettes quite strongly. 'Who's been smoking?' I demanded, of course. All of them know there is to be no smoking. And then, to my surprise, Justin started laughing, and then they were all giggling like children, and Tigger said, 'I'd better own up, it's me,' and then they all laughed even harder. And I said to Mary, 'It is bad for Tigger,' and she said, 'Miss Henman, he is not a baby.'

And then perhaps I raised my voice a little, and said to her, 'Don't tell me about my husband!' Which is embarrassing, in retrospect.

Because Trevor turned on me. Men do. They feel no loyalty to women. He said, in that quiet voice he uses when he's cross, 'I have not been your husband for twenty years. And Mary has a point, actually.'

So then I felt entirely alone. It was weak of me, but I wanted to cry, because they had all behaved so badly, but instead I closed the kitchen door rather firmly and went into my study to work.

I sat for two hours, staring at my laptop. This is my house, but I felt like a prisoner, afraid to set foot outside this room in case they were lurking there, smoking and laughing.

It is Mary's fault. She has been here too long. And I am paying her a fortune. I have been too soft, she is taking advantage.

At first I went back to my novel again. It seemed so feeble, untrue and unhelpful. I did not feel it was connected to me.

Then something odd happened, one of those weird glitches the brain comes up with when one's over-stressed.

My novel had a heroine called Emily who was leaving home to go to university. Somehow I slipped into the first person, and I found I was writing about the village. The things I was writing were all about me. The fear and the excitement, the loneliness of leaving (I suppose all these quarrels must have left me feeling lonely).

And so I slipped back, for a moment, into childhood. The sounds I remember from the village. The wind in the cornfields. The tractor straining. The ominous bees by the buddleia. The chickens' fretful squawks from the hen-house. My mother's sheets snapping on the line, when she wasn't ill, when I was little. My mother calling me in from the garden. And I forgot about Emily; and for a moment, I was perfectly happy, even though, when I had finished, my mind circled back to Mary.

37 Mary Tendo

£1,270. I am ahead of schedule, because of my new wages, which I negotiated, like a lawyer (and to be fair, Miss Henman tried to be generous). There are still many weeks left before Christmas, so I could go back with three thousand pounds! Which is nine million Ugandan shillings.

And yet, this morning, I just feel afraid. I have not seen Miss Henman since she was so angry. I think she is jealous that Justin likes me. She shouted from the window as if she was drunk.

I find myself thinking, buy presents for Jamil. And I tell myself, do not do this again, but I find I am going out of the house, with all my clothes on, and my thin orange coat, and seventy pounds tucked in my purse, and I try to stop myself, but I cannot. It always happens when I am not happy. I must not let myself be unhappy. Compared to the great unhappiness, nothing matters, everything is light. Yet the small unhappinesses scratch at my soul.

I do not like these arguments. In Kampala, I never argue, or only with my friend the accountant, and then we kiss and make up straight away. And twice with Omar, on the phone. For Omar does not like to phone me, and phoning from Libya is sometimes hard. It was nearly two weeks before he phoned to tell me the bad news about Jamie. Why didn't Omar ring when Jamie first ran away? I cursed my husband, and then I was sorry. And yet I still blame him. I cannot help it. My son has become a stone in my heart.

Every day of my life, I think about Jamie.

Kampala is a place of many rumours. Perhaps the pain is too great, and you speak. A small whisper, a hiss of hurt. A week later, the rumour returns, like a wreath of snakes around your shoulders.

I know Miss Henman will send me away. Last night when we were smoking she was very angry, and I was afraid she would dock my money. But this only makes me more eager to spend it. Jamie, Jamie, something for Jamie.

Because I am afraid of ending up with nothing. And the British will keep all the things that they have, their houses, their gardens, their lawns and roses, their cupboards full of fine shirts and blouses, the ruby-red walls of wine in the beer shops, their pictures, their books, their colleges, the way they speak English as if they are princes, as if it is the only way to speak English, and the bus conductors do not understand me, but say 'What?' or 'Sorry?' as if I am a fool – which makes me afraid my language is nothing, although Ugandans speak excellent English, and write it too, like Moses Isegawa, our novelist who writes beautiful books, but here I have met no one who has heard of him.

They will send me away, and keep it all. Their squares of white buildings as big as a whole village, where water bursts up and wastes in the sun, their tame stone lions, so proud and calm, whereas ours eat goats, and fishermen, their supermarket

MAGGIE GEE

palaces, heavy with food, twenty sorts of coffee, thirty sorts of bread, long fridges like fishing boats groaning with fish, thousands of fat-cheeked, featherless, chickens as bald and blank as *bazungu* faces, apples from Cape Town, beans from Kenya, all the best food in Africa –

They will keep the fruit, and give me a stone. And I will have crossed the world for nothing.

Because when we were in the garden last night, and the Henman was so angry, and shouted from the window, I saw that Justin was sorry for her. I saw that if there were a really bad argument, he would forget me, and side with her. Because in his heart, of course, he loves her. It is always the same with a son and his mother.

Jamie, Jamil. He loved his mother. He liked to press his cheek against mine, even later, when he developed stubble, when he was living with his father. Even when his father had the new wife, even when Omar cooled to me. And this is the thing that makes me wince and frown as I press into the chill of the UK winter. Did Omar grow cold towards our son, as well? He became too ready to think badly of him, too ready to think he was corrupted by others. Was it because the new wife had a new baby? Did Jamie leave because he didn't feel wanted? Did he know how much his mother loved him?

And yet in the end I could not protect him. Love's not enough. It is strong – so strong. My heart could tear its way out of my chest. It could beat so hard that my life would end. It is strong, and yet it has no power. It cannot bring him back to me.

I last saw Jamie two years ago. His father gave him money for the flights to Entebbe. I was there to meet him, with Charles, and the car. When I saw Jamie coming I ran to hug him. He was still narrow-bodied, as sixteen-year-olds are, and he walked out alone, with his untidy baggage, and I felt there was only me, in

204

all the world, to help him, and I hugged him so hard my arms became numb. We were talking so fast that Jamie didn't hear when I introduced him to my friend the accountant, who sat in the car, waiting for us, but I didn't realise till we got to my flat and he said, 'Mummy, you must pay the driver.' He thought that Charles was a taxi driver! And when he understood, he looked upset, and afterwards Charles said he thought he was sulky. But I said, 'Charles, you must understand. Young men feel shy when their mothers have boyfriends.' And we were careful, but not careful enough, because Jamie knew that Charles was my *kabito* when he caught us kissing in the kitchen. Perhaps he told Omar I was a whore. I do not think so. Jamie was kind (I could not stop him giving money to the beggars). And yet his parents stopped loving each other. He knew that both of us loved other people. Did Jamie think that we loved him less? Did I make him unhappy, in Kampala?

The wind in October is horribly cold. It is thin and sharp and it makes me lonely. It screams and howls as the Henman does. I do not want to hear what it says. I miss the friends that I have at home. Even if they gossip, at least they know me. I miss the strong *chai* that we drink together, Beverley from the flat above and Ruth next door with her new small dreads like stubby, soft little heads of puppies. I miss the faces I saw every day, old Mr Lugira with the weighing machine his son brought back from America, standing smiling by the side of the road, and often he would weigh me for free. And Karim Hussein, my friend at the bank, who always treats me like a lady. And my other friends in the street where I live, and even the maids at the Nile Imperial, who are nice to me, for whatever reason. The youngest, Benedicta, was like a daughter. I miss my home. I miss Kampala.

And the trees have begun to look lonely now. It is strange,

and sad, to see them naked. I had forgotten how the trees become naked. In Uganda, the trees keep their leaves. I do not want to see everything naked. And last night in the garden, Justin took off his clothes, and I was no longer sure he had got better. He shook and trembled like a tree in the wind. They are not so strong as they like to think, these tall young men, these fine young men. Do they realise this, the young western women, when they laugh at the boys and make them feel small? When I last saw Jamie, he was not full grown. They are easy to hurt. Maybe easy to kill.

I rarely hurry, but my feet go faster, because I must keep ahead of the voices, whispering things I do not want to hear, whispering things that someone has told them. My friend the accountant, he knows also. But it was not him who told the maids. I have shown them the photos of Jamil in my purse. We all show photos of our children. I make myself hurry, not to think about it, to keep the cruel voices out of my head, that say all day long, at the back of my mind, *her son is lost, her son is* – no, I must run away, I will keep ahead –

But when I try to hurry, I become breathless, and my heart beats too fast, and I have to slow down. It seems that England is making me ill. Why should my flow be like pink water? I suppose the sickness comes from my heart, because recently I am too sad to go dancing, and even in church I am sometimes lonely, unless I go east, to Waterloo, but the buses are slow, and the underground eats money, so usually I go to the local church and sit with the other black people, Nigerians, Somalis, Ethiopians, Jamaicans, and they only say 'Hallo' and 'It's cold' and 'How are you?', because they do not really know me, and last week I stayed to have coffee with the vicar, Mr Andy, who asked all newcomers to stay, but he was too busy to talk to me, so I had a stale biscuit and went away. (But still next week I will

go back again, because it is Harvest Festival.) If I am still here.
If I am well.

Perhaps this city is poisoning me.

Perhaps Miss Henman is poisoning me.

I miss my son. I miss my son.

Now I go to the market and start to buy shirts. Pale blues
and greens for a gold-skinned boy. The jeans are long-legged
and lean-waisted. I do not really know how tall he is, I do not
really know how slim he is – I do not know the face of my own
son, but I smile at the stallholder and manage to stop crying. I
imagine Jamie wearing them: the girls would love him. He will
still have brown eyes that glow like amber, and run as swiftly
as the wind. He used to race against his dog, Liquorice, but
soon he grew too tall, and too fast. Surely all the girls want to
marry him. And I will have gold-skinned grandchildren. But
the wind shakes the stalls and the clothes fly like kites, flicking
out like whips, loud and spiteful, and there are white jackets
and white trousers, kicking –

I hurry on to spend more money, although everything here
is very expensive, ten times as expensive as in Kampala. Still,
Jamie must know that his mother loves him, that only the best
would be good enough, that I shall never stop loving him. Shall
never, *ever* stop loving him.

The seventy pounds disappears very quickly, and
afterwards, my purse is empty, and I feel empty, and my hands
are shaking.

I do not want to go back again to the house where the
Henman and Justin are waiting together, where she is waiting
for me with her son, and she has everything, and I have nothing.
Perhaps she will be nosy, and look at my presents, and perhaps
she will be angry, and send me away.

And if she is nosy, what will I tell her? How could I bear

to share my sadness? She would peck at it. She would dirty it. And then I would not even have that. She would wave her busy little hands at me, and say we must search, and telephone people. But nothing would happen. He is in God's hands. In the hands of the God of glory.

I will not tell her about my trouble. How Omar phoned, and his voice had grown old. He told me that our son had gone missing. And this was at the time when the city of Tripoli was boiling with anger against America, because of the war against Iraq. There had been big marches. The young men were in a passion. Jamie went to all the demonstrations. There were arguments at home, more arguments. Omar insisted he did not lose his temper. Then one morning, Jamil was not there. And Omar had heard that a few of the young men, those rich young men with their empty lives, had set off for Iraq to volunteer, travelling through Syria, by bus, overland, burning to fight in their own *jihad*. I did curse Omar, which was unfair. He swore he had tried to restrain our son, but sometimes restraining him made him more angry. In any case, nothing at all was certain. No one could confirm where Jamie had gone. Omar has heard nothing since Jamie left, or if he has, he has not told me. I long for his call. I dread his call.

Besides, there are other possibilities. That Jamie was trying to find me in Uganda. But he had no money to fly to Entebbe. Better if my son has gone to Iraq. Because no one can cross, by land, into Uganda, not from the north, where the boy would be. Only Kony's devil army and the children they capture.

If Jamie did that, he is no longer alive.

If Jamie did that, my life has been wasted.

I will not tell my secret to the Henman, who has her son, and complains about him, and wails and moans, and is pleased with nothing.

And so, although my feet are weary, although my legs are like lead this morning, I catch a bus towards Zakira's flat. Perhaps she will come back with me to the house. I will bring her back with me as evidence that I am a good and helpful person.

Of course I am afraid that the Henman will sack me. But surely, not if I can bring her a grandchild. Although Zakira is frightened to meet her, because she is a Muslim, and Moroccan; but she grew up in England, and has a degree, and will soon be rich, with her MBA. And the child will surely be beautiful, with parents like her and Mr Justin.

The wind is deafening, shouting and battering, howling his name, *Jamie, Jamie*. I ring the bell as loud as I can. Zakira must let me in out of the cold.

After what seems like days, Zakira comes to the door, and she asks me inside, but she does not smile. 'Sorry to keep you waiting, I couldn't turn the tap off, it's driving me mad, *drip drip dripp*ing.'

When I ask her to come with me, she looks serious. 'Look, I've thought about it. I was mad, last week. I can't just butt in there, eight months pregnant. Have you told him about me?'

'You said I must not.'

She has made me some tea, but I still feel empty, and I ask her, has she got bread, or a biscuit, and she gives me some biscuits, and I feel better, and the tap keeps dripping, like a tiny gun.

Then I think, how hard Zakira's life must be, here all on her own, with the baby coming, and the wind howling around the windows. And then I start to feel more cheerful, or perhaps the biscuits were good for me. I start to forget about my shopping. I start to feel like myself again.

Because Mary Tendo is a happy person. When there is a chance, I am always happy.

Zakira tells me, 'It is all hopeless,' and this reminds me of Mr Justin, who said it was hopeless when I told him to ring her.

And yet, I know that nothing is hopeless.

(*Except only some things are completely hopeless. Zakira is lucky not to know about them.*)

I say to her, 'Zakira, nothing is hopeless. I do not know how, but I am going to help you.'

And then she smiles, and says, 'Mary, I believe you.' But still she refuses to come with me today. 'Besides, the pipe under my sink is leaking. I have to get everything out and clean it. The flat must be right before the baby arrives.'

And then I think about Trevor and Justin. 'Zakira, I can find someone to help you, who will mend your tap, and the pipe under your sink.'

'Thanks, but at the moment I can't afford it. It is a hundred pounds to get a plumber.'

'These men are my friends. They will be your friends too.' I am so excited that I can't wait to call them, and Trevor's card is in my handbag.

But Trevor is booked for the next three months. 'I'm a popular chap. You wouldn't believe it. All over London, they're crying out for me. No one can mend their own things any more.' But when I explain it is a friend of mine and Justin's, he promises to try and do it sooner.

'And Mr Justin must come as well.'

'Well, maybe. He doesn't help every day.'

'Because it is his friend, it will be good for him,' I say, as strictly as I can.

'If you say so, Mary. Catch you later.'

As I walk home, the sun comes out. Together, Zakira and I are stronger. Suddenly the bare trees are very pretty, like the fine black lace I saw in the market. We do not make lace in

Africa. I don't feel so cold with the sun shining.

I realise I have forgotten my shopping, but it doesn't matter, it never matters, I will not think about it, not think. Because I must get on with my life.

And so I must make friends with the Henman. I do not mind if I have to say sorry. Pretend to be humble, as she would wish. The woman is wrong about everything, and yet it is true that smoking is not healthy. Perhaps that is why I am out of breath.

Still, I stop at the Henman's newsagent – the owner, Dinesh, likes talking to me; he left Uganda when he was twelve, when Idi Amin sent the Asians away, and perhaps he misses Kampala, like me – and buy cigarettes with the Henman's money.

38 Vanessa Henman

That African sweetness I had almost forgotten. Like the children who ran along the side of the road when we drove in our jeep towards the west of Uganda, yelling, 'Good morning, *muzungu*! How are you?', and smiling, though I would never see them again, their voices like bells, and those huge white smiles, even when the driver was grumpy with them, pretending that they were after my money. I know that it was just their innate good nature. You would never see that with English children. Africans smile so much more than we do.

And Mary Tendo is pure African. I am ashamed of myself for forgetting, and getting such small things out of proportion.

She came to see me with her head bowed, looking not so very different from the shy young woman who answered my advert in the newsagent, sixteen or seventeen years ago, though this time she didn't call me Madam! But she said 'Miss Henman', and was very polite.

She admitted she was in the wrong. She said she knew smoking was bad for her, and I said, 'Of course everyone smokes in Uganda,' and she looked puzzled, but said, 'Yes, I am sorry.'

'You see, I do worry about Tigger. He isn't as young as he was, you know.'

'Yes, he is not as young as before. I am very sorry about Mr Trevor.' Her mouth was twitching, and just for a second I thought she was making fun of me, but then I realised she must be upset.

'Never mind, Mary. It is OK … and Justin is really too young to have started.'

'He is too young, and Mr Trevor too old. Yes, they should not smoke, it is true.'

I felt rather silly, when she put it like that, but Mary was a mother, she understood.

'I'm sure you wouldn't want Jamil to smoke. Honestly, Mary, it's very dangerous.'

And then Mary nodded, submissively, and said, with passion, 'They must not do it.'

And so I said, 'Mary, let's forget all about it.'

Because that is the only grown-up way, and someone in the house has to be a grown-up.

'Forget all about it, please, Miss Henman. I want us to be like a family.'

'Of course, Mary. We can be like sisters.'

Though obviously I would be the older sister. I felt more touched than I would have expected. I wondered if this was the moment to hug her.

'Vanessa,' she said, with that quick shift of attention that characterised Mary Tendo's conversation, 'what are those papers on the table?'

'Oh, just work from my Life Writing students,' I said. I did not imagine she'd be interested. She waited, and then said, 'That is interesting.'

'I like to help our students get published. I am sending these extracts to an agent. Quite a famous one, in fact. One of the best. She will come to visit the class after Christmas.'

(Of course I did not tell her my little secret. I've decided to enclose a few pages of my own, from the thing I was writing about leaving my village. With a pseudonym, naturally, 'Emily Self'. I thought the name was rather clever.)

'That is interesting. You are very helpful,' she said. Her eyes were very big and very bright.

'Oh well. I mean, it's a lottery. I just have to pray that the good ones get noticed.' Emily Self, I thought, for instance.

'Next week let us all go to church together,' she volunteered, with her wonderful smile, her teeth like bright ivory, her gums deep pink. 'Then we can pray together about the agent.'

She had said this before, and I'd turned her down, but now seemed exactly the moment for bonding. And, certainly, praying hard about the agent! After all, it was a very sweet offer. Although I am not formally religious, I do have a sense of spiritual beauty. And, though one feels shy of saying so, love. Even if one's behaviour sometimes falls short. 'Yes, Mary. Why not. You and I will go together.'

'And Justin as well. And Mr Trevor.'

'Oh well, I don't know about them, Mary. But thank you very much for asking me.'

I wanted to reciprocate in some way. With her very recent raise, it couldn't be money. So I found myself saying, 'There's something else. I would like to invite you to come with me to my village. I come from a village, you know, as you do.'

It is one of the things I know about Uganda. I talked to the people at the embassy, and they said, 'Remember, when you meet Kampalans, the important thing for all of them is the village. Even though they are city-dwellers, they all belong, at heart, to a village.' I suppose it is where she spends her weekends, but I was too busy to go and see one. Perhaps one day I will go back to Uganda, and Mary will take me to her village.

'Yes, Miss Henman. We shall go to the village.'

And that *was* the moment, and I gave her a hug. She was shy and hung back, quite stiff in my arms, but I hugged her harder to show that I meant it, and somehow we bumped our heads together. 'Sorry, Mary.' 'OK, Henman,' I thought I heard, but then she added '*Vanessa*'. She did seem to smell very faintly of tobacco, but cigarettes cling through several washes.

39

Vanessa is putting things in her diary. It is covered all over with birds' feet of writing, scratchy and criss-crossed, a busy woman's diary. In fact, there is hardly any white space. The only blank page is in 'Reading Week', when the students at her college have a mid-term break to try and read around their subjects. Into that week she might fit some writing, but she quickly inks something over it. It coincides with the party in the village, when she wants to go and stay with her cousin: perfect. Her pen pecks hard at the empty space. If she goes for three days, there will be four days left. She rings up Fifi and agrees to go to Paris, and then she scratches over the last bit of whiteness, cross-hatching it with Eurostar times and places, and then she thinks briefly about her writing, and the pleasure in her busy-ness is tinged with guilt. Perhaps she will take her laptop to France.

The maddening Arab is ringing again, the one who thinks she is Japanese. 'There is nobody here called Mistendo,' she snaps, and puts the phone down, as she has before, but this time, because she said the name out loud, it suddenly clicks:

of course, he wants Mary. Vanessa never thinks about her surname. Mary has always been simply, well, *Mary*. How can Vanessa have been so stupid? But she is too busy to call him back. Next time he calls, she will put him through. She returns to her in-tray, and forgets all about it.

Vanessa's especially busy because she is going to church at eleven, with Mary. In theory she's looking forward to it, but in practice she fears she is going to cry. Memories of her mother's funeral, when the village turned out in sympathy, and suddenly she felt part of a multitude, when all her adult life she has been alone, just she and her son against the world.

Yet that is the ideal state for a writer, as she recently told her new intake of students. 'Most modern writers are exiles,' she said. 'You see exile can be a very personal thing, to do with a kind of willed isolation. I speak from my own experience.' (She was quoting, in fact, from a book she had read.) 'How many successful women writers are married? Almost none, I think you'll find.'

Beardy seemed to bridle when she said that. He stayed behind at the end of the class, pretending to pack up his papers. Once they were alone, he'd taken her on. 'Do you think you should be warning these young ladies against marriage?' he asked her, with his old-fashioned, playful twinkle. 'I mean, I myself have been through a divorce, but I try not to put my daughters off it. I miss being married. I don't write any better.'

'I think your writing is improving somewhat,' Vanessa had said, repressively. (She's never quite told him how good he is, because she finds him a little threatening. His comments in the seminars are too sharp; he is starting to gather a coterie. Older students can be controlling.)

'You're single, are you?' he smiled at her, but his tone was coarse, bubbling with laughter. 'You've mentioned a son.

But of course you are. Has it helped you write your Pilates books?'

Vanessa's mouth had gone tight and thin. 'I have also written two highly praised novels,' she said. 'Exactly what point are you trying to make?'

'I think I've made it,' he said, with a laugh, and bowed ironically, and left the room, but at the last moment, he turned back, and said, no longer laughing, apologetic: 'In fact, I have read both your novels. I think you're really talented. But when are you going to write another? Does being single really help us to write?'

And then he was gone, leaving her winded.

And yet, Vanessa knows she's right. This morning, she needs to be alone, herself, in charge of her desk, in charge of her life, before she can submerge herself in Mary's.

She wishes she had not agreed to church.

She is changing her clothes – because what do you wear? A skirt, surely, but not a hat, and too much jewellery would look vulgar, but none at all might look a bit bare, so she finds her pearls, and the pink wool suit she wears to chair departmental meetings, and a matching pinky-pearl ring and bracelet – when Mary knocks on the bedroom door. Vanessa's white silk vest is half over her head. She stares at Mary through the neck-hole.

'You look stunning, Mary. Is that tribal dress? I mean … is it … indigenous?' She is not sure they still talk about tribes. Her voice is muffled by the vest.

'Of course it is not dangerous. It is a *gomesi*, Miss Vanessa.' It has a wide sash and peaked, puffed sleeves, which stick up from her shoulders like butterfly wings. It is golden bronze. Mary's skin glows against it.

Vanessa decides not to explain. She slips on her jacket and her pearls. 'It's very nice. You look, well, delightful.'

And Mary smiles back at her appreciatively. 'And you, Vanessa, look like a Jamaican – '

Vanessa does not know quite how to take this, but Mary continues, '– because, I have noticed, the English do not like to look smart in church. It is not the fashion, for white Christians. Best of all, they like jeans and sandals. They think it makes them look more humble. But Jamaicans and Africans look very smart. We do not like this scruffiness. We do not believe the white Christians are humble. They sit at the front, in the very best seats. Thank you for looking smart, Vanessa.'

Sometimes Mary sounds surprisingly sharp. Vanessa is glad she has cut the mustard.

'Now we must find some food to take,' Mary says, briskly, and sets off towards the kitchen.

'Oh no, Mary, really, we don't do that,' says Vanessa, laughing once more at Mary's innocence.

'Because, Vanessa, it is Harvest Festival. The Reverend Andy asked everyone to bring some.'

'Oh, Harvest Festival, wonderful.' Vanessa brightens considerably, remembering long-lost feasts of colour, being sent to school with marrows and apples. And thanks to Mary's new regime in the kitchen, they soon assemble an impressive display: black and orange plantains, a Savoy cabbage so yellow green it is almost golden, frilled and tightly-layered like the bodice of a dress, three baking potatoes as big as Easter eggs; a feathery-topped, fluted column of celery.

They pause in the hall, just before they go out, and see themselves framed in the circular mirror. It is a picture of harmony: silver-blonde Vanessa in her pink and pearl, smiling broadly with her new shiny teeth, her white hands clutching the speckled plantains, the pale rod of celery under her armpit, and next to her, the intense dark figure of Mary, dressed in the golden bronze butterfly dress, her hair caught up in a swathe of gold fabric, taller than Vanessa, even in her pink heels, broader than her, but with her arm around her, and it sits on Vanessa's pink woollen shoulder, surprising her with its heft and weight, and Mary's other arm holds the green and yellow basket she brought from Uganda as a present for Vanessa, with the cabbage and potatoes brightly peeping out.

'We're fertility goddesses,' Vanessa says, very taken with this image of the two of them, but Mary looks stern, it is the wrong kind of godliness, so 'Sisters', Vanessa tries again, and smiles at the glass, and Mary laughs to herself, and repeats it, so softly that Vanessa hardly hears it.

Sometimes, she thinks, Mary is almost timid.

A moment later, Mary shouts, 'Justin!' at a volume that does not seem credible. Vanessa looks at her amazed, but in seconds there appears at the top of the stairs a combed and tidied, pink-faced, Justin, wearing a white shirt and linen blazer his mother hasn't seen him in since the breakdown.

'Present and correct,' he smiles at Mary.

Mary hands her loaded basket to Justin, and Vanessa stops herself from protesting, for after all, he must be stronger now. The three of them head towards the door. 'Mary, we're going to need umbrellas,' says Vanessa, as the hissing sound of rain comes closer. She looks out of the window: deep metallic-grey, with weeping fringes of navy blue cloud. The wind is rattling the rose against the glass. She opens the door to get a closer look, but as soon as she does she sees Tigger is waiting at the end of the path with his big white van.

He comes down to meet them with a golf umbrella. 'Minicab, Madam,' he says to Mary, and the two of them laugh in such an intimate way that Vanessa has to tell herself not to be jealous.

So now we are all here, even the men, Vanessa thinks, bringing up the rear. Justin seems cheerful, though he squints at the rain. She hates the idea of going in the van, but she does not want to make a fuss. She hopes it is not covered in paint and brick dust. Knowing Tigger, it probably is. Though even Tigger looks smart for him, in a sports jacket over a black polo-neck jumper, with Mary Tendo smiling and clutching his arm.

But how does Mary manage it? Vanessa asks herself, puzzled. Do we actually all do whatever she wants?

And they follow her meekly into the church and down into a pew at the back, where everyone but them is black. Indeed this whole segment of the church is black. Vanessa wonders if she will be unwelcome, but a glance at Mary's face shows she isn't bothered.

'Why do all the black people sit over here?' she asks Mary. 'Is it because English people are racist?'

Vanessa feels proud to have used the 'R'-word. It is the beginning of their new frankness. After all, if they are friends, there must be no secrets.

But Mary, who was praying for Zakira and the baby, the granddaughter of whom Vanessa knows nothing, just laughs, and points at the radiators. 'It is because the heaters are here at the back. English churches can be very cold places.'

Mary has many things to pray for today. First of all for Jamil. Always Jamil. For Zakira and Justin and the baby. And for herself. For her own secret. The autobiography that she is writing. And about the agent. As she promised Vanessa, she is going to pray hard about the agent. Though Vanessa does not have any idea why.

It is Vanessa's first time in a church since she sat by her father for her mother's funeral. 'It's what she would have wanted,' she remembers him saying. According to her father, they used to go often, when she was just a tiny girl, before her mother's world was warped by illness, and perhaps that accounts for the shock of love Vanessa feels this morning when the second hymn turns out to be a rousing 'We plough the fields and scatter'; and though she is wary of sentiment, she finds there are tears pricking in her eyes. She is part of the singing, and part of the people, and part of all people everywhere who have ploughed the fields and loved the earth, who have scattered the good seed on the land, who are watered by the Almighty hand; and somewhere in that surge of feeling is an almost forgotten love for her father. The congregation belt the hymn out, and she is surprised to hear Justin singing, a fine tenor voice, and she squeezes his hand.

But Mary is looking at the harvest display, which is on a table in front of the altar. Can the Reverend Andy be pleased with it? There are small ziggurats of tins, rows of packets, a pineapple with a label still on it, some faded, supermarket-style apples, and somebody has brought a pumpkin, but for some reason, it's been tucked behind the tins (in fact, Andy's female curate hid the pumpkin, at the last moment, as they all came in, because of the association with witchcraft). Mary and Vanessa's offerings stand out well against this patchy, unsatisfactory landscape.

I was the child who came with the harvest, Mary Tendo thinks, half the world away. But it seems that in UK, they have forgotten how to grow things. One day they will starve, like Ethiopians. Although they have rain, and this is not a desert.

As usual, Mary tries to listen to the sermon, but Andy speaks as if to small children, making jokes about TV that are not very funny (though maybe she is wrong, because Justin, who watches TV all day long, laughs happily, pleased to be included, and so do some of the scruffy white people). Soon her attention wanders again.

Not everything in England is better, Mary thinks. Perhaps it will be different in the country, when I go to the village with Vanessa. Perhaps there are still harvests in the country.

Mary's never been to the English countryside, though twice she and Omar went to the seaside, and stayed in what they called a 'B and B'. They were the only black people, and everyone stared, in that English fashion where the eyes flick away and then they pretend they are not interested, though they were kind to Jamie, and not unfriendly, and Jamie loved the water, and played on the sand, and he could be naked, and no one bothered …

She sees him, suddenly, gilded by the sunlight, maybe three or four, running for the sea, and his laughter is blown back towards them by the wind, and his sturdy body gets smaller and smaller as his little legs pound down the firm sand, and she suddenly sees he will run straight into the water and sets off after him, hurrying, but he goes faster, and the tiny black figure plunges into the wide band of wavery silver and screams at the cold, then disappears, and she runs faster, and at last she finds him.

Omar was untroubled, reading a paper. Omar thought Allah would look after him.

And she prays, silently, fiercely, clearly: *Jesus, please bring me news of my baby. You who see everything, find him, please.*

Vanessa sees Mary staring fixedly at their offerings on the meagre table, and whispers in her ear, 'Well done, Mary. You saved the day.'

Mary blinks at her, startled, far away. 'I don't understand.'

'Your Savoy cabbage. Look. I'd say it's the absolute star of the show.'

'Thank you, Vanessa.' Yet her face is almost haughty. 'Vanessa, it is time for the collection.'

'Oh heavens, Mary, I hope I've got some money.' Vanessa starts digging through her handbag. Mary knows there is always money in that handbag, untidy bunches and sheaves of notes. She decides to help Vanessa get into heaven.

'It is OK, Vanessa. Twenty pounds is enough. If you have not got anything larger.'

Vanessa draws her breath in, sharply, but the maroon brocade bag on its wooden handle is almost there, carried by an ancient sidesman, and resignedly she finds a twenty, and pushes it in to the maw of the bag, though she's almost sure Mary only gives five, there is a glimpse of blue-green in Mary's dark pink palm, and further along the row she hears the chink of coins, and she wonders why Mary Tendo is smiling.

And then Vanessa thinks of the phone-call this morning, and the voice, so unfamiliar, drops into place, a voice she knew from over a decade ago. 'Mary,' she hisses, 'I've just remembered. Somebody rang. I mean, once or twice. I think it might possibly have been your husband.'

She is not prepared for Mary's ghastly face, the smile dying, the sharp intake of breath.

And now Mary Tendo starts praying in earnest, she sinks to her knees on the hard stone floor, there is no time for the embroidered hassocks which hang unused on the back of the pew, and she squeezes her eyes into concentrated darkness, she prays for light, she prays for help: *Please not now, Jesus. I cannot bear it.* Mwatttu sikati yesu! *Jamie is young, he understood nothing. Please take this cross away from me.*

But even as she prays, she knows it is hopeless, she has known ever since the first news came of her son leaving home in Tripoli. And yet, if she hears Omar say those words – if she must hear her husband, and Jamie's father, saying the words she fears so much –

Lord, take this cup away from me. But if it is your will –

Mary cannot go on. She fixes a polite smile on her face, pushes along the pew, passing Vanessa and Trevor and Justin with the faintest acknowledgement, because they have slipped into a world of ghosts, and walks out of the church, the swing doors crashing.

40

She runs all the way home, breath tearing, heart thumping, Mary who never hurries, never runs, and rings her husband in Libya, which Vanessa owes her, and has always owed her, she thinks, as she furiously punches out the numbers: 'Omar,' she says, as his familiar voice answers in guttural Arabic. 'It is I, Mary. Is there any news?'

Omar sounds strange, surly, in rusty English. 'I have been ringing you since three weeks … Mary, you promised to give me your mobile number.'

'I lost my mobile. I will give it to you now.' (But even his surliness is a relief. If Jamie were dead, he would not be surly.)

Omar's story is long and fractured, full of 'if' and 'perhaps' and 'maybe'. There has been a possible sighting, in Baghdad. But it comes at three or four removes. The source is 'a crazy boy called Mohammed', the cousin of a cousin of Omar's new wife – Omar is going to meet him tomorrow. Mohammed is one of the rash young men who trekked to Iraq as volunteers, hoping to fight the Americans. He came home, injured, some time after the war, and spent months in Tripoli recovering. 'He says the volunteers had a terrible time. No one in Baghdad was ready to trust them. The civilians were worse than the military. You see, people think they are suicide bombers. No one was going to let them fight – '

'I do not care, Omar. Tell me about Jamie.'

'There is a zoo, you know. A zoo in Baghdad.'

'What are you talking about, a zoo? Is Jamie alive? Do not torture me.'

'Be patient, Mary. Let me finish my story.'

And so she stands and suffers, clutching the phone, while the story continues at Omar's pace.

Baghdad Zoo was in a desperate state, because of the bombing, the shortages. There was a blind bear, some mangy wolves that once belonged to Saddam Hussein's son, everything half-starving or half-mad. 'According to Mohammed, a Libyan was there. He heard about him from another volunteer. This boy was young, like Jamil, and from Tripoli, helping out because there was no one else. Mohammed is not sure of his name. But then Awatef asks Mohammed if it could be Jamil, and he says maybe. But only maybe. Then I ask him on the phone, and he says he thinks it is.'

'He is not certain.'

'He is not certain. I think he never met him, he just heard about him.'

'It could be nothing,' says Mary, slowly.

'It can be everything,' says Omar. 'You know our son, how he feel for the animals, how he wants to take care of them.'

'If it is him,' asks Mary, suddenly agonised, 'why hasn't he rung us? Does he hate us, Omar?'

'Perhaps he is ashamed of running away. Perhaps he is ill. Or perhaps it is not Jamie. Mary, I am going to Baghdad next week. I could not go before, because my wife – my other wife – is ill, Mary. I cannot leave her with the little son.'

'The other son,' says Mary, sadly.

She sits, face blank, the tears streaming steadily, for several minutes after putting the phone down.

News. Some news. It is better than nothing.

But it is so much worse, as well. Stirring up all she has tried to bury. Hope is painful, like the pains in her hands after going outside in the UK winter – the worst pains come when she is back in the house, when the blood pushes slowly back into her fingers.

Mary goes upstairs and washes her face, and puts on lipstick, and starts cooking lunch. Whatever happens, people have to eat. She hears the door open as the Henmans come back. 'Coo-ee, Mary. Are you all right?' And in fact, in an hour or so, she is all right.

But a little hope can grow too quickly, even in darkness, with nothing to feed it.

She prays to Jesus, 'Help me to hope. But help me not to hope too much.'

41

Two days later, Vanessa and Mary Tendo set off for the village, with Mary driving, since she's always enjoyed it, and Vanessa responsible for map-reading the puzzle of lanes at the end of the journey. Justin is not coming, after all. At the last minute he has cried off, claiming to have a painting job to finish for his father. (It is true, but he also means to sleep with Anya, who does two hours on Saturday morning. He's noticed *she* means to sleep with *him*. Justin has almost stopped being depressed.)

'You are coming as a friend, and not to work,' Vanessa says to Mary, regally, as the two women pack the car. 'I wish that Justin would come as well, but he is being obstinate.'

'I think he has something to finish for Trevor.'

'Oh honestly, Mary, it's not a real job. Tigger's only getting him to help as therapy. He could sometimes try to please his mother.'

'He has to be a man now,' says Mary.

'As if I did not want him to be a man!' Vanessa stares at her, indignant, but something in what Mary says strikes home, and settles there, so they do not quarrel.

Mary has remembered something she needs. 'I have forgotten my Bible,' she says to Vanessa.

'Oh honestly, Mary, you won't have time to read it. The whole village will want to talk to us.' (As Vanessa says this, she hopes it will be true, that they won't think her weird for bringing Mary, that they won't be, well, *racist,* that Mary will be happy.) 'In any case, we really must get started.'

But Mary looks unhappy, and gazes at the house. 'There is something else that I have forgotten.'

'I'm sure you'll be able to buy it in the village. Now get in, Mary, we have to go.'

'Vanessa, I think it is important – ' But Vanessa's in the car, and has slammed the door.

So Mary gives up, and climbs in beside her. God will protect them, if he chooses to.

Soon they are whizzing down the motorway. Mary Tendo loves speed, and drives rather fast, mouthing Luganda oaths at men who try to cut in. She leans forward slightly, towards the windscreen, and seems to scan the far horizon. It is as if by leaning, she can make them go faster, like a sprinter dipping towards the tape. She uses the horn with brutal vigour, marking each time she changes lane.

After a bit, Vanessa says, 'You don't look awfully comfortable like that, Mary. If you keep leaning forward, you'll strain your neck.'

Mary smiles and nods, but she keeps leaning forward. They are going 90, and burning up the distances, but Vanessa is anxiously aware of the lorries, enormous as houses, thundering beside them. It is as if Mary enjoys a good race. She never willingly yields her space. Of course, she must be a competent driver. When she was younger she drove Justin everywhere.

'Perhaps we could slow down a little. We don't have to fight to stay in the fast lane.'

The volume of traffic is slowly mounting as the late October day gets underway. If anything, Mary is leaning further forward, her eyes screwed up tensely, her dark head bowed.

'Mary, honestly, that is a very odd position.'

'But Miss Vanessa, I must drive like this. Do not worry, I am a very good driver.'

'Why must you, Mary?' Vanessa is indulgent. Perhaps it is a Ugandan style of driving. (But wasn't Uganda famous for car crashes?)

'Because, Vanessa, I am very short-sighted. When I lean forward, I can see the road.'

The speedometer is showing 95.

'What do you mean? Don't be ridiculous!' Vanessa shouts as Mary swings out and edges a petrol tanker out of their way. They both have to shout; the noise is deafening, and Mary is adding to it, blaring her horn. 'Do you actually know what short-sighted means?'

'Yes, Vanessa. It means I perhaps need glasses. I sometimes wear glasses when I am driving, but today I left my glasses in the house.'

'You're crazy! You should have gone back for them!'

'Miss Henman, you said that we must leave.'

As the argument intensifies, she seems to go faster. Vanessa sighs, and shrinks back in her seat, and consults the still safe surface of her map, and attempts to fold herself into that miniature world, to ignore the thunderous, terrifying racetrack, but when she shoots a glance across at her driver, she sees that Mary is enjoying this, she is gripping the wheel in her strong broad hands, her eyes gleaming, her lips curving upwards or muttering gentle encouragement to herself as she cuts up yet another juggernaut, and leaves another man making gestures in her mirror, the impotent rage of the defeated male ape.

Vanessa shuts off. They will live, or die. She cannot always take control of things. At least, now, Justin is finding his feet, in however feeble and hopeless a way. So if she did die, it would not be so awful. And perhaps her novels might survive in libraries. And her cousin would know that she tried to come back, and did not entirely forget her family.

Her mind wanders away to Beardy. Or Alex, to give him his proper name. He did say that he admired her novels. Of course he was aggressive, as many men are, but in his short story, he had described her as 'tensile, like a dancer. And 'in a good light, beautiful'. Vanessa is feeling rather old today, because she is anxious about going to the village, where her coevals may look younger than her, where her pretty cousin may still be prettier, where everyone who once loved her may have vanished, where people may think her a sad old stick …

But a man in London thinks her beautiful. Reads her novels. Believes in her.

The car swerves left, but she knows they'll survive.

42

Vanessa arrives at her aunt's in a state. Things went wrong once they left the motorway. Here was the straight, noisy main road that had always cut the village in two, and then the patchwork of lanes on the map she expected to know like the lines on her palm. But she recognised nothing. They drove in a circle, and ended up back on the main road.

She found her landmarks: the steeple, the old school, perched like toys athwart the rushing traffic. But they didn't help her when all around them was a sprawl of raw red, which meant nothing to her, small modern houses with small tight gardens spread along the lanes like beads on a necklace. Everything looked different. Where was the centre? There didn't seem to be one any more. She tried to rotate her brain, but all it did was make her feel giddy. For a moment she thought it was the wrong village, and stopped a cross cyclist who grunted the name, and it *was* her village, although he was Indian. 'Where are the shops?' she called after him, pleading, although he was already two metres away. 'What shops?' he asked, and grinned unpleasantly. Evidently he had not understood her. The traffic was so loud that he probably couldn't hear. 'Garage,' he called back over his shoulder. 'Over there', but Vanessa was too deafened to hear him.

But they did find the garage – at least there was a garage. It sold sweets, papers and birthday cards. She recognised, with a leap of the heart, the glitter-scattered card that Lucy had sent her. The man behind the till had a local burr and was probably not much older than Vanessa. Or maybe around the same age as her. She showed him the address, which she had written down, and he scratched his head, as if it meant nothing, but when she asked for her cousin by name, his face lit up. 'Oh, Lucy Henman! I've known the Henmans all my life. The old man isn't doing so well. And who may you be?'

'Vanessa Henman.'

'Oh, I heard about you. Didn't you go off to Cambridge? Course I was only a kid at the time.' He gave her directions, and touched his cap, and she would have felt better if they had then found it, but Mary seemed obstinate and obtuse and didn't listen carefully to her instructions, so they ended up driving in more circles.

Then Vanessa focussed. It was there, like a dream. 'Stop, Mary! We're here!' The old gate, the blue door.

'Miss Henman, you said we were here before.'

But this time she is right. It is the same house. Yes, that is her Aunt Isobel's house, the house where she has always lived with Uncle Stan. It looks different because the trees have grown up, two great dark yew trees which obscure the windows and make the house look smaller than before. Not that it has ever been a very big house. Vanessa's village does not have big houses.

Lucy is putting up two of her daughters, so they have to stay with Lucy's parents. The front door is the same peeling sky-blue it used to be when Vanessa was little. They ring the doorbell. Inside, there is a crash of furniture, and then the slow movement of something living, a shuffle and drag of someone coming to the door, and the minutes exacerbate Vanessa's nerves, but then the door opens, and there is her aunt, a hundred years older, but wreathed in smiles, her very own aunt, and this is her welcome, she's enfolded in laughter and soft, solid flesh that smells of lilacs, and something medical.

'Nessa, dearie. How lovely to see you. We're all at sixes and sevens here. You know Stan's not well. He sometimes knocks things over ... Who's this?' She peers puzzledly at Mary, then says, 'Oh yes, nice to see you, dear, Lucy did say you would be bringing a friend, but she didn't mention – I see, never mind. Come in, come in. You're too thin, Vanessa. We'll have to feed you up. Of course we hoped that young Justin would come – '

So they are swept in, and back in time. To smaller rooms and narrower stairs. To unshaded bulbs and yellowed paintwork, to thin, cheap towels in deck-chair stripes. Here they are still living in the 1950s. Nothing, it seems, has been thrown away, though they do have a huge flat-screen television. 'We rent it, actually, we ought to buy it but you know how it is, we never quite have the money.' Uncle Stan watches it most of the time, and his contribution to the lunchtime conversation is a lengthy digest of the plots of the soaps, which he delivers anxiously, in his soft new voice, as if his own life is not good enough.

'It's the effect of Parkinson's, the way he talks,' whispers Isobel, in the dark kitchen, which seems like a period film set to Vanessa. Old electric cooker with solid hot plates, enamel bread-bin, little calendar with spaniels, glossy ears drooping over circled dates next to which are pencilled 'DOCTOR' or 'HOSPITAL'. 'He's making a big effort, but he's very tired. They don't think he's got long to go – ' And although her aunt speaks matter-of-factly, as if of a race with a gallant jockey, Vanessa realises it's death she means, death that hovers by the stained formica underneath the wall cupboard with its layers of cream paint. Suddenly that cupboard is very familiar. Was it where her aunt kept homemade ginger biscuits? Sweet and tacky, misshapen as puddles. The taste returns to her, buttery, hot. '– But it's bound to buck Stan up, seeing you. And your friend. She's very nice. She seems just like us. You know we've never had an African in the house. '

It is a shock to Vanessa that they are poor. Oddly enough, she had not expected it, as if the wash of prosperity in London would have flooded over and found every village and changed the lives of the people here. In fact, they are no better off than they were. Indeed they must be worse off, since everything's the same, just older and darker than before. This house has no videos, or dimmer switches, or mixer taps, or bathroom suites. There is the same curved bath, with rusted feet, which they could have sold for a fortune in London, and the separate loo, with its high dark cistern. The chain is mended with ancient string.

'I'll show you to your room,' Aunt Isobel says, after they've drunk cups of sweet milky coffee. 'Oh, don't you take sugar?' she asks, too late, spotting Vanessa's wince of distaste.

'It's fine, Aunt Isobel, it's just that I get toothache. No, never mind, I'm enjoying it.' And she is, in a way. It takes her back in time; her mother used to make the same mild, sweet fluid.

The two of them follow the old lady upstairs, checking themselves at every step as she heaves and pants her way to the top, then turns and smiles at them; one tooth is broken. 'Slow and steady wins the day.'

And then Vanessa has her second shock. For she and Mary

will be sharing a room. Of course, she should have expected it. The house is small, and there are only two bedrooms, for the one where Lucy and her sister once slept has now been turned into a junk room. Isobel explains this as she opens the door to a small bright room with a double bed.

And so they will be sharing a bed.

There is a vase of roses on the bedside table. 'Your Aunt Becky crocheted that bedspread,' says Isobel. 'I had to clear their house out after she died. She would have liked to be here to see you.' And then, seeing something stunned in Vanessa's expression, she says, 'Will this room be all right for you? I thought, seeing as the two of you are such friends … In any case, it's all we've got.' And just for a moment there's a flash of something that Vanessa remembers from when she was younger, when she went to college and her cousins did not, when her aunt thought she'd got above herself, and told her mother, and there was a row. Hurriedly she says, 'That's quite all right.'

'It is very nice,' says Mary, laughing. 'I do not mind sleeping with Vanessa. Though sometimes Omar says I kick people.'

Vanessa does not laugh. She takes most of the hangers, and the side of the bed with the bedside table.

In the evening they all go to Lucy's house, except Uncle Stan, who 'has a programme to watch', or so he says, but his wife whispers, 'Well, the old boy never goes out.'

Lucy lives in one of the modern houses that have appeared along the lanes. It has an air of recent ruthless tidying; the beds in the garden are freshly dug over, spanking new winter pansies in brilliant islands upon a background of immaculate brown. They are building an extension at the back: it is large and white and nearly finished, with a round conservatory on the end.

Lucy is nervous, but full of laughter. Pretty from a distance, with a cap of yellow curls, close up her fine skin is wreathed in smiling wrinkles, Vanessa is relieved to find, as they kiss. Her blue eyes are kindly, but not the cornflower pools that used to lure Vanessa's boyfriends away. And I am slimmer than her, thinks Vanessa. And surely I dress decades younger. She begins to feel better, to relax.

Lucy welcomes them into her pink front room, rather too pink, but very bright. There is a rose three-piece suite and a low carved coffee-table covered with a sheet of gleaming glass. It is loaded with things on cocktail sticks, sausage rolls, olives, bijou gherkins. There is a bottle of sparkling wine on the table. The late sun flashes on a set of crystal flutes. Lucy shows them her house with self-deprecating pride: it is light and bright and well-organised, a world away from Aunt Isobel's (though Vanessa notes there are very few bookshelves, and she would never live in a 1980s house, with cubes of rooms and double-glazed windows). There are sunshine-yellow fitted units in the kitchen, with matching blinds, kettle and toaster. Vanessa says, 'Lovely,' but thinks *too yellow*. 'You don't think it's too yellow, do you?' asks Lucy. The floor is an eye-popping yellow and white check. Vanessa is determined to be nice to everyone. 'Lovely, Lucy. You must clean it every day, how marvellous' *(but I would be far too busy)*.

Lucy gives her a slightly quizzical look. 'I'm afraid not, Nessa. I have a cleaner. Nearly as old as Mum, but she keeps going.'

It turns out Lucy pays half as much as Vanessa, and the cleaner comes for twice as many hours as Anya. 'One day I'm moving to the country,' says Vanessa. 'You can't imagine how hard it is, in London. I mean, cleaners have us over a barrel, they aren't even English, and we pay through the nose – '

Of course it's OK to say this to Lucy, who lives in the country, and will understand. Then Vanessa remembers, with a sinking heart, that Mary is standing listening in the doorway. 'I don't mean you, Mary, of course,' she blusters.

Mary smiles at her, enigmatically. 'Of course not, Vanessa. You cannot mean me. I am not your cleaner. And remember – when I was your cleaner you paid me very little.'

Vanessa hopes that Lucy did not hear her.

'I hope you'll be all right at Mum's,' Lucy says. 'She does her best, bless her, but Dad is exhausting, it's not his fault, but she has to do everything. I would have had you here but then the girls said they wanted to bring the kids for the knees-up, and I have to say, I'm the original doting grandma – I think that's them!' And she rushes to the door.

And there they are, the next two generations. The daughters are stylish, handsome women; one is a solicitor, one a doctor; one is a Chloe, the other a Serena. They are warily friendly, at first, to Vanessa, as if they have heard too much about her. The grandchildren range between two and eight, and all have cut-glass middle-class accents, and either have nannies or go to prep school. The daughters are protective of their mother Lucy, and make a fuss of her, and praise her food, and admire her garden, so Vanessa does too, and they all get mildly tipsy together. Mary chats intensely to Serena, the solicitor, who turns out to have done VSO in Kenya, and Vanessa ends up with a grandchild on her knee, and there is a lot of shouting and laughter.

The first night, Vanessa says, aside, to Mary, 'Mary if you don't mind, I will have a bath. As you know, I have headaches when I don't get my exercise, and the hot water helps me to relax.'

Mary doesn't demur, though she is sweaty from driving.

But when Vanessa makes the same speech to her hostess, Aunt Isobel's mouth tightens on a drawstring. 'Oh no, we don't really have baths at night. The water's gone cold again by now. I expect we could manage one in the morning.'

Vanessa washes glumly in the bathroom. She's asleep by the time Mary joins her in the bedroom. Vanessa jerks awake and looks at her watch. It is nearly midnight. 'Mary, what have you been doing?'

'I was talking with your aunt and uncle. They are very interested in my life in Uganda.'

'Really?' asks Vanessa, disconcerted. She feels vaguely cheated by this news. Surely Mary should talk about Uganda to *her*? 'I too am very interested, Mary, you know. Particularly as I have been to Uganda.'

'Yes, Vanessa, you have mentioned it.' Mary goes to sleep smiling, and does not say, 'But you never asked me about life in Uganda. You were always too busy telling me about it.'

When Vanessa comes down to breakfast next day, Aunt Isobel is in the kitchen. She gestures conspiratorially at the garden, smiling, showing stained and broken incisors. 'Look who's managed to get outside. And your friend's with him. Heart of gold, that girl.'

'Really?' Vanessa goes out to join them. *She* has a heart of gold, as well.

Stan and Mary are propped against the garden wall, looking down the path towards the bird-table. And they are smoking. Mary's doing it again. Vanessa stares at her, mute, accusing.

'Ah, Vanessa.' Mary smiles, and blows smoke. 'Stan has asked me to join him for a cigarette. Although, as you know, I have given up smoking. But of course, I respect your uncle very much. I think it is a cultural thing, to join him.'

'She's a laugh a minute, this girl,' says Stan. His voice

sounds stronger, although he is coughing. 'See, Izzie's given up, so it's nice to have company. I'm showing her my birdies, look there, down the garden.'

'I like the blue and yellow ones,' says Mary, indicating them with a flourish of her fag.

Not to be outdone, Vanessa joins in. 'Your tits are absolutely wonderful, Uncle.'

And Mary quickly seconds her. 'Very nice tits.'

Both of them are puzzled when Stan bursts out laughing, choking and heaving against the wall. But this visit is going really well.

Soon after, the day dissolves in grey rain. Mary and Vanessa try to wander round the village, but Mary has no Wellington boots, and the traffic soon sprays them with thin slurry. After a bit they give up and go back. The house feels small for the four of them.

Mary Tendo volunteers to help Aunt Isobel with the ironing, though Vanessa whispers, 'You don't have to, Mary.' She demolishes a mountain of linen in an hour. 'I am an expert,' she says, when Isobel thanks her.

After tea they get ready for the village party.

'My outfit is OK?' Mary asks Vanessa. Her dress has a high neck, and a knee-length skirt, but to Vanessa it seems slightly too red and too tight, and generally makes Mary Tendo look too – what?

Too pretty, she realises, ashamed. Mary looks really pretty in her smart red dress. It shows off her curves, which have surely grown curvier. Surely, in London, her bosom has grown? Vanessa inspects her own spare, lean form. 'Tensile, like a dancer', she remembers. Men didn't like women who were – *blowsy*. Did they?

43

'So nice to meet new family,' Chloe shouts at Vanessa, trying to rise above the noise of the band in the revamped village hall, which is fast filling up with people. 'We really enjoyed yesterday evening at Mum's. And you are, you know, from the old village. I don't know who half these people are.'

Vanessa is flattered, pleased to be welcomed. 'Well Mary and I don't know a soul.' (But in fact, Mary has quickly made friends with two men who are laying cable under the road, men with shadowy jaws and big muscles and sharp, metropolitan haircuts. They are the best-looking men in the room. She is dancing energetically with both of them, shimmying her hips in a frank, rhythmic fashion that makes Vanessa wince and look away. Though Vanessa can dance with the best of them, and so she would, if anyone asked her – Why don't they ask her? She is looking nice. She isn't so much older than Mary.)

Sighing, Vanessa turns back to Chloe. 'I wish you could have met my Justin. All of you children would get on so well.' She realises that she actually means, 'You have all become middle class, you children, everything about you, your voice, your style, whereas your mother and I ...' It was a small miracle.

Then Serena comes up. 'Someone's dying to meet you,' she says, and leads Vanessa towards the kitchen.

On the way, they pass Vanessa's first boyfriend. It is Raymond Biggins, now fat and red-faced. She recognises him by his fleshy lips. He surely looks twenty years older than she does. But he stops and stares. 'It can't be Vanessa. Hallo there, darling … Bloody hell, you've aged.' 'Don't worry, sweetheart, he's fucking pissed,' shouts his equally fat wife, slapping his bottom.

'Ah,' says Vanessa, a little shaken. She swigs at her drink, and tries to smile. Ray Biggins always was a loser. And aggression could be a sign of desire.

In the kitchen, a large grey-haired woman is sitting drinking on her own. When she sees Vanessa come into the room, she puts down the glass, slowly, deliberately, and peers at Vanessa, and then she smiles.

'Do you recognise me?' she asks Vanessa.

The woman has a long face like a bloodhound, and deep brownish bags under her eyes, but there is a familiar curl to her lip, and that horse-toothed smile – Vanessa struggles to place her.

'I'm a wreck now, of course, but when I taught you, Vanessa, I was a hopeful young sprig of thirty. And now we're both old biddies, eh?"

'Miss Tomlinson,' Vanessa gasps, struck. 'You taught me English. You encouraged me.' But she is unsettled by that 'old biddy'. She bolts the last of her gin and tonic.

'Yes well, I thought you had talent, then. I retired, of course, five years ago. But I hear you've gone and become a teacher. Always told you girls never to teach.'

'Oh I don't really teach,' says Vanessa, ashamed. 'Just part-time Creative Writing, you know. Really I'm a writer, as you said I should be.'

'Read your first novel,' the woman says. A silence follows. And extends. She seems to be swaying slightly on her feet. Vanessa remembers they all called her 'Tommers'.

'You didn't happen to read my second?' Vanessa is sure the second is better. 'Shall I send you a copy? It's not a problem.' *Because I have three hundred copies at home.*

Tommers holds up her hand as if to ward off demons. 'Don't bother. In fact, you sent one for the library.' She hiccups, and smiles, her mouth crooked.

'Did you read it?' asks Vanessa, breaking her own rule: never ask people if they've read your books. If they have, and like it, they will let you know.

'Started it.' Tommers leans closer to Vanessa, as if she is going to confide a great secret. 'Not sure anyone else took it out. The girls will only read famous names. Or things which are, you know, exceptional.' Now Tommers is breathing into her face, a ghastly cocktail of wine and cheese. 'Do you mind me asking, did you mean it to be funny?'

Neither 'Yes' nor 'No' seems a promising response. Vanessa decides to move away, but her old teacher sees her escaping.

'Jus' got myshelf a bottle from the bar. Would you care to take a glass with me?' Her accent is suddenly very genteel.

Vanessa is slightly too drunk to say no. Besides, Tommers's rudeness has a riveting quality, like watching a juggernaut run you down.

The two of them find a seat in the corridor. Vanessa tries to drink as fast as her old teacher. They discuss many things: Jane Austen, diaries. Tommers becomes quieter and less abrasive. Vanessa starts to dominate the conversation. Soon her old teacher falls totally silent. She seems to be asleep, but Vanessa prefers it. She hears herself say what she's never said before. 'I think I might write about my life. I'm teaching an Autobiography course. I've just given a chapter or two to an agent. A fairly high-powered one I happen to know. I do sometimes wonder what's the point of novels – '

At which, the older woman jerks into life, waving her arm wildly and splashing her wine. 'Thash right,' she says, staring straight at Vanessa, although her eyeballs aren't moving quite together. 'There's no bloody point. Unlesh you're fucking Cackfa. Kafka. Cackfa. Whish you're not.'

Vanessa realises Tomlinson is paralytic.

'Autobiog. Og. Og. Ogra. Ography', the woman says, triumphantly. 'You'd *shertainly* have a lot to write about.'

'What do you mean by that?' asks Vanessa.

'BARKING mother. IDIOT father,' Tomlinson shouts, as if it is obvious. Now other party-goers are falling silent and pausing to stare, curious. 'Feel I can be quite frank with you, Vanesha. All friends here. S'right, issn't it?' She clamps her arm around Vanessa, looks suddenly serious, and opens her mouth. There is a burp, then a raspberry trickle of wine. 'Jus' write the truth about it all. Thing ish, you've done *fucking* well, Vanesha. Got to fucking Cambridge from our fucking awful school. Father who could hardly even write his name. Mother should've been in the fucking loony bin. You were practically a fucking servant, at home. OK, your novels aren't fucking Proust – '

And at that, she slides gently on to the floor, and falls asleep, smiling cherubically.

Vanessa snatches up the last of the bottle, turns on her heel and returns to the party. She will talk to anyone who isn't Miss Tomlinson. Drink blunts the contours of the conversation. Tommers was jealous and an alcoholic. Besides, Vanessa despises swearing. Within half an hour she is singing karaoke, and half a dozen people are clapping her on, while a few young men in the corner are jeering. But Mary is leading a loud conga round the hall, her red hips swinging from side to side, her face glowing, her smile very white, at the head of a great sweeping 'S' of people.

In fact, Mary seems to be the star of the evening. Vanessa drinks more in the hope of being jollier. Surely she can be as much fun as Mary, on her home ground, in her own village. Ray Biggins sways up to her, with his coat on. By now his face is more plum than crimson, but she knows he is going to apologise, and she offers her cheek, beneficent. Instead he smacks her on the lips, wetly. 'You were always a good kisser, Ness. What I've come to ask though is …' (pointing at Mary) 'is she really an African princess? That's what she told my mate Gonzy.'

Vanessa's last, unreal memory is of saying goodnight to Lucy's daughter Serena, who is trying to apologise to her. 'I do hope Miss Tomlinson wasn't a bore. When she is drunk, she does tend to swear. She's been very bitter since her girlfriend left.' 'Oh she can fuck off,' Vanessa shouts, cheerily. Serena stares at her, appalled.

Then begin the long trials of sobering up.

In the early morning, her head spinning with wine, many things she has forgotten come back to Vanessa. How often she missed school to look after her mother. How once when Miss Tomlinson was her form mistress, Vanessa went to school late with her nails raw and bleeding because her mother had begged her to bleach the kitchen. How she never went on trips. There was never the money. She would watch the others setting off, excited.

And yet, she got to Cambridge. That was really something. The only girl ever from this village.

It wasn't nothing. It was surely something. Even if her novels weren't any good …

No good, no good. Her life was no good. She hadn't been good to her son, or her husband.

Your novels are hardly fucking Proust.

The words come back to her, at three, at four.

When Vanessa finally starts to nod off, Mary starts snoring with imperial grandeur, then runs her feet in the bed like a hamster, until Vanessa says loudly, '*Shush*', when Mary says, puzzlingly but distinctly, 'I'm sorry, Justin', turns over and farts, so obviously she is fast asleep.

It is a loud and very smelly fart which makes Vanessa burn with indignation. Somehow it seems to smell of Africa, and everything she doesn't like about Mary. In any case, the fart has staying power; it is salty, peppery, meaty and fatty as all the sausages and bacon at the party. Perhaps that makes it an English fart. Why didn't Mary do it before she turned over? The line of her cheek almost seems to be smiling. After that it is even harder to sleep.

It is an odd sensation, waking up with Mary. The first night they arrived, Vanessa was so tired she had slept dreamlessly through until morning, then got up hastily and put her face on before Mary could wake and see her, pallid. But the day after the party, Vanessa jerks awake with a thumping headache at half-past nine, and Mary has got up and drawn the curtains, so the morning light blazes full in her eyes. Vanessa is aware she must look dreadful. Mary stands peering down at her. She is dressed, and her eyes and teeth gleam white. She looks big and healthy. She has lipstick on.

'Good morning, Vanessa,' she almost sings. 'Have you slept well? Did you like the party?'

44

'So you're off today,' whispers Uncle Stan, at breakfast. Aunt Isobel has gone to see off the grandchildren, so Vanessa finds herself cutting up his toast, and feeding it, patiently, morsel by morsel, in through her uncle's trembling jaws. There is a cavern of blackness behind his false teeth. He dribbles, slightly, from the corners of his mouth. She tells herself she is glad to do it. It makes her feel better, after last night. She is being useful, as a niece should be, and she's never known what to do for him, she's never done anything for her family, she left them behind, all the aunts, the uncles, her elderly parents, her school, her friends … Mary is watching her from the doorway. There is an odd moment when their eyes meet. Vanessa has a moment of *déjà vu*, remembering how Mary used to sit and feed Justin, when he was little, spoon after spoon.

'You should take your friend to see where you lived,' Stan wheezes, as Vanessa gets the last bit in, and then he coughs it out again. She picks up his coffee, and tests it for heat. 'Still standing, I hear. Just about. Apparently they're going to demolish them all. All the old tied farm cottages. Wouldn't mind a last look myself.' But he knows he will not get to the village again. What would that mean, to be imprisoned?

'Odd to think we never owned that house,' says Vanessa.

'Oh no. It was one of your mother's complaints, that he never paid for the roof over your heads. But of course that's how it was with farm workers. That was how they paid them, with those old tied cottages.'

'I don't really know if I can bear to see it,' says Vanessa, wiping her uncle's chin. 'Maybe we should get off back to London.'

'Vanessa, I think we should visit your home,' says Mary, and comes round and pats Vanessa's shoulder. Vanessa sits passively and lets Mary touch her.

'Vanessa, I will drive us. I think you are tired.'

'Of course not, Mary. I must have exercise.' And, just like that, she is Vanessa again.

And they do walk, although the car's already packed, and Mary has found the errant glasses in her pocket, and actually popped them on her nose to prove it, little gold moonlets that make her look younger.

The cottage is along the old main road. Vanessa sets off at a swinging pace, plunging off the lane into the river of traffic. 'Don't worry. There's a pavement all the way,' she instructs Mary, who looks doubtfully at the dwindling strip of tarmac where they have to walk in single file. Mary hangs back behind Vanessa and watches the stick-like figure of her employer battling forwards in the autumn wind.

Though every so often, Vanessa half-turns and gives a boisterous 'thumbs up' of encouragement, the truth is, she isn't enjoying this either. The tarmac is cracked and overgrown with weeds. Every two seconds, another loud vehicle screams past her shoulder, and the air buffets her. At first the hedge on their left looks pretty, scattered with red hawthorn berries, fat wild rose-hips, old man's beard and the last blackberries, but within a few paces it becomes her enemy, reaching out thick savage tentacles of bramble that block the pavement and wave towards the road, forcing Vanessa out into the traffic's lethal slipstream. The brambles she manages to bend sternly forwards spring eagerly back and whip at Mary's face.

Everywhere they see enormous notices. 'SLOW THROUGH THE VILLAGE', '40', 'SLOW DOWN', and one forlorn 'THANK YOU FOR DRIVING CAREFULLY'. But in fact all the cars are doing 70 or 80, and Mary, sullenly bringing up the rear, fervently wishes that she could join them, that she could be part of this giant rally that cuts the English fields in two, instead of a tiny, deafened walker with snakes of vegetation clutching at her ankles.

Now Vanessa has turned, and her mouth is opening, and she is pointing and shouting something, but a full-tilt, cliff-high furniture van carries her words away into the future.

'Over there!' Mary finally makes out, and with that Vanessa darts with staccato urgency into a narrow gap in the traffic, and reemerges, to the squealing of brakes, across the road by some kind of hut. Taking her time, to express her disapproval of this whole life-threatening manoeuvre, Mary picks her way across to join her.

'This is where I grew up', says Vanessa. Not looking at her, looking at the ground. The place is half-boarded up, and half broken-into. Some windows are smashed, and some are nailed shut. But it is not possible, Mary thinks, Vanessa can never have grown up here. The walls are covered with purple graffiti, the same crude signs that she sees in London.

Whatever its present state might be, this house can never have been other than small. In fact, it is more like a hut than a cottage. The roof is low. The front door is mean. Even in Mary's village, this would not be much.

The garden is half the size of where they have been staying, and it is entirely overgrown with weeds. There is the remains of a bird-house like Stan's, but its wood has turned green, and bits of jungle throttle it. There is a pond, but it is full of dark leaves. Beside it, a rusted tangle of chicken-wire.

Suddenly Vanessa begins to cry. Mary has never seen her cry. Vanessa walks away firmly, her face averted, but Mary can see Vanessa's shoulders are shaking. After a minute, she follows her. She does not touch her, but she stands near. 'Are you thinking about your parents?' she asks. Mary herself once cried for her parents. Not so long ago. Three years ago.

'No no, not exactly … Yes. My mother always used to put bread for the birds. Even when she was really ill. Mum liked all of that, frogs, squirrels. She worried about them more than people. And the chicken run – she liked getting the eggs. Her lawn, and the beds … her garden. Poor Mum – you see, she loved her garden. She would be so upset to see the garden.' Each time Vanessa says 'garden', she sobs.

And Mary says, 'I see. I am sorry,' but in fact, she thinks crying for gardens is silly. Birds eat your fruit, and frogs are disgusting. Mary herself has much worse things to cry for, but she would rather die than tell Vanessa. Slowly she begins to feel angry again. Up country at home there are more things to cry for, and yet Ugandans rarely cry in public. Her own village, half-emptied by AIDS. The nearby villages wiped out by war.

They cry for their parents, we for our children.

How did she end up in this strange part of England that seems as if war has never touched it, where growing old is normal, and many have white hair? (And at last night's party they were dancing to the band, the white-haired couples, or holding hands, as if they had a right to a long life together.) Where nobody seems to have the Slim disease, and the cars on the road are all four-wheel-drives, even though the road is flat, and straight, and smooth, and none of them walk, because they are too lazy, and if you do walk, you might get killed?

Mary thinks with longing of the roads of Uganda, the straight red roads that sweep away to the horizon, and vehicles come, two or three an hour, but the people throng all along the roadside, the mothers in *gomesi*s, the girls in bright frocks, the babies tied to straight backs with strong cloth, the bicycles loaded with green bananas, the boys with yellow plastic cans of water, the skinny cows with their enormous horns, and everyone talking and laughing and staring, where there is still time, and space, to move, and if one of the jeeps, full of tourists, or soldiers, comes along too fast, there is no problem, there is all the world to spill across and fill, there are fields and forests, not hedges and pavements, and everyone walks and runs and pedals … The British have caught themselves in a trap. Soon their bodies will no longer move. Perhaps that is why Vanessa is so frantic, driving herself to go faster and faster.

Mary does see it's sad, Vanessa's ugly village, where the children are fat, which would be strange in Kampala, where only businessmen's children are fat. There are no real shops here, no businesses, no stalls selling flowers or vegetables. The beautiful church, with its fine tiled spire topped with a golden chicken spinning in the wind, which Mary had hoped they would attend on Sunday, has been turned into flats, so Uncle Stan told her. He whispered that only half of them have sold. 'It's a joke. No one round here can afford them.'

Mary's anger ebbs away. They are what they are. And with

a slow upsurge of pity and pride, Mary finally starts to believe it. *The house where Vanessa grew up is poor.*

Perhaps she is embarrassed for Mary to see it. It is actually smaller than her own family house, the house where Mary grew up in Uganda.

So she and Vanessa are not so different. In some ways they are almost the same.

But Mary does not feel she worked hard as a child. There were always aunties and cousins to help. For her, there was so much sun, and laughter. And all the doors and windows were open. And nobody drew on the walls of houses.

And without planning it, or wanting it, Mary puts her arm round Vanessa's shoulder, she draws her to her, and Vanessa cries. 'I did the garden, I hated it, but the garden never looked like this ... I cleaned the house, I cleaned the house.' She is almost hysterical, she keeps repeating it. They stand together in the autumn wind, and Vanessa clings, and Mary comforts.

On the way back to Aunt Isobel's, Mary spots something she did not see on the way out. It stands opposite the point where their lane turns off the thundering steel ribbon of road. At first it looks like the eye of a fish, silver and glassy, a thing on a stick, then as they get closer, it's the mouth of a fish, a silver gape with a grey open mouth, seen from the side, a lateral V, and then she sees that the grey is the road, the ribbon of road reflected in a mirror, and it is some kind of fish-eye mirror that she has never seen before, put there to show drivers that there is a turning where tractors might suddenly come out.

Vanessa spots it at the same time, and as they stand there, waiting for the stream of metal to stop and let them back into kinder country, the sun comes out, and illuminates it. Both of them stop and stare at it, side by side, pressed close together by the tiny gap between the thorns and the lorries. It is a tiny, radiant disc of sharp beauty, with a huge blue sky and swelling white clouds, a convex circle that shines like a world, and they are there, minute, in the bottom right corner, at the end of a road that slopes away into the distance, at one precise vortex of time and space, and the world is enormous, and they are tiny, and their ant-like bodies vibrate with the traffic, two small living things on an enormous planet, and Mary has crossed the earth to this place, and when she turns again, ten feet down the turning, the two of them merge into the same bright dot.

45

On the way back to London, Vanessa drives, silent, rejecting Mary's offer to drive, discouraging her attempts to talk. Yet both of them know they have grown closer.

Approaching the front door, Vanessa is anxious. 'I only hope Justin's all right,' she mutters.

'It will be OK, Vanessa,' says Mary. 'Anna was coming in to clean. And Soraya said she would cook him dinner.'

'And who is Soraya? Oh, the Indian girl.'

'No, Vanessa, she is not Indian. I have met Trevor's friend. She is a white woman.'

The house seems normal, no fire or flood, and Justin's room is tidy, but empty. At seven he comes back, and seems pleased to see them, and actually calls Vanessa 'Mum', and tolerates ten minutes of news about the village before he wanders away again.

For Vanessa it is a quick turn around. At seven tomorrow she will be on the Eurostar, sitting opposite Fifi, off to Paris.

'You'll be all right, Mary?'

'Yes, Vanessa.'

'It's only three days. Nothing will happen.'

'Nothing will happen,' Mary agrees.

In fact Mary hopes that a lot will happen. Because Vanessa is going away, Mary has fixed for Trevor and Justin to go and do some work for Zakira.

But Vanessa thinks, soon this will be over. Justin is practically normal again. I just need to edge him towards a real job, or possibly he should go back into education, a Master's in something, I would pay his fees …

The worst is over. I am fond of Mary, we've become fast friends, but soon she'll be gone. One day I shall visit her, of course, in Uganda.

46

Next day Vanessa sleeps on the train to Paris, though Fifi is nervous, and wants to talk. She is going to visit her ancient grandmother, who has recently been taken into hospital. Fifi, who has never liked spending money, has arranged for them to stay in her empty house. There is a complex chain of negotiation; a cousin has given her spare set of keys to another cousin's neighbour's friend, or perhaps the gardener of the neighbour's friend. There are instructions about lights, and locks, and bedding, 'such a bore' for Fifi, who has other things to think about, for instance, payment for the cat-sitter who will be feeding Mimi organic cream and chicken livers.

'I must say the family seemed rather reluctant. And almost suspicious of my motives. I mean, it was my therapist told me to go. Of course I couldn't tell them that. But anyone would think I was after Grandma's money. I admit she has rather a lot of money, but for heaven's sake, there are ten of us grandchildren, and all the others have done better than me, they have all podded, there are scads of great-grandchildren. I am hardly competition for them. In any case, I *am* a grandchild. I do have a right. I have a right to a family.'

Vanessa pretends to fall asleep. Fifi is tiring when she talks about rights. Besides, Vanessa needs time to herself, she needs to drink deep of her own story, the bittersweet time-warp of her days in the village … it's like sipping medicine, remembering Miss Tomlinson. The things the woman said about Vanessa's parents.

The sour dark house where Vanessa grew up. Yesterday it looked so cramped, so poor.

Mum's poor strangled garden, Vanessa thinks, remembering the nettles, the rusty wire. But then, Mum could never look after herself. Which meant we had to look after her. Dad's awful, clumsy tenderness. I despised him because my mother did. It wasn't comfortable, despising my father.

Then later, having to get away. Being forced to reinvent herself. The difficulties when she came home from Cambridge, and Lucy and the others laughed at her new accent, which she herself wasn't even aware of.

Forty years later she's still hot with shame.

'Vanessa, you're not listening!'

She forces her lids open on the flat French countryside, the nondescript land between Lille and Paris, and tries to listen, but inside her head she is remembering the cleaning, always the cleaning, before school in the morning and when she came home, the only way to keep her mother's nerves at bay, since Dad or Stan used to tramp the mud in, the floor in the kitchen was usually swimming, the old chipped sink bloomed with vile yellow stains … Her mother's pale fretful eyes would be searching, restlessly looking for mess and dirt, more proof that life on earth was a nightmare, a hellish test she could not survive. Vanessa had to work hard to save her, for without her mother she knew she would be finished, since Mum was the only one who knew she was clever, too good to be a farmworker's daughter.

I tried to make everything different for Justin. Only the best was good enough. He had every chance that money could buy.

Somewhere along the way, it went wrong.

'So, did you enjoy your little trip to the country?' Fifi asks her, as they draw into Paris. 'Wasn't it awkward taking Mary?'

'No. In fact, Mary was rather a hit. Everyone wanted to dance with her. My Uncle Stan was very taken.'

Vanessa tries not to think about the fart. She would rather die than tell Fifi that. And it wasn't important, in the longer view. Bridges had been built, chasms crossed.

And, left on her own, while Fifi goes to see her family, in the tall, stuffy house where Fifi's grandmother lived, Vanessa feels renewed, and hopeful. She sits down at the desk in the bedroom with her notebook. What she has learned will surely bear fruit.

But in fact, for some reason things go against her. That weekend there's a miniature Indian summer. The thick heat of August returns, and clings. Most of the windows are impossible to open, the wood dried and twisted in an airless clinch, and when she finally attacks one with a knife, prising at the frame with fierce determination, the paint flakes off, and then the wood splinters, and she cuts her hand before she gives up. Small beige moths flutter out of tall cupboards like rags and tatters of exploded lace. The polished walnut swirls uneasily with faces. On the dressing-table that was once Fifi's grandma's, a cloudy cut-glass bowl of pink face powder sits uncovered, breathing at her. Vanessa feels she is inhaling human dust.

When she looks for respite at the walls, almost every centimetre is covered with photographs, framed and unframed, large and small, curled photographs of smiling children, proud parents, sprinting dogs, a crowded world of happy strangers that is slipping very slowly into the past. This family's life seems like a long, sunlit picnic; they meet up in parks, in woods, in gardens, there are always at least half a dozen of them, and they dance and prance for the photographer, they hug each other and play leap-frog, they hold up small babies and exquisite toddlers, they ride donkeys or have swimming parties, cut big cakes or raise a diadem of glasses.

However, when Fifi briefly returns, it is to complain of being snubbed or excluded. 'You know what they're like, Parisians! They pretend they don't understand a word, when as you know I am practically fluent, you heard me talking to that taxi-driver … And they expected me to pay for myself. In any case, the restaurant was filthy. And Tante Clothilde was rude about my mother. Now I see why she wanted to escape her family!'

When she leaves again, Vanessa stares at the walls. Those happy childish faces haunt her. Movies that have turned into still photos. Colour that is fading towards black-and-white, so she can never quite get to the reality of it, never find out if Fifi is right –

But it's painfully different from her own lost life, locked up in that low, dark house in the village.

She thinks, it's not that I'm envious, exactly. It is just that haunting sensation of other lives. We only live once. Has my life been all right? Have I really done my best for Justin? Did he have enough friends, enough happiness? Did we ever go for sunlit picnics? I wasn't a great one for seaside holidays. I never let him keep a dog or a cat. I was an only child, so he has no cousins …

Their life seemed thin, empty, cold, compared to the frieze

around these walls, the children feasting on life's banquet.

Vanessa is crushed and stifled by ghosts. They brush at her consciousness like bruised moth-wings as she tuts and sweats in the warm soft heat, writing, or not writing, because the pen moves slowly, and she starts to imagine she hears childish voices, a high silver humming that torments her ear, but when it finally drives her out into the kitchen she realises it is just something electric, but she still cannot find it to switch it off, so it goes on vibrating like a thousand crickets as the sky outside the shutters turns indigo, a thousand insects or a swarm of lost children, the ghosts who should have played with Justin.

I should have played with him more, she thinks. I shouldn't have handed him over to Mary. But I had to work to pay the mortgage. I still have to work to keep my son.

She stays there, grimly. She is a professional. 'Bums on seats,' she always says to her classes. 'If you sit there long enough, the writing will come.' But she sits there, solidly, and nothing happens. Outside the window, Paris calls to her, grey and silver, infinitely delectable, singing *come on, you are still young, dance with me, dance, Vanessa* –

But Vanessa closes her ears, and sighs, and makes another wretched cup of instant coffee, though outside the doors there are glorious *crèmes*, in wonderful cafés, and *kir*, and *frites*. She will not give in. She can sit this out. Like a terrier, she digs in, and waits.

On their last evening, Fifi returns upset. 'Today she did actually recognise me, *Grandmaman*, and she was sweet … But now Grandpa is dead, she will never come home. She thinks she will, she talks as if she's going to, but her daughter Jeanne said to me it's impossible, the stairs are too dangerous, she can't live alone … So tell me, what is the point of all this? All the books and pictures and music and photos? All the *objets* she's chosen with such exquisite taste? Just to end up in some wretched almshouse. By the way, darling, how has your writing gone? Why didn't you go off and see the Louvre?''

'Oh you know, a writer needs time on her own.'

But the journey back is rather subdued. They agree that amassing possessions is pointless. Fifi makes a note of this in her expensive new palmtop, whose merits she then explains to Vanessa. Vanessa declares she is going to have a clear-out. She sits and lists things to do in her notebook, the one in which she had planned to write. But while Mary is there, she may as well make use of her. Together they can really make a difference. Mary can hardly say she is busy –

Vanessa only half-knows she is fending off depression. 'Kissy kissy kissy,' they say at Waterloo, but Fifi feels Vanessa hasn't been supportive, and Vanessa is restless and frustrated.

It isn't so easy, facing up to the past. Tomorrow she has to go back to teaching. The precious empty week is gone.

47

She comes home in a black taxi at three pm. The driver complains about immigrants, and they have the mandatory argument. The fare of twenty-five pounds is outrageous. She walks even faster than usual up the path, bumping her suitcase along the concrete. She rings the bell, but they're too lazy to answer, so she drags her keys out of the bottom of her handbag and jerks them irritably into the keyhole.

'Mary!' she shouts as she comes in through the door. 'Justin! Where is everybody?'

In fact, she finds Mary out at the back, standing on the lawn, wearing a winter coat of Vanessa's, which blows open to show the annoying blue nightdress that Anya had found in Justin's room. 'Hallo, Vanessa.' She seems friendly, but startled. 'I thought you were not coming back until this evening. Sorry, I have put your coat on.'

'That's quite all right,' Vanessa says, but she can't quite get rid of the feeling that Mary isn't totally glad she is back early. (She's right: Mary had been planning to call Libya on Vanessa's phone.) 'That is rather a smart coat for the garden, Mary. Why don't you borrow my anorak?' *Or else put more of your own clothes on*, she thinks to herself, but does not say it.

'I shall make you a cup of tea, Vanessa,' Mary Tendo says, with a queenly smile.

On the way back in, Vanessa pauses and takes a proper look at the garden. She is dismayed to see that a lot of it is bare. It is certainly tidy, but where are her peonies? What has happened to half her roses? Her heart sinks as she realises. Besides, there are sticks all over the place, thin bamboo sticks at odd angles which she supposes must mark new plants. Some of them project from the fence like spines. She pulls one out: it is oddly barbed. It looks familiar, but she can't take it in. It almost looks like a kind of arrow. This must be a technique of the Ugandan farmer. Or else Mary has been murdering squirrels.

'Mary, I didn't ask you to *garden*. Just a little pruning was all I wanted.'

'No, Vanessa, but I knew you would be happy. Because you said your mother liked the garden to be tidy, I finished the gardening while you were away.'

'I see.'

Mary Tendo has her back turned, boiling the kettle, unaware that there is anything wrong.

Vanessa swallows rising fury. After all, Mary was trying to be helpful.

'How was France?' Mary asks her. The tea she has made is too strong and black. Sighing, Vanessa pours herself more milk.

'Oh well, you know, it was just Paris.' She has been to Paris a dozen times. There have been better and worse trips to Paris.

'Vanessa, I have never been to Paris. I think that one day I would like to go.'

Vanessa thinks, it's maddening how she makes me feel guilty. Even when she's blatantly in the wrong.

'I have come back with lots of new resolutions,' she says briskly, swilling down the tea in one gulp, burning her throat unpleasantly. 'I want you to help me clear everything out. We've got too much rubbish. Far too much stuff. I think you once said something like that yourself, that English people's houses are full of *things*. Well I want to get rid of a lot of it. But first do you think you should put some clothes on? And where is Justin? Justin can help.'

'I want to talk to you about him, Vanessa.' (Mary's feeling happy, and proud of herself. The meeting with Zakira was a huge success. Justin and Zakira were in each other's arms within three minutes of their arrival. While the two of them were kissing and hugging in the kitchen, Mary had filled Trevor in on the back story. 'I thought that boy was a bloody fast worker,' Trevor said, but she could see he was worried. 'What is the old girl going to say?' After two hours with Zakira, he had relaxed. 'She's a lovely girl,' he told his son. Soon the necklace was back on Zakira's neck. The amber glowed on her blue-black skin. The tap was mended, the sink no longer leaked, and Justin stayed behind at the end. Mary is ecstatic. She has pulled it off! Justin's up and dressed, with a job and a girlfriend. She cannot wait to tell Vanessa.)

But Vanessa's in the grip of the hyperactive state that is her only way of fending off depression. 'Not now Mary, we have to get on.'

In this mood, Vanessa carries all before her, but Mary and Justin seem slow and stubborn.

When Vanessa asks Mary to clear out the cupboards in the sitting room, ready for Vanessa to sort, Mary says, 'But Vanessa, that will make a mess, and Anya – there is a little

problem with Anya. I am not sure she is coming on Wednesday.'
(The problem is that Justin's slept with Anya, the night before
his reconciliation with Zakira, and Anya is in love with him.
Whereas Justin just thinks she is quite a nice girl with whom
he has made a little mistake. Or not so nice a girl, once she has
kicked his television, and said he is a *Dummkopf*, and a loser.
Justin thinks Anya might not be coming back.)

'Mary, we are *clearing up* the mess. If we make a little dust,
there are dusters in the cupboard. I hope you know where the
cleaning things are.' Vanessa is aware that she sounds rather
sharp, and makes a last-ditch attempt to sound reasonable. 'I
myself am not too proud to clean up. By the way, I really think
you should take my coat off.'

Mary removes the coat, which reveals the maddening nightdress, which is semi-transparent and looks – slatternly.

'It is Anya's job,' Mary says, politely. 'It was Anya's job, to
do the cleaning. It seems her name was Anya, not Anna. If she
has gone, we will find another one. In fact, she was not even
Australian.'

'For God's sake, Mary, put some clothes on. Are you saying
you are not willing to help me?' Vanessa's voice is beginning to
rise, to steer its way up through the unstable octaves. Her heart
begins to beat unsteadily. There is a certain blind pleasure in
losing her temper.

'I am not saying I am not willing,' says Mary, but her jaw
juts mutinously.

Vanessa is too cross to listen properly. Mary's double
negative just sounds like 'No'. 'I think I have been fair with
you,' she says. 'I have treated you like a friend, Mary.'

Mary's eyes go dead. It is starting again. 'Yes, Miss Vanessa.
We are like friends.'

'So don't you think that you ought to help me?'

Mary looks at the floor. 'I ought to help you.' She thinks of the money. She is still hundreds short. She has to survive in this house until Christmas. And yet, the Henman is a madwoman. You do not start cleaning in the afternoon.

'So do we understand each other?' Vanessa victorious. She's full of adrenalin now, she is speeding. Sometimes these points just have to be made. She can't let these people walk all over her. When you are too soft, this is what happens. She rides her crest of unhappiness; nobody likes her, not even her son, nor Mary, nor Miss Tomlinson.

'Yes, Henman,' it sounds as though Mary says. 'We understand each other, yes, Henman.'

Mary goes to the sitting-room and opens the cupboards and starts to pull everything on to the carpet, bulging files, table mats, half-finished knitting. A box of old pens and broken pencils. A foot-high pile of old Christmas cards. A yellowing turret of ivory napkin rings. She doesn't think, she just pulls it all out. In the end, almost the whole carpet is covered. She gives it a small but savage kick.

But as she does it, she can hear the Henman screaming. The Henman is trying to get Justin to help. Whatever his response, it is not enough. Her rage, her grief are beyond all bounds. 'You are useless, useless, you've always been useless. Why are you such a hopeless son? You have *disappointed* me and your father. Get up, will you, do something!'

In the end, Mary can bear it no more. She leaves it as it is, the ruined sitting room, and goes upstairs to see what can be done, if anything can still be done to save Justin.

'Miss Henman, do not upset yourself. If he will not do it, I will do it. '

'It's quite extraordinary,' Vanessa says, in a voice that skates between laughter and tears. 'All I've asked him to do is collect the photographs, the photographs of his own childhood, the photographs of our life as a family. It doesn't seem a lot to ask. He has been dossing here for twenty-odd years. He has never given his mother a penny. He has never lifted a finger to help. Now I ask him to do one simple thing and he claims I am hysterical. I will get hysterical if you all want, I am *ready* to become hysterical – '

'Miss Henman, please, do not shout any more.'

'You are telling me not to shout at Justin. I am his mother. I care for him.'

'Yes, Miss Henman. You are his mother. Of course, Miss Henman, you care about him. But please, Miss Henman, no more shouting.'

And Mary helps her, and they get the work done, and the dustbin is left bulging with paper and celluloid, duplicate photographs, dusty drawings; Justin sleeps with his pillow over his head (and feels he has a right to: the day before, he and Trevor worked a thirteen-hour day, finishing a painting job for a deadline); and slowly Vanessa wears herself out, and the terrible storm in her brain subsides, leaving the beginnings of unease and guilt.

They do not go to bed until after midnight.

'Goodnight, Mary. I know you have helped me.'

'Yes, I have helped you. Goodnight, Henman.'

Curious how she still couldn't manage the name. 'Vanessa, *please*.' And Vanessa disappears, smiling an anxious, placating smile.

But Mary Tendo sits downstairs, brooding.

48 Vanessa Henman

I am sitting in my study, too tired to write. I have just had another ghastly day. Sometimes it seems I am surrounded by fools. All day I have felt as if I was hung over, possibly because of yesterday's argument. It wasn't my fault, not entirely my fault, I was stressed from Paris, and Mary was – slow …

And yet, one doesn't like to lose one's temper. One doesn't like to raise one's voice. And Mary is well-meaning. In the end, she helped. I wouldn't want to jeopardise the very real friendship we were starting to achieve when we went to the village.

Still, I'm sure by now she has forgotten all about it. One can't be good-tempered all the time. Perhaps I will offer to cook, tomorrow. Though actually, I am too busy to cook.

And today at college was an utter waste of time. I sometimes wish I was teaching something real, nursing, astrophysics, not Creative Writing. I sometimes wish I had *learned* something real. I always felt superior to my father, and yet he knew real things, he was a farmer, he knew about the fields and the animals, he knew about machinery, like Tigger.

Is it possible that I have underestimated Tigger? He swears that Justin has 'found his feet'. He says the boy has a wonderful eye, and might have a future as an interior designer, which sounds like a glorified painter and decorator –

But if Justin is happy. Really happy …

Maybe I have always got things wrong.

Derrick came to see me (it's becoming a habit) and wanted to read his new story out, something he'd written in the reading week, and apparently it couldn't wait till the class. I particularly wanted to be left alone, because now I am really getting going with my writing, and I do think the stuff about my father might be good. So much so that I'm going to take a risk and send the agent, rather naughtily, another extract by 'Emily Self'. (I think I'll say she's 'quite promising'!) If there were no students, I could finish it by spring. But the young are selfish, and sap one's energy. They think we only exist to serve them.

I'm afraid Derrick reads in a monotonous voice, stopping every so often to see if one likes it, cocking one of those thick black brows. (At first I found his hairiness appealing. Not any more, not any more.) Also, he does smell strongly of sweat. Perhaps he was nervous, I don't know, but his manner was – over-confident. Maybe I have given him too much encouragement.

I had to be honest with him in the end and say I found the subject-matter difficult. It was about a red-headed woman who kept hens, and killed them by hacking through their necks with a knife. Very detailed, with too much blood. I said, 'I'm not sure of her motivation,' and he said, 'She hates birds, and, like, thinks she's a fox. That's why I made her a red-head, obviously.'

It wasn't entirely obvious to me. 'I'm not *absolutely* sure about the chicken motif.'

'You said you loved my metaphors. But you said I was writing too much about pigeons.'

'Well, yes. Perhaps I meant, "birds generally". (I was having to suppress my irritation. How much did he know about this subject? After all, we had a hen-house in our garden. And not a word of Derrick's story is true.)

'Didn't you dig the bit where the chicken goes on running and her head is like flying around on its own, like a balloon with the air rushing out, and the woman sucks up the blood from the knife? It's a metaphor for oral sex, obviously.'

The metaphor had passed me by, thank God.

He looked hard at me, with a small smile. If they find one attractive, it's because one is a teacher. I said, 'I wasn't *entirely* persuaded. Most women do not like raw hen's blood.'

'See, I'm not writing for most women,' he muttered, staring at his knees.

'Surely you are not just writing for men?' It is bracing for the young to meet a feminist.

'No.' There was a pause, while he pulled at his neck as if he was trying to strangle himself. 'Thing is, I am writing for you, Dr Henman.' And then he looked me right in the eyes. His eyelashes were thick, and black, but there was something odd about those hot dark eyes. 'I have found your comments very inspiring. No one has encouraged me before. Everyone else always thought I was mad!'

There was a long silence. I could not think what to say. Now he was patting himself like a puppy. I wished I had been franker with him.

'It's just so great that you appreciate me. I've never, you know, had that before. Thanks to you, I'm writing, like, all the time, obviously. I just can't get enough of it. You know, I once showed some stuff to my psychiatrist. He told me it was better "not to fixate on it". Don't you think that's amazingly funny? In fact, he suggested I take up football!' He hooted with mockery at this suggestion. 'What kind of criticism is that?'

'You have a psychiatrist?'

'Obviously.'

I suggested he go away and write something different.

'Say, from the point of view of the pigeon? That bug-eyed Daisy girl would really go for that!' Something in my expression must have stopped him, because he held up his hand, and mimed shooting his temple. 'Sorry, I mean the point of view of the chicken!'

'*No birds.*'

But I can see it is hopeless.

Despite his long dark lashes, he is just another nutter.

Whereas Beardy – Alex – is really very interesting. I did completely underestimate him. Although I am usually a good judge of character. He brought my novels in for me to sign. I heard him praising them to the other students. When I think about that, it makes me feel better.

I must try to see the funny side of Derrick. Whenever I tell Tigger about my students, he seems to find it hilarious. True, that has always irritated me. In fact Tigger is *exactly* like my father, who was kind-hearted, but understood nothing.

But what if he understood more than my mother? What if the same were true of Tigger?

And suddenly, I am free to start writing. I start with the chickens. We fed the chickens. Their soft red wrinkly combs, their pink strutting feet, my father's big hands throwing the corn, the patient way he let me help him, although my mother didn't want me to get dirty.

After that I write for an hour without stopping, my very first memories of my father, my father in the garden when a bee stung me, my father picking me an apple from the tree. But somehow I know that the chickens are best.

By the time I stop, I am feeling much better. And this is the piece I shall send to the agent, the second submission by 'Emily Self'.

I haven't seen Mary since our little quarrel, and Justin will be in bed, I suppose. The house is quiet, although I can't help imagining I hear that thumping which unsettled me so, that regular bumping from Mary's bedroom, but really I must not imagine things.

In fact, now I have managed some writing, I find I am no longer annoyed with them.

At least no one here is as mad as Derrick. I know I was a trifle sharp with Mary. I would say sorry, but I think she'd be embarrassed. I shan't forget to tell her I'm grateful.

Yawning, I push open the door to my bedroom. I put on the light, and it is ghastly, awful, absolute horror has come into my bedroom, at first I can't scream, I just stand there, not breathing.

They are all on my bed, black and sinister, sitting in a row like shrunken heads, beady eyes staring, teeth bared, waiting. Some of them have bodies that are short and stunted, stumps of limbs or hands like man-traps, crawling all over the place where I sleep. At first I don't even understand what they are, it is as if they have climbed out of the depths of my head, come swarming up from some hideous cellar, but after a moment I recognise them. They are my African masks, my own possessions, and some little figures I found in Uganda, which Mary has always objected to, pretending she thinks they are bad for Justin, and now she has taken them off the walls and brought them in here to terrify me!

And I have to admit they are horrible, sitting there grinning and staring in the darkness. I stand there, frozen. My mouth is open, and noise and dribble are coming out. I hear myself screaming, a long way off. I cannot stop, and I cannot touch them.

But then something happens I could never have expected. I suppose I did make a lot of noise. There are feet on the landing, and then he appears, in green pyjama bottoms, his chest-hair golden, and his eyes are soft and anxious, as they used to be, and then his arms are actually around me, and Justin says, 'Mum, darling, what's the matter? Are you all right? Speak to me.'

And I sink against his chest like a homing bird, and my tears run down, warm and salty. Just for a moment he solaces me. As a good son should, as a good man can.

Then Mary pushes in through the door. 'What is the matter, Henman? Why are you screaming?'

Which made me lose my temper again. 'What the hell are these things on my bed, Mary? What on earth do you think you are playing at?'

And yet they are already not quite so frightening, now Justin is here, now I see what they are.

But Mary herself. Mary is frightening. 'How dare you try to frighten me?'

'You told me you wanted to get rid of everything. You told me you wanted a new beginning.' Her eyes have got that strange, purblind look, which means she cannot see or hear, as if I am not a person to her. Africans can be racist too. 'I did not have time to finish my work. I was going to put them on top of your cupboard.'

Now Justin's arms are releasing me. 'You see, Mum dear,' (that gentle *Mum dear!* It is balm to me, but he goes on talking) 'it's just a mistake. It's nothing, really. It's all OK. Don't shout at Mary.'

'You're taking her side!' I start to feel hurt. I have been betrayed. Justin's turned on me. I can see the two of them exchanging glances, as if they have discussed me before, as if I am just a joke or a problem, and I feel left out, as I was at school, when everyone thought I was weird, and ignored me, but as an adult, I won't tolerate it! And I am the person who pays all the bills! I have paid this woman to abuse me!

'Get out of my room! Both of you!' And I see them leaving, almost side by side, his arm touching hers, his broad naked shoulders – of course I don't really want him to go, to leave me here with these horrible objects –

And before I know quite what I am doing, I find myself throwing stuff after them, hard, and a mask hits Mary on the head, and a pot-bellied manikin gets Justin on the shoulder, and then the door closes, and I just keep throwing them, crashing them hard against the painted wood, till the empty stupidity of what I am doing makes me too weak to throw any more.

And then I sit and cry and cry.

But the door opens, and Justin comes back. Justin comes back to comfort me.

Part 5

49 Mary Tendo

Two thousand three hundred and twenty pounds. I keep it in cash, in my bedside table. The money is beautiful, thick and smooth, not thin and worn like Ugandan bank-notes. It has the sheen of wealth and hope. By Christmas I shall have nearly three thousand. By Christmas there will be ice and snow. I have had to spend money on warm jumpers, and I wear Miss Henman's anorak. She told me I could wear it before she was angry, and now she is embarrassed to change her mind, though I see her looking at it thoughtfully. Also, at the moment, we aren't really talking. So I carry on wearing her anorak, and gloves.

Omar has gone to Baghdad, to look for Jamil. I am happy because he is doing something. We are looking for our son, we have not forgotten him. Even if he doesn't want us to find him. Even if indeed he is not there. Because since the first rumour things have grown less hopeful. Jamey's friend Idries does not think it is him. Idries told Omar he was almost sure that Jamil had gone south to find his mother – but that is too bad to think about, because if so, my Jamie is lost. In southern Sudan or among the Acholi, in the battlegrounds of northern Uganda. Kidnapped by the Lord's Resistance Army – it is impossible to contemplate. The God of love would not allow it. *Ntekisobola okugwa ku mutabani wange.* And yet, people whisper. They hiss, in Kampala. They list the horrors of the northern war, where Kony makes children kill each other, dipping them deep in blood so they can never escape him –

Perhaps Jamie never even reached the border. The desert has killed so many young men. The *suq* lorries are unpredictable. Perhaps he never got beyond Wau –

This could not happen to my son.

So I am happy when I think about Baghdad, when I let myself picture Jamil at the zoo. My Jamie was always good with animals, knew how to talk to them, to calm them down. It was part of his kindness. Part of his goodness. Jamie deserved better parents than us. If we had not divorced, he might be at Al Fateh, starting his veterinary course. Did he leave because he despaired of us?

Five years ago, not long after the divorce, I went to Libya to see him. I spent a year's wages on the flights to Tripoli. He had shot up a foot in eighteen months, but still he was not as tall as me. He was polite and awkward, and had nothing to say. I thought, I must go, I am giving him pain. We were sitting together in his father's hot courtyard. People seemed to be watching from every window. He did not know how to behave with me. Then Omar's new wife came out and took pity. 'You should go for a walk with your mother,' she said. The road roared along by the side of the sea. Big liners docked there, alongside the mosque. Everything was green to honour Ghadaffi, and his face grinned from posters, and I felt he was mocking me. We walked in silence, then Jamil started talking. He wanted to explain his new country to me. Tripoli was a modern city which was rapidly starting to go out of date, because they couldn't get parts to mend things, because they had angered the US and UK. Jamie's voice warmed up, and his English came back. He took my arm, beside the river of traffic, and the sky was blue, and so was the sea, and just across the channel was Malta, and suddenly I felt entirely hopeful, for the world was all about us, and one day he would be free. The feeling didn't last, because my head was uncovered and my blouse, though decent, didn't have long sleeves, and the cars started hooting, and some drivers called out, and Jamie was ashamed that I was his mother, or ashamed of the hooting, I didn't know which, perhaps he just wanted to protect me – but he was a boy of thirteen, how could he? And I said, 'Dearest son, we should turn back. One day we shall meet in Kampala, or London. Never forget you were born in London. Never forget you are half-Ugandan.'

I think that the world was too painful for Jamie, this complicated world which tore him in two. He said, 'I hate the UK, but I still love London.' I think he was saying he still loved me.

And later he came to see me in Kampala, the last time that we saw each other. I will never forget how tightly he held me, and I held him, we held each other, when we picked him up at Entebbe airport, and there he was, dwarfed by his sprawl of cases, and then getting bigger as I ran towards him, and when I got there, he was taller than me, and everything I wanted was in my arms.

If he never comes back, I know he loved me. I am lucky that my son and husband loved me.

And even now, perhaps I am lucky. I can go on waiting for the phone to ring.

I have asked my friend the accountant for Christmas. My

friend has been to London before, when he got his qualifications in Britain, and when he travelled here for business. He will probably be able to get a visa. If he pays enough money, he will get a visa. He can give my address, and show photographs of us, and prove that he has a good job to get back to. Britain need have no fear of him. I have not told Miss Henman, in case he doesn't come. But if he does come, he can sleep in my bedroom. She said to me, after Zakira came to visit, 'Your Ugandan friends are always welcome here,' thinking because she was black she must be Ugandan. And if I had not understood Miss Henman so well, I would probably have thought she really wanted them to visit. It does not matter, she has given permission, and if she makes a fuss, I can remind her. Charles can eat fish and chips every day from the chippy. He can eat them in my bedroom, and throw away the paper.

And yet, I do not feel quite easy.

But soon after that, we will fly home together, and go to my village, with the car full of gifts. And so my mission will have been successful. And also, I have written about my childhood, thousands of words about my childhood that will make a book when I get home. Uganda has its own publishers and bookshops. Uganda has its own writers and readers.

But still, I also hid two chapters of my book among the writing of Miss Henman's students, which she was sending to a famous British agent. Perhaps the agent will like my writing. Mary Tendo, the Ugandan discovery! Maybe my book will find a British publisher. Maybe my book will win a big prize. African writers sometimes win big prizes. Then people are surprised, and jealous.

I heard Miss Henman talking to her friend (I do not like this friend, called Fifi, at all. I think many people would say she was pretty, but her smile is like a caterpillar wriggling on concrete.) They were discussing a writer from Nigeria who had been shortlisted for a big prize. 'It's only because she is black,' said Fifi. 'Come on, darling, let's not pretend!' Miss Henman laughed, but she did not deny it.

I think, if I won, Miss Henman would be jealous.

But also she would be able to boast. 'Oh yes, did you know she was my cleaner? I found her an agent and a publisher.' (Although she does not know she is finding me an agent.)

But still, if it happens, we might both be happy. I do not mind if Vanessa is happy. In fact, I would rather she was happy. When we were in the village, I was sorry for her.

And yet, at the moment we are not happy. She has not forgiven me about the masks, and I have not forgiven her about shouting. So I have not told her about Justin and Zakira. I tried to tell her when she came back from Paris, but she would not listen, she got in a temper.

I would like to tell her she is very lucky. I would like her to know she will soon have a grandchild. It must be the happiest time, for a mother. I remember my mother being happy in the village, although she had so many children, although she never left the village. So many children and grandchildren, even now that a few of them are dying.

In England, people never have enough children. It is as if here they have Slim in their brains. Something that makes them forget to have children. Here people have things instead of children. If I'd stayed in Kampala, I would have three children.

But Miss Henman is lucky to have her son. Miss Henman is lucky to be loved by Justin. Miss Henman is lucky to have a grandchild.

Maybe I will never be so lucky.

For two months or more I felt sick every morning. I knew

MAGGIE GEE

I was being poisoned by London. And my flow was thin, and weak, and scant, as if I had become an old woman. But I bought some herbs from the African shop, and I prayed in church, and now I feel better.

So life is long. My son might ring. I am not so old. I might have more children.

Justin goes to Zakira's every day. He takes her shopping, and looks after her. He has got a haircut and he looks much better. I asked him why he did not stay with her, but he said, 'I don't want to worry my mother. Besides, I would miss you, Mary darling.'

But I said to him, 'Justin, you must do without me. Soon I am going back to Kampala. You must bring Zakira to meet your mother.'

But he pulled a sulky face like a child, with his lips like Cupid, and went away.

In some ways, he is still a baby. For instance, Trevor wants him to drive the van, because sometimes there are things to fetch from the store. 'He still won't have a go at it, Mary,' Trevor told me. 'He's lost his nerve. One day he'll have to. I mean, it's important. It gives me the willies, the way he sits there.'

Perhaps he will be better when the baby is born. Then there will be room for only one baby. Justin will have to be a man.

I am reading the book that Trevor lent me, *My African Journey* by Winston Churchill. Trevor did not want to lend it me, he changed his mind and became embarrassed, but I wanted to read it, I am not a baby, who cannot do things in case they upset me. I do what I please, I am not like Justin.

And I find I am enjoying Winston Churchill. He is a good writer, and very funny, and says what he thinks, as a young man should. Although of course he gets many things wrong. And some of it is funny by accident. But at least he is not frightened to say anything at all, or always saying sorry, like most English people, which makes it impossible to know what they mean.

And sometimes I want to laugh aloud, and shake young Winston by the hand. This is what he says about Ugandan man: 'does he loll at his ease while his three or four wives till the soil, bear the burden, and earn his living?' I think I know the same men as Winston! Though my friend the accountant has always worked hard, and my father tried, until he fell off the bicycle (admittedly because he had been drinking *waragi*).

And this is another thing Winston said: 'the all-powerful white man is a fraud.'

50

'Oh, one of your students rang,' says Justin, when he meets his mother on the stairs.

She looks at him, critically. His hair is short; he is fully clothed; his eyes look clear. She can't deny it's suiting him, helping his father. But the lists of MA courses are still there where she left them, lying 'casually' upon the table. Perhaps there is an MA in Interior Design?

'Which student?' she asks.

'Oh, I don't know. He wanted your address, to send something.'

She wonders whether it was Beardy – *Alex*. He has been so attentive in her recent classes. She feels he is going to ask her for a drink. Perhaps he wants to send her something personal. A Christmas card. An invitation. Roses.

But she tells herself to stop dreaming. It will just be an appalling script from someone. 'You shouldn't really give them my address,' she says. 'Never mind, Justin. You're looking very handsome.'

She decides to ask him about Christmas.

'I've had another letter from Lucy. You remember, my cousin, the cousin in the country? Daughter of Aunt Isobel?'

He nods, vaguely. He wants to go out. He has promised to come round and give Zakira a massage. Rubbing warm oil into her wonderful belly, her huge belly, so big with his child. Now his mother seems tiny, irrelevant.

He realises this is a very good feeling. In an odd way, it lets him feel fond of her. How can she ever have seemed so important?

'She's invited us to go for Christmas. The extension will be finished, there is room for us all. One of her daughters will be in Australia, but Serena is going, the one who is a lawyer … She might have contacts that would be helpful for you.'

It's like half-watching a programme on the television. He knows the set is on, but he's somewhere else, wondering which is the best oil to buy, wondering if it will be nice for the baby, wondering if it is a girl or a boy. He, Justin Henman, is going to be a father. The world is changing, utterly. His mother understands nothing of this. And he is glad that she understands nothing. Last time she only caused problems with Zakira. For the moment, it needs to be entirely his, this new, this magical beginning of a family.

'Will you come, Justin? Are you listening?'

'Um, yes.' He means he is listening, though it isn't true, and he's already gone downstairs. But Vanessa thinks he is saying 'yes' to Christmas.

'That's agreed, then, darling. Have a good day.'

Now Vanessa feels a little surge of joy. For she will have a child to show off to Lucy. It was rather odd turning up with Mary. This time she will drive up proudly with Justin. Vanessa will have to do the driving of course. Justin is still not driving again. But at least they will be safer than she was with Mary.

'The twenty-second,' she shouts down the stairs. 'Coming

back on the twenty-eighth.' She thinks she hears a grunt before the front door closes.

There is a note from Mary on the kitchen table: 'I have gone shopping. If anyone telephones, please tell him I will be back soon.'

It's unusual for Mary to leave notes. It is unusual, indeed, for Mary to give any information at all about what she is doing. And who is this 'him' she expects to call? Vanessa remembers the shouting, cheerful man who rang one morning from Uganda. She can't quite remember what it was all about, though she does remember how annoying it was that Mary took the phone-call on her bed, before Vanessa had officially got up. *She planted her great bottom right on my pillow. Right on the place where I put my face.*

Mary must be thinking about going home.

Vanessa realises how much she wants this. They've had a wordless truce since the night of the masks, but underneath it, she senses they are both making plans. Mary has been out of the house a lot, or talking to Justin or Tigger in the kitchen, and they still fall silent when Vanessa comes in, which brings back Vanessa's old sense of isolation. There is really no more reason for Mary to be here. Yet Vanessa hopes to bring things to a graceful conclusion. If they cannot be friends, they should not be enemies. She feels a kind of duty to Uganda.

Yet the money she is paying out is enormous. Not that she resents it: it makes her feel better about bringing the whole chapter to a close. Should there really be notice, with an arrangement like this? After all, it has been informal, friendly.

Mary's note gives Vanessa an idea. The easiest thing would be to write her a letter, and slip it underneath her door.

She goes to her study and begins to write, but after a moment, she tears it up. A handwritten note seems a tad too casual. There is just the possibility, the tiniest worry, that Mary will not be keen to go. After all, every week Vanessa's handing over money, great bundles of notes, cash in hand. In a way Mary's on to an easy number.

Vanessa tries again on the computer, a formal but friendly letter of notice. 'Obviously I'll pay you until the New Year, and this will hold even if you decide to leave sooner.'

Yes, she could not be fairer than that. The blunt truth is, she doesn't need her any more.

There is a ring on the door. That will probably be Mary, who has a tendency not to take her key. It is one of her more annoying habits. Vanessa goes rather slowly to the door, and opens it with a reproachful smile.

But it isn't Mary. The day is cold, and dazzling. The shape of a man, blank on the light.

A young man. Standing too close to the door. He is in her face. For a moment she is startled, but then her eyes grow used to the light, and she sees it is just Derrick, the boy from college, hunched in a navy military jacket. He looks thinner than ever, and his hair is too short, which makes the bones of his face show through. His eyes are rather bright, today.

She steps back, instinctively, and says, 'Oh, hallo,' as he steps forward, half across the threshold.

'I have brought something to read to you.' He is already unfastening his bag, he is in.

She says, 'I'm sorry, I'm rather busy. Really you should bring me work at college,' but he laughs, a short, strange laugh like a dog, and pushes straight past her down the hall. And yet he is her student. She will have to be civil.

'Where do you write?' Can his voice be trembling? 'I want you to show me the place where you write.'

She realises he is merely nervous. 'Why don't I make us a cup of tea? I mean, I can give you twenty minutes or so. Just this once, but really, in general – '

'Show me your study, please, Vanessa.' Now he is talking more quietly, but there is still that tell-tale tremble. Yet Vanessa has never meant to be frightening. Probably the context is over-awing. She smiles at him, trying to look kind and maternal and yet, at the same time, authoritative. He cannot make a habit of doing this.

She leads him to her study, and indicates, with an airy hand, her chair and desk. 'It's all ergonomic, of course,' she says. 'Worth thinking about, once you have some money. Makes such a difference to one's working day. Now sit yourself down and I will put the kettle on.'

'I don't want tea,' he says, too vehemently, and sprawls on her turquoise futon sofa, though she had pointed him towards the armchair. 'I have things to read to you, and things to show you.'

Vanessa remembers the annoying voice with which he reads, too loud and too slow. She really can't put up with that now. 'I think it would be best if you just give me an outline. Then we can discuss any problems you have, and I will read the whole thing in due course.' She sits on her typing chair, which means she looks down at him, and instantly begins to feel better. 'Shoot,' she says, feeling brisk and powerful.

'It's a short story. Called "Creative Fire", but I think that might be a bit old-fashioned. I might call it "*Feu*", or "Liver".'

'Liver?' says Vanessa, taken aback, but then, smiling, on automatic pilot, 'very striking. Yes, much the best title of the three.'

'Do you remember you talked about using myth?' he says. He is sounding calmer now. 'In our last class. You told us to make modern versions. Well, I researched Prometheus on the net. The guy who went and stole fire from the gods. I guess, in a way, this dude could be a writer. So I changed the name to "Metheus". You get it, don't you? Me, *Metheus*.'

'That's good,' she says. On the screen, to her left, she can glimpse the text of her letter to Mary. She finds her mind is wandering.

'So Metheus needs to have creative fire. In the time of the Greeks I guess you couldn't do drugs, so he goes and steals it from Mount Olympus. He writes two or three really big sellers, but then he gets caught by the father of the gods. Who is really, you know, just this dude's Dad. And then of course Metheus gets punished.'

Vanessa starts to see where this is leading. After all the times she has told him not to!

'So his Dad gets Metheus staked out on the patio, with his liver being pecked by – ' Something dawns on him. He looks at her anxiously, and finishes, '… his liver's being pecked by a – *rabbit*. No, a rat.'

'You know perfectly well that it is an eagle. Everyone knows about Prometheus. I said to you, Derrick, please, *no birds*.'

But he ignores her, he rushes on by. 'And then Metheus has to defend himself, and defend, you know, the creative spark, so he gets a knife, and kills the eagle.'

It is out. He looks at her, sweating, triumphant. 'Do you like the way I have rounded it off?'

Some of them are totally unteachable. And yet he is a little too worked up for her liking. Vanessa decides she had better be tactful. 'Derrick, I have said you must broaden your palette.'

'You didn't like Metheus. You thought it was shit.' He is rummaging compulsively in his bag. Oh God, she thinks, he's going to take it out and read it. Instead he drags out something big and heavy, wrapped in a cloth and puts it on the floor, beside the futon. 'I'm serious,' he says, and unwraps a knife. It makes a heavy, clunking sound on the floorboards, a serious knife that could cut through bones, a butchery knife, a killing knife, not a silly knife in an invented story. The blade is long and very shiny. 'I'm a serious artist. This inspires me. Remember you wanted us to show you the things that were important to our creativity.'

'I don't like knives. Please put it away. And I think you should write another story.' Vanessa can hear herself talking on empty. What do you say to a boy with a knife? 'I mean, this one has verve, and pace, and you have a beginning, middle and end – '

'You think I'm stupid, don't you?' he says. He moves forward on the futon so his knees touch her calves. His eyes are darting all round the room, his lips are working, smiling, nervous. And there is something strange about his breath.

'You're like everyone else. You think I am mad. You're just too cowardly to say so. It was obvious, when I read you my story about the chickens. You didn't really like it at all. You didn't understand the metaphor. You just pretended to encourage me. I trusted you. I respected you.'

'Let's talk about this,' she says, but it's hard, her breath is short, the words don't sound right. 'I do want to help you with your writing. First you must put that knife away. Perhaps I was a little too negative.'

'Well, are you sorry?' he demands, voice breaking, of everyone who has ever upset him, parents, policemen, therapists, teachers – stupid, lying, greasing teachers –

'Sorry, sorry,' Vanessa breathes.

And before she can react, he is kissing her, his large wet tongue pushing into her mouth and his thin hard hands grabbing her shoulders, and she falls sideways off the chair, so for a moment her mouth is uncovered, and she gasps, 'Derrick, will you stop being silly,' before his fingers cover her face, he puts his whole hand over her face – They struggle, unsuccessfully, clumsily. Vanessa is fit from her exercises, her arms are sinewy, her calves are strong, but she is no match for a fit young man. He is saying, 'What's the matter, I just want to kiss you, I love you, you know, I really love you – ' His mouth tastes horrible, of metal.

Then Vanessa thinks she hears a sound in the hall. Derrick has his back to the doorway of her study, but she's facing it, and with a lurch of the heart, between the bars of his fingers, through her stretched, hurt lids, she sees the front door opening, a lifetime away, and the dark, solid figure of Mary coming through it –

Agonized, she watches it disappear again, Mary's tired, everyday, unfrightened face, carrying her bags through into the kitchen, and at least it seems the boy has heard nothing, for he's busy, dragging off his jacket with one hand while he holds her down on the floor with the other – but what really makes her cry out with pain is the moment he tries to change position and places one knee on top of her thigh, so his whole young weight bears down on her femur, and she grunts a stifled 'No!' because she feels it is breaking –

And then her door bangs hard against a pile of books which knocks over another pile beside it, and they fall like thunder on the struggling couple as Mary pounds into the room. Derrick's hand relaxes and the fingers peel off. Oh *Mary, Mary*, nostrils flared with fury –

'What are you doing?' Mary shouts like a man, her voice hoarse and strong, but she sees in an instant, she snatches up the knife and flings it hard across the room, out of reach, then hits the boy with the flat of her hand, a hand made hard by decades of work, once, twice across his bony temple, and he staggers off Vanessa, stunned, and then Mary punches him hard on the nose, and a rose of blood bursts out of the nostril, and then with a furious cry in Luganda, she knees him with brutal force in the balls.

He collapses forwards on to the carpet. Mary is holding him down by the neck. Vanessa staggers to her feet, but the leg Derrick knelt on does not seem to be working.

'We will call the police! *Ono mubbi! Mutemu*! Stinking thief and murderer!' says Mary, panting. 'You will sit on him, Vanessa, while I call the police. Did you steal my money?' she shouts at Derrick, but the blood is pouring from his nose, he is gathering himself, one hand over his face, and he pushes her off him and staggers from the room, no longer human, a wounded hyena, yelping angry, inaudible swear words, with Mary after him, she has him by one shoulder, she shouts, 'Villain, villain!' and pulls his hair, but seconds later, he is through the front door while she aims one last kick at his legs, his bottom, and he crouches for a moment, winded, on the porch, with the garden path sunlit and ordinary behind him, framed by the door, which is gaping open on an everyday, astounded morning, and the rose leaves bob towards his face, his blood-stained, sorrowful, hurt child's face.

'Leave him, Mary,' Vanessa gasps. 'Just let him go.'

'But he is a thief. In Kampala, we deal with them! Every week, the crowd catches someone on the street. Next day they report a death in the papers!' Mary is shouting this at Derrick. 'Villain, I will kill you if you take my money.'

'He hasn't taken anything.'

Now he is limping away down the path. Mary is torn between following him and running upstairs to check on her money. But she sees the outside broom in the porch and snatches it up and throws it after him, whirling the head like an Olympic hammer-thrower, and hits her mark, and he yelps again, and then he is gone, and the tall hedge hides him.

Vanessa has crumpled on to the floor, and sits in the hall, her head in her hands. Mary is erect, regal and glowing, full of the passion of the fight.

'Thank you, Mary, I don't know how to thank you – '

'Are you all right, Vanessa? You are not bleeding?' Mary crouches, briefly, and looks her over. 'Now, Vanessa, I will check my money.' Mary goes upstairs two at a time, faster than Vanessa's ever heard her move. Indeed she did not know that Mary could run, but she returns in her normal leisurely fashion. 'I was in time, he did not take my money.' When Mary tries to lift her, Vanessa collapses.

The rest of the day passes in a dream-like fashion. The police, Trevor, Justin all come. Mary is heard giving stirring descriptions that always end with the rescue of her money. Everyone is full of praise for Mary. Vanessa is taken off to hospital for an X-ray on her painful leg, not in an ambulance, as she had expected, but in Trevor's van, which is white with plaster dust, and she is not too ill to complain. 'Sorry, old girl, no one gave me notice.' But Trevor is loving, worried, kind, and Justin is almost too upset to talk.

Still Vanessa is left with a puzzled feeling that somehow Mary is the centre of all this, that the heroic role, which was surely hers, the stoical, plucky victim of attack, has passed to Mary, and will not come back, however much she tells her own story.

The police pick up Derrick not far from his lodgings. He turns out to have a history of violence, and has been seeing a psychiatrist since he was eleven.

And most people begin blaming themselves. Justin is frantic

that he gave him her address. 'No, it's my fault for giving him my telephone number,' his mother tells him, meaning it. But Vanessa cannot bring herself to confess that she did it because Derrick was young and handsome. Because she wanted him to feel special. A little flirtation varied her day. *The trouble is, flirting wasn't what he wanted. My fault, my fault.* 'It's my fault, Mother,' Justin groans, insists.

But Mary tells him not to talk nonsense. 'All over the world there are villains,' she says. 'At least this young man did not steal any money. You just be thankful for Mary Tendo!'

'He told me he had a psychiatrist,' says Vanessa. 'I took no notice. I just thought, they're all mad.'

She is sitting in Emergency with Trevor. The NHS does not think she's an emergency, despite Trevor's best efforts on her behalf, though they say, 'You could fetch your wife a cup of tea.' They seem surprised when he asks directions, as if most of the patients come with maps. 'It's downstairs, turn left, left again, cross the courtyard, in through the red door, not the first, the second; then upstairs, straight down, across the next landing, you'll see it after the children's ward. If you get to surgery, you've gone too far.' But Trevor decides he cannot leave her. Her back is hurting, and her face, and her neck. Her left leg makes her limp, and sigh.

'You're all right, old girl,' he keeps telling her. 'Thanks to Mary. She was a cracker.'

'I kept my head,' Vanessa assures him, but he does not take the hint and praise her.

When a doctor finally examines her, he is sympathetic, and briskly thorough, but 'It could have been worse,' he assures her, annoyingly, after she and Tigger have told their story. 'You've got some bad bruises. Time will see to that. If you like I can prescribe something strong for the pain.'

'Will I be all right by Christmas?' she asks.

'Oh yes,' he says, startled, as if it is obvious. 'I wouldn't advise you to drive home today. But of course, your husband will be able to drive you. ' Normally Vanessa would be the one to correct him, but this time it's Trevor: 'Ex-husband,' he grunts. Vanessa feels the doctor is taking it too lightly; she wonders if she'll ever recover. The police have offered her counselling, but she doesn't want to talk to someone stupid. Still, the tired young doctor, as they struggle through the door, with Vanessa leaning heavily on Tigger, manages a final moment of kindness. 'You ought to be right as rain by Christmas.'

'How right is rain?' Trevor asks, rhetorically. Outside the door it is raining, hard, and Vanessa clutches him uncomfortably as they limp together across the carpark, like some eternal three-legged race. She weighs upon him. He needs to escape.

Besides, he is feeling a little bit guilty. He's been talking to Mary about village wells. As a plumber, he knows a lot about water. She has had an idea that he could come out to Uganda and train villagers to look after a well, but she's made him promise not to tell Vanessa, in case she decides she would like to come with him. Tigger felt disloyal agreeing to this, but he'd love to do something good in the world, and he'd love to have a look at the Pearl of Africa. Soraya knows he's never got beyond Calais; she's happy to spare him for a month or two. It would be good for Justin to run the business. And as for Vanessa – he needs a clean break.

51

The weather worsens rapidly. The British are glad, in their aching bones. It gives them something to complain about. Also, a proper cold snap will kill the mosquitoes that make it feel like somewhere foreign, the new clouds of fruit flies in airless kitchens, the whispering indices of climate change. This is Great Britain, not Africa. December *should* be a chilly month, then they can show character by putting up with it. Pleased, they rush out to buy hot-water bottles, and middle-aged men are indignant to be offered winsome covers like small furry animals. 'Sorry, sir, it's all we've got.' Trevor walks away shyly with a garish Pooh Bear, which he thinks at least will give a laugh to Soraya. He intends to pay her more attention. She's a lovely girl, bright and loyal. Soraya wants to have his children. Now trade is so good, he could almost afford it. After he's done his bit in Uganda.

Mary Tendo, however, looks grey and grim. She wears all her clothes and still feels cold. Vanessa goes out and buys her a jumper, since Mary ignores hints to do this herself. There has been no more mention of Mary leaving. The jumper is pretty, and very expensive, a peach-coloured mohair that tickles Mary's neck. It has a matching scarf. Vanessa feels generous.

But she is no longer in charge of the future. Justin seems evasive when she talks about Christmas. Mary Tendo reveals no plans. And Tigger almost seems to be avoiding her, now the bruising has faded, and her leg is better. Though the college was horrified about what happened, and sent memos about 'putting in place new safeguards', the Dean said privately that you can't protect women stupid enough to give out home phone numbers. There is a meeting of Convention (Vanessa isn't present) where scathing things are said about Creative Writing and the mental state of both staff and students. 'It never was a real subject, in my view,' says die-hard Dr Harding, Social Studies, who has never been offered a Readership, who tried to write a novel, twenty years ago; besides, Vanessa once snubbed him, in the bar. All round the room, there are murmurs of assent.

Within the seminar group, people are appalled and thrilled. A garbled version of the story gets about where Vanessa was raped and nearly murdered. Daisy is responsible for these embellishments. It must be true: Derrick has disappeared. The men look at Vanessa assessingly, tenderly, trying not to imagine the scene in detail. She has said the least that she can get away with, attempting to sound neutral, like a policewoman: 'You may have heard that some events took place involving a member of this class. He is having psychiatric help. There is no reason for anyone to be anxious.' Yet she herself is still jumpy at night, and prefers it when there are people in the house.

But Justin seems to be staying away. His mother senses he has hardly been here, ever since the strange night when she met him on the stairs, perhaps ten days after she was attacked, and his eyes were shining, and he was wreathed in smiles, and when she said, 'Justin, you do look happy,' he hugged her so hard that she gasped with pain and he backed away saying, 'Sorry, sorry, I am just so clumsy, what's the matter with me?' And yet, he went on looking radiantly happy.

'Would you like a cup of hot chocolate?' his mother had inquired. She was curious, and she wanted to talk. But he said, vaguely, 'I'm just in and out. I'm actually staying with – a friend. *Two* friends!' And then he laughed out loud with pleasure. Perhaps he was drunk, but he didn't seem it, although there was definitely wine on his breath. 'I just popped back for some, uh, some blankets.'

And before she could ask any more, he was gone. Vanessa went back to her bedroom, thoughtful. She is not afraid, because she knows that Mary is somewhere, down in the kitchen or out in the garden, having the bedtime cigarette that she no longer tries to conceal from Vanessa, and which Vanessa accepts is her due.

But minutes later she's convulsed by fear to hear Mary Tendo screaming, loudly.

It seems the screams go on and on, and Vanessa gets ready, she pulls her shoes on, her heart is thumping like some straining engine –

But then she hears that Mary is laughing. Mary is laughing and shouting with Justin. And this time Vanessa feels more sad than envious: Mary Tendo and Justin are friends. Perhaps all that time Mary spent with Justin, all those years ago, when Vanessa was busy, have given them something both precious and ordinary. (It wasn't her fault. She was always so busy. She didn't choose it, she had no choice. Surely, though, Justin's love for her is special?)

For several days the house seems full of laughter. Vanessa would like to be a part of it. But since what happened, she's felt oddly muted, incapable of going on the attack. The world seems to have become illogical, surreal, as if she is living at an angle to it.

One day there is a phone-call from a bubbly, husky-voiced woman who says a loud, two-tone 'Ha-llo!' like an old friend, but then asks to speak to Justin.

'He's rarely here at the moment,' sighs Vanessa, at which the woman says, with odd intimacy, 'No, of course, I quite understand ... My name is Jasmine. Call me Jazz. And you must be – let me see – Vanessa! Vanessa it's so nice to talk to you. I have excellent news for you and Justin. You have been selected from hundreds of callers to take part in next month's "PARENT SWAP"!' She delivers this announcement on an ear-bursting crescendo.

'This is some advertising thing,' says Vanessa, but Jasmine forges on, cheery, brazen.

'Look at it this way, Veronica. This is great opportunity. It's your chance to tell your side of things to thousands of people who only know Justin's – '

'Stop bothering me,' says Vanessa, and puts the phone down. When it rings again, three times, she ignores it. Of course, it is just another nuisance call, and yet it is disquieting. She sits there for a few minutes, puzzled. Justin's side of things, indeed! How would 'thousands of people' know about Justin? What could it mean, a 'parent swap'? She means to tell him about the call, later, but is overcome by a strange inertia.

Small candle-flames brighten these dark days. First, in a simple, childish way, Vanessa is looking forward to Christmas. Once she realised that Mary would not be leaving, Vanessa has simply asked her to join them, and Mary agrees, demurely, saying only, 'But Vanessa, I am waiting for a call from Uganda. It is possible that my friend will come.' Vanessa doesn't take much notice of this, since Mary has been waiting for a call for weeks. Lucy seems happy for Mary to come. So the three of them will drive up together, Vanessa thinks, with some contentment. A real Christmas. A country Christmas.

Secondly, in the last session of term, bearded Alex takes the bull by the horns. He stays behind and hands over a Christmas card. 'Look, this is probably not the best time for this, not after, you know, whatever happened, which we are all sorry to hear about, but I've put my phone number on this card, and if you felt like going out for a drink … I promise not to talk about writing. Maybe we could do a film, or a show.'

It is sweetly old-fashioned, this talk of a show. Vanessa blushes with pleasure and smiles. The smile keeps warming and extending, on its own, and their eyes meet; older eyes; briefly unguarded. They like each other: a man, a woman. Maybe this time they will get on.

She takes the card without committing herself, but she knows she will give him a ring after Christmas. Perhaps they will go to a pantomime. Something non-verbal, unintellectual. Perhaps she can get him to shave off his beard … but she catches herself, and changes her mind. She will only suggest the lightest trim.

52

But Vanessa's new calm is badly shaken by two events in the run-up to Christmas. She is sitting in the dining room one morning, ripping open cards with her usual elan, trying to get through ten envelopes a minute, when she realises one of them isn't a card. It is a letter from the high-powered agent, suggesting a January date to meet the class, and responding to the extracts she's seen. Vanessa's heart starts to beat unsteadily, thumping at her ribs, drumming at her temples. She spots 'Emily Self' in the middle of the page.

She forces herself to read from the beginning. 'Several very talented students ... tribute to your teaching methods ...' Then something that makes her choke on her coffee. 'Perhaps the most gifted, as I'm sure you're aware, is the African writer, Mary Tendo. Marvellously fresh, vivid descriptions of growing up in Uganda ... certainly like to see more of it ... though strictly between ourselves, Vanessa, the multicultural bubble may have burst ... could be, frankly, just a little bit "last year"... Not that it's relevant, but is she photogenic? It will be very good to meet her ... and Emily Self. Thank you for drawing her to my attention. The second extract was the better of the two. She doesn't, of course, have anything like the panache and style of Mary Tendo, but I really do think I could do something for her. The feeling is that "poor white rural", sort of post-*Cold Mountain* with a nod to *Deliverance*, is going to be very big next year. That father with the hen-house is wonderfully sinister.'

Vanessa reads it again and again, at first unable to understand. Coffee and bile rise in her throat –

So Mary is a secret writer. *Mary Tendo has been writing a book*. She has smuggled some chapters in, like a cuckoo. Mary has charmed someone yet again. Mary Tendo 'the most gifted'!

It is all too much for Vanessa to bear. And Emily Self 'doesn't, of course, have the panache and style of Mary Tendo …' It was the 'of course' that hurt so much.

But Mary need never see this letter, Vanessa thinks, crumpling it. No, Mary never *will* see this letter.

Then she uncrumples it, and reads it again.

On the other hand, Emily Self could be big. 'The father in the hen-house is wonderfully sinister' (even though Vanessa thought she'd made him touching). 'I really do think I could do something with her.'

That means, she must believe she can make me famous.

I am always said to be photogenic. So that's one less thing to worry about.

Vanessa needs time to take it all in. For a while she cannot bear to look at Mary. The thing she has done is so dishonest. Passing herself off as one of my students! Taking advantage of my trust!

Mary, for her part, has no idea why Vanessa has started glaring again. But Mary feels guilty about having seen the grandchild, so she is submissive, and tries to placate her. It should be Vanessa who is holding the baby, Vanessa, in Mary's place, gazing down on his quick brown eyes and long tear-slicked lashes, watching him kick like a little pink frog. Vanessa, who doted on frogs in the garden. Though she hadn't always been good with young children –

But no, Vanessa would love this baby. Mary feels bad for her about the baby, but Justin is stubborn as a mule.

Then, the night before they are all supposed to be leaving for the country, Justin tells Vanessa he isn't going. 'I'll have to come up later, on my own. There's stuff I have to finish, Mother.' Vanessa questions him very closely, but all she can establish is that somewhere or other, a young couple need alterations for their new baby, or else they will not get in for Christmas. Justin's enigmatic: 'Like, no room at the inn.' She wonders yet again if he is on something: he seems so giggly, so absurdly happy, yet at the same time he has a sleepy look, though he's up every morning and out of the house. His bedridden days seem to have gone for ever.

'But darling, you can't get to Lucy's on your own.' Because since his breakdown, Justin has not driven. Despite all Tigger's attempt to encourage him – 'Come on lad, you're a bloody good driver. You passed first time, which is more than I did' – despite Tigger's pleas that he needs help with the van, Justin's still afraid of the driver's seat. 'I can't do it, Dad. I might kill someone.'

And so it is arranged he will follow with Mary, who will drive Justin's superannuated Jaguar, if it will move, after six months in the garage. Mary likes the idea, and spends a happy afternoon getting it purring over again; she turns out to be a competent mechanic. Vanessa will drive up tomorrow as planned: Justin and Mary, two days later. 'And Mary, for God's sake, don't forget your glasses!' Vanessa sounds as sharp as before the attack.

Vanessa leaves in the morning, waving manfully, and yet she has a mournful, anxious look. Mary and Justin feel touched and guilty, seeing Vanessa's small stiff figure manoeuvring herself into the driver's seat, with two suitcases of what she calls 'essentials', plus bags of food, clinking bottles, rolls of wrapping paper, carrier bags of presents, a holly wreath, and a great hollow box of crackers, shining with cellophane, a cube of decorated air, two dozen titivations of crepe and gold paper in which a few paltry plastic giftlets rattle. She is so small compared to the bulk of her possessions. They wave to her as she shrinks down the road.

'So when will you tell her that she is a grandma? Of the most beautiful baby in the world?' Mary asks Justin, hugging him. 'Poor Miss Vanessa, I am sorry for her.' It tempers the faint pleasure of outwitting her employer (but the baby, in himself, is so glorious: pinkish-skinned, though it will darken later, red-lipped, stormy, but easily comforted, topped with a shock of straight dark hair).

'I'm going to tell her. All in good time. Once we're sorted out, I shall bring them both to see her.'

The next day, the weather's sharply colder. There are alerts of imminent snow. The bookies taking bets on a White Christmas close their books, and exhausted housewives fight back into the shops to buy more thick soups, more Christmas puddings. Now all the furry hot-water bottles have sold out. There is a miniature run on bedsocks.

Vanessa, in Sussex, starts to worry. 'If it gets any worse, you are not to come,' she instructs Justin, when she gets him on the phone, though for the past two days he has hardly been at home. 'Mary is not to drive if it's snowing. She isn't used to snow. She's African.'

'Oh, Mary and I aren't frightened by snowstorms,' says Justin, grandly. Yet it keeps getting colder. Zakira has the baby in a soft cocoon of blankets. He and Mary shiver as they pack the car. He does not want to leave his woman, his baby, but he still can't say so to his mother. Will he ever learn to say 'No' to her? One day, he thinks, I shall just be myself.

But it isn't so easy to be himself. Maybe having a family of his own will help; a new family, to escape the old one.

They had firmly intended to leave before dark, but Justin receives a call from Zakira: her nipples are hurting; she needs something from the chemist. With a stricken expression – she must not be in pain – he shoots out of the house before Mary can take him and does a tour on foot around the three local chemists, who sell him half a dozen useless remedies, and then Mary drives him to Zakira's. It isn't easy to leave his new family; Zakira seems fretful, almost reproachful, so by the time they are really on the road, it is sunset.

The air is full of Christmas petrol: it has a poisoned, leaden feel. The sunset is magnificent but also lowering, red flames shooting between mountainous clouds which are the brownish purple that presages snow.

As they turn out of their street, the white dance begins, first big light flakes, individual as flowers, and then slowly quickening, multiplying, twisting, till within thirty minutes their car has been sucked into a sifting forest of grey-white shapes, as soft and thick as if cut from flannel, which burst into brightness at every street lamp, then fade again, instantly, whiten then darken, so everything looks different, hides and shifts, and the solid stream of traffic melts and blurs into a series of whispering spectres, and deepening the white is the indigo evening as night blues over the afterglow.

'Your mother said I shouldn't drive if it was snowing, but

it didn't snow till we had already left,' says Mary, smiling, but she isn't quite happy, though Mary believes in being happy.

Firstly, her glasses, though nearly new, bought from a friend who no longer wanted them, keep steaming up, and pinch her nose. She has to take them off and wipe them, and on one occasion, nearly loses control, and Justin reaches across to grab the wheel. 'Be careful, Mary,' he says, crossly, sounding suddenly unpleasantly like Vanessa.

Secondly, Mary had forgotten snow. Her memory had turned it into something minor, something sweet and flat and docile, like icing. She is taken aback that it is eating the world, surging up all round her, in four dimensions.

Thirdly, her *kabito* hasn't called. Four weeks ago, he telephoned to tell her he was coming, he had the tickets and was 'sure of a visa', but since Ugandans don't believe in a visa until it is in their jacket pockets, he promised to call again to confirm; but the second phone-call has never come, and she's been unable to track him down.

So Mary is doomed to spend Christmas with strangers, in a village a world away from her own village, far from her church and her friends in Kampala, away from her beloved friend the accountant, who grows more dear now she isn't going to see him. She misses him badly, longs for him. For the first time she thinks, 'I might marry Charles.' But she cannot marry him until she locates him. Will she ever see him, or Uganda, again?

'Read me the signs,' she says sharply to Justin, who is humming and staring in a blissed-out fashion.

'It's cool, Mary, we're heading for the motorway.'

On the motorway, thinks Mary, things will seem more normal, the lights will be brighter, the traffic streams steadier, and I will get my bearings again. Unconsciously, she starts to drive faster. Soon she is going very fast indeed, revving at the lights, overtaking, and she bombs on to the motorway without a pause, and Justin wakes up and sits bolt upright.

He remembers, with a shock, Zakira and the baby.

'Look, Mary, you'd better slow down, since it's snowing. See, the overhead signs are saying 40.'

Mary shoots a glance across at him. He is a young, fit man. He should be driving. At any rate, he should not be taking it for granted that driving will be done by someone else, while Justin sits there handing out instructions. Mary feels safer when she drives faster, in control at last, skating through life, leaving everything behind, the mess, the exhaustion, the years of slow, insurmountable work, going inch by inch, a snail with a duster. If Mary can stay in the fast lane, she will, and in any case, today the roads are dream-like, the whole of England has become insubstantial, her early feelings of doubt and panic have been replaced by a dreamer's calm: nothing will stop her, nothing can hurt her.

But Justin's voice nags in her ear. She manages to stop herself snapping at him.

'Justin, I love you, but soon you must start driving. You will see later, with the baby. It will be useful if you are driving.'

His full red lips, so like the baby's, look suddenly sulky, lower lip jutting. He has made an effort; he has got better; he is working hard, he has become a father, he's making an attempt to please his mother, he's trekking to the back of beyond for Christmas ...

Now Mary expects him to drive the car!

'Mary, I love you, but you are my driver.'

She looks at him narrowly through newly wiped glasses, which show every pimple, every flaw. This tall young man with his pout like a baby. That greedy mouth which had dragged at her nipples.

'Mr Justin, I am not your driver.'

But he only laughs, in his Justin way, a charming cherub, and pats her dark hand, stroking it as it clutches the wheel, the hand of the woman who has mothered him, served him, cleaned up his vomit, given him her breast, this black woman guiding him through a snowstorm, in the midst of a reindeer herd of cars, all chafing forwards in the snowy darkness, their headlights dipped on the new white like eyes.

'They can't have done the gritting. The snow is settling,' says Justin, reflectively, looking at the road.

Then suddenly he is clutching her wrist, as he has pulled at Mary a thousand times before, pulled at her skirt, her sleeve, her arm – 'Watch out, Mary. We have to slow down.' They are shooting down the slip road to their second motorway, and Mary once again shows no signs of braking to dovetail into the slipstream of the traffic – 'Mary, honestly, it's dangerous!' He has spotted, lying on its side like a beetle, a gritting lorry on the hard shoulder, with flashing lights and three hunched men.

And all his life he has been tugging at Mary (she feels as she screams across the shuddering lanes and, as if by magic, other cars avoid her) and she's never minded, it was only Justin, her second baby, Jamil's little brother – but now he is so much bigger than her, and he is still tugging and begging and ordering, and thinking it is funny to call her 'my driver', and Jamie can no longer make everything right.

'Justin, be quiet. I am a good driver. I have driven you ever since you were a baby. Now will you please stop bothering me.'

Her authoritative voice works on him. He falls silent, and then he dozes. Sleep has always been his way out. He only wakes up when he feels the car slowing to a standstill, and his first thought is, 'Thank God, we're here.'

But he looks out of the window, and sees motionless traffic, just visible through endlessly cascading snow, and he looks upwards, and it comes forever, falling from roofless grey halls of snow, and suddenly it fills him with vertigo, the blind gyres of snowflakes bearing down on him, rushing so fast the car can never escape them, the sky has pressed the whole world to a standstill, and it keeps on coming: the snow, the snow.

'What's happening, Mary?'

'I don't know. We have been standing here for half an hour. Maybe there is an accident.'

Mary is writing in a small green notebook. 'What are you doing, Mary? Shall we play Hangman?' When he was a boy, Justin taught Mary Hangman, and the two of them used to play it for hours.

'Perhaps later, Justin. I am writing something.'

'Is it a shopping list?' It makes him smile. How many times, when he was smaller, has he helped Mary write the shopping list? And she always added the things he asked for, the sausages and beans, the crisps and jelly, though she kept them in the cupboard with her cleaning things, where he knew his mother never looked, and it was one of their special secrets, and Justin remembers how much he loves her, and she is here with him now, in the snow, and they'll save each other, of course they will, and it will all be a great adventure (his mother is miles away, as usual).

And then he remembers, no, it is Christmas, it's much too late for shopping lists.

And Mary seems a little distant. 'No, Justin. It is something different.'

He takes her hand, playfully, and tries to stop the pen. She snatches it back with surprising force. He looks at her, hurt: 'Don't be cross with me.'

'I am writing my *Autobiography*.'

'Oh yes, that thing you were doing in your room, and Dad had to help you with the computer. Did you keep it up, then? How is it going?'

She imagines she hears a note of lordly indifference. 'I will soon finish it, and publish it. That is why I work when I get the chance. When it is published, you can buy a copy.'

It is starting to get a little cold in the car. Outside, there are desultory outbreaks of hooting. People switch their engines on and off. One man has got out of his car, and peers forwards, but the snow is too thick for him to see anything.

'What if the Jag won't start again?' Justin asks her. He just wants reassurance.

And Mary runs the engine for a bit, so the heater comes on, and the minutes pass, and her pen whispers over the lined paper, and Justin drums his fingers on the dashboard and wishes the tape deck were not broken, and the snow *shushes*, *shushes* outside the window, and the wind moans dog-like down the white blocked lanes. And Justin thinks, we could sit here forever, and it isn't entirely an unpleasant thought, because he's always found Mary's presence so soothing; but today there is something different about her.

She is preoccupied, almost impatient, as if she has better things to do, but he knows he can tease her out of this mood; he has always been the centre of Mary's world. She went back to Uganda but she never forgot him. She came back and loved him the same as before. Secretly, he thinks she loves him more than Jamil. Of course Jamil grew in Mary's belly, but Mary was always there for Justin's bedtime, and Justin's birthdays, and Justin's illnesses – which means she can rarely have been at Jamil's. Jamil has always been his ghostly rival – he has only met him on five or six occasions – but Justin is pretty sure he's still ahead. Mary has mentioned Jamil less this time.

'Are you going to write about me and Jamie?'

Her pen stops writing. She stares at the dashboard as if it is a television. 'Yes, Justin. I shall write about you.'

'Have you bought Jamie a Christmas present?'

'Yes, I am always buying him presents.'

'Have you bought me a Christmas present?'

But Mary will not answer him.

Suddenly there's movement, way up in the distance, and other engines fire into life, and under the shimmering scythings of snow, the whole scene shudders into motion again, but this time it's a halting, wounded motion; the whole herd knows that for now, life has changed, survival has become part of the challenge.

'I need the bathroom,' Mary says, primly. 'We'll have to stop at a Services.'

Their progress is, to Justin, reassuringly slow. There is no more possibility of Mary speeding. The traffic flow moves in stops and starts, at 10 or 20 miles an hour, a great suffering, disintegrating caterpillar, assaulted from above by hordes of tiny white predators, and Mary and Justin desert the jerky caravan and move with a relative turn of speed down the road towards the blankness of the Services' carpark. A field of churned snow, with a few white-fleeced cars crouched at random angles in the emptiness. The town is reverting to countryside. The world of machines is losing its grip.

Inside, the Services seem ghostly. The personnel have a haunted look that goes oddly with their coronets of tinsel, their fluffy reindeer ears, their enormous necklaces of glittery red and green Christmas balls. They stand and stare out of the plate-glass windows. 'I'm only supposed to be on duty till nine,' a harassed-looking teenager confides in Mary. 'But nobody's thought about how I get home. I've got a baby waiting for me, you see.' She looks far too young to have a baby. 'Where are you making for, anyway?'

Mary tells her, and the girl looks self-important. 'Forecast's like really crap,' she says. 'Excuse my language. They're saying, like, nobody oughtn't to be driving tonight.'

'We shall be fine,' Mary says.

'Good luck,' the child calls after her.

But part of Mary is not sure she is fine. She sits in the ladies' using her mobile. Mary has several people to contact, and does not want to do it in front of Justin. She needs to call Omar, though her heart is heavy. The phone calls to Libya have never been easy, hard to get a connection, hard to talk to Omar, but now there is the nagging fear of bad news. She needs to call her friend the accountant, to tell him where she is, and what is happening. She wants to tell him that she loves him, since she has never told him that she loves him, and perhaps she will never escape this place, this endless journey through corridors of ice, this long middle passage between two strangenesses, and even when she arrives, she will be far from home.

But first she must do what she dreads, and ring Omar. She shivers as she puts in the number, and manages to misdial three times. The line is appalling, racked with howls and moans. Her ex-husband is out, and Awatef seems distant. 'He could not look for ever, Mary.' And so he came home. 'Baghdad is still dangerous, do you understand?' The boy in the zoo had already moved on, and Omar could not even confirm he was Libyan.

Omar has come home, without Jamil. Without Jamil. Hope, drags, curdles.

'Mary, believe me, Omar has tried ... but he must also look after his family.' 'Once he had another family,' says Mary, but

Awatef doesn't hear, and Mary doesn't repeat it. Instead, she says, 'Tell Omar I am sorry.' She is not surprised, but she shivers more severely, shaking so hard that her teeth knock together. So cold, so pitiless, this grey country. She sits and stares blankly at the concrete floor. Then she rings the number Vanessa has given.

'Mary! I have been mad with worry! Is Justin all right? What on earth has happened!'

The voice is broken up, it is fizzing with snow. Mary thinks that her little employer must be frozen. (But in fact, Vanessa's sitting in Lucy's front room, telling her cousin all about her life, cradling a large balloon of brandy that both of them agree they 'wouldn't have usually'. Fortunately Lucy is a good listener. Vanessa is having a lovely time. Lucy makes her feel glamorous. Now she in turn feels benign towards Mary. After all, poor Mary's writing was a little old-fashioned, even though the agent did her best to be kind. Vanessa is the one who is tipped for success. She's already drafting the blurb in her head – *'a raw, riveting tale of rural lust ...'*)

'It is snowing, Vanessa, the road is not easy, but Justin is fine. He is eating chips and drinking his tea.'

'Where are you?' The voice sounds suspicious now.

'Crossroads Services, near Freemantle.'

'You've stopped at the Services? That will hold you up. I do hope you're not going to get here too late.' There is a silence. Mary turns her eyes to the window shivering against the night, its glass shaking and straining in the wind, barely managing to hold back the wild white weather, the unfriendly distances of which Vanessa knows nothing.

Perhaps alerted by her silence, Vanessa tries again. 'Of course the main thing is you're both all right. It's just that, you know, *preferably*, I'd rather you didn't wake up Lucy.' She cocks one eyebrow at her cousin, who makes polite demurring faces: they mustn't worry, it is quite all right.

'Yes, Miss Henman.'

'Oh really, Mary, by now you must have learned to say Vanessa.' She means it to be friendly, but it comes out wrong, as if she is saying that Mary is stupid, and Mary's voice echoes back through the snow, muted, stubborn: 'To say Vanessa. Yes, Miss Henman.'

'It isn't actually snowing here,' Vanessa says, as if that makes it better. 'But the forecast did say it was on the way. Isn't it exciting, a White Christmas! You'll be able to tell everyone in Uganda you had a real White Christmas with us!'

Then Mary starts to know she will not be going. A voice in her head says, *Never, never*. 'Yes, Miss Henman. A White Christmas.'

(But where did that voice come from? Of course she must go. But it speaks to her again: *Go home, go home*.)

'Well anyway Mary dear, safe journey. Give my love to Justin. Kissy kissy kissy.'

53

Vanessa puts down the phone frustrated, but dramatizes it into a laugh, for Lucy. 'That was Mary. Of course, my African friend. Yes, the heroine who saw off that infatuated student. We are very close now, but as you know, she was my cleaner for years and years. They don't find it easy to be treated as equals. Even now Mary occasionally calls me Miss Henman. As if she were a child, and I the teacher!'

And Vanessa starts to glow with her own importance, the power of ruling and then renouncing, the touching affection Mary feels for her now, which 'must mean I'm not completely ghastly!' She laughs at the absurdity of that thought. 'She saved my life, Lucy, you know.' And then inspiration carries her along. 'But I have been able to give something in return. Living in the house of an established writer has encouraged Mary to write about her life. Now I've put her in the way of a top literary agent. Of course in my job I have all the contacts. It isn't certain she'll be able to help her, but if Mary gets published, won't it be wonderful?'

'Wonderful, wonderful,' says Lucy, yawning. 'It's very

exciting, all these famous people. Now if you'll excuse me, I'll tear myself away and go up and finish wrapping my presents. I've left them out some ham and potato salad.'

Real snow starts falling, light and lovely, in the blank central space of the double-glazed window that Lucy has framed with spray-on snow and little bunny-scuts of glued cotton wool. 'Oh isn't it glorious, magical,' Vanessa enthuses, as Lucy goes to bed, and then settles down alone with a double gin, the TV controller, and a mug of cocoa. She feels heroic, waiting up for them.

But she falls asleep, frightened, and still on her own, as the temperature plummets around two am.

5 4

Now Mary is ready to ring her accountant, but she looks at her watch: already ten pm. Midnight in Uganda: too late to ring. She longs for Kampala's warm earth, tender heat, the sheen of round brown arms in the moonlight. She hopes Charles is being faithful to her.

She switches to 'Messages' to send him a text, but finds to her surprise that he has left her one. She clicks on it, and reads, and reads again, flushes the toilet, and shouts 'E-e-eee!' She looks in the cold mirror of the loos, and smiles, and then laughs, and an elderly woman who had peeked around the outside door, gingerly, draws back again. Mary's all alone in this sterile grey space, but her smile is big and warm enough to light up the room –

Because her friend the accountant is already in London. Charles is at Heathrow! He has cleared Immigration. Because of the weather, he is putting up for one night at the airport, but tomorrow he will come to 'the white woman's house', *enyumba eyo mukyala omuzungu*.

Mary's smile dies. The house will be empty. There will be

nowhere for Charles to go.

Meanwhile Justin is sitting waiting in the café. 'I thought you had left me,' he says, with mock pathos. The humour of it is lost on Mary. He is just a baby, a baby man. As they come out of the Services, the icy wind hits them, and flurries of snow attack their lips and noses, and both of them skid on the pristine white surface, and Justin clings on to Mary's arm. It isn't clear if he is using her or saving her, but Mary feels Justin is dragging her down.

And now her consciousness is torn in two, as the future pulls her in opposed directions. She knows she must drive Justin to Vanessa's village. She has promised to do it. She has to do it. Justin is incapable of getting there alone. It is one of the last things she'll do for Vanessa, a kind of final handover, and then – Vanessa will carry the load on her own.

But Mary also knows that she is going back to London. She imagines herself hugging her friend the accountant. She can almost feel his strong arms crushing her. She knows they will soon be together again.

For the moment, the snow is enough to cope with. She's reluctant to leave the kingdom of light, the reassurance of the other human faces, and reenter their box, and restart the race, the snails' race over the earth's glassy surface, which is slowly being covered with a skin of black ice, so that every so often, the car slips very slightly. It feels colder now: they keep their coats on. Justin has a picnic blanket under the back seat, and when he sees Mary shivering, he plunges like a dolphin and brings it up, and drapes it carefully round her shoulders.

'Thank you,' she says, and gives him a smile, the first real smile for several hundred miles. 'I am happy I have borrowed your mother's boots.'

'Oh?' Looking down, he sees she is wearing his mother's best boots, which are wildly expensive. The grey suede boots his mother had bought with the money from the third Pilates book. They look plain and serviceable, broad and blunt-toed, but Justin knows they are a fashion item. He thinks, 'My mother will not be pleased.' But the grey boots look quite good on Mary, kitted out, as she is, like an Andean Indian, with at least six layers of clothing on.

This time, they are driving at 5 miles an hour. Justin starts to notice that when Mary skids, she tries to correct it by steering against the direction in which they are sliding, and so the car just keeps on skidding.

Which doesn't matter while the skids are small.

'Mary,' he says, but tentatively. 'I don't suppose you're used to driving on ice.'

She is concentrating, but she still laughs. 'Justin, we do not have ice in Uganda, unless you are driving in the Rwenzori mountains. And I have never been to the Rwenzori mountains.'

She thinks, one day I will go with Charles. One day I will have another life. One day I am going to have enough money to do the things I want to do. And she thinks with pleasure of the money she has earned, the money she carefully hid under the carpet after it was spared by Vanessa's attacker. It is a start. More will follow. And her friend the accountant makes good money. He would earn more if he diversified less. She will encourage him to concentrate. Once they are married, it will all come true. They will give what she has earned here away to the village, but then there will be more. Together, they will make it. And maybe more children. It's her dearest wish. She had always longed for a brother for Jamil. For years she wanted it, but now that is over. God in his terrible wisdom did not want it.

For now she is trapped, in hostile country, and a thought flies across her mind, like a heron, a sharp dark heron on its way to the horizon, *Now is no time for me to die. Lord Jesus, please do not let us die.* And she prays, also, for Zakira and the baby, all babies, every small suffering thing.

And she finds herself praying once again for Jamie. Whom the world and its wars took away from her, like all the other sons from all the other mothers. After this, she tells God, she will resign herself, yield up her hopes and accept His will. But just one last time, she begs for his life. Because it's all that matters, to be alive. Not who he is with. Not what he does. Not what he believes. Just that he lives. *Just give me a sign, please, Jesus ...*

And then she waits, staring straight in front where the headlights shine on the blind red eyes of car after car pushing on into the future. But all she hears is the snow, and the silence. And then she knows he is not alive.

And so she is there. The place of utter darkness. There, in the middle of the meaningless whiteness. She needs to look it in the face. There is a terrible comfort to it, after all the hoping, and wishing, and praying, and hoping again. If there is nothing, it can come to an end.

But, nagging at the edge of her consciousness, Justin is still trying to tell her something. 'Mary, when we slip, you must drive into the skid. If you steer against it, it makes it worse.'

'Justin, please do not give more advice.' And in any case, the traffic has stopped.

The car begins to seem small, to Justin, who's grown used to being driven in Trevor's van, with the windows open and music playing, and Trevor driving casually, with one hand. Mary's style of driving is very tense. And her face, grimacing forward at the weird snow-light, looks big and mask-like, not like herself, her jaw sticking forward, almost a skull. She looks like death; wooden, awesome. She could be ninety years old, at this moment. He wonders, for the first time since he has known her, if Mary could ever actually dislike him.

But his inner voice rejects it, instantly. This is his Mary. Mary loves him.

And then suddenly, she shakes herself, and her face softens, and she comes back to life.

For more than ten minutes they've been stationary. If possible, the snow is coming harder now, one solid assault from a great sack of grey feathers. Mary looks at her watch, but not at him. 'Justin, shall we put the radio on?'

They get a local station, which is playing a song called 'Call off the search', which isn't encouraging. Then there is a break for traffic news. Justin grips her arm as he hears 'M23'. They listen. Drivers are being told to avoid it. A 20-mile tail-back has developed. Cars at the front are becoming snowed under. Though in the opposite direction, cars are still moving, people are still managing to drive to London, 'gridlock' is the word that's being applied to them. And yet they are only 50 metres from an exit; if they wanted to escape, there is a way out; but they are all locked in the grip of duty, all of them are going to parents or siblings, aunts or uncles or expectant children, bearing cargoes of effortfully chosen gifts. If they give up now, it is surely all wasted. Christmas fever has them in its grip. It is the time for duty, the once-in-twelve-months when British people remember the family. In hundreds of cars, there is *esprit de corps* as they huddle together against the night. In just as many, quarrels are starting. Older men talk about 'Dunkirk spirit', and teenagers snigger, and turn up their music, and blame their parents for getting stuck, and tell them which *totally important* TV programmes they are being forced to miss.

Mary looks longingly out of the window at the stream of traffic pressing on to the capital, where Charles is sleeping on the edge of the airport, beside the quiet beds of the aeroplanes, the beautiful great birds which, after the snow, will soar up into the red sky again, to warm Entebbe, to Uganda. And she wants to be in them, flying away, she is filled with desire for the skies of home, to look up at the *kabakanjagala* tree, the tree whose name means 'the king loves me', its red flaring generous mouth in the sunlight, and Charles loves me, the king loves me …

Then Justin is shaking her by the shoulder. 'You're asleep, Mary. Don't sleep, don't leave me.'

'It doesn't matter, the traffic isn't moving. Maybe it will never move again.'

'You have to stay awake in case we get going.'

She looks at him, coldly. He is a great baby, but he isn't a baby, he's a rich young man. His cheeks look loose, his mouth is sullen. He is too old to say, 'Don't leave me.' She isn't his lover, she isn't his mummy, and she has been driving for nearly seven hours. Mary has had enough of him.

'Justin, I want you to listen to me. I need to sleep for an hour or two. Probably the traffic isn't going to move, but if it does, you will have to do the driving.'

'Mary!' he whines, in explosive panic, 'you have to be joking, you know I can't drive, my mother made you promise to look after me!'

'Yes,' says Mary. 'Nineteen years ago. But now it is over. You are no longer a baby. I do not have to look after you. Now I shall get out so that you can take over.'

She is wrapping his blanket tighter round her shoulders, she is opening the door, she is getting out –

And Justin starts sobbing and panicking as the snow and the night whirls in through the breach, the terrible terror of adult life, where he will be cold, and no one will love him. The harsh air saws at his nose, his throat. 'Where are you going! You can't get out!'

And she shouts, into the loud buffeting wind, 'I'm not getting out, I'm just making space so you can move into the driver's seat,' but she sees him still sitting there, shouting and sobbing, his face going pink as he gets more indignant, and she suddenly realizes he'll never do it, while she is there he will always be a baby who expects Mary to be his nanny, his second mother, his cleaner, his driver – the wind howls around her ears, pure pain, and in thirty seconds her fingers are freezing. She shouts, 'Move across, or else I'm going,' and he doesn't move, he just sits there shaking, a boy in a bubble, a frozen boy, and Mary suddenly knows what to do.

'Goodbye, Justin, I love you,' she says. 'Remember that you are a good driver. Tell your mother I tried to look after you. But now you will have to take care of yourself.' And with that, Mary firmly closes her door. She plods to the right of the bonnet of the car, going slowly, sternly so as not to fall over, and makes for the central reservation, and Justin half rises in his seat, Justin half tries to follow her, because on her own she will surely be killed, and on his own he will surely die, and he shouts at her 'Mary, Mary, be careful', but he sees her climb sturdily over the barrier, a moving mountain of coat and blanket that slowly gathers a veil of snow; then she crosses, deftly, through the north-bound cars, though as each one passes Justin gasps and winces; and he is still slumped in the passenger seat, in a solid ice-field of south-bound traffic, when he sees a big lorry in the northerly slow lane veer over in Mary's direction, then stop, and he thinks, some great trucker will take her away, some man with great muscles and a dark blue chin, but after a few minutes the lorry starts up again, and Mary's still there, still plodding northwards, and as she gets smaller, she looks like a peasant, huddled under her hump of blanket, and he can no longer see her face, and she trudges along like all the earth's peasants, fighting their way north through a world of snow.

Justin feels terror, and impotent anger, and hot tears rush into his eyes, but as he watches her recede in the distance, moving doggedly but infinitely slowly, he suddenly thinks of Zakira, pregnant, in the lumbering slowness of her final weeks. How she needed him to look after her. And he discovered that he could do it. That he could be a man, a father. He flexes his hands. He peers forward and assesses it. Only 40 or 50 metres to the exit. Justin slides over and takes the wheel.

Mary knows inside that she is strong as an ox, that she can walk for ever, all the way back to London. When her friend was ill in Kiwoko hospital and she was a student at Makerere she often walked half a day to visit her, carrying melons, sliced bread and clean clothes. If only she had gloves. In all her life she has only owned one pair of gloves, a rainbow-striped wool pair she wore in winter in the early morning life she led as a cleaner, and they must have fallen apart long ago, she screws up her eyes and the lids make rainbows, rainbow strands of nothingness, there must be ice on her lids, her lashes, and her hands are like ice, they have no separate fingers, two blockish things that she raises with difficulty, trying to fend off the moths of sleep, the cold soft wings of the hungry spirits …

Jamie is dead. She can go to him.

She keeps on walking, though she's going slower. She remembers the walk in Vanessa's village, when the brambles caught them and the thorns scratched them. Looking back from the present, it seems bathed in sunlight. They knew where they were going, everything was easy. Mary intends to hitch to London, but only one vehicle has stopped to date, a thin white-faced man in the cab of a huge lorry who indicated she should suck his penis, and she mimed back that he should fuck himself, which at the time gave her a feeling of freedom, but now she no longer feels free, or brave, and the exhilaration of her choice has gone.

Now she no longer feels anything at all except the heaviness of keeping on walking, and even if she wants to hitch, she can't, because she can no longer lift her hand, or turn her head towards the traffic behind her, but every time a car passes, she wobbles, almost knocked sideways by the weight of cold air, and now the worst pain has passed from her hands and is turning her ears to lumps of hot ice, two growing tumours of burning coldness, pressing her eardrums until they must burst, and then even that pain begins to grow numb, and the noises turn to a single roaring, a single battering, stunning loudness.

So that when someone drives up the hard shoulder behind her, blowing loudly on his horn again and again, letting down his window, waving and beckoning, at first she hears nothing, then the car is upon her, and for a moment she thinks she will be killed, and then she realizes, it's Justin, laughing.

'Get in, Mary. We are driving back to London.'

55

Vanessa's woken at nine by a worried-looking Lucy, still in her pyjamas, frowning gently down at her: she has been listening to the news in bed. 'They say about five hundred motorists are trapped. Their motorway completely froze up. There are snow-ploughs and ambulances out.'

'Is anyone hurt? Tell me nobody's hurt. Nobody's dead. Please tell me that.'

Lucy's stricken face seems to say the opposite. Vanessa enters the zone of horror.

So when Justin telephones, nervous, guilty, at ten o'clock, having got four hours' sleep, and tells his mother that they had to turn back, they will not be coming, but they are both safe, she does not complain, she sobs with relief, and when Mary comes on the line to speak to her, Vanessa doesn't care that some Ugandan will be staying, she says 'Yes' at once, 'Yes, yes, of course', and says Mary must help herself 'to whatever', and 'of course, Mary dear, take care of Justin.'

'Vanessa, Justin will take care of himself.' Mary Tendo is laughing, softly.

'Thank you, dear Mary, for everything.'

'For everything. It's OK, Vanessa.'

On the swell of relief, Vanessa longs to be generous. She takes a deep breath before she speaks. 'Oh, and Mary. I received a letter – a letter came from my friend the agent. The Christmas post is very bad. I think you may have, uh, accidentally included some of your writing with my students'… Of course it was a surprise to me. I would have encouraged you with your writing, but you didn't tell me. Which is a pity. But in any case, the agent liked it.'

'The agent liked it. What did she say?'

'She said it was vivid. Really, you know, very promising, Mary. She definitely liked it.' For some reason, Vanessa finds this hard to say. 'It was one of a few she especially picked out. And this, my dear, is a very good agent.'

'And will she sell it?' asks Mary Tendo, calmly.

'It's early days, but who knows, maybe.'

'Who knows, maybe,' Mary laughs. 'Thank you, Vanessa. We will see. First I will have to finish my book. I am tired now, Vanessa. I have to sleep.'

'Mary, the agent would like to meet you. And I – I would like to come and see you in Uganda.'

'Ah, in Uganda. Goodbye, Vanessa.'

Vanessa puts the phone down, and passes the news of their safe arrival on to Lucy.

She stands lightly brooding, looking out of the window at two sparrows skirmishing over a nut. She had thought Mary would be more excited. Why wasn't she dazzled by the thought of an agent? Why wasn't she, well, just slightly more grateful?

In fact, Mary is sitting in Vanessa's front room with her feet up on the sofa, singing softly. The agent liked it. She especially liked it. She picked it out from the *bazungu* students. Mary finds she is singing herself to sleep. She holds Justin's blanket against her chest. Even the mightiest eagle, she thinks, can sometimes come down from the treetops to rest.

'Are you all right, Mary? Oh, you're singing. What did Mum have to say to you?'

'Nothing important. Just … something nice.'

'Mary, stop being mysterious. You know that I know all about you.'

'Not everything, Justin. You are still young. I know things you can never imagine.' She smiles at him. 'Now, go to Zakira's.'

56   Mary Tendo

Today is Christmas Day. It is a great day. The snow is still falling like mist in London. I think the sun is shining on Kampala. Soon we are going home to Uganda. God has smiled on his servant, Mary. *Katonda Mulundi*. He is really good.

£3,005.75! I have earned myself a small fortune. In every way I have been successful. There is a firm bulge of money under my carpet. I have counted it with my friend Charles, and we smiled as we reached £1,000, then £2,000, but the number kept rising, and when we got to £3,000, I whooped with joy and danced on the landing. Over nine million Ugandan shillings! Soon the money will fly back with us to Kampala.

Before Vanessa returns, in three days, I shall be gone. She will learn to be a grandmother on her own. She is very lucky. Her grandson is a wonder. He looks a little like Trevor, and a little like Justin, and a lot like Zakira, except for his hair. And the colour of his skin is like shiny pink roses. He does not look white as old maize, like Vanessa. He is chubby, not skinny. His face is sweet and round. He cries like rain, and then stops in an instant. He does not screech and wail, like his grandmother.

And yet he looks clever, as his grandma does, and he has little bandy legs, like her, and busy, wriggly hands and fingers. Soon he will be playing with his mother's amber necklace, which his father used to wear, when he was lonely. I think that the baby will make Vanessa happy. For the moment they call him Abdul Trevor. (I hope it is a joke; it is a very silly name. But the baby will make them more sensible.) Justin says they will welcome his mother home. Zakira will cook a big meal for her. Little Abdul Trevor will entertain her. Vanessa too shall have her party.

I am happy for her, since yesterday. For God has smiled on his servant, Mary. I have been blessed, I am full to the brim.

My happiness makes me want to sing, although I know I have a squawking voice, worse than mouse-birds squabbling in the mango tree. And it makes me want to shout, and then I shush myself.

I am so lucky I am almost afraid. The last shall be first, the least have most. I thought my fruit had returned to dust. Now I have been blessed, I have been renewed. *Katonda anjagalanyo.* Praise God!

Something I am holding safe under my rib-cage. Something that makes me hug myself, hard, and yet I must be gentle with myself.

It is almost too precious to share with anyone, although Charles knows, and his eyes became moist, something I had never seen before. He brushed the wet away, and said it was a fly. But he could not speak, and he kissed my belly.

And now I must get up, and walk around the house, this big strange house I have been living in, with its books, and its pictures, and its piles of paper, its dust, and its shadows, and its photographs, its heavy old radiators making the air warm, because the sun does not shine on England. I walk around, and I think about it all. I walk upstairs, slowly, and down again. I walk into Vanessa's sitting room. There are so many Christmas cards, maybe a hundred, although Vanessa does not have many friends, but these people are so rich that to send a card is nothing, and perhaps these people do not really like her.

Today I like her. Today I nearly love her, although it might be different if she were here. But if she were here, I would have to tell her, and I am almost sure that Vanessa would kiss me, as she did at the airport, when I did not expect it, and I know I hugged her, as the planes flew over. When we do not think, we like each other. And maybe thinking does not always matter.

I have discovered why I felt sick before. When I came to England, I was already pregnant.

I was not being poisoned by the air of London.

I was not being poisoned by Vanessa.

I, Mary Tendo, am pregnant again.

My friend the accountant is kind and clever, though he is no good at family planning (but he just smiles and says the condom was faulty, and it is true that many condoms are faulty in Kampala). It was he who noticed that my body was different, that my nipples were larger, that I had a new belly. And then we found a chemist, the only chemist still open in this part of London, and bought the test, which was very expensive, but worth each penny, since it told us good news.

My friend the accountant is completely happy. 'How many shall we have? Three, four?'

He doesn't understand that one is a miracle. It is a world of change: from nothing to something. It is the future, leading us out of the past.

And there is something else that he does not understand. 'Now you will no longer think about Jamie.' Of course, he says this because he loves me. He wants me to think about him and the baby.

I do think about them, and my heart swells with joy, but still, every day, I think about Jamie. I shall think about Jamie every day of my life. Till I know where he is, I shall carry him with me.

I have sent Charles to the kitchen to check on the chicken. He is very pleased that I'm cooking a chicken. Perhaps he thinks I have killed it for him. But in fact I took it from Vanessa's freezer.

We are watching the television together. Soon we are going to see the Queen. It is a long time since I have seen her. Perhaps she will be thin and small, like Vanessa.

It is Christmas Day. It is the best day. It is the first of many great days. I took my friend the accountant to church, and we sat together, and looked at the stable, and he was happy because of the baby. 'Mary, we will call him our English baby.'

I'm not sure that the English will call him that. In any case, he was conceived in Kampala. I am happy to be having a Ugandan baby.

I always wanted a brother for Jamie, but it is too late for them to play together. I do not say this to my *kabito*. I shall not shed a tear on Christmas Day. I think he will know his brother in heaven. Perhaps I will see them run to each other. And all the trees will be in flower.

But now Charles is coming through from the kitchen. He is bringing the chicken, steaming hot. It smells of baked salt and lemons and spices. I learned this recipe from Zakira. After lunch we are going to see Abdul Trevor.

I am very hungry. The food is delicious. Charles opens a bottle of champagne. When I told him to take the wine from the fridge, he said 'We shall buy our own wine, Mary, I have changed enough money, I am not a pauper,' and I agreed, we are not paupers, we have enough money, and so forth, et cetera. But still, Vanessa would want us to have it. On the phone, she told me to 'help myself'. I raise my glass to her: 'Cheers, Vanessa.' (I hope Dom Perignon is a good make. I think she would not mind – it is old, it is 'Vintage', indeed the date on the bottle is 1990, so she will be glad that we have drunk it.)

And now the TV plays the national anthem. Charles starts to get up; he is fond of the Queen: but the plate on his lap spills a little gravy, and so he smiles and sits down again. They do not play all of it, just a little. Our minds turn towards the Ugandan national anthem. In our country, we play the whole anthem. 'We are walking together down the road of education, marching towards a better Uganda ... '

And now the Queen is talking and smiling. She has not got tiny and old, like Vanessa. She has tidy hair and a skirt and jumper.

'I like the cut of her jib,' I tell Charles. When he looks puzzled, I laugh, and he laughs, politely. 'Ha, ha. English English is amusing,' he says. But Charles likes the look of the Queen, as well, though he slightly prefers our own Nnaabagareka Sylvia Luswata, the young, pretty bride of our King Ronald.

We watch Queen Elizabeth meeting people. 'There are a lot of African faces,' says my friend the accountant. He drinks more champagne. 'The Queen has a lot of African friends.' He is pleased with this. He burps and chuckles.

'They show more Africans at Christmas,' I say, because I have drunk less than Charles. I think of the Ugandans in Forest Gate. They don't spend their days at Buckingham Palace.

Then I think about the Bible teachings on slander. Christmas Day is a time to be happy. So I try again, with a mouthful of chicken, which is plump and delicious: soon I'll suck the bone.

'Maybe the Queen has grown tired of the English. I myself have had enough of them, for now. Soon we will go home again.'

'Perhaps the Queen will come and see us in Uganda.'

And I think about Vanessa, who said on the phone, 'I should like to come and see you in Uganda.' And I smile, and say to Charles, 'Perhaps she will.'